THE DRAGON & THE FIEND

SERIES STARTER OMNIBUS
THE DRAGON GATE
THE EVER FIEND

RANDY ELLEFSON

Evermore Press/Llurien Books
GAITHERSBURG, MARYLAND

Evermore Press, LLC
Gaithersburg, Maryland
www.evermorepress.org

The Dragon and the Fiend / Randy Ellefson. -- 1st ed.
ISBN 978-1-946995-90-2 (paperback)
ISBN 978-1-946995-61-2 (hardcover)

CONTENTS

The Ever Fiend

ACKNOWLEDGEMENTS

Cover design by Miblart

INTRODUCTION

T his series starter bundle, *The Dragon and the Fiend*, brings together two fantasy novels by Randy Ellefson, each the first in a series (the *Talon Stormbringer* books are not sequential and can be read in any order).

THE DRAGON GATE
(THE DRAGON GATE SERIES, #1)

Ryan and his friends only learn that Stonehenge is a portal to another world when it pulls them through it. Arriving on Honyn, they are mistaken for the Ellorian Champions, four adventurers of unusual talent, skill, and questing success. They have been summoned to close the Dragon Gate before a horde of dragons can fly through it and destroy all life.

Trapped there until the quest is complete, they set off to master magic and the sword, to call on gods, to evade traps of men and monsters, to seal a gate and their fate. To save a world – and save themselves.

THE EVER FIEND
(TALON STORMBRINGER, #1)

Only a fool steals from a wizard.

Talon Stormbringer thought he knew the risk of stealing from Viland Shadowbreaker – until he got caught. The wizard will spare him if Talon fetches the deadly silver elixir from the Everway, a supernatural land of lost souls and worse, ruled by the Ever Fiend. Talon had assumed none of it was real but agrees to go despite a band of people he can't trust accompanying him. Of all the things they might discover on their journey, one is the hardest to learn...

Only a fool steals from the Ever Fiend.

FREE BOOK

Anyone who joins my fiction newsletter mailing list receives a free eBook of *The Ever Fiend (Talon Stormbringer)*. Visit http://fiction.randyellefson.com/newsletter/

The Dragon Gate
The Dragon Gate 1

ACKNOWLEDGEMENTS

Edited by JJ Henke

Maps by Randy Ellefson

Cover design by Miblart

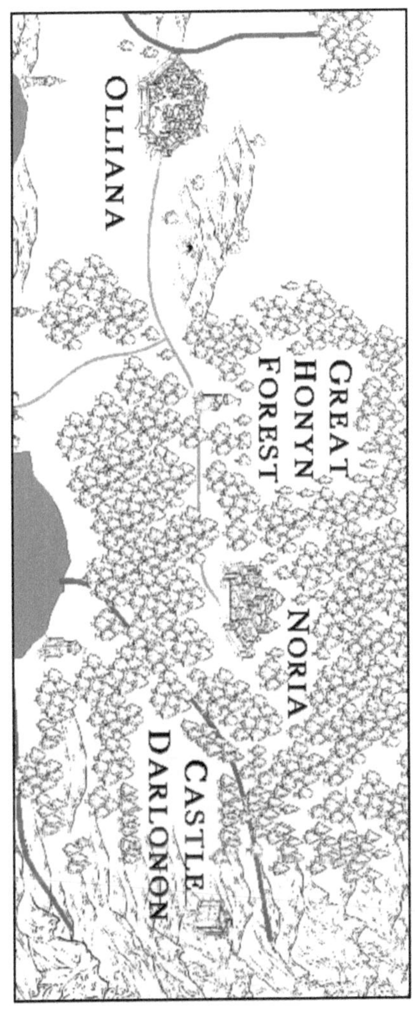

Partial Map of the Kingdom of Alunia, on Honyn

View a larger, full color map online at http://fiction
.randyellefson.com/dragon-gate-series/the-dragon-gate/

THE LONE SURVIVOR

Lucion stared unseeing into the campfire. His ears strained to hear past the rustling treetops and creaking boles of the dark forest. Gusts of wind tore through the woods as if searching for him, the noise drowning out the chatter of his four companions. If anything else was moving out there, his group would never know it. The coming storm didn't concern him, but the ogre footprints did. They looked a week old and likely meant no trouble, and he was certain enough of this to have lit the fire and slapped deer meat over it, but the value of alertness wasn't lost on him. His own prey lay chopped in pieces before him.

The hunter's gaze shifted to the ruins of Castle Darlonon perched among the looming mountain peaks overhead. For a moment, he thought lights twinkled in some of the windows. A cautious glance at Rogin showed his brother hadn't noticed the lights, which was just as well. Rogin had told enough stories about people going up there and never coming back that no one believed much of anything he said anymore. Just minutes earlier he'd sworn a dragon had appeared in the night sky, but of course that was impossible. As Lucion turned the deer haunch over,

Rogin walked off into the woods to relieve himself and the darkness swallowed him. As if to celebrate, the woods groaned loudly, and the wind howled through the treetops. Lucion shivered.

"It smells so good here," said a woman's voice, and the men turned in surprise, seeing an elegant woman breathing in deeply through a pert nose, her full bosom straining against the red silk of an evening gown. Golden hair framed a heart-shaped face and tumbled past her petite waist. She stood at the clearing's edge, her radiance making the shadowy woods seem all the more dark. Her green eyes boldly danced from one man to the next, appraising them. Captivated by her allure, they hardly noticed she could not have been more out of place so many miles from any settlement.

"I haven't smelled such fine meat in so many years," she purred, eyeing Lucion. He could've been the most handsome man alive for the way she gazed at him.

Mesmerized by her attention, he pleasantly replied, "It is only fresh deer, my lady, not even seasoned, but you're welcome to your share of it and all that we have."

Her bright eyes locked onto his as if the others didn't exist. He wished that were so, for he wanted her all to himself and trembled as she came nearer. Fine words had never been his to command and he stood at a loss, adoring eyes saying more than words ever could. As she stopped before him, her feminine scent washed over him. He smiled like a schoolboy.

In the silence, she kindly asked, "Why so quiet? Dragon got your tongue?"

Not noticing the subject had come up again, he stammered, "Uh, n-no, my lady. Dragons, well, they uh, they don't show themselves around here no more."

Eyebrows arched in surprise, she asked, "Is that so?"

"Yes, my lady. They were banished by the Ellorian Champions some years ago, to another world. The Dragon Gate up there in the castle keeps them away. You'll be safe here, that I can promise you." And he meant every word, for his heart would burst if anything happened to her. He didn't mention that the champions had disappeared without a trace some years ago and that if the dragons ever got loose, no one would be able to send them back. The planet would be destroyed. There was no sense in worrying her.

Seeming amused by his assurance, she asked, "So then you haven't seen a dragon recently? Tonight, for example?"

Startled, he wondered how she could have known and replied, "Oh no, nothing like that. Uh, Rogin here did think he saw something in the sky earlier, but it was nothing." He couldn't tear his eyes away long enough to look for his brother. It was good that this was so, for he might have noticed Rogin was still missing and alerted her to this.

"What did he think he saw?" The seductress slowly ran a finger down his chest. The long, bright red nail was sharp enough to cut through his shirt and draw blood he didn't notice.

Lucion hesitated for fear of causing concern, but then she leaned closer and breathed him in long and deep, clearly enjoying his scent. Aroused, he confessed helpfully, "A dragon."

As if expecting that, she smiled in satisfaction, her green eyes finally leaving his to look over the others. They stood as mesmerized as Lucion, who felt as though a pleasant heat had ceased bathing his face. The sudden coldness startled him. His devotion faded long enough that he wondered aloud, "Who are you?"

Her gaze returned to his playfully. "Someone who doesn't like witnesses," she purred.

Before he had a chance to understand what she meant, his head flew from his neck, a bemused smile still on his face. It was still rolling across the ground when she went for the nearest man, who stared stupidly at the long, gleaming nails dripping with Lucion's blood. She raked open his belly, shoving a hand inside to pull out organs that she bit into with delight, dark blood spurting across her face. As he collapsed beside the fire, the others fumbled for weapons and the woman spoke a strange word.

Her appearance morphed and grew as they watched in awe, golden scales reflecting the firelight as two enormous, leathery wings blotted out the dark sky. A sinuous neck lifted her giant head into the night, two baleful eyes glaring down on them with lust. Four thick legs and feet ending in talons supported a huge golden body that no normal weapon could pierce. She took her time, snapping up the next man in her fanged mouth and cracking him in half. She hadn't tasted such warm blood in years and relished it like wine. The last man turned for the woods, but her barbed tail snaked out to impale him where he stood, holding him aloft. The dragon chewed slowly as if savoring every morsel, her forked tongue licking her lips as she gulped them down.

Her jaws weren't the only ones agape, for out in the bushes knelt a staring Rogin, horror riveting him to the spot. As he watched, the golden dragon lifted into the night air with a powerful leap and thrusts of leathery wings, scattering embers across the clearing. Then she sucked in a great breath and blasted fire down on the evidence, setting the forest ablaze so that Rogin crept away on his hands and knees, his back awash in heat. With a snap of her wings, the dragon turned and soared away to Castle Darlonon, where she rose into the sky and then plunged down inside to disappear.

And Rogin ran. He ran as far down the road toward Olliana as his legs would carry him, finally collapsing before a startled farmer, tales of dragons, fire, and death pouring from his mouth. At first no one believed him, but soon lights appeared in the ruined castle at night and ogres trolled the woods, chased from the peaks by mercenaries at Darlonon. Just the one dragon had been seen, but the others couldn't be far behind now that the Dragon Gate stood open. Someone had to close it, but only the long-missing champions could.

CHAPTER ONE

RENFEST

With thundering hooves, the golden knight's steed charged, lance aimed left toward the tilt separating him from his quarry. A dummy on a pole held forth a small metal ring for him to pluck free, and with a clink it slid down the shaft as the crowd politely cheered. He lifted the prize aloft, cantering around the stadium to a smattering of clapping. He wasn't what they really wanted and he knew it, cheers turning to jeers in his mind. As more knights thundered in and the crowd roared for the main event, he left the small arena, unable to watch the other knights charge each other. But he heard the battle screams, the cracks of lances shattering on plate armor, the clatter of plate armor as men crashed to the ground.

Sighing, he dismounted and pulled off the blue-plumed helmet, his feathered blond hair hiding the ear buds that were wirelessly tethered to the smartphone tucked inside his armor. Any signs of modern technology were strictly forbidden at the Maryland Renaissance Festival, or "Ren-Fest," as the locals called it. It ruined the illusion of the time period. Like all performers, he was supposed to show bewilderment when guests pulled out a camera. It was as if the whole faire, population included, had been transplanted from Medieval times and was unaware it wasn't somewhere in England around the 1500s.

Ryan led the white gelding to the stables, feigning smiles at young, busty women trying to get his attention, their pushed-up bosoms tempting his blue eyes. Being tall, handsome, and muscular readily attracted women, even without the costume, and pretending to be a hero got him more attention. If they knew the truth about him, they'd look the other way.

As he pulled the saddle off, a familiar figure arrived beside him. Eric Foster stood dressed for his role as a jester at RenFest, wearing a parti-colored jumpsuit of red and blue, a matching three-pronged hat, and pointed shoes, all with bells. He looked ridiculous and had to be almost as uncomfortable as Ryan in the brutal August heat.

"How'd the joust go?" Eric asked, taking off the hat to wipe sweat from soaked, black hair. "When are you gonna move on to the real thing?"

"When I'm ready."

"Why aren't you ready now? You're better than the others at that ring thing you just did. I'd think that makes it easier to hit bigger targets like them."

"Can't argue that."

After an awkward pause, Eric asked, "Worried about getting hurt?"

Ryan opened his mouth to say no but realized it was close enough to the truth. "Sort of. People getting hurt comes with the territory."

Taking a sip of water, Eric observed, "You always seem to avoid contact sports. I'm still surprised you weren't on the football team in school. It's not that big a deal, you know. I get hit every day. You get used to it."

"It's not me I'm really worried about," the big man confessed, wincing as someone un-horsed a knight in the stadium. He realized his answer wasn't entirely true. He'd seen his brother paralyzed for life and the idea chilled him. To be dependent on others for so much was a helplessness he couldn't imagine. It gnawed at him every time he tended to his brother since the day of the accident so long ago.

"I guess that's better than being a wimp," Eric remarked lightly, "but if you really want to do something, you shouldn't let that hold you back. Accidents happen."

Ryan frowned. "Yeah, but we don't have to invite them. I should just forget it and accept I'm never gonna do it."

"How's that going to make you feel better?"

"It's not, but it's better than the alternative."

"Which is?"

"Let's go."

Ryan led the horse into a stall and latched the door. As they exited the stables for the faire grounds, he realized that Eric would never understand, not when he did martial arts every day as an instructor. Ryan didn't know how he could stand it, but Eric proudly admitted getting beat up all the time as a kid until learning karate. Ryan had little experience with violence, but all of it was bad. He'd never been struck by anyone except the one time he stupidly wondered aloud what a real punch felt like only to have Eric show him. He smirked at the memory.

As they strolled along, Eric deftly picked the pocket of a father of two, then returned the wallet to the surprised man as people chuckled nervously. Ryan watched with mixed feelings. His friend had never given him a reason to distrust him, but Eric had spent years on the streets after his parents abandoned him. Eric's last foster parents had turned him around, but it was a hard life for a rich kid like Ryan to imagine, sneaking into places, stealing things, and spending time in jail.

They stopped at the knife throwing contest, where Eric mocked a teenage boy's inaccuracy until the booth worker took his cue and reacted.

"Think you can do better, Fool?" the man asked, handing Eric the knives. Ryan stood back, having seen the pair reenact this every weekend for a month. He knew what was coming and tried to play his role, feigning surprise by the skill the jester was about to demonstrate.

Eric said, "I have more experience dodging these than throwing them!" He casually tossed one at the tree stump target and hit the bull's eye. Acting startled, he did it again, then switched hands with the same result as people applauded. Again and again he struck the target, even tossing knives over one shoulder, under a raised leg, and blindfolded, though his accuracy dropped.

Finally, Eric turned on the booth worker amidst the cheering. "Is this some kind of trick? They all hit the target. I want my money back."

"You never paid."

"Oh. Right. Well then, I, uh, guess I had better be going." He turned.

"Hey! Get back here!" The booth worker called as Eric ran away. Turning to Ryan, he demanded, "Sir knight! Do something!"

Unsheathing his sword with a grand gesture, Ryan turned and called after Eric, pretending to give chase. He pushed his way through the crowd, watching Eric disappear but knowing where he was probably going.

Eric heard Ryan's voice fading and stopped running. The big guy would find him soon enough. He walked by the Market Stage, the Boar's Head Tavern, and the strong man pole where Ryan sometimes slammed the mallet down so hard that the bell at the top not only rang but practically flew off. He ignored the shops selling trinkets, his eyes fixed on a fortune teller to one side. She had long blonde hair and hazel eyes in a face that turned heads, and his pulse raced on making eye contact and seeing Anna Lynn Sumner grin at him. He stood in line for his turn with her, and when the last kid was gone, Eric flopped down across the scarf covered table from her, bells jingling.

"You know I have to read your palm while you're here," she said in greeting.

"Of course," he said, handing it over. "So, what can you see?"

"A bunch of bruises," she replied matter-of-factly. "You need to take better care of them."

"It's kind of hard in my line of work," he replied, "but that's not what I mean. Tell me my future, oh Mistress of the Heavens."

Chuckling, she said, "You know I don't believe in that sort of thing."

"Then why are you giving palm readings all day?"

"Because the kids believe it and it's fun to see them dream."

Feigning exaggerated sadness, he asked, "Don't you dream anymore, poor Anna?"

"Of the supernatural that doesn't exist? Hardly. I outgrew that sort of thing."

"Don't let Ryan hear you say that, or he'll call you a 'godless one' again."

She laughed. "Yes, I know. He's funny with that. Religious people and their desire to save the world. How can we stand to live among them?"

He smiled, for they'd talked about their mutual atheism before and tried not to bring it up before Ryan too much. The big guy was reasonable unless someone questioned the existence of God, but at least he didn't go around quoting Scriptures. Few people could stomach that, least of all Anna. They knew she saw plenty of fallout from religious beliefs at the hospital where she worked as a medical resident. She sometimes complained that some people avoided real care in favor of some superstitious belief or other nonsense. Either that or they took matters into their own hands with some harmful treatment and made it worse. That reminded him of something.

"Are you ready for tonight?" Eric asked, turning a little more serious.

She pursed her lips. "I guess. If convincing him doesn't work, then we'll all just go without him."

Between her gaze going over his shoulder and the clinking of plate armor getting louder, he knew that the man they spoke of was approaching. "Still meeting at your place about it?"

"Yeah. Remind Matt. He's the key to it."

Eric grinned. "Don't sell yourself short. You could convince *me* to do anything."

Anna rolled her eyes. "You're an impossible flirt."

Deciding to quit while he was ahead, Eric rose, bowed, and added, "Your faithful servant," before stepping away as Ryan joined him, sword sheathed again. The knight nodded at her.

As they stepped away, Eric cried a loud protest to those in line, "She said I have no future, that I'll be imprisoned this very night!"

"No surprise there," remarked a passerby.

They went in search of Matt Sorenson, whom they found beside the nearby Lyric Stage, ready to assist another performer doing magic tricks for kids. Eric had taught him some sleight of hand that he still struggled with, but Eric knew that this wasn't the reason Matt looked nervous. He had stage fright and had joked that if he could do magic for real, the first spell he'd cast would be something to cure him of this condition.

Eric saw Matt's green eyes spot him and Ryan. Matt made a sign with his hand. *Hi*, the fingers said.

Eric made his own gesture. *Hey. You'll be fine. Picture them naked.*

No thanks.

Suit yourself. There's a hot redhead at your one o'clock.
Eric saw Matt look that way and waited for the reaction.

Dick.

Made you look. Remember, tonight at Anna's.

Ok.

See ya.

Right.

Matt watched them turn away in search of bored people to entertain, wishing he could do the same. Just then the other illusionist called to him for help, and he steeled his nerves to step on stage. A sea of faces and applause greeted him. Everywhere he looked eyes met his. They were inescapable. His heart fluttered and suddenly his stomach churned, and he fell to his knees, vomiting all over the floor. Thinking it was part of the act, the kids cheered while shame over-came him and he retched again and again. Kneeling over the mess he'd made, he realized making his lunch reappear was the closest to a magic trick he'd done before an audience.

CHAPTER TWO

THE PENDANT

Ryan plowed down River Road in the wealthy suburb of Potomac, Maryland at twenty over the limit, the radar detector silently watching for cops. He'd gotten enough speeding tickets to earn a suspended license before, but now instead of slowing down, he just drove prepared. As he made an illegal pass around a Sunday driver, the Dodge Charger roared like his pulse, but the questioning look Anna shot him made them go quiet again

"What?" he asked defensively, feeling guilty. He knew he shouldn't do it with her in the car, at least, but he couldn't help it. "I did it safely. No one was coming." When she didn't say anything, he added lamely, "C'mon, I made that pass in two seconds, and there wasn't even another car in sight."

"Yeah, I know," she admitted, playing with a pendant around her neck. He'd never seen her without it; it was some sort of family heirloom, a square-cut diamond surrounded by a rectangular silver frame. "I'm just surprised you keep doing it. You're always so careful about everything else, but then you drive like a maniac. It doesn't make any sense. I thought you were afraid to get hurt."

He stifled a frown. It was his own fault people believed that, since he let them, but it frustrated him anyway.

"What's the rush?" Anna asked.

He shrugged. "I need to get home to Daniel."

She sighed. "Didn't you just talk to him? Your brother will be fine until you get there. You don't have to get us killed on the way."

He looked sideways at her and eased up, so they were going all of two miles per hour slower. It was a gesture of conciliation without really ceding the point and he sensed more than saw her wry look. They finally turned off the road, having passed many mansions that paled in comparison to the LaRue estate. He noticed Anna gawking like she'd never seen it before, especially when they pulled up by the six car garage, where a red '77 Lamborghini Countach, a silver 2020 Aston Martin convertible, and a yellow '79 Ferrari 308 GTS were just some of the mint condition cars sitting idle. Ryan ignored them as he thrust open the car door and put a foot out before the Charger even stopped.

"C'mon," he said, exiting agilely despite his height and physique.

As she struggled to keep up, Anna looked back at the black car with the huge dent in the driver's side door. "Why don't you drive one of these other cars?"

"Because I don't deserve them," he muttered.

"What? Why?"

He opened his mouth to explain but realized it might lead to a subject he didn't want to discuss. "Long story."

"You could be driving one of these and yet you bought that car with a dent already in it. And you won't fix it. C'mon. Level with me." When he didn't respond, she added, "You're a strange one, Charlie Brown."

He nodded to himself. Maybe it was true. That was the problem with secrets. They made you do things but not explain them, leaving people to invent a new truth and a new you along with it. It made him keeps friends like Anna at arm's length. He suddenly felt lonely as the mansion's shadow swallowed him.

The main house had two wings where Ryan's rich parents entertained senators, foreign dignitaries, and "old money" like the LaRues or business owners who sought their favors. Those who hadn't been here were seldom aware of his family's wealth. Part of him resented the money and he knew perfectly well why – all the money in the world wasn't saving his brother.

The three-story foyer had a massive chandelier and polished, decorative tiles like a public government building or fancy hotel. Crystal figurines and marble busts stood on elegant cherry furniture in the halls, and Ryan tried to ignore them as he strode by. He always felt like he wasn't supposed to touch anything, which was one reason he liked the dented car; it was already screwed up. On some level he knew he and it were the same and had felt drawn to it the moment he saw it, the same way this house repulsed him the second he turned into the driveway. Urgency brought him here at a clip, but something deep inside him made him want to get away just as soon as he arrived.

They found Ryan's brother in the large, gourmet kitchen, where he sat tilted way back in his custom, powered wheelchair so that he faced the ceiling. It let him take the pressure off his legs and butt to avoid sores, though Ryan knew that wasn't why he liked it. His long black hair was pulled back to reveal two pierced ears. On his left forearm lay a tattoo of a snake coiled around a knife. Such displays went against their un-cool parents, but they'd always let Daniel get away with certain things due to his injury, a fact his brother took advantage of and resented at the same time. Ryan did, too, because he saw them as signs of his brother's unhappiness and wanted Daniel to be at peace.

Daniel flashed a grin at Anna while flicking a raisin at Ryan's head and joked, "I knew it was you from the screeching tires. You should be careful. You don't want to end up like me."

Ryan got down on one knee beside him and squeezed a hand. "If I could trade places with you, I would."

Daniel rolled his eyes. "I know. I should know better than to joke with you about it. How'd RenFest go?"

"Where's Susan?" Ryan asked, looking around for the live-in nurse and ignoring the attempt at changing the subject.

His brother nodded to another room where a TV could be heard. "Watching the tube."

"Susan!" Ryan called, rising. "Come in here!"

Daniel shot him a look of annoyance. "She doesn't have to be with me every second, you know. I told you to stop that. I don't even need her. Or at least not for that anyway," he added suggestively.

Ryan squeezed his shoulder. "Don't get so worked up. I just wanted to talk to her about how you're doing."

"Yeah right," muttered Daniel, using the joystick to reposition the chair upright. While he was a quadriplegic, he had full use of his right arm and hand, but his grip with the left was too weak to do much with. He still had control over his bladder and related areas, but he'd never walk again and really had no need for the 24/7 nurse Ryan had insisted on hiring. He was in no danger of respiratory failure or similar life threatening complications, but Ryan was deaf to guidance on these matters, even from world renowned doctors, for once he'd gotten it into his head that some quadriplegics could die suddenly, he'd never forgotten it. Not all quads were the same, but telling that to Ryan was pointless.

Anna leaned over to kiss Daniel. "Hello. How have you been?"

"As heartbroken as always that you won't kiss more than my cheek."

She shot back, "Isn't that why Ryan got you the nurse?"

While Ryan cocked an eyebrow, Daniel said, "I wish," and rolled out of the room as the nurse arrived.

Patting Ryan's arm, Anna said, "I'll watch him," and hurried after Daniel, who she found doing donuts in his wheelchair on the hardwood floor. "Don't run me over, please," she said.

He stopped and sighed. "Only if you were Ryan."

"He drives you crazy, doesn't he? Would you like a long break from him?"

He looked surprised. "Are you kidding? I'd *love* that. Planning to kidnap him? It's the only way."

She laughed but not without concern at the truth of it. She knew Ryan frequently called or texted to check on him and that the well-meaning attention caused tension and arguments. "Me, Matt, and Eric are going on that trip to England that we've been planning for forever. Ryan's been planning, too, but never committing to it."

"On account of me."

"Yeah. He doesn't want to leave you despite all of this." She gestured at the luxury around them. "Has he ever gone on a trip without you?"

"No. I haven't gone more than eight hours without seeing him since I was a little kid, so I don't know how you'll pull that off."

She played with the pendant around her neck. "We have an idea, but you might find it intrusive."

He laughed. "Not more than his hovering. Let's hear it."

"We thought to install web cams here in the house. Matt's a techie and good with that sort of thing. If Ryan can see you in the cameras when he wants, maybe he won't bug you so much when he's away. And he might just agree to come with us."

"That's actually not a bad idea. He can check on me without me knowing it. And I can randomly give the cameras the finger when I feel like it, just in case he's watching. And it sorta fits this whole thing."

Failing to hide a smile, she asked, "How do you mean?"

"It's a nanny cam, basically, like I'm a frigging baby." He seemed amused, at least. "That's how he treats me."

"We don't mean it that way, of course."

He waved that off. "But Ryan would. I'm all for it. Shit, you should've done it sooner."

"No objections from your parents?"

"Nah. I know Matt's good with security."

"Do you think Ryan will go for it?"

"Oh, I'm sure he'd love it, too. But as for him going to England with you because of it, I don't know."

"Me either.

"Seriously though. It would do him more good than me to find out I'll be fine without him."

Anna nodded. "Wish me luck."

"You're gonna need it."

———— ✦ • ✦ ————

A fortnight later, Ryan, Anna, Matt, and Eric stood in the English countryside, the giant stone monoliths of Stonehenge looming nearby in the dark. The place was deserted. It had closed hours earlier when they'd been here for a private tour that allowed them to walk among the stones, and Anna had lost her pendant in the grass during this tour, or so they surmised. They hadn't been anywhere else but the big SUV Ryan had rented, and a search of that had turned up nothing.

Ryan sighed, staring at the little glowing screen of his iPhone in the dark. He still had no connection to check on Daniel. It had taken a week of enjoying the web cams back in the U.S. before Ryan had finally, and very reluctantly, agreed to make the trip. So far it had worked, and he was just starting to relax a bit, but out in the middle of nowhere, a flaw became apparent.

Suddenly a hand closed over the screen and he looked up, startled. Matt was frowning at him. "C'mon," Matt whispered. "Put it away. You can check on him later. Anna needs our help. At least make a show of looking even if you don't really care."

"Of course I care," Ryan muttered, putting the iPhone into a pocket with an effort. He knew the pendant was more precious to Anna than even his golden cross was to him. It was a family heirloom that her aunt had given her, and she'd confided that inside the diamond were strange letters that only a jeweler's glass let you see, but no one could read them. Losing it had been bound to happen sooner or later, as she was always pulling the pendant back and forth on the chain, stressing the fragile lock. His eyes went over to where Eric was leading her by the hand toward the monument, a large flashlight he'd found in the car sweeping back and forth.

Matt turned toward them. "Then let's go."

"Right." Ryan fell in beside him as they marched up the gravel path, passing the circular earthen bank and ditch and a ring of holes in the ground to enter Stonehenge. Few of the center stones remained and most of the larger sarsen stones that he recognized from pictures were gone, too. "So what did they say this place was for?"

"Solstice rituals or something."

"It's a lot of trouble to go through just for a ritual, isn't it?" Ryan asked, laying a palm on a cold stone. It was huge, ponderous, and formidable. Someone had put a lot of work into this. "They must weigh a ton."

"Twenty-five tons, to be exact," corrected Matt. "The big ones came from twenty miles away. It makes you wonder what they really did here. It does seem like a lot of work for just a ritual."

"How long ago was this built?" the big guy asked.

Matt smirked. "You weren't listening at all earlier, were you? Something like 3000 to 1600 BC."

Ryan glanced around at the open countryside, wondering if a passing cop car would see Eric's flashlight and show up to arrest them for trespassing. Then he noticed something and went off to investigate, stepping around a toppled stone to discover that the air beyond it tingled strangely, like he'd walked into an electrical field. A faint light shone near a pair of giant stones with a third stone lying across the top. On the trilithon's surface, a few feet above the ground, three oddly shaped lights were glowing blue. Had the moon shone brighter he might never have noticed. When he stopped beside them, he found Anna's pendant lying there in the grass, reflecting the glow on its silver parts. He picked it up absently, staring at the trilithon.

After a moment, he realized they'd stopped here earlier to see an ancient carving of a dagger and axe on the stone. The glowing symbols were beneath these and seemed vaguely familiar, though they hadn't been here before. He'd seen such symbols in fantasy role playing games.

"Norse runes," he said to himself, trying to remember how to read them. They were a form of alphabet used for communication, divination, and magic. With every moment, more lines of text appeared on the once dark and silent stone surface, letters swirling around the monolith to cover all sides.

"Guys!" he called in amazement. They turned to see words of blue fire igniting their way up the stone surface, covering the lintel stone on top.

Eric called, "Get away from there, Ryan!"

He blinked at the suggestion and then realized Eric's instincts about danger were infinitely better than anyone he knew. He backed away, but on seeing looks of fear on their faces, jogged toward them, meeting at the center of Stonehenge.

"What the hell is going on?" Matt asked.

"I think we should get out of here," Anna said, taking the pendant from his hand.

Moments later, every monolith burst into blue flames. An arc of fire spread between them and to places where missing or fallen stones now reappeared like ghostly apparitions from the past. The outer ring of sarsen stones encircled them as flames raced around the lintel stones on top, starting at the original entrance to the site and coming around again. They were the first ones in ages to see the full shape of Stonehenge as it was meant to be, but they didn't have long to admire it. As the flame wave circled to where it started, everything disappeared in a blinding flash.

Ryan could hardly see for all the swirling and flashing lights surrounding them, a vortex of air drowning everything out. It looked like Anna was screaming. He tried to step toward her but couldn't move his feet. He looked down and saw only blackness below him. The earth was gone, as were the huge stones and the sky.

While he watched, Matt's jeans and shirt changed to a long, dark robe, a staff appearing in one hand. Startled, Ryan looked at Eric, who now wore leather from neck to toe, a bandoleer of knives across his chest and a short sword at one hip. Then this disappeared and for a moment he was naked before his Earth clothes returned. Ryan's eyes went to Anna just as she switched from bare to her normal clothes, and a moment later she wore a long white robe. He glanced down at himself and saw a suit of golden armor, a big sword strapped to his waist and a golden lance in one hand. Then the noise, wind, and darkness abruptly stopped.

Squinting and shielding his eyes in the bright sunlight, Ryan tried to make out his surroundings. The air tingled and he felt invigorated and refreshed, as if awakening from a deep sleep. Words of blue fire were fading from the stone pillars around them, but it wasn't Stonehenge. These were a foot in diameter and well kept. The tallest were at the back and they decreased in size to an inch high in the front. A raised dais lay underfoot, where more decorative markings faded from view. Above them in a towering hall of grey limestone, sunlight poured in from huge stained-glass windows depicting dragons, elves, knights, and other fantastic sights.

And there were people, standing at the far end of the room, staring in amazement. Dressed in finery befitting a royal medieval court, scores of them stood against the tapestry-covered walls, fur-lined or silken tunics and leggings as well-kept as their brushed hairs and trimmed beards on the men. In the room's center stood a tall, robed figure, white hair and a matching beard flowing past his belted waist. A large book lay open on a podium before him. He lowered a staff similar to the one in Matt's hand to the floor and looked every bit the wizard. Behind him stood a pair of thrones, one empty, the other bearing a regal woman in an elaborate gown, a golden crown upon her head. Nearby stood people that looked like they might be her advisors, one of whom rose and came toward them with an outstretched hand.

"The gods be praised! They have come!"

The crowd murmured and the queen rose slowly, eyes moving from one arrival to the next, studying their faces. Ryan didn't know what to say or do and sensed that little of either was probably best. At last the queen raised her chin regally.

"Welcome," she began in a clear voice, a smile growing. "Welcome to Olliana, capitol of the Kingdom of Alunia, on the world of Honyn. I am Queen Lorella, ruler of this land, and I have summoned you for a noble quest, to free our land of dragons as before, and return peace to our world."

While a round of cheers greeted this announcement, Matt leaned over to Ryan and quietly repeated, "Quest?"

"Did she say 'dragons'?" Anna whispered, wide-eyed.

"Yes," replied Ryan in amazement, wondering if they were sharing a delusion. He was dreaming. That was it. He was back at their hotel room having a cool dream. He relaxed.

"We are most excited by your return to Honyn," the queen continued, "and word will go forth at once that the Ellorian Champions have answered our call, for so many worlds depend upon your aid that all will rejoice at your return after these many years." She paused expectantly and Ryan realized all the important-looking people were staring at him. The queen clearly thought they were someone else but now was probably not the time to ask who. He cleared his throat.

"Thank you for this reception, Your Majesty," he replied, voice booming off the tall walls as he played a part just like at RenFest. Improvising this sort of thing now came naturally. Why couldn't all of his dreams be this awesome? "What is the nature of this quest?"

Queen Lorella announced, "You must fight your way to the Dragon Gate, defeat the dragon guarding it, and reseal it. If you fail, every life on Honyn shall perish, as shall each of you."

Under his golden armor, a sheen of sweat soaked Ryan's clothes. Kill or be killed? Dream or not, that struck a nerve and brought up old, painful memories. Distracted, he slowly became aware that Anna was urgently whispering his name and that everyone was waiting for his response. He cleared his throat. "We're honored to answer your call," he said, projecting confidence, "and look forward to fulfilling your quest."

That brought happy murmurs from the crowd but not Eric, who whispered, "Ryan, don't promise anything like that."

Fingering the lance, the supposed knight murmured, "Well I had to say something, didn't I? Besides, this isn't real."

"Well, maybe not," Eric began, seeming less confident than usual, "but watch what you say."

"You are most welcome, Lord Korrin of Andor," Queen Lorella replied to Ryan. "Please accept our invitation to a great banquet in your honor tonight. While your suite is prepared, my Prime Minister and the Arch Wizard of Olliana, Sonneri, will explain what lies before you. The quest will begin tomorrow." She regally turned to leave, an escort of pages following.

"Great, this dream will probably end without anything cool happening," observed Ryan. He pinched himself, surprised that it hurt. It felt real.

As the queen disappeared, a tidal wave of chattering sycophants plunged toward them until guards intervened, cleaving a path for Sonneri and the queen's Prime Minister. The latter wore golden trousers and a sash over his embroidered tunic – a rectangular piece of cloth slipped over the head and belted at the waist. Sonneri's pine staff thumped on the floor as he approached, one hand on his prodigious belly, grandfatherly eyes bright. He pulled a pipe from his blue robe and lit it with a snap of his fingers. He looked pleased as he bowed.

"Greetings," said the wizard in a gravelly voice. "We are most surprised to see you here."

"So are we," Matt wryly observed.

"If you, uh, summoned us," began Anna, coming forward, "why are you surprised to see us. Were you expecting someone else?"

He bowed even lower to her. "My lady Eriana, no one could possibly come in your stead, but you have not graced a world with your presence in many years, and so we did not expect you to come."

"I see," she said. Her eyes lingered on a slender figure observing them from beside the empty thrones. As if noticing this, the man turned away, the cloak on his back swirling to reveal an embroidered tree. Fluid, graceful steps carried him away.

Sonneri continued. "If you'll come with us, the Prime Minister and I will answer your questions about the quest."

Ryan gestured for the others to precede him as they stepped off the dais. Dreams always centered around him and yet the others seemed focused on everything *but* him. And he had to admit that this felt real. He felt the heat of the sun each time he stepped into it. The voices around him had an accent he couldn't have imagined if he'd tried. He took a deep breath through his nose and caught a subtle but acrid smell of sweat, as if those nearby didn't bathe often. If this was a dream, his senses were far more alive than usual. A nagging feeling told him something was wrong and he began to frown.

"After this meeting," he started, addressing Sonneri, "we could use some time alone to discuss matters, if that wouldn't be too much trouble."

"Certainly," agreed the wizard.

Ryan brought up the rear, noticing that his finely carved, golden plate armor fit perfectly and was well adjusted despite the number of straps holding it together. Even the underlying chain mail was the right size. A golden sword sheath hung from one hip, where a helmet held fast to his waist, tightly tied to keep it from bouncing. That's when he noticed how quiet the armor was. His RenFest made all sorts of noise, chain mail clinking and straps squeaking, but not this one. It seemed designed for stealth and actual usage.

As the throne room disappeared behind them, he cast a glance back, wondering if stepping onto the Stonehenge-like dais would send them home. That's when the similarity between it and the monument struck him along with a suspicion as to the real nature of England's most famous archeological site. Maybe they'd learned what it was really for after all.

CHAPTER THREE

THE QUEST

Eric entered the War Room behind the wizard Sonneri and Prime Minister, the others trailing him. He had already noticed that his comfortable black leathers were supple and well worn. Metal studs designed to deflect swords dotted both the tunic and the arm bands that covered his black linen shirt. His fingers discreetly picked his own pockets, discovering coins, an unworn ring, some small tools he guessed were lock-picking aids, and a hidden knife. Other blades were scattered about his person, some in view like the dagger and sword on opposite hips and the bandoleer of throwing knives across his chest, but smaller ones lay along his forearms, thighs, and even the back of his neck. He suspected more knives were in places he couldn't reach now, like the soundless black boots that fit better than any he'd ever worn. A pouch at one hip held a white powder that reminded him of the chalk he used when rock climbing.

As he moved to a large table, he was caught between wanting to study every last item he saw, playing a part that he sensed required more nonchalance and confidence than he felt, and blurting out questions to his friends about their opinion of what was happening. He knew this was no dream, and yet how could it be real? Now appeared to be a chance to get answers from those who'd brought them here, so he focused on that. Getting reactions from his friends would have to wait. In fact, he hoped their own sense of decorum kept them from saying the wrong thing. Ryan in particular looked like he wasn't taking this very seriously up until now, when Eric saw him frown and look concerned. He fixed each of them with a stern gaze, wishing that more than he and Matt understood sign language. He took the opportunity to sign a few comments to his supposed wizard friend.

He signed, *I don't know what's going on but take this seriously until we're alone, okay?*

Yeah, no problem.

Try to influence the others with demeanor, etc.

Especially Ryan.

Exactly.

Eric saw Anna watching him intently, a question in her serious eyes, and he sensed she was on board.

They stopped around a large hexagonal table where Prime Minister Diam spread several maps of Olliana, in Kingdom Alunia, and nearby kingdoms. Along the walls hung swords, lances, other weapons, and tapestries of battle scenes. The standing suits of armor showed signs of use and suggested historical significance. Glass cases lined the room and presented peace treaties and other scrolls. Ryan leaned his lance against one wall, gazing up at the banner tied to the end. Eric wondered what was on it.

"It's been some time since your last visit," began the Prime Minister.

Eric tried to hide his surprise. If they were thought to have been here before, didn't anyone recognize this wasn't true? Did the four from Earth look enough like whoever had been expected that no one could tell the difference? That was a question he couldn't ask.

"Yes, it has," Eric said. "Can you remind us of the situation then and since?"

"Certainly," the Prime Minister replied. "While both good and evil dragons exist on some worlds, only the latter existed here on Honyn. They long terrorized villages and towns in all kingdoms, but they generally acted alone, so the threat was manageable if not entirely satisfactory. Trouble arose years ago when a strong leader coerced coordination from the others. A female named Nir'lion rose to power and was the most aggressive we've ever seen. The resulting campaign of terror was so fearsome that when we last summoned you, you determined they had earned a banishment from Honyn."

Eric saw his friends look surprised. They needed to control their expressions better. He tried to divert attention to himself by asking, "And is that what we did? Banish them? To...another world? It's been a while. Please refresh our memory, almost as if we've never been here before. We won't be offended if you tell us something we remember."

"Yes, Andier."

The martial artist cocked his head. "How did you say that name?" he asked as if it wasn't pronounced correctly.

The Prime Minister looked concerned. "Did I not say it right? I beg your pardon."

"Well, let me hear it again and I'll tell you."

"Andier of Roir, the Silver-Tongued Rogue."

Great title, Eric thought. "And do you have my companions' names learned so well, too?"

Matt discreetly made signs with his fingers at him. *Nicely done.*

"I would certainly hope so," the Prime Minister replied. "The knight is Lord Korrin of Andor, the Golden Knight, whose charming smile dazzles the ladies more than his gleaming armor. The Dragon Slayer, the Lord of Hearts, the Pride of Andor. A man whom women want, and whom men want to be."

On hearing this, Ryan raised an eyebrow and began to grin until catching Eric's eye and receiving a subtle but stern shake of the head. The supposed knight pursed his lips in amusement.

The Prime Minister turned to Matt. "Soliander of Aranor, the Majestic Magus, the Flaming Hand, the Lord of Power, a wizard so potent that whole armies have been known to balk at your name. Few have dared challenge you, and none have been the victor." Matt nodded as if unimpressed.

With a nod at Anna, the Prime Minister said, "The lovely Eriana of Coreth, a golden-haired beauty whose healing touch brings life to the dying and hope to the lonely. Said to be favored of the gods, perhaps even a lover, for the strength that flows through the Blessed One is unmatched among mortals. The Lady Hope, you've left many a warrior smitten by your healing hand." He bowed and then turned back to Eric, who tried not to grin at the atheist Anna, who wore an expression of muted annoyance.

"And finally, Andier of Roir, the Silver-Tongued Rogue. With a mind full of tricks, an ear for the unsaid, and a knack for entering places uninvited, the Slippery Serpent can learn more about you than your own mother."

"Very good," replied Eric, thinking they were in an awful lot of trouble. "And you refer us as the champions, not by any other name? Some places give us nicknames."

"Not here, Andier. You are, of course, the Ellorian Champions, from the world Elloria, though most simply call you the champions. With your permission, we may continue?" The Prime Minister pointed at the map. "You recall there is an old castle, Castle Darlonon, nearby in the mountains. It's a ruin and therefore largely forgotten, and so it was here that you created a device with a dual purpose."

Sonneri interjected, "As you no doubt remember, this device, the Dragon Gate, would not only remove the dragons from Honyn but prevent them from returning. The details of how to operate it were not revealed to us, and only Soliander knows how it works." He looked at Matt, who looked uncomfortable with the revelation.

"Or so we believed," added the Prime Minister. "Two weeks ago, a dragon was seen flying over the peaks east of here. Investigation revealed there is great activity at Castle Darlonon when there should be none, and that the gate stands open. We believe the escaped dragon is Nir'lion, and it's a certainty that she intends to release the remaining dragons, which must be prevented."

"Only one came through?" Ryan asked.

"We think so," admitted Sonneri. "We suspect that whoever released her has a plan that requires only Nir'lion for now and that the others continue to remain behind, but that is conjecture. Suffice it to say that if the rest had come through, we'd be battling for our lives."

"You don't know who released her?" Anna asked. The men shook their heads.

"What about the Dragon Gate?" Matt asked. "What condition is it in?"

Sonneri replied, "We believe it's intact."

"You haven't seen it, then?" Eric confirmed.

"Not directly, no, nor has anyone else. The castle is guarded by members of the Dragon Cult and mercenaries they've hired. No one has been able to get inside except a magical spy I sent."

"Who is this cult?" Ryan asked with distaste. Eric knew he didn't care for them because the ones on Earth often perverted God's word, according to his friend. He couldn't disagree. They were typically nut jobs.

Sonneri sighed. "They are fanatical dragon worshipers who believe this world rightfully belongs under the rule of dragons. The banishment outraged them and they vowed to release the dragons and seek revenge on not only you four, but Olliana, as well."

"Perfect," said Eric wryly.

"So do you think they're the ones who freed the dragons?" Anna asked.

"Doubtful," replied Sonneri, puffing his pipe. "They have some wizards among them, but none powerful enough to unweave the spells Soliander wrought."

"Then who?"

The wizard Matt answered, "We're hoping you'll discover this."

How are we supposed to that? Eric wondered. Unless whoever did it was standing there at this Dragon Gate when they arrived, how would they know? It wasn't like they even knew anyone here to begin pointing fingers.

"At this time," the Prime Minister began, "we believe Nir'lion doesn't know we're aware of her return, and we intend to keep it that way."

"Probably wise," Eric interjected.

"She seems intent on staying out of sight," the Prime Minister continued, "and if she's openly discovered, she may hasten the release of the others. We also have an advantage if she doesn't know we're prepared. However, a secret of this magnitude is hard to keep, and word has spread across Honyn. Some foolish men have tried to reach Castle Darlonon in a reckless attempt to kill her, but we've stopped everyone who's tried with a force of men guarding the castle road. Doing so is precarious due to the danger of being detected, however, so time is of the essence. Another factor is that other kingdoms have concluded that we're responsible for her release and are in collusion with the dragons to attack their lands."

Eric frowned. Another kingdom getting involved only worsened things. "Why would they believe that?"

"Because they are fools," muttered Sonneri, glaring at the map.

The Prime Minister sighed. "When Olliana last summoned you and you completed the quest on our behalf, great attention and praise were heaped upon us. The stature of Kingdom Alunia rose considerably and we became a more powerful and influential kingdom. This was not viewed favorably by all."

Sonneri interjected, "In short, they became jealous and have assumed that Alunia is power mad, and madness it would be if they were correct. They believe a wizard of Olliana freed the dragons at the request of Queen Lorella, who subsequently made a deal with Nir'lion that Alunia is not to be attacked. Instead, we will wage war with the dragons upon the rest of Honyn."

Looking confused, Anna observed, "But that doesn't make sense. Why would you have summoned the, uh, four of us before to banish the dragons if this is what you wanted?"

Sonneri replied, "Banishment was your decision, not our request. If you remember, the previous quest's requirement was to control the dragons so they could not work together against our world, and to nullify them permanently."

Tall order, thought Eric. *The four we're impersonating must be really powerful.*

"Also," continued the wizard, "the assumption is that Alunia became power mad after that quest and only now made a deal with the dragons."

"I see," said Anna, looking concerned.

The Prime Minister pointed at a region on a map. "Most recently, a neighboring kingdom, Rokune, has threatened action against Olliana and this hastened our attempt to summon you. They are not the only kingdom preparing for war, but they are the nearest. Since you have not answered a summons in many years, our announcement that we would try was considered a shallow, empty gesture. However, now that you've arrived, the queen's messengers are quickly sending out the news."

Perfect, thought Eric, wondering if now was a good time to confess. Being sent back probably required Sonneri's cooperation, so they had to stay on his good side.

"Since this began," the Prime Minister continued, "tensions are high and the queen hasn't quite been herself. I must beseech you to resolve matters quickly." He looked expectantly at Ryan. On seeing this, Eric realized the big guy was the apparent leader of these champions. He wasn't known for decisiveness.

Matt asked, "Is there an historical record of what we did here before? It could refresh our memory." Eric looked at him in approval, thinking it was a fantastic idea.

"Yes," answered Sonneri, looking apologetic, "though I must confess we made a copy of the scroll you provided before locking away the original, which was regrettably stolen years ago so that its secrets are likely known. I will have the copy delivered to your suite along with a scroll describing our gods and religions for Eriana to re-familiarize herself with, as is customary, of course."

Anna exchanged a look with Eric, who knew what she was thinking – there was no master plan, destiny, afterlife, ghosts, or any of that other baloney. He'd let her vent to him later. Now was not the time and she seemed to know it. Sonneri's words also suggested that Eriana, and now Anna, had to learn the gods of each world she visited and commune with one, getting familiar, before being able to have one heal through her. Being able to ask someone about such concerns would've been nice, but everyone thought they were the real Ellorian Champions, who would know such things.

As they exited the War Room, a court page advised them that Queen Lorella had arranged for a castle tour. It could have been an innocent excursion were it not for the noblemen and women who were let loose upon them. They spent an hour fending off questions about past exploits, where they'd been, what it was like to be so revered, what they thought had happened to let the dragons loose upon Honyn again, and more importantly, what they were going to do about it. After Ryan tried to be helpful and answer these questions despite being clueless, Eric took over to deflect the inquiries, claiming they needed to keep certain things to themselves. People kept asking anyway, and it was with some relief that the tour finally ended.

Along the way they'd seen much of Castle Olliana, a living home full of royalty, dignitaries, pages, scribes, and people on court business, including knights and wizards who asked questions they deflected. White towers swirled gracefully into the sky, spiraling up to blue domes topped with silver points. The four large, corner towers served the royalty, the knights and their squires, priests and clerics, and finally the kingdom's arch wizard and followers. But they saw signs of the dragon rampage in that some buildings were destroyed and others seemingly permanently burned by dragon fire. Their suite lay in the royal wing a few halls away from the queen's, a prestigious location. A steward advised them of various housekeeping matters before leaving and closing the doors, which Eric crept up to, listening to the footsteps fading away.

"Okay," he said at last, turning back, "we're alone."

CHAPTER FOUR

FRESH WOUNDS

Anna had seldom if ever seen Eric look serious, as he was so often quick to joke, but she knew of his troubled past and that there had to be more to him than one-liners and sarcasm. His demeanor since they'd disappeared from Stonehenge had made more of an impression than Ryan's casualness, though that had since vanished. The strain of pretending to be fine over the past hour, with all those people asking questions and looking to them for help, while a growing dread had been filling her had made her relieved to be alone with her friends. But she excused herself, looking for a bathroom and heading through an adjacent doorway, where she found only four bedrooms, none with toilets or a sink. Each had a tub, washbowl, and chamber pot, to her dismay. With a frown, she closed an ornate door behind her.

As she walked, she caught her reflection in a mirror and stopped a moment. While she'd noticed elements of her outfit, the full picture only now became apparent. Golden patterns and symbols she didn't recognize covered the bottom edge, cuffs, neck, and hood of her white robe. Her long blonde hair was now in a French braid, a golden pin through it. She wasn't wearing much else except a few rings, a bracelet, and an amulet that depicted one figure kneeling beside another that was rising from a supine position. No sign of her pendant. Seldom one for much makeup, she noted that all of what she'd been wearing on Earth was gone.

She had already sensed she wasn't wearing much beneath the robe, including a bra. The undergarments proved to be just a thin, long shift, skirt, and white leather boots. What had happened to her Earth clothes? The thought made a rush of questions and anxiety seize her and she desperately wanted to talk to the boys, so she rinsed her hands in a bowl, not finding soap, and headed back. She returned to where she'd left them, finding them talking quietly together. They turned as one and she saw only serious expressions.

Letting out a sigh, she sat on a couch that looked like the expensive furniture at the LaRue estate, albeit in medieval style. Out the window behind her waited a balcony that she wanted to check. It might be nice to view their setting without onlookers asking questions she had to dodge.

She asked, "What did I miss?"

Eric pursed his lips. "Well, we've agreed we're not dreaming or having a shared delusion of some kind."

Ryan added, "At first, I thought it was and didn't take it at all serious. I wish I had. Now I promised that queen we'd do something."

"Yeah," said Matt. "I kind of wished you hadn't."

"How was I supposed to know?"

Matt joined Anna on the couch and pulled what looked like a spell book from a bag he'd arrived with. As he flipped through it, she thought that any artist could have drawn the fantastic pictures, but the pages had the look of frequent traffic. There were spills and stains, bent corners, and torn pages. Someone appeared to have *used* this thing. Extensively.

Anna remarked, "Something tells me this isn't even Earth."

Eric pulled out the short sword he'd arrived with and examined it while saying, "This…wizard, Sonneri, can probably tell us how this summoning thing works, to send us back, though I doubt we'll understand it. It appears to be magic."

"Or science that they think is magic," observed Matt, not sounding like he believed it.

"If it's just science," Ryan began, pulling out his own sword, "there'd be more of it, right?"

Anna nodded. "Right. I saw no electricity, air conditioning, even plumbing. No planes or cars. Out the windows I only heard wagons and horses' hooves on stone, and I saw people buying things with gold, silver, and bronze coins, not credit cards or even paper money. There's certainly no internet, TV, or smart phones. If we're still on Earth, we've gone back in time, which is just as implausible."

At her own mention of smart phones, she cast a look at Ryan, but he hadn't reacted. They didn't need him realizing he couldn't check on Daniel right now. Seeing his scrutiny of the sword, she looked and bluish-silver steel, with elegant, golden script flowing down the blade. Similar script curled around the shaft of Matt's staff and graced the pages of the book he continued flipping through.

Eric interrupted her thoughts. "This sword is perfectly balanced."

"This one, too," said Ryan. "Really light, too. It's surprising. It doesn't seem like any metal I've ever seen."

"I hope you don't need them," Anna remarked.

"Hard to argue with that," admitted Eric, putting it away and feeling around his outfit for something, which she realized was throwing knives when he pulled several out, testing their balance in his hands. "Whatever happened at Stonehenge could've been technology we just don't know about. You know, something like motion sensing lights could seem like magic to the ignorant. Even Sonneri appearing to light his pipe by snapping his fingers could just be technology that reacts to sound."

Anna knew they might have indeed traveled by science regardless of what anyone on Honyn thought, and maybe it was better for people here to think that whatever the truth might be. After all, performing magic took skill, talent, knowledge and discipline, which were all reasons Matt was no Soliander. But science required none of these things. Once someone smart enough to build a device had done so, anyone could use it. People with automatic guns didn't need skill to kill a highly trained Samurai. It was how the weak could defeat the strong and upset what some considered the natural order of things. Then again, magic items allowed unskilled people to cast spells, too, but within limits. If Soliander's staff, which they apparently had, possessed some power to facilitate this Dragon Gate closing, maybe they stood a chance of doing that, but it was an unknown and far too risky.

"So what do we do?" Anna asked. "We can't really do this quest."

Eric nodded. "If this is for real, and we just decided it is, then there's a real dragon out there, too, and it sounds like she wouldn't hesitate to kill us for trying to screw up her plans."

Ryan said, "True, but this world is in serious trouble, and they think they can't protect themselves and we can, so we'd be turning our backs on them."

"Not really, because we're not who they want," Matt observed, "and they don't even know that. They've got to send us back and try to summon these four people again. Maybe it will work this time."

Anna nodded, thinking she'd almost like to stick around and watch the result. "Yeah, it's the only responsible thing to do."

"Yeah, you're right," Ryan agreed. "So when do we tell them?"

"Before this banquet tonight," suggested Anna, feeling guilty. "We've got to do it before everyone gets too excited."

"I think it's a little late for that," Eric remarked ruefully, rising. He cocked his head and Anna had the impression he'd heard something from another room. That impression grew when he started moving in that direction.

"Sonneri's probably the one to send us back," Matt observed, "so we should approach him in private, I think."

"Good idea," said Anna. "Maybe he can even help us figure out how we got substituted for these people when we tell him."

While Ryan carefully swung his sword, Anna's eyes followed Eric as he reached the doorway of a bedroom. He suddenly leaned back sharply and she thought something had narrowly missed hitting his face. Then his arm rose swiftly, meeting and blocking the arm of someone swinging a dagger at him from inside the bedroom.

"Eric!" Anna yelled in panic, rising.

The martial artist retreated and a figure in black followed, lunging from the doorway. Eric grabbed the man's forearms and fell back, pulling the intruder onto his upraised foot and throwing him headfirst behind him. A table shattered under the assassin as Eric rose to go after him, with a quick glance into the bedroom.

"Ryan! Another guy coming in through the window!"

The big man stepped into the doorway, a knife meant for Eric's back bouncing off his golden armor. Startled, he backed away and yelped, "What do I do?"

Rushing the first guy, Eric replied, "Stick him with the sword!" With that he kicked the first assassin in the face and the intruder flew backwards, dropping another dagger.

Anna backed away from the fight, caught between wanting to help and running. Matt had risen and come to stand near her. Together they moved behind the couch toward the balcony.

Also wearing black, Ryan's foe drew a sword, prompting the knight to raise his own without the confidence Anna had seen him use at RenFest. Those were staged combats where he knew every last move his opponent would make beforehand, having practiced it together for hours. How would he fare when someone meant to kill him? The intruder's blade sliced at him much faster than Anna expected and he barely blocked it, backing away. "There's another one coming in!" he called.

"Oh my God," said Anna.

Ryan's attacker glanced behind before resuming almost recklessly, forcing Ryan back. He leapt away from the knight and turned just as the third man entered. This one wore brown and green leathers and hardly spared Ryan a glance as he leapt after Ryan's attacker. Their blades met with a loud ring.

"Is he helping us?" Matt asked.

"Think so!" Anna answered in relief. Her eyes lingered on realizing this man had slanted eyes, a delicate heart-shaped face, and otherworldly gracefulness. She could've sworn a pointed ear sometimes peeked out from under the blond hair. The word "elf" popped into her head.

Ryan exchanged a startled look with them before moving around the room to guard them. "Stay behind me."

"You don't have to tell me twice," remarked Anna, clinging to Matt. She pulled her eyes off the apparent elf to Eric, whom she'd never seen fight for real. A round of flying fists happened so fast that she couldn't follow it, but then the assassin drew a sword and so did Eric. Did he know how to use it? Eric blocked a swing, the blow jarring the blade from his hand to the floor. Anna gasped, but he kicked the man's wrist and that sword fell, too. His attacker punched him in the jaw with the other hand, knocking him back, then threw a knife that struck his chest, bouncing off the studded leather.

"Son of a bitch!" Eric looked a little disbelieving, then angry. He grabbed his own throwing knife but hesitated to throw it. His attacker drew another, raising one arm, and Eric flicked his wrist. The knife stuck in the man's stomach. Another followed into his upraised arm. Then Eric leapt forward and up, spinning in the air, his foot slamming into the man's face and hurling him backward into the wall before ricocheting him forward to the floor face first, where he lay unmoving.

Anna just stared at the aftermath until Eric turned to the other fight unfolding. The second assassin's back was to them, which apparently gave Ryan an idea for the way he quietly approached them, raising his sword high. He brought the pommel crashing down on the assassin's head. The blow thrust the man forward and right onto the elf's sword, which impaled him through the chest. The assassin fell back, almost striking Ryan, sightless eyes staring at the ceiling.

"Oh my God," the knight said. "That's not what I wanted!" His eyes danced about the room, from the dead man's eyes, to the blood pooling on the floor, to the pity in the eyes of those looking at him, and finally to the sword that had done this. He dropped it with a clatter and clamped his eyes shut, one hand over them.

Anna saw crimson spreading out beneath the man Eric had fought. Despite being afraid to go near, the medical student in her took over and she went to check his pulse, not finding one. Eric helped turn the man over. He'd fallen on the knife in his abdomen. He was dead. Anna exchanged a stunned look with Eric before they rose. Matt had gone pale, holding onto the couch to steady himself. The elf knelt to wipe his sword on the other victim's clothes and an awkward silence filled the room, broken only by Ryan's distressed breathing.

"Thank you," Anna started, struck by his piercing green eyes, delicate nose, and graceful, efficient movements suggestive of strength beyond his lithe, tall frame. Long blond hair fell behind his pointed ears, some of it braided.

"Who are you?" Eric asked, another knife ready. "What are you doing in here?"

"I observed them climbing the walls and followed," the man replied in soft, musical voice. "Their intentions were clearly ill."

Suspiciously, Eric asked, "How'd you come to see them?"

Anna thought he should be more polite, given that the elf had saved their lives, but she wanted to know, too. Was he spying on them? Paranoia seemed appropriate.

"My suite is across the courtyard from yours," the man answered, gesturing out the balcony.

Anna looked and saw a dimly lit window with a terrace, from which hung a long tapestry that had partially torn away during the man's descent on it. She came forward. "You were in the courtroom before," she observed, remembering the man with the tree-embossed cloak.

"Yes."

"I'm..." she hesitated, trying to remember her supposed name, "I'm Eriana."

He looked her in the eye and frowned. "No, you are not."

She hesitated, unsure what to say.

"I appear to be the only one not fooled by your charade," the man continued, looking from one to another, "presumably on account of the length of time those you impersonate have been absent."

They exchanged a nervous look.

"Why does that matter?" Matt asked faintly. If he didn't look at the bodies or all that blood, maybe he wouldn't pass out.

"Four years is a long time to humans and your memories fade."

"So..." Eric started, "four years is not a long time to you?"

"Correct."

"Because... you're an elf?"

"Of course."

Ryan pulled his hand down and opened his eyes. "An elf?" He scrutinized the man and finally said. "Are these supposed to be real, too?"

"Do you think I'm an illusion of some sort?"

"No," replied Ryan quietly, "I just don't think you're for real."

"I am of the flesh."

Eric interrupted. "We can discuss this later. The important thing is these men just attacked us, and everyone thinks we're Andier, Eriana, Korrin, and Soliander, but you don't. Why don't you tell us what's going on?"

The elf cocked an eyebrow. "I was hoping you would tell me. I am Lorian of the House of Arundell in the elven city of Noria, in the Great Honyn Forest. I have known the champions on several occasions and know you are not them. However, it may be best to continue your charade with others until we can speak further."

Eric nodded, suggesting, "We need to get some guards in here in case there are more of these guys." He looked at the bodies in consternation and Anna knew he had to be upset about having killed someone, maybe less so than Ryan, but still. Any curiosity about this champion stuff had abruptly ended.

Lorian put away his sword, bending over a corpse. "We must inform only the Queen's elite guard. Few others can be trusted."

Surprised by that, Anna asked, "Do you think someone here sent these men?"

"Possibly," replied Lorian, turning down the collar of one to reveal a tattoo of a dragon silhouette. "These are Dragon Cult members. It is interesting only two were sent. For such a formidable group as the champions, this is absurd. Professionals would not have been so easily dispatched, either."

"That was easy?" Ryan asked quietly.

Matt asked, "Does that suggest these men knew we aren't the champions and could be more easily killed with just two assassins?"

Lorian turned appraising eyes on him. "Excellent question. I do not know."

Eric observed, "Either way, this means the cult knows we're here, and they're likely to tell the dragon we're coming if they're in contact with her. The element of surprise is gone."

"That was unavoidable from the start," Lorian remarked matter-of-factly. "With the queen's announcement of your arrival, they'd have known long before you reached the castle. They'll be expecting you."

Anna hadn't thought of that, but it wouldn't matter with them going home soon.

Eric lent a hand as the elf dragged one body to the other. As Lorian picked up the dead man's sword, Anna noticed it was badly nicked from contact with either Ryan's sword or the elf's, but Korrin's was unscathed.

"Now might be a good time to decline the quest and be sent home," suggested Anna, worried about Ryan but unsure what to say.

The elf cocked an eyebrow. "That is not possible."

"Why?" Anna asked.

Lorian looked confused. "You cannot refuse a quest. It is woven into the spell that summons you and requires completion before the counter spell, that which sends you back, will work. If you refuse the quest or fail in it, you will remain here until your death."

Ryan went pale and a stunned silence followed. Anna's eyes fell on the dead.

"And if we accept," she said, "we'll all get killed."

A CONSCIENCE RIDDLED

After the attack, the elf Lorian had fetched the Prime Minister and a few elves to discreetly remove the bodies and blood-soaked rugs. They'd been given a new suite to the relief of both Matt and Ryan, one for being squeamish about blood and the other to escape the reminder, though it didn't help. Death had left no room to think this wasn't real.

Lorian had convinced Queen Lorella to let him lead the quest through the elven woods to save time, help them approach Castle Darlonon unseen, and to let Lorian gather elves to assist. They didn't mention wanting to speak more in private and Ryan wondered if the queen had suspected something from the long look she gave before agreeing. Perhaps politics were at play, yet another thing about which they knew nothing here. Maybe they shouldn't tell the truth about anything except to Lorian.

Now they nervously waited for the banquet, unsure what was expected of them. Each wore new finery courtesy of the queen, Ryan and Eric in tunics and tights, Anna in a lovely gown that had required a maid's assistance to get into, and Matt switching his somber, black robe for a more pleasant white.

"You know," started Matt, "we should all be really tired by now, since it was night when we left Earth and we've been here for half a day it seems, but I don't feel that way."

"I noticed that, too," Eric said. "It's probably four in the morning on Earth."

Matt suggested, "Do you think the summoning spell rejuvenated us in some way?"

"Possibly. It did change our clothes."

"And trapped us here," Ryan interjected sourly, breaking his silence. He hadn't spoken much since the attack. Anna had privately consoled him for a few minutes, but it hadn't helped, partly because he didn't let it.

Matt asked, "Do you think we can we trust this Lorian guy?"

Anna shrugged. "He's an elf."

Ryan shook his head. "How do we know he's not human with prosthetics taped to his ears?"

"Oh, come on," Anna chided. "Didn't you take a good look at him? There's no way he's human."

No, Ryan thought, *I was too busy looking at the man I just killed.*

Matt fingered his staff. "It wasn't just the ears or the eyes, either, but the way he moved, and something I can't put my finger on."

Ryan said, "Even if that's true and we accept that elves are generally good people, that still doesn't mean he doesn't have his own plans or agenda. We can't just trust someone because he's an elf."

Anna nodded. "True, but saving our lives goes a long way." At the mention of saved lives, Ryan frowned.

As someone knocked on the door, Eric said, "I think tonight we should all sleep in the same room, with one of us on watch."

"Good idea." Matt went for the door, adding, "Let's stay together at this dinner, too."

Eric nodded. "Or for that matter, until we're back on Earth."

They followed an escort down halls and an ornate, grand staircase, celebratory music growing louder until they reached the banquet, when the music stopped and all eyes turned to them, applause and cheers erupting. The Great Hall stood seventy feet high, with large tapestries of hunting scenes covering the limestone walls. The musicians sat on a balcony at one end opposite an enormous fireplace. In between stood six tables long enough to sit fifty people each, every seat filled but theirs.

They soon sat at a prominent place near the queen, Prime Minister, and the wizard. Ryan as Lord Korrin and the Anna as Lady Eriana sat on one side, Matt as the Majestic Majus Soliander and Eric as the Silver-Tongued Rogue Andier on the other. Lorian and two elves looked on nearby. Queen Lorella made some suitable comments regarding the occasion, during which Ryan noted the food looked familiar – turkey legs and breasts, hot breads and buns, chopped and whole vegetables like carrots, radishes, and ears of corn, stuffing, roasted boar, some kind of fish with the head still on, a pasta dish in red sauce, and wines and meads. While dining, Ryan first evaded questions with mouthfuls of food as an excuse, but soon he deflected people with his own questions, particularly those of several knights asking about his equipment or battle strategies. They seemed pleased at his inquiries and eager to brag, so he let them, but their related exploits ground everything in stark reality, reminding him he was an abject novice and imposter.

After dinner, when servants cleared the floor for dancing, Korrin became the object of many a woman's – and in truth, a few men's – fancy. Ryan's upbringing had included lessons in this kind of ballroom dancing, and though he didn't know the steps, he learned more quickly than Anna and Eric. He wasn't in the mood for it, and while some of the small talk with strangers distracted him, others kept asking about Korrin's exploits, reminding him of death.

During dinner, Eric had sipped wine while discreetly observing the attendees, from wait staff to guards, nobles, elves, and even the queen, whose eyes weren't the only ones on them. Glances came from all corners, but one group had felt out of place to him, their manners less refined, their glances too obvious. They seemed less like courtly fops and more like those living by their wits and sword. A rather dashing man among them had caught his eye and exchanged nods. Eric knew when someone was keeping an eye on them and hadn't liked it.

He hadn't failed to notice Ryan's preoccupation since the attack. Their talk at RenFest about Ryan not wanting to hurt anyone stayed fresh in his mind. Perhaps the big guy really meant it, though he didn't know why that was such a big deal to him. You had to draw the line at people trying to kill you. If the attacker ended up dead as a result, it was their own fault; they should've thought of that before attempting murder. Ryan had been right to do what he'd attempted, and while being remorseful was one thing, beating yourself up was another. He'd seen Anna console him too, and he was a bit annoyed that he'd gotten all of her attention. He'd killed someone, too, and just because he didn't let on so much didn't mean he wasn't also upset.

Once dancing began, Andier's mischievous nature apparently attracted its own kind of women to Eric, and while most were subtle about wanting amorous attention, others weren't. They seemed to think it was all right to be honest with Eric about their desire to be naughty, and he wondered just who this Andier fellow was. Maybe he had a reputation Eric needed to uphold. A glance at Ryan suggested the wholesome women had gone after him as Korrin while the sexed up ones went for Andier. Eric could live with that – or so he thought until he saw Anna's dance partner. It was the dashing man he'd noted earlier, and from the way he was looking at her, he clearly had naughty ideas of his own.

"My Lady Hope," began the man to Anna, bowing as he cut in on someone. "What a pleasure it is to meet you. I am Cirion of Ormund." One rough hand took hers while the other found the small of her back, both suggestive and possessive. She thought his mysterious, dark eyes seemed amused and probing, dancing a fine line between making it clear what he wanted and giving himself plausible deniability. He cut a lean figure in a green tunic that hugged his broad shoulders, black hair catching on the turned up collar of his black shirt. He seemed somehow nimble and quick, as if he'd never let himself be still long enough to get complacent. The phrase "a rolling stone gathers no moss" came to mind, his strong jaw suggesting he was in full command of his journeyman life and would have it no other way.

"To what do I owe the pleasure?" Anna asked, knowing a guy who wanted to bed her for what he was. She had to admit he was rather charming and she smiled despite herself.

"You waste no time, I see." He smirked knowingly.

Catching his meaning, she replied, "Well, you have until the dance is over to do your business. I'm sure that won't be a problem for you."

He laughed a rich baritone. "I assure you I can last quite a few songs."

"Perhaps, but maybe I'll be bored by then."

He laughed more genuinely. "Ouch! My lady, I had no idea you had such wit, and so cruel, too. Perhaps your title of Lady Hope is a misnomer, as you've surely tried to dash mine."

"But I haven't succeeded, I see."

"Well what kind of man would I be to give up on the first try?"

"Do you really want me to answer that?"

"Not really." Cirion paused. "Perhaps you'll be more amenable to other hopes of mine."

"Ah. Here it comes."

"Yes, you see, it's been some time since you visited Honyn and you might benefit from a guide on your way to Castle Darlonon, not to mention inside."

Her eyebrows arched. Was he a Dragon Cult member? "You've been inside?"

"Certainly. Not since the dragon returned, of course, but after your last visit."

She noticed he didn't say why. "And why did you go in? Didn't you know we strictly forbade such entrances?" This was a little tidbit she's picked up from Sonneri.

He smirked and ignored that. "I wanted to see this famed Dragon Gate, of course, but as you know, I couldn't reach it."

"Not man enough?" Anna asked, wanting him on the defensive as much as possible. Better him than her.

He grunted. "More like not wizard enough. I can cast a fair spell or two, but Soliander there can put up spells even an arch-wizard can't get by." He looked over at a young, red-robed wizard who was approaching Matt.

Curious what they'd encountered, Anna asked as if testing his truthfulness, "And what did you find there?"

Cirion seemed to catch her intention as he replied, "Well, for starters, the castle gate was unguarded, presumably to lure people to that courtyard, where the tiles burst into flames if you put your foot in the wrong place. Nasty trap, that one. We didn't get much farther despite getting by the main doors. The stairs were clearly unwise unless you wanted to visit for a rather long time, but the way forward was no better. We spent two days in the maze beyond it before escaping. After that, we were rather tired of the whole affair."

"Is that all it took to defeat you?" Anna asked, wondering how they would get past these defenses. "Why would you want to guide us? What's in it for you?"

He smiled, pearly white teeth dazzling her. She knew that in medieval-like times, such fastidiousness was rare. "Aside from the pleasure of your company and wicked wit?" Cirion replied. "Why, to see you slay the dragon. Few have seen the legendary Ellorian Champions in action."

Making up stuff, she replied, "We don't generally allow spectators. They might get killed. You wouldn't want that, surely?"

"Naturally not."

"Then why do you really want to go?"

He paused. "As I mentioned, I'd like to see this Dragon Gate."

"Why? For what purpose?"

Seeming put off, he sighed slightly. "Haven't you ever admired something purely for its beauty?" He looked her up and down suggestively.

"Yes, but not when it might kill me," she replied, giving her own suggestive look.

Smirking, Cirion replied sagely, "Without risk, there can be no reward."

"And what reward do you expect?"

"Well," he began expansively, "if you must know, being in the company of the famous champions when you seal the gate would allow me to say, and rightfully so, that I was partly responsible, and my improved reputation would allow me grander adventures of my own and all the subsequent fortune and happiness." He smirked at her. "Surely you wouldn't deny me this?"

Turning the tables, she pressed against him suggestively. "Don't be so sure of what I'll deny you. Why didn't you just tell me this before?"

He leaned close. "I didn't want to seem greedy," he confessed.

Anna feigned surprise. "You?"

He smirked again. "I do have pride, my lady."

"So I noticed." She rolled her eyes, then decided to cut this short as the dance neared its end. She felt comfortable to make this decision without the guys. "I'm afraid I can't allow you to come with us. We can't be sure what we'll face, and what risks we'd expose you to." Cirion nodded his understanding, and when the song ended, excused himself, to her relief.

As Matt watched his friends from beside the dance floor, he sipped from a wine glass etched with dragons and ogres. He tried to look unapproachable because he'd never danced a step in his life, but he was in luck, for Soliander wasn't the target of anyone's fancy, and therefore neither was he. He'd noticed big men who were probably knights talking to Ryan and had noted in relief that there appeared to be few wizards in attendance, though he wasn't sure. Were they required to dress like him? That made it easier to notice them, but if not, there could be more than he wanted. On one hand, he was eager to ask others about this, but he sensed Soliander was the one who'd get the questions, so he hoped to evade it altogether.

He fingered the ornate, mahogany staff in one hand, having sensed that leaving it behind was unwise, considering its nature and how powerful it could potentially be. Elegant gold script he couldn't read flowed down it, a bluish-silver steel prong atop it holding a fist-sized diamond. In the cloth bag he'd arrived wearing over one shoulder, he'd found two tomes that had proven to be spell books. Inside his soft black robe, numerous hidden pockets held several vials, tiny bags, and oddly shaped items he couldn't identify by touch and hadn't had time to examine yet. Several rings, a bracelet, and a necklace beckoned his curiosity, since they might have been magical.

As he stood hoping for a chance to explore these items, a red-robed fellow a few years younger than him stopped beside him, looking every bit the young wizard, a wooden staff in one thin hand and several pouches hanging from a golden cord at his waist. Matt had noticed him before. Gold rings and bracelets peeked out from the sleeves of his well-worn robe, which depicted a magic wand and staff over his heart. Tall and skinny, he seemed awkward and nervous, one hand brushing the long brown hair from his thin face. His brown eyes were deep and intelligent, alert, but discreet.

"Greetings, Soliander," he said timidly, bowing his head.

Matt nodded at him and tried to use his best alpha male tone, which was pretty weak, to intimidate the guy into going away. "Greetings, wizard."

"My name is Raith," said the young wizard. "You begin your quest tomorrow?"

"That is correct."

"It would be most interesting to see you in action."

"Perhaps," replied Matt evasively.

"Um, well, I've, I've been thinking it might be a great help to Honyn, and yourselves, if you were not the, um, only one able to work the Dragon Gate. This way, the four of you would no longer be summoned simply to close it."

For a moment, Matt thought that was a great idea, but then he thought better of it and gave Raith a hard look, knowing where this was going. "It's not that much trouble," he said dismissively, "and we might have no other reason to visit your fair world."

"That is true. Hopefully nothing else would require your assistance, as much as we are honored by your presence." He paused. "Still, what if you are unable to come and no one can close the gate? You could be away on another quest, or... or..." He stopped.

Matt arched an eyebrow at him. Was he suggesting Soliander might be dead and unavailable? That was bold. "You needn't worry about that," he replied, feigning disapproval.

Raith hesitated and Matt had the impression he was choosing words carefully. "I'd very much like to learn how the Dragon Gate works," Raith began sincerely, "and accompany you on your journey. I could lend assistance, freeing you for more important tasks."

He wore such a hopeful look that Matt took pity and lightened the attitude. "I think it's best that no one but me knows how to turn the gate on and off."

Raith nodded. "Yes, and pardon me for remarking, but it seems that someone else has already figured that out, Great Magus."

Now there was a good point, but there was no way Matt could give this guy what he didn't have – knowledge of how the gate worked. It wasn't really his decision to make anyway, but that of the real Soliander, despite his apparent disappearance and abandonment of the gate and any other concerns. Fortunately Matt had a better point. "And you see how much trouble this person has caused?"

Raith bowed his head. "You are wise beyond me. Perhaps you could merely show me how to activate it, not deactivate it."

Matt conceded that was another good point, except it was possible the same thing turned it off and on. "That is possible, but I'll make that determination after the quest, not before."

"You are too kind. Perhaps if you saw me in action yourself, you'd entrust me with this task more readily?"

Matt shook his head inwardly. This guy didn't give up easily, but Matt was resourceful, too. Changing the subject without seeming to, he asked, "Maybe. Why don't you tell me about your schooling? How did you become a wizard?"

Raith looked flattered by Soliander's genuine interest and soon became engrossed in relating his experience, which Matt helped with a barrage of questions to keep him distracted. A life as a wizard's apprentice or formal schooling sounded fascinating. Raith had been on his own a few years now, and it became clear he wanted to learn from Soliander, but Matt was having none of that. He skillfully avoided questions to the point of rudeness, but with such a deferential admirer, it was easy. He forgot to keep an eye on his friends, but he wasn't the only one getting distracted.

Awash in perfume, caresses, and flirtatious looks on the stone dance floor, Ryan felt the effects of so much feminine attention on him. Normally it didn't work, but the sheer volume of young women vying for him was unusual. The subjects they raised didn't help, like how much land their fathers owned as dowry, or what title he'd assume upon marriage, or their family's proximity to the throne. While they clearly wanted a husband and perhaps a trophy one at that, their looks promised no shortage of bedroom frolicking. These weren't just girls, either, but full-bodied women, all dressed to kill.

The only sobering aspect was that it wasn't really him they wanted, but Korrin, the Pride of Andor, and that his courage in battle was the reason for his desirability. It was the single greatest difference between them, and why these women found a violent man so attractive mystified him. They must surely be romanticizing the whole hero idea and ignoring the bloody truth they never saw. He was sure that the reality of a dead body would've taken the romance out of their looks in an instant. It had surely done so for him. Every dance step became a bitter reminder that the man he'd killed would never take another step again.

The women took turns with him, casting looks of thinly veiled hostility toward each other, though one seemed rather unconcerned with any dagger-like glances thrown her way. She caused a hasty retreat in the one she replaced, and from the muscles bulging under her golden gown, she could apparently take care of herself. Her gaze was direct like that of a man, and she seemed powerful, dangerous, and sleek like her jet black hair. Rough calloused hands added to the sense of vigor, suggesting she was a swords-woman, and an agile one at that, for her dance movements were smooth and nimble.

"What's your name?" Ryan asked, feeling a firm grip nearly crush his hand.

"Nola, the Fair Raven," she replied, her dusky voice stirring him. Her mysterious dark eyes lent weight to her nickname.

"You are strong," he appraised her, "and yet gentle."

"As are you, Lord of Hearts," she purred. "It is no wonder women throw themselves at you."

"I'm a good catch," he replied, but her blank look indicated the joke fell flat, so he moved on. "How did you develop such a physique?"

"Swinging swords at men who wouldn't take no for an answer."

"Then I guess I had better be civil."

"I'm sure my skill is nowhere near yours, Pride of Andor," she reassured him, "so you needn't worry. I *would* be grateful for the chance to cross swords with you, if only in jest, of course." She pressed against him suggestively, her bosom pushing up more in her low-cut gown, but even that couldn't take his mind from his conscience. The thought of pretend violence made him frown.

"I'm afraid time is short for swordplay," he replied quietly, "as I leave first thing in the morning."

Nola asked, "Are you headed straight to the castle?"

He paused before replying. "Yes," he answered, having remembered the side trip to Arundell with Lorian was a secret. "I don't know of anywhere else we'd want to go."

"Aren't you traveling with the elves?"

The accuracy of the question startled him. How did she know that? From her slight smirk, he suspected his expression, whatever it was, had answered for him, but he tried to lie anyway. "Uh, no," Ryan said lamely. "Why would you think that?"

She smiled. "My mistake. I saw you dining with them. I guess a big strong man like you doesn't need help from a bunch of scrawny elves to kill the dragon. You're the Dragon Slayer after all."

He looked down and away. Why did everyone have to remind him of the expectation to kill over and over? His thoughts strayed to Daniel back home, the loss of his smartphone and any way to use it a gnawing worry. He had to get back. He needed to quit dancing now and go blurt the truth out to Sonneri. Maybe Lorian was wrong and they could go home now anyway.

"Why the long face?" Nola asked quietly, breaking his thoughts. She seemed sympathetic and he realized he'd dropped his guard. "Does something trouble you, Korrin?"

Their eyes met and the kind look in hers disarmed him. He couldn't really tell her the truth, but did he have to pretend he wasn't upset? Did it matter? He shrugged noncommittally. "It's nothing."

She pressed against him more, as if offering herself as consolation. "If it dampens your spirit despite all these ladies pursuing you, then it must surely be something.

Would you prefer to discuss it in private? I have a suite to myself here in the castle and you can unburden your noble heart to me." Her hand stroked his hair tenderly and she laid a sweet kiss on his cheek. Sudden, turbulent emotion welled up with him, threatening his self-control.

"You're very kind," he started huskily, intending to regretfully decline, but she interrupted.

"I've only just begun to show you kindness, Korrin," she replied gently, and with that she whispered sweet, compassionate words in his ear and leaned into him. It seemed that all his life he'd kept his torments to himself, for in those few moments when someone saw his angst, he'd kept quiet like so many men so often do. Culture demanded men deal with pain alone, but her embrace promised a release he increasingly felt unable to restrain. His guard fell. Even Anna, for all their friendship, hadn't gotten past his defenses, but he felt himself falling into this stranger's care. As the dance ended, she led him from the floor, past the guards and away, and he went readily if not eagerly.

Out on the dance floor, Eric struggled to keep his wits about him. Naughty thoughts raced through his mind every half second, in no small part because women put them there. Andier might be the Silver-Tongued Rogue, but now Eric was either tongue tied or it was hanging out of his mouth, figuratively speaking. It had been too long since he'd been with a woman and the desire they aroused was strong. It was all he could do to tear his eyes away to keep tabs on his friends, and this time he didn't see Ryan. His eyes searched again, less discreetly, and finally he dropped all pretenses on realizing the big man was gone. He caught Matt's gaze and moved his fingers behind his dance partner.

Did you see Ryan leave?

Matt put his wine glass down. *No. He's gone?*

Yes. Eric figured Anna was too distracted to have noticed and Lorian was too embroiled in conversation. The guards, he realized. They ought to have noticed.

He excused himself and sought one at the entrance. The young man snapped to attention. "Did Lord Korrin leave this way?"

"Yes, my lord."

Eric hadn't expected the title. Only Ryan had gotten that so far. "When?"

"Just a few minutes ago."

"Where did he go?"

Looking apologetic, the guard answered, "He did not say, but he was headed toward the Blue Crest Wing."

"Was he alone?"

"No, my Lord. He escorted Nola of Ormund, presumably to her, uh..." He faltered, looking pained.

"Her suite?" Eric finished.

The guard pursed his lips. "Yes, my lord."

"Where is that?"

"I'm not sure, sir, but probably in the second level of the Blue Crest, directly down this hallway." He gestured and Eric took off at a jog, worried and wondering what Ryan thought he was doing. It didn't occur to him that he'd allowed himself to be separated from the group as well, but someone else in the Great Hall noticed.

Watching Eric leave, Cirion excused himself from a different young lady who'd just been flirting with Andier at his direction. Like all the others, she didn't have anything interesting to relate about the rogue anyway, for Andier didn't give much away, but distracting him had been the real goal. To his surprise, Eriana had been a harder mark than he would have believed. He'd had other reasons for talking with her, one being the chance to bed her despite her reputation for chastity. He had conquered unattainable women before, but she had proven her womanhood wasn't the only thing she guarded well. He hadn't learned a thing from her, and that was rare. A glance revealed Raith still had Soliander's attention, and Nola had succeeded with Korrin where he had not, so if at first you don't succeed....

He headed for Eriana, but as he closed in, a familiar figure intercepted him.

"Cirion," began Lorian smoothly, offering a goblet of red wine. "I know your love of elven wines and have brought you a glass of our finest. You must try it."

The dashing man looked at him first in annoyance, then impatience, feigned cordiality, and finally resignation. "You're too kind," he replied politely, taking the glass and casting a regretful glance at Eriana. Elves were famous for subtlety, but he saw the knowing smirk on the elf's face and made a note to watch out for this one. How much did he know? He didn't have long to wonder. From the corner of Cirion's eye, he saw two elves moving quickly through the crowd, then take off running in the same direction Korrin and then Andier had gone. Cirion silently cursed and returned his gaze to Lorian, finding a look of barely hidden steel in the eyes.

CHAPTER SIX

LORIAN

It wasn't until he reached the door to Nola's suite that Ryan realized he was lost. He hadn't been paying attention, his mind a swirl of death and affection, blood and caresses, remorse and hope. Nola looked up at him suggestively as she aligned the gold key with the lock on her suite's door and slipped it inside. Her lips brushed against his so that he hardly noticed being drawn into her scented room, an odd mixture of steel and roses in the air.

Suddenly two hands yanked him backwards, breaking contact with her so fast that it startled him. He blinked in surprise and turned to see a short figure with black hair glaring at him. A moment passed before he recognized Eric.

"Didn't you hear me?" Eric snapped, pulling him further into the hall. "I must've called your name four times."

Ryan heard himself mutter something even he didn't comprehend.

"C'mon," said Eric the rogue, "we have a big day ahead of us tomorrow and don't have time for this."

"But–"

"No buts. Let's go." Eric pulled him by the arm and Ryan followed, still off guard and confused. "Goodbye, my lady," the rogue called to Nola. "He's not the sort to call the next day anyway."

As Eric led Ryan down the hall, two elves appeared out of the shadows ahead, looking alert until seeing them. They slowed, stopped, and became far more casual in demeanor. Ryan realized that not only had Eric come after him, but the elves, too, possibly at Lorian's suggestion. Suddenly he remembered the pledge to stay together, but even now, he saw no harm in going with Nola. He sighed in frustration, which worsened when Eric spoke again.

"What did you think you were doing?" Eric asked. The elves waited until they passed before trailing along at a discreet distance.

Offended, Ryan replied irritably, "You wouldn't understand."

"Try me."

"Bug me about it tomorrow. I'm not in the mood."

"But you were in the mood to get laid."

Ryan shoved him away with one hand and kept walking. "Asshole. That's not what this was about."

"Well, what then?" Eric asked, following.

"I told you later. Just leave me the fuck alone." He sped up to put distance between them, relieved that Eric seemed to let him go on ahead. He followed the noise toward the banquet hall and then wandered off toward their suite, fairly certain he could find it. Not until reaching the door and opening it did he look at his pursuers, seeing only the two elves. He sighed and closed the door, feeling lonely. Would they stand guard outside to keep other people out or him in? He didn't think it mattered as long as he got to be alone – and no one snuck in to try killing him.

Once inside, Ryan struggled for some way to calm down, but the lack of modern entertainments like television or the internet left no room for distraction. He stood alone with his dark thoughts, eyes moving from silken pillows to ornate, mahogany furniture and rich rugs. The lavishness seemed somehow shallow and empty, matching his outfit style for style so that he tore at the tunic to get it off. He soon found himself on his bare knees beside his bed, head bowed, hands clasped before him, smoke from the snuffed out candles curling through the dark room. He hadn't done this in a long time and didn't question whether the God of his Earth could hear him here or not. It didn't really matter, for the forgiveness he sought for killing someone had to come from within and he doubted that would happen anytime soon, if ever.

He wondered how Daniel was doing and if he'd ever see his brother again. In the strangeness of the arrival here, the attack, and the man he'd killed by accident, he'd hardly had time to wonder about Daniel. All these years of worrying about his brother and now it was his own life that might suddenly end. That was always true in a sense, but courting danger like this raised it to a whole new level. There was no easy way out of this. He went to bed and suffered through a restless night that left him tired in the morning, and the last to rise despite being the first to bed.

The next morning, Ryan entered the sitting room to find the others, dressed for the quest, talking quietly. From their glances and the sudden silence, he surmised the subject had been himself. His dark mood had lifted some, enough to pretend he was fine anyway. Trying to ward off any well-meaning remarks, he flashed an insincere smile.

"Does anyone know where I can get some coffee?" He scratched at his stubble, wondering what to shave with.

"I already asked," Matt complained. "There isn't any. They don't even know what it is. This is going to be miserable."

Anna chuckled, picking at some fruits. "You'll get used to it. I have to admit I was hoping this was a dream when I got up."

"Or a nightmare," Ryan added quietly. "I wish I knew how Daniel was doing."

Eric gestured to a ceramic bowl of water on a silver tray, a short blade for shaving next to it on green towels. "They dropped off this stuff earlier," he said, sitting down. If he harbored any resentments about the night before, Ryan couldn't tell and appreciated a lack of attitude. "We already used it, but you'll want to warm up the water on the fire. It's not the most sanitary thing, but I think we're okay."

Ryan took the bowl and left to shave, his thoughts on his problematic role of a knight. They would never return home if they didn't succeed, and the quest undoubtedly required all of them. Matt couldn't cast spells, nor Anna heal anyone with magic, which left him and Eric. If he refused to fight, it was all on the martial artist. As impressive as Eric was, he wasn't going to punch a dragon into submission. Ryan would have to help and be willing to use deadly force. Even if he didn't, he'd still be condoning whatever Eric did if he just stood there and watched instead of stopping him. It was unlikely they could seal the Dragon Gate at all, with or without a fight.

He couldn't do this. There had to be another way. If refusing meant living out his life on Honyn as a shamed coward, that was better than killing anyone else. He could live with that, but the others might share in his fate and he didn't have the right to decide that for them. Maybe he could just quit and let them go without him. If this Lorian guy could bring enough elves with him, Ryan wouldn't be needed. The idea brightened him. He'd talk to Lorian privately when he got the chance.

After a quick breakfast, they left the suite to see Lorian, following a guide through the castle halls. Matt walked more briskly than the others, his head full of questions about the summoning, wizardry, and anything related to magic. The elf was the one person he could ask about such things, since everyone else would expect him to already know. It wasn't that he wanted to cast a spell – well, he did, but that seemed as improbable as anything else – but the talk with Raith the night before had filled him with ideas. Besides, he needed to know how to fool people or give plausible excuses that he wasn't going to cast a spell when they expected him to. When they arrived, the elves wasted no time. Two let them through a door to Lorian's suite. The elf promptly greeted them and got right down to business.

"It is not safe for us to speak of your true identities in this place," he began, motioning them to sit on sofas embroidered with forest settings, "but my brethren have cleared the area of possible spies. We should have a few minutes, at least."

"So they also know who we are?" Eric asked, walking around the room and peering through doorways. Matt looked at the balcony and see an elf there, his head scanning back and forth.

"They know who you are not," corrected Lorian, slanted eyes watching him, "but only two of them, who would have discovered your charade on seeing you. It is important that such individuals be told the truth and cautioned to remain silent, else they might remark upon it aloud in front of the wrong company."

Eric nodded, remaining standing while all but Lorian sat. "And the wrong company would be everyone, except elves?"

"Elves who knew them, yes, and some dwarves."

"Dwarves?" Matt asked. What else was on this planet? Despite the danger that would get closer by the day, his curiosity was rising even more.

Lorian replied, "Yes. Elves and dwarves are likely to remember the details of the champions' appearance better than humans. Four years is long enough for your kind to forget, and it is not unreasonable to mistake you for them, considering the similarity of your appearance." He looked at them one by one. "I must say, the resemblance is re-markable, as you're each the same basic height, build, hair color, and have similar features. You are nearly the same age, a bit younger. This is undoubtedly why they chose you. Only those with whom they'd spent considerable time are likely to discover the deceit, and on most worlds, they acted very much alone."

"Chose us?" Ryan asked, looking like he hadn't thought of that before. Neither had Matt, who had assumed this was all some sort of accident.

"Yes," said the elf, leaning against a chair. "Those you impersonate. I'd very much like to know why the four of you have appeared in their place."

Ryan glanced at his friends. "We were hoping you could tell us that."

Lorian's slender, blond eyebrows arched. "You do not know? Didn't they tell you?"

"Who?" Matt asked, fingering his staff. "This Soliander and the others? You think they sent us?"

"Of course," answered Lorian. "How else would you come to be here in their place?"

"We don't have the slightest idea," replied Ryan in frustration.

The elf asked, "They didn't tell you?"

"No," answered Ryan. "We've never even heard of these people until we showed up in the court. We certainly haven't met them."

Lorian looked from one to another, measuring them. "Then they didn't send you."

"No," answered Matt, realizing Lorian didn't know what was going on any more than they did. "Not that we know of, anyway."

"And you haven't met them." Lorian paused, eyes troubled. "Then you do not know their whereabouts?"

"Right," said the wizard, sobered by the elf's reaction.

The elf sighed. "I was hoping we'd finally know where they've been since we last saw them."

Anna asked, "Are they missing or something?"

"Essentially, yes." He looked at them as if something had just occurred to him. "You say that you've never heard of them. How is it that possible?"

Matt glanced at the others, but no one answered. "Why is that surprising?"

"There must be some connection between this world and yours," started Lorian, "for the summoning spell to have brought you. Their existence must therefore be known there, and they are a legend on every world to which they are known. You therefore should have heard of them."

"Well, I don't think anyone's heard of them back home." Matt was tempted to make observations about the lack of magic and knights and all that, but decided not to get into it. He wondered how the champions could have ever been to Earth, not to mention recently. Magic, had it ever existed, had died out centuries ago. Then again, that was pure speculation as much as anything else. Maybe people secretly practiced it. "Are all these worlds they go to places of magic, knights, castles...elves?"

"Yes, of course." Lorian paused. "Is your world not such a place?"

Ryan snorted. "No. There's nothing like this on Earth."

The elf asked, "Earth? Is that the name of your world?"

"Yes," Anna replied more politely, frowning at the knight.

Lorian looked at the big man. "This would explain your disbelief that I am an elf?" Ryan nodded, and the elf looked at him curiously. "But you say elves don't exist there and yet you've heard of what an elf is."

Eric said, "Yes, we *have* heard of elves, dwarves, dragons, and magic, but they aren't real in our world."

Lorian spread his slender hands. "But then how could you have heard of them?"

A long pause followed that. Matt figured that the likely reason was that storytellers and authors had invented them, but elves were real on Honyn. How could they be real in one place and an invention of the mind in another, and yet be so similar? They had to be the same, which meant that somewhere on Earth, at least in the past, elves, dwarves, dragons and all manner of fabled beings had really existed. And maybe still did.

He remarked, "That's a good question, especially considering we were clearly summoned by magical means from Earth. Magic must work there after all."

"I don't know about that," disagreed Anna. "The magic was performed here on Honyn. Besides, it could've just been technology we don't understand, remember?"

Eric shook his head. "Whatever it was, I assume it had to work on both sides, so if it was magic here then it was magic there. You know, if magic works on Earth, people could hide that fact as long as they avoid doing it in public, but elves, dwarves, and dragons would be hard to hide."

Lorian suggested, "The dragons could have been banished from your world as well."

Matt perked up. "That's true."

Nodding, Eric admitted, "Yes. And technically, dwarves exist. There have always been little people on Earth."

Anna nodded. "They don't act like that, though, living underground, the long beards, being grumpy."

The elf smiled at her and turned toward Ryan. "But no elves?"

The big man spread his empty hands as if to apologize. "'Fraid not."

"There are a lot of deep forests that are seldom traveled," Matt started, "so they could always be hiding in there."

"I don't think that's so true anymore," Eric said, "but anyway this is all beside the point."

Lorian nodded. "Another thing I want to know is where you were when summoned."

"A place called Stonehenge," said Matt. "It's an ancient monument thousands of years old. No one knows what it was really designed for."

"Describe it, please."

"It's a circular monument in an open field, with giant monoliths of stone standing upright, some with other stones on top, connecting them."

Lorian seemed to think he'd said enough. "It sounds like a Quest Ring. Most look roughly the same, being circular monuments, similar to where you found yourselves upon arrival. Champions are summoned to a Quest Ring on every world and is usually the place from which they depart for home. Magic words are embedded into the material from which the Ring is made—usually stone."

Matt glanced at the others. That sounded a little too familiar. "There were words in the stone, but they usually weren't visible." He described what happened when the words of fire erupted and they vanished.

The elf gazed at him thoughtfully. "Interesting. That suggests they were on a quest on Earth, but you were sent back instead. Maybe they're still there."

Eric asked, "Do they need to be in a, uh, Quest Ring, to be summoned, like we apparently were?"

"No," said the elf. "They could be anywhere, be separate from each other, even on different worlds. The spell brings them together, delivering them to the Quest Ring of those summoning them. However, the summoning spell would fail if they were engaged with another quest. It may have been coincidence that you stood at that particular Quest Ring when summoned."

Matt absorbed that in silence like the others before the elf broke this thoughts.

Lorian said, "Something of more immediate concern is that Cirion of Ormund and his mercenaries spoke with each of you last night, probably to glean information." Matt saw blank looks on everyone's face except Anna's. She looked startled. Lorian elaborated. "Cirion danced with Eriana while his young wizard, Raith, spoke with Soliander at some length. Nola, an exceptional warrior in her own right, targeted Korrin and nearly succeeded with some design, from what I understand." His eyes met Ryan's and the knight flushed. Lorian turned to Eric. "Andier was not a target except as Cirion could get you distracted, as your predecessor's ability to spot trouble is legendary. A parade of lovely women sought your attention at Cirion's behest."

It was Eric's turn to look startled, then a little embarrassed, even angry. Maybe resentful. Then something seemed to occur to him. "The dashing man who danced with Anna?"

"Yes," said Lorian.

"Who is he?" Anna asked. "What does he want?" She blushed after asking and Matt knew what she was thinking because he'd watched them. Cirion couldn't have been more obvious about one desire and he stifled a smirk.

"One of this world's would-be heroes," began the elf, "who try to earn a name with quests. He hides his questionable ways well, understanding appearances. Others of his ilk have demonstrated their misguided attempts to reach the Dragon Gate, which is no doubt his aim as well. Cirion's mercenaries arrived hours before you and were no doubt unhappy with your arrival, for it should have signaled the end to their aspirations, but it seems they were intent on interfering with you in some way." He looked at Korrin pointedly.

The big man looked uncomfortable. "But I thought she just..." He trailed off and then flushed, seeming indignant, then angry. Matt had never seen the big guy mad before. He looked especially dangerous standing there in that golden armor, a sword on one hip. Matt knew he was a gentle giant, but if Ryan could learn to put on that face on purpose, that and Korrin's reputation might stop some people from messing with him.

Anna asked, "What happened? Did I miss something?"

Ryan and Eric exchanged a look, making Matt wonder what passed between them.

"She lured me to her rooms under the guise of..." Ryan hesitated. "Of making me feel better about having killed that man, but Eric stopped me at her door." Anna let out a slow breath through her nose. Ryan heard it and met her disapproving eyes before looking away. "I'm sorry for wandering off," he said sincerely. "I know we promised to stick together. It won't happen again."

"It had better not," Anna replied quietly.

Rescuing the knight, Matt changed subjects. "That wizard was asking me how to manipulate the gate, but I didn't know anything to tell him even if I'd wanted to."

"Cirion wanted to lead us to the castle," said Anna, "but I refused him. He also said he'd been inside, not long after the, uh, champions left, but he couldn't get by some sort of maze. Do you know what we might run into?"

Lorian nodded. "Mostly Dragon Cult members. I suspect Soliander's traps have been dispelled by whoever opened the Gate. If not, the way will be harder."

A nearby bird call prompted an elf to enter from the balcony, exchange a look with Lorian, and return. "Attention has begun to focus on your presence," said Lorian.

CHAPTER SEVEN

WIZARDRY

As he always did, the dark elf hesitated three strides from the richly carved mahogany door of his master. Fantastic scenes of dragons, knights, and wizards doing battle graced its surface, but none were more heart-stopping than what he had personally seen in the room beyond. Daunting forces had been summoned by the wizard within, and despite the ferocity of each, whether it be demons, wraith lords, or even minor deities, the wizard had commanded obedience. The thought reminded the elf not to falter in his devotion, for an urgent message had arrived at the black, looming castle.

He was a dark elf, so called to distinguish his kind from wood elves, those beings of light and goodness, the very thought of which made his lip curl in a sneer. There was power to be had in darkness, and it was his kind that sought to harness it. Long ago they had given themselves up to it and found their skin turning nightmare black, the hair whiter than the palest moonlight, eyes of blood red staring from their now sinister features. The same delicateness of wood elves remained, but what passed for a tender, supple nose there gleamed sharp like the blade of a dagger here. So, too, with their grace, no longer like a breeze through the trees but like a knife sliding into flesh. Dark things were their province, and yet what lay beyond the door was darker than anything his kin sought. All seemed still at the moment, but that could change in an instant.

Steeling himself for the unknown, he quietly rapped on the door, which opened silently, orange firelight washing over him from within. As he entered, a quick glance confirmed no magic was afoot, though the dark granite floor bore the residue of powdery markings inside a circle of still-flickering candles. Bookcases full of ancient tomes lined two walls, vials, jars, and jugs of every shape filling another. Bright flames roared in the hulking stone fireplace, and an enormous black desk seemed to cast a pall over the room. Behind it sat a slim figure in a dark robe, unremarkable in its lack of adornment, and yet anyone trained in magic would have taken notice of the man at once. The reek of power coming from him struck like a blow.

The sorcerer bent over a large tome, his features lost in the shadows, a dark orb of swirling colors on a small stand beside him. The room was far too dark to read, but the words and drawings were written in light. The dark elf waited for what seemed like an eternity, a line of sweat trickling down his back while he fought to remain still and silent. Only a fool reminded the wizard of their presence. Finally the wizard favored him with a glance.

In a quavering voice, the dark elf said, "My lord, I have important news."

The master commanded, "Speak it."

"The Queen of Alunia on Honyn attempted to summon the great Ellorian Champions."

The sorcerer interrupted in derision. "She's hardly the only one. Even children attempt this."

"Yes, my lord," the dark elf answered, knowing it was a common fantasy of children, "but she was successful."

The wizard's head snapped up. "What?"

"She was—"

"I heard what you said," the robed figure interrupted. "What do you mean? Be specific."

The elf steadied himself. "The four champions answered the summons and are embarking on a quest."

The wizard frowned inside the hood. "Four? Not three?"

The elf felt confused, wondering at that but knowing better than to ask. He'd seen those who didn't know their place burned to a crisp or frozen and then shattered on being toppled to the floor. "Yes, four of them."

"And they claim to be Eriana of Coreth, Andier of Roir, Korrin of Andor, and Soliander of Aranor?"

"Yes." The elf paused, then ventured, "There has been no suggestion in Olliana that they are imposters."

Only silence greeted this, for the dark magus was not one to share his thoughts. "What is the quest?" he asked, fingers touching on a newly fashioned amulet of priceless, bluish steel, made from a rare material that the dark elf knew no one else had ever possessed.

"To banish the dragons again. The device holding them—"

"Yes, yes, I know what happened." He waved a dismissive hand.

The elf wondered how the dark magus could have known, but he was often aware of things transpiring far away.

"When did they embark on the quest?"

"They have yet to do so."

"Leave me."

As the dark elf turned toward the door, his eyes darted to the rosewood cabinet in one corner, where no one dared go. Those with magic power could sense the foreboding protection around it, and those without power just felt unwell the closer they got. He suspected a demon guarded it, for he had a bracelet that pulsed when one was near and had discreetly tested it just by wearing it into this chamber. He knew better than to even look too long, for he'd seen a man killed for that. But this was the first time he'd been in here in some days and he had the unmistakable impression that the cabinet had been disturbed. As he closed the door behind him, he risked a glance at the wizard and saw glaring eyes on it, lips set in a resolute grimace.

In the azure sky high above Castle Olliana, the white wizards' tower drew hopeful eyes to it like none other, for the tower's residents were known to practice their art from its highest reaches, creating fantastic displays for anyone lucky enough to be watching. Those within had a rare sight to behold, too, for the topmost windows provided view of the swaying green treetops of the Great Honyn Forest and the jagged, snowcapped peaks in the distance. In the last fortnight, Sonneri had spent many hours watching those peaks for dragons. Even with magical vision enhancements that put telescopes to shame, nothing unusual had appeared to magical watchers like the one he now stood instructing for a different purpose.

"I want you to discreetly follow them," said the wizard to the black crow, whose impassive black eyes stared back with unusual intelligence. "It's imperative you not be detected. The rogue is likely to be just as alert as the stories say, and the elves are wise to such surveillance."

"Of course," squawked the bird, impatient. This wasn't the first time it had spied on people.

Sonneri fixed it with a serious stare, used to more respect. "Keep your distance, for the wizard's magical sense is formidable and extends farther than you'd ever imagine. Change your shape each time you come near them."

The crow became a robin, then a mockingbird, and finally a peregrine falcon, and he nodded, satisfied.

"Report back often and don't dawdle in the elven lands."

The falcon bobbed as if bowing and turned on the pine perch before launching itself through the open window. Sonneri stepped to the window, reaching out for its bronze handle. A loud brass fanfare rang out far below and he peered down into the teeming courtyard, where a throng of people cheered. It seemed the Ellorian Champions were leaving.

⁕ ⁎ · ⁎ ⁕

Castles weren't designed with dragons in mind. That much was obvious. Even well-kept keeps kept their occupants only one step ahead of discomfort, the hard stones cruel surroundings. Drafty, ruined castles fared worse for the lack of upkeep, though they did have the advantage that if you felt compelled to knock down a wall or rip through the ceiling with your claws, no one would complain, but there was only so much you could do to one and leave it standing. Interior decorating dragon-style had its limits.

Even with her recent modifications to the long-abandoned Castle Darlonon, Perndara the dragon was grumpy. The Grand Hall was big enough for her enormous bulk, and the hole in the floor a good place to dangle her barbed tail, but she wanted to be outside. Dragons weren't meant to be indoors any more than castles were meant to be their homes, and she desperately wanted to fly again.

She'd been spotted last time, however, and though she'd devoured most of those hunters, one had gotten away and Nir'lion hadn't exactly been amused with the result. Now their plans – well, all the plans were really Nir'lion's – had been ruined and Nir'lion was off dreaming up some way to turn the situation to her advantage.

In fact, just this morning, news had come that the Ellorian Champions were on their way. Perndara's spirits had soared for the first time since Nir'lion had practically torn her golden scales from her thick hide. Shortly after the pair first escaped through the Dragon Gate, Nir'lion learned of the champions' apparent disappearance, threatening the revenge she so badly wanted. But now that goal had returned.

Perndara had been so happy that she'd roasted the poor messenger and then slurped him down in one gulp, savoring the flavor of fresh human. That was a chief complaint about the land of their banishment, there being nothing but wild livestock. Dragons loved to play with their food, and nothing fought back like sentient races. Humans were good, dwarves not so much with all that nasty hair, but the elves were delicious, the marrow sweeter and more succulent than even their blood, which was like wine. She was pleased to know some elves were expected for supper in a few days.

She had to avoid eating too many of these Dragon Cult members in the ruin, however, though the stupid fools seemed to consider it an honor. The cult had never been bright. They knew enough not to flaunt danger, however, and had been avoiding her when in dragon form. It was one reason she changed now, her large body shimmering briefly as she vanished like an illusion. In her place stood an elegant woman of exceptional beauty, golden hair tumbling to her slender waist, full breasts straining against the silken gown, and jewels of shining brilliance about her sinuous neck. The only hints of her true nature were the golden eyes that faded slowly to pale green. As all dragons could, she snuffed the sensation of magical power emanating from her so as to pass for human. But as she had with those hunters, sometimes letting the power exude had its advantages.

Perndara slowly climbed a staircase at one end to look down on the Dragon Gate. A large oval nearly twenty feet high and twice as wide, it lay on its stand almost flat, tilted toward the blue sky. Dragons were pulled down into it through the ragged opening in the castle roof, the crumbled ceiling having made this an ideal spot for the gate. Newer rubble had lain scattered about the floor – most likely Soliander's doing when setting up this device – until she'd ordered the cult to move it to a corner. They had dutifully cleaned everything but the gate upon her order. The last thing she wanted was the door to their prison kept in good shape. If she could have destroyed it, she would have, but it was impervious to her magic or dragon fire. She had no idea what it was made of and hadn't seen anything like it. It was unadorned except for a peculiar looking hole above the three steps at its base. She surmised this related to its activation but wasn't really interested. Once the dragons were free, they'd bury the thing under tons of rock. For now, they waited, the force of Nir'lion's will strong enough to keep the remaining dragons on the other side despite the door being open.

The sight of the gate renewed her thirst for vengeance. She'd been told not to harm the champions too much, for Nir'lion wanted them alive. After all, these were the four who'd trapped them these long years, and revenge was to be had slowly. Still, accidents were known to happen, especially with such powerful forces being tossed about, and Perndara was in fact known to be somewhat careless. That's how she'd come to be seen flying over the tall peaks, so it wouldn't be too surprising if one of the heroes met an untimely end. Yes, that's how she'd put it to Nir'lion. The knight had simply not been fast enough. He was unable to escape her fiery breath, or a sweeping claw, or the clamp of her long fangs on his tender flesh.

She had healing powers, like all dragons, and was prepared to answer the question as to why she didn't heal the knight after accidentally wounding him. In the heat of battle, she'd say, she was too distracted and hadn't noticed the grievous nature of his wounds. Oh, and the priestess Eriana, well, she had been knocked unconscious during the melee and unable to heal the knight. By the time she roused, he had perished.

And it had to be the knight, if for no other reason than that title he proudly wore, that of Dragon Slayer. She would see about that. If this puny human thought he'd be slaying a dragon here, he was in for a surprise. More importantly, it was he who truly led them, regardless of any counsel or help from the others. It was that knight who had guided them into this banishment, she was sure of it, and for that he was to pay with his life. Nir'lion would have to settle for the other three and Perndara's best rendition of an innocent apology from a timid, careless, twit of a dragon who was nothing of the sort. She knew perfectly well what she was doing and the wrath that would come with it, but let it come. It would be worth it. Lord Korrin of Andor was going to die screaming in her fanged mouth.

CHAPTER EIGHT

AFFINITY

As the horses cantered into a stand of evergreens, Olli-ana disappeared behind them and with it, a kingdom full of hope. Ryan breathed a sigh of relief, settling in to enjoy a ride through beautiful country. He'd been an avid horseman for years, but his friends looked quite out of place. Anna had some experience, but the elves had taken the reins from Matt and Eric, leading them along for now. Some basic horsemanship lessons were in order.

An embarrassing fanfare had accompanied their depar-ture. Beyond the blaring horns, crowds of people had lined the streets to see them off. Some threw bouquets of flow-ers to Anna and garter belts to the men, particularly Lord Korrin. Outwardly, Ryan had appeared to enjoy the atten-tion, hiding his consternation. The number of people de-pending on them daunted him, and he'd settled for waving and concentrating on holding the lance in his stirrup, the deep blue banner snapping in the warm breeze. On it, a golden dragon breathed fire toward a fearless golden knight. He hoped the depiction was pure fiction but began to rethink his decision to stay behind, for all the looks of hope, especially on children's faces, made him realize all these people were counting on him in particular. The thought of letting them all get killed wasn't acceptable, his loathing of violence notwithstanding. He suddenly felt selfish.

There'd been no sign of Cirion, Nora, or Raith, which both worried and relieved him. An unseen troublemaker wasn't good. He doubted they'd simply turned tail and gone home. If headed for the gate as expected, maybe Cirion's mercenaries would spring any traps the cult had set for them. It would serve them right.

Cirion wasn't likely to arrive first, however, for his mercenaries couldn't take Lorian's shortcut, which shaved two days off the eight-day trip to Castle Darlonon. Lorian's family controlled that area, his estate in its center, and the elf sent a messenger to warn of wayward humans matching a certain description. Cirion, and anyone associated with him, weren't welcome in the elven woods, where borders had been tightened in advance of war. He could try anyway, but elves appeared to be far less amused by smart talking rogues than humans were. Since only the queen knew they'd visit Lorian's estate, they'd spend one day there, still arriving at Darlonon a day before expected. It gave them time to learn self-defense, at least.

For the first day, they rode in silence through open fields and peaceful autumn foliage, reflecting on the situation and what might be happening back on Earth in their absence. The days on Honyn seemed shorter, the nights longer – and the season happened to be the same – but Ryan's friends could have sworn this day in the saddle lasted forever. At times only the frequent moaning broke the quiet.

"Oh man," said Eric during a break, standing beside the horse and holding onto the saddle to keep from crumpling to the ground. "My legs are rubber. I would've thought all the martial arts would've had me in better shape. How am I supposed to fight anything when I can't even stand?"

"Nothing prepares you for so much riding except riding. You'll limber up after a few more days, Eric," Ryan advised. Despite his experience, his legs hurt, too, but he refused to admit it.

"I seriously doubt that."

Lorian asked. "Is that your real name? Eric?"

The rogue nodded. "Yes. I guess we had better tell you our names to avoid confusion."

The elf suggested, "On the contrary, you should use your assumed names, and only those, in case someone overhears you. And if no one else knows your real names, we can't use them by accident."

"Good point," agreed Eric, wincing.

The cobblestone roads near Olliana soon gave way to dirt as they pushed hard across rolling hills and wooded trails. Their band of armor-clad elves and humans attracted no attention until stopping at a roadside inn for the night. Firelight shone through ground floor windows, two chimneys pumping smoke into the starry sky. As Ryan looked for constellations he knew wouldn't be there, he thought the stars shone brighter, whether from the lack of city lights and haze or just proximity. Among the stars drifted three moons, the best evidence they weren't on Earth so far, the impossibility of faking that sinking in. He took a deep breath, noticing the fresh air. Everything seemed more natural, from the unprocessed foods to the handmade garments, though the lack of modern accommodations, especially toiletries, almost negated any pleasure derived from that naturalness. The idea of spending twelve days on the quest frustrated him, for that was two weeks of knowing nothing about Daniel.

As they filed into the inn, the elves stabling the horses, Ryan secured four of the bedrooms for the four elves and four champions, as they'd be sleeping two to a room. In doing so, he flashed more gold – courtesy of the court –

than the innkeepers probably saw in a year. Eric quietly suggested more discretion. The innkeepers were quick to realize their identities. Korrin's golden armor and Soliander's staff didn't help.

They gathered for a meager dinner in the inn's cramped common room, pushing two well-worn corner tables together for a meal of day-old bread, slightly stale ale, and tough beef, with apologies from their hosts. Ryan hadn't eaten such poor fare since he'd tried cooking for himself on a few misguided occasions, but he expected it would get worse once camping. The generous tip he gave was more charity than deserved, but the owners looked like they needed a break. He asked that they not be disturbed and got his wish.

Lorian had introduced his three elven companions along the way, but only one, Morven, chose to speak with them. At one hundred fifty years old, he was still a teenager among elves, making Ryan wonder if it was awful to be a teenager for so many decades. Tall and skinny, he showed none of the awkwardness of human teens, being all grace if not poise, brown hair flowing freely to his waist and sometimes across his delicate features, hiding shy green eyes. He spoke quietly if at all, as if unsure of himself, but his words nonetheless conveyed conviction in his thoughts. The elf's specialty was archery, yet another skill they lacked, and the knight wondered just how many skills the champions had that they didn't. If Morven and other elves didn't come with them, they'd never succeed or see Earth again.

While the others made small talk, Ryan pulled out the vellum scroll the real Soliander had written about their previous time here, unfurling the painted case to see a scribe's bold and elegant script. After skimming a few lines in the dim lantern light, he whistled and said, "Listen to this."

At the time of our summoning by the King of Alunia's arch-wizard, Aurilon, the dragons of Honyn were rampaging. Under the leadership of Nir'lion, the dragon horde had laid waste to hundreds of towns across Alunia and the neighboring lands, with Alunia suffering the worst. No village was too small to escape their fiery breath, no town too sacred, no outpost too remote. Castles, temples, schools, homes, and farms were equal targets under their wrath, and the only reprieve came when they had gorged themselves on humans, dwarves, and elves so fully that they could not continue for a time.

"They *eat* people?" Anna asked.

Ryan nodded slowly, thinking he'd always avoided swimming in shark-infested waters or going other places where humans were considered food.

Eric asked, "So Sonneri was not the arch-wizard at the time, and there was a King?"

Lorian nodded. "Yes, the king died several years ago, and his wife became queen. Shortly thereafter the wizard retired and has since perished. Sonneri was an apprentice of Aurilon's and long a confidant of the royal family. His assumption of the role at the queen's request went unchallenged."

Ryan turned back to the scroll, trying to keep his voice down so the serving girl wouldn't overhear.

With the countryside in disarray, people fled to the cities. As if waiting for this very thing, the dragons set upon these fortified population centers en masse. The city of Trisune in Nurinor was razed to the ground in just hours. Across the sea, the Empire of Perthia lost the great port cities of Gharili and Tuunark, and here in Alunia, Vollunia, Hexia, and Ferralon fell in quick succession, inspiring our immediate summoning.

As is usually the case, many great warriors and wizards sought to solve the problem prior to our arrival, to no avail. Upon our briefing, we made our own determination after investigating. Rampaging dragons do not respond to reason and cannot be subdued, and with Nir'lion's leadership keeping them engaged, this was especially true. We suspected that even with her death, the dragons, now used to their rampage, would continue for an unacceptable time before reverting to their usual "every dragon for itself" attitude. Thus, we determined that something must be done about all of them.

The quest as stated indicated we must not only halt present hostilities, but eliminate the possibility of such actions in the future. This latter item is an aggressive request, so much so that its improbability renders it potentially invalid. Such invalid quest requirements may be safely ignored, meaning the questors can still depart at the conclusion of the quest's other requirements. However, it is difficult to know this will be the case and it behooves us to make some attempt at resolution, even if the solution does not satisfy the exact parameter as stated.

We therefore decided upon banishment.

Ryan looked up, several questions on his mind.

As if reading his thoughts, Lorian offered, "Some quests are impossible to perform, and the summoning spell knows this, in a sense, and will make the summoning fail. However, some quests have multiple requirements where only part of the quest is impossible. Such requirements can be ignored by the champions. Other times, a requirement cannot be met as stated, but some approximation of it can be accomplished and the questors are obliged to achieve what they can. Sometimes this impossibility results from a poorly phrased requirement where the intention was not stated accurately, and it is up to the Ellorians to determine the true intent."

Anna remarked, "It reminds me of those genie-in-the-bottle stories where the genie grants the wish but it's never what you meant."

Ryan nodded and returned to reading Soliander's scroll aloud once more.

In my own travels, I had previously come across an unin-habited world suitable for the cause. It is lush with vegetation and wild stock, mountainous enough for dragon lairs, and yet no sentient races exist there, or even non-sentient humanoids. The dragons could live and thrive.

However, this world was not without concern. On it I had discovered a unique ore I named soclarin, an ancient magic word meaning "vessel of power." In addition to being impervi-ous to the elements, such as fire and ice, it also resists magical energy, and yet magic items created with it are of significantly greater power. It was this ore that allowed me to create the Dragon Gate, a device powerful enough to not only banish the dragons but serve as a lock on the planet Soclarin. Only the most powerful of wizards can fashion items from it, but I am its discoverer and only I know how to do so.

For the banishment to be effective, neither dragons nor anything else should be able to leave Soclarin, since dragons can change shapes and impersonate other beings. However, locking a planet in this way takes tremendous energy. Without the soclarin ore, it would be extremely arduous if not impossi-ble. However, choosing Soclarin as the place to banish them presented a problem for me, as I have used the ore to fashion other items and would no longer be able to access it once the gate was active. For this reason, I traveled there one last time to retrieve a suitable quantity of ore for the foreseeable future.

Two gates were created, one upon Soclarin and another here on Honyn in the ruined castle of Darlonon in the Tarron Mountains of Alunia. The Soclarin gate does not contain a lock for the obvious reason that the dragons have no need of operating it, and the Honyn gate locks both. I formed the Honyn gate in such a way that only my staff – or a similar item made of soclarin ore, of which I believe there to be none not in our possession – could unlock it. Items made from so-clarin appear bluish grey or silver if fashioned into a blade, being lighter than expected and virtually indestructible.

The description reminded Ryan of Korrin's sword, which was bluish silver, unusually light, and had been completely unmarked after the sword fight in their suite. His opponent's sword had been badly nicked.

Eric leaned forward. "This says only Soliander could open the gate, or someone with a soclarin item, which again means him, unless someone stole something of his."

"Well, with him being missing," added Matt, "it's obviously not him, and since he's not around to guard his stuff, someone might've tried to steal something of his."

Morven shook his head, a brown lock of hair falling off his shoulder, green eyes moving from one champion to another. "The magical protection around his dwellings is reputed to be truly formidable and includes demons and the like. It would be madness to try."

Fingering the staff, Matt said, "I guess all we need to close the gate is this."

"Possibly," agreed Lorian, "but the staff usually facilitates spell casting and does not replace it. There might be more needed still." He frowned. "Since you have it, and the rest of you have their remaining items, they clearly do not also have them. It does not bode well for them."

"Maybe the spell is in one of the books." Matt pulled out one bound in red and silver and started flipping through it despite the unfamiliar language. Archaic-looking symbols graced many pages amidst probable directions and maybe ingredients for potions, identifiable by the quantities listed. Depictions of dragons, unicorns, monsters, and other mythical beasts – or maybe not so mythical – adorned the pages. Most of the text was in one of two scripts, the first aggressive and somehow suggestive of being ancient, the second smooth, elegant, and flowing, beautiful to look at even if not understood.

Lorian, who sat next to him, said quietly, "It is written in elvish."

"Why elvish?"

"It is common among human wizards to write spells in another language so that ordinary folk cannot understand them, whether it be the incantations or the accompanying descriptions. Most humans cannot read elvish."

"Yes, it's working, because I can't read any of it. These books aren't going to help me much."

"I can teach you both elvish and the language of magic, , Nu'Eiro."

Matt perked up. "Really?" Then his face fell. "How can I learn anything useful in a few days?"

"There are magical means to acquire the ability quickly," replied Lorian.

"That reminds me," Eric began, "I've been meaning to ask how we can all speak English, our language back on Earth, and you guys do, too. I know the worlds are connected, but it seems a huge coincidence."

The elf nodded. "You are not speaking English. Just as I can cast a spell to allow you to speak and understand another language, the summoning spell has this built into it. Soliander added this to make it easier for them. Otherwise they might often arrive somewhere and be unable to communicate. The summoners must specify what language is expected and the spell adjusts accordingly."

"This summoning spell sounds incredible," Matt remarked.

"It is, and among the most sophisticated spells ever cast. It is one reason the soclarin ore was needed to enable it."

Eric asked, "So then what language are we speaking?"

"Vortunon, the common tongue of this continent, of the same name."

"But I feel like I'm speaking English."

"That I cannot explain, but I would imagine that, now that you are aware of the difference, you could speak in English and switch back to Vortunen if you tried."

They exchanged a look, with Matt the first to say something in English. The others followed suit, then switched back to Vortunen.

Eric asked, "So if we're summoned elsewhere, we might gain the ability to speak that language?"

"Yes."

"Is this permanent?"

"I do not know."

"So if elves summon us..."

"You gain elvish."

Matt said, "Wow. That's awesome. I want to learn how to do this kind of spell."

Lorian chuckled. "As would many. First, I must test your affinity for magic to see whether you have anything more than the rudimentary powers everyone possesses. Otherwise there won't be much point in instructing you. I brought materials to administer the test." Lorian looked around the inn and added, "Now would be a good time if you are agreeable to it, but not here. Let us go upstairs."

Matt nodded and rose, taking the books and staff with him. Eric got up to go, too, gesturing for the others to remain. Matt looked at him inquisitively.

"No going off by ourselves, remember?"

Matt shrugged. Lorian appeared trustworthy but being cautious didn't hurt. Neither would a witness. Minutes later, Lorian and Matt sat facing each other in the elf's room, Eric watching with his back to the closed door. The floor creaked as he shifted to brighten a wall lantern. They weren't used to it being so dark inside at night. They needed to maximize the daylight hours, rising early. Being a night owl lost its appeal when there was nothing to do and you couldn't see anything.

From a woolen bag, Lorian retrieved a rectangular tray of black metal divided into four recessed squares, a split, recessed circle in the center. The elf placed the tray on a three-legged stool before pulling six glass vials out, one holding a deep red sand he poured into one corner, where it flattened by itself to form a level surface. That got Matt's attention. They had yet to witness anything supernatural after the summoning. Sparkling light danced from within the next vial as Lorian poured it into an adjacent space, where the liquid softly glowed. Another bottle of clear liquid seemed unremarkable until he poured it and it ignited into a low, golden flame. The next glass held a swirling, smoky atmosphere that drifted down to the fourth quadrangle, softly stirring as if alive.

"The four elements," realized Matt, wanting to touch them.

"Yes," Lorian approved.

"And in the center?"

"The essences of magic and spirit." Lorian held up a glass with a thick, glowing, golden liquid. It wasn't smooth like a fluid, but multifaceted like crushed foil. It slowly oozed into one half of the center circle, looking for all-the-world like solid gold. The last vial held a similar, shimmering liquid like molten silver.

"Which is which?" Matt asked, staring.

"The silver of the moons is of the spirit, which is why silver weapons hurt the undead. Magic, the fire of the soul, is golden." He took the tray in both hands and uttered several phrases that didn't sound elven from they'd heard today as the elves spoke among themselves. The tray glowed briefly. Then Lorian pulled out a small knife and gestured for Matt's hand, which the techie warily extended. "I need six drops of your blood, one at a time for each test."

"Why?" Matt asked, feeling lightheaded as the blade approached his fingertip. He'd seemingly been born averse to the sight of blood.

"It is the gateway to the soul," Lorian answered, "for how is the soul released except by the shedding or stilling of blood? It connects body and soul, and being part of both, allows us to touch your soul's magic energy through the flesh." He reached for Matt's hand and chose one finger to hold steady. The knife snaked out to slice a small cut before the wizard-to-be could flinch. Lorian pulled Matt's finger over the sand and gave a short squeeze. A single drop fell to the sand. After a moment, the red sand rose to form an elegant house, which then dissolved into a village of many houses, then a city, a continent, and finally a small planet showing continents and rotating on its axis.

"What does it mean?" Matt asked, the blood forgotten.

Lorian's wide eyes fell on him. "You have a strong connection to the earth. The weakest would see only a hut form, or a house. The stronger see a town, a city, maybe a kingdom."

Matt wasn't sure he wanted to understand the implication. "But, this shows a planet."

The elf nodded slowly. "I have only seen one stronger, showing many planets. It was Soliander himself."

Matt whispered, "Wow."

Eric shifted and Matt glanced at him, seeing a look of concern he didn't share. The rogue said, "I'd like the results of your testing known only to us."

Lorian said, "Very wise. Agreed. Let us proceed."

He pulled Matt's finger over the tray again, this time to the fire, which had been softly crackling. Another drop of blood fell, landing with a sizzle. The flames turned dark red, then brightened to orange, yellow, and finally a white so bright it hurt the eyes. Matt leaned back from the heat as arcs of white flame lashed out like a solar flare. Though the test concluded and cooled, the globe still spun slowly. A sun had formed.

"That was awesome." Matt breathed, anxious to see what the other tests did.

"Great power over fire," observed the elf, gesturing for him to proceed.

This time Matt squeezed out a drop himself. The fog stirred as shapes began to form. First were archaic-looking symbols he didn't recognize, then a dragon flying through the clouds, and finally his own face staring back. A swirl struck the visage and tore it apart, a spinning vortex growing wider as others formed, the tornadoes merging to form a huge hole of swirling blackness, the roaring air and thunder audible as cracks of lightning flashed light upon the watchers.

Matt recognized a hurricane from TV. A glance at Lorian confirmed his high level of affinity for air, too. "What did the symbols mean?"

"Symbols?" The elf looked confused. "Where?"

"In the fog," Matt answered. "It was right at the start, before my face appeared."

Lorian and Eric exchanged a look. Matt realized from their glances that only he had seen them. "Describe them," commanded the elf.

"On the left was a circle with a man inside it, lightning surrounding it. In the middle was a square with each line bowed inward toward a little star-like point in the middle, with something sticking out of it. The right one showed one sword piercing two hearts, each with a drop of blood falling from it. What do they mean?"

"I'm not sure," evaded Lorian, frowning. "The first two are unknown. The last is bleak."

"Meaning?" Eric asked.

"Death," Lorian announced, "though that could be death of an idea or a cause, not necessarily the one who sees the symbol. It can also mean rebirth. Its meaning is possibly changed by the others, but I do not understand them. What seems clear is that two lives will be at stake."

Matt sighed. Things kept getting more complicated. Hopefully this wasn't some sort of omen, especially since his life was likely one of those at stake.

"Please continue," suggested Lorian.

Matt squeezed a drop into the crystal water, which splashed upward to form a fountain from the blowhole of a whale that materialized beneath it. As the water descended, it formed a wooden ship-of-the-line as the whale vanished. The ship's sails unfurled with a snap and it surged forward on the wind, slicing through the white-tipped waves. Dolphins leapt ahead of it.

"That's amazing," said Matt.

"You can master water, if you desire," said Lorian, appearing impressed.

Matt wondered if he was jealous and how much power the elf had. Something occurred to the young wizard. "These keep showing great things, but what happens when someone is not gifted?"

"It varies from person to person," the elf replied, green eyes thoughtful, "and can sometimes be interpreted as fortune telling, though that is not its purpose and it cannot be taken literally. In the case of water, I once saw a whirlpool open and swallow the ship depicted. The fog has shown someone lost within, walking in circles, unable to find their way. The fire has shown nothing but charred ash. The signs of weakness or failure can be subtle, since these can be overcome and are uncertain, but the signs of power are unmistakable."

Eric asked, "How much interpretation is involved. What is the chance you are wrong?"

"It's always a possibility, but I see only signs of great potential here."

Lorian nodded at Matt, who squeezed a drop onto the silver, which reached up to catch the blood, then lay still. Smoke stirred on its cold, silvery surface, forming a floating torso and ghostly head with wild hair, two arms reaching toward Matt as the figure howled and shrieked. Two pinpoints of hateful red light looked into his. Then it stopped as if truly seeing the wizard for the first time. It became a peaceful, hooded figure with a bowed head and arms outstretched in supplication. But when its eyes, now blue, looked at Matt again, the figure turned and hurled itself away, slamming into an invisible wall along which it desperately slid, searching for escape. A low, terror-filled moan filled the room and gave way to a whimper as it raised one hand as if to ward off a blow.

"The dead will respect and fear you," remarked Lorian in amazement, "not the other way around. I have never seen such a reaction."

Matt wasn't so sure about that. The first figure had certainly made an impression on him. Then again, so had the last.

Lorian gestured to the gold liquid. "The final test, for magic, is the most important."

Too distracted by the fantastic to be concerned about blood, Matt eagerly squeezed out a last drop. It landed with a clink as if striking solid metal, and there it stuck, still shaped like a droplet. The gold beneath it simmered as if melting, the blood drop smoldering, then oozing out across the now molten surface and sinking. A hooded, robed, golden figure rose from within, carrying a staff topped with a crystal that burst forth with golden light that swirled around the room before settling on Matt as the figure knelt and bowed. It wasn't as spectacular, but Lorian gasped.

"The master wizard has bowed to you!" The elf's eyes were wide and he looked from Matt to Eric with what seemed like alarm. "I would not tell even your friends of these results. Even if you trust them with your life, others have means of extracting information from even the most determined captives."

Matt raised an eyebrow at Eric and received a nod of agreement. The young wizard trusted his opinion above all others. Both leery and eager, Matt asked, "Will you be able to teach me anything between now and the castle?"

"Certainly," the elf replied, thinking safety had to prevail, more so in Matt's case than usual. "We must prevent witnesses, however. After all, Soliander is not in need of instruction. Keep this private as well. We must be very careful, not only with the knowledge of your potential, but of your need for training."

"How dangerous is Matt?" Eric asked, arms folded, and the wizard-to-be looked at him in surprise. A look at Lorian showed the elf wasn't surprised by the question. He pursed his lips and appeared to choose his words carefully.

"Right now, he is not, and we must ensure that only those he wishes to harm are affected by anything he does."

Eric nodded and seemed to have heard what he expected.

They returned to the common room long enough for Lorian to suggest everyone retire for the night. As they filed back upstairs, Matt realized they hadn't divvied up the rooms yet, so he suggested Eric stay with him. He wanted to talk about the test and what it meant. He also felt safer with Eric around than anyone else. He'd always respected his friend, but after that martial arts display when they'd met the elf, this had soared. If they had a leader, it was Eric, who was more decisive than everyone else and more able to handle himself. Then again, after what Matt had learned about his potential, maybe he'd soon be the strongest of them all. He went to bed intending to fantasize his way into sleep and dreams of power.

CHAPTER NINE

ARUNDELL

Across the hall, Anna couldn't say the accommodations surprised her. The low, rickety cot was a far cry from the previous night's lodging. Getting accustomed to the lack of amenities would only worsen once the camping started, as she assumed it would in a day or two. The idea that it was all downhill from here and that she should be pleased right now made her smirk. Ryan had closed the door and dropped a sack of supplies beside his bed.

"Do you need help with your armor?" she asked, moving closer in the dim light.

"Not really, but you can help."

"Okay, what do I do?"

He showed her how to loosen the straps and unhook pieces, and as she removed the big back plate, she placed it on his bed, across from hers. She hadn't shared a room with any of the four before but trusted them, maybe Ryan more than the others. Or at least Eric. When a guy flirted with you as much as the rogue, you couldn't help wondering if there was something to it, even though he did it to every girl. That didn't necessarily mean it didn't mean anything.

"I think you can handle the rest. I'm going to change out of this robe. Just don't turn around."

"You don't want me to step outside?"

"No. I trust you. And I don't think I want to be alone except when using a chamber pot, and even then..."

Anna quickly changed into a sleeping gown with one eye on her companion, who never peeked, as expected. He had the honor part of being a knight down, at least. He busied himself stowing armor pieces in the sack.

"Okay," she started, "I'm done. Do you need any more help?"

He shook his head. "A man should take care of his own armor."

She rolled her eyes. "You and your 'man's work'. When are you going to join the rest of us in the 21st century?"

Indicating their surroundings, he remarked, "It's more like 13th century, so maybe I'm just being hip."

Amused, she said, "Next you'll tell me that women want a man to take care of them. We can take care of ourselves perfectly fine, you know."

"Maybe, but women like it when a man takes care of them, whether they admit it or not, and to be honest, I prefer the kind of women who admit it."

"Would you feel better if this quest was to rescue a princess?"

"Actually yes, I would," he admitted, closing the sack of armor. "Not only would I not have to kill a dragon, but she'd be grateful instead of resentful or something."

She teased, "Ah, I see. You just want her to sleep with you after you rescue her."

"No, though that never hurts," he joked. "I just like it when a woman lets a man be a man and she can be a woman herself, instead of fighting it."

"And what does accepting it mean? Being barefoot and pregnant?"

He scowled. "I never said that, and that's not what I mean."

"What *do* you mean?"

He sighed. "Not dressing like a man, and being feminine, for example. Being seen as a woman is not the bad thing some women make it out to be."

Anna had to admit he had a point but decided to end the banter. She climbed under the grey, wool blankets and rolled away from him. "Well, you can change now and I promise not to look. That way I won't see you as a man."

With a chuckle, he asked, "Afraid you'll enjoy it?"

She turned back and looked him in the eye. "Oh, I'm sure I would."

"Turn around," he ordered, smiling.

"As you command, my lord."

In the morning, Eric stood on weak legs and knew it was going to be a long day. Soreness set in despite the stretching he'd done the day before and before bed. The others had watched in amusement, but today it would be his turn to laugh. He peered through the dirty window, seeing the sky lightening to one side. He'd risen near dawn without an alarm. Life without a timepiece seemed more relaxed as long as he didn't have appointments or a schedule. In the castle, people had come to get them or wake them as needed, and he suspected Lorian would set their schedule from here onward, but he longed for a way to be certain of not oversleeping.

With Matt asleep, he tried to discreetly use the black, wrought-iron chamber pot, but the sound of a liquid stream hitting metal woke the techie, who rolled over and groaned.

"My legs hurt and I haven't even stood up yet," Matt complained, pulling sheets over his head.

"Maybe Anna can heal you," Eric replied helpfully.

"She doesn't believe in God, remember? How's she going to heal anyone?"

Eric grunted and buttoned his leather pants, which he'd slept in, though he normally slept in the buff. Then again, he lived in a temperature controlled environment, not a heat-impaired wooden inn. The court had given them sleeping gowns, but they weren't really appropriate for traveling and corny anyway.

"That's a good point. I hadn't thought of that." He sat on the bed to pull on his leather boots. "I'll leave so you can pee. I wonder what time checkout is." Matt smiled at his reference to Earth hotels.

"Check the weather on the TV while you're up, and please, please, please get me some coffee. I'm dying here."

"I didn't see a Starbucks," started Eric, heading for the door.

"You'd be surprised," Matt interjected. "They're everywhere so Honyn has to have one somewhere."

"I'll be downstairs checking my email at the concierge desk."

"We *are* the news," Matt remarked, laughing.

Eric paused as the truth of it struck him. They were indeed. And when they failed, they were also going to be the news.

This was not going to end well.

——— ❖ ∙ ❖ ———

In the Great Honyn Forest, a buck stepped quietly through the underbrush, picking its way so silently that any humans or elves wouldn't have noticed had they been near. The estate of Arundell lay just yards away, but those inside paid no heed to natural things moving beyond the wall surrounding it, for it was enchanted to let wildlife pass through and onto the grounds. The wall reformed behind the buck as it entered the grounds and it glanced over its shoulder as if acknowledging the wall's anomalous behavior.

As for the buck itself, it was of unusual coloring, being dark black with white streaks through its fur, with wicked antlers of ebony, and bold demeanor. It strode with a purposefulness uncommon in wildlife, even passing elderberry, greenbrier, holly, and other delights without a glance. Nearby white-tailed deer took one look at it and bolted, for something never before seen was not to be trusted. The buck spared them not a glance as it reached a clearing. In the distance, the rooftops of Arundell's manor appeared. With a bound of energy, the buck headed straight for them.

A winding dirt road brought the champions to the crest of a hill overlooking the Great Honyn Forest, green treetops and pines stretching away, the craggy, snow-capped peaks of the dark Tarron Mountains on the horizon. The peaks' distance made Ryan realize he had days before his trial truly began unless something happened on the way there. And it likely would, for Lorian confirmed that ogres, orcs, goblins and other fantasy creatures they'd heard about existed in the woods they now cantered into, on alert for trouble.

Hours later, only a tree blazed with a head of two pointed ears indicated they'd entered elven lands, no enormous trees with a city built high into them in sight, for only Noria stood this way. Ryan's desire to quickly get home to Daniel muted his hopes to visit later if they survived this quest; a bad dream about his brother had upset him.

As night approached, they stopped in the trail, Lorian turning to one side and speaking a strange word while flashing an amulet. The tall grass parted and low hanging branches lifted up and back to reveal a wrought-iron gate with the elven word "Arundell" carved in gold above it. The gates swung inward, and the elf rode his horse through, the others following. Ryan glanced behind to see the gates closing, foliage returning to position.

They entered a wide clearing with deer grazing, a herd of elk drinking from a pond farther off, and elves playing various war games on the lawn. Covering hundreds of acres, the property had a river, archery range, riding trails, its own farm and winery, plus separate buildings for staff, guests, and the manor house. The latter stood atop a hill, a garden twice its size surrounding it and threatening to consume it entirely, gazebos, trellises, and walking trails amidst natural spring fountains and fish-filled pools. Trees that seemed to stand behind the house from a distance were actually inside and poking through the roof.

Stopping by the stables, Lorian remarked, "I know you're weary of riding, but you three could benefit from instruction while here, preferably tonight." He indicated all but Ryan as elven stable boys took the horses away, house servants grabbing the saddle packs. Another elf tried to take Matt's staff until the techie waved him off. Then the elf went for the bag of spell books, and for a moment Matt let him before Eric caught his eye and shook his head.

Anna winced as she dismounted. "Can we start lessons tomorrow?"

Lorian looked amused. "Yes, but Andier should not wait. If there's to be fighting from horseback, you must be ready."

Eric's eyebrows rose as he and Anna followed the elf inside. "Is there expected to be any?"

"No, but you must be prepared for the unexpected."

"He sounds like a boy scout," observed Ryan to Matt, patting his horse farewell as they followed.

The wizard nodded. "He's probably light years ahead of any boy scout."

Ryan had been a decent scout but not taken it seriously, since practical application for all of it was hard to come by, but that was different now. "Maybe I can learn tracking from the elves or something," he said.

"Maybe you should," Matt began. "Eric, too, just in case something happens. We're completely dependent on them to get there and back. I mean, what if all the elves are killed?"

Ryan hadn't thought of that. How would they get back from Castle Darlonon? "I'll mention it to him," he answered, having a worse thought. *What if all of us are killed?*

Before dinner, they moved into separate but adjoining bedrooms with the softest pillows, comforters, and sheets Anna had ever known. After the attack in the castle and with so many people around, she had never felt comfortable there. Something about this elven estate was beyond peaceful, and she drifted off.

In the meantime, Eric suffered through some basic horsemanship lessons from Morven, focusing on forward propulsion and direction control. The fine balance he'd honed via martial arts paid off as he kept a good seat and control with his hands. Still, any experienced rider could see the mistakes, from moving his hands too much to poor leg position. Every time he focused on one thing at Morven's reminder, something else went wrong. As he got off, Morven suggested continuous lessons during the quest and the rogue quietly muttered to himself as he walked away.

Wearing the finery given to them by Queen Lorella, they were greeted by a surprise when they gathered for dinner. Before leaving Olliana, Lorian had sent for a dwarven friend to meet them here. Rognir of Vodavi not only lived in the dwarven community in the nearby Tarron Mountains, but knew the land around Castle Darlonon and had been inside. The dwarves had built it for Kingdom Alunia long ago, so he'd learned its layout and secrets the last time the champions came.

Rognir made an impression despite being just four feet tall. His bulbous nose was the most obvious feature of his rough-hewn face, which was so covered in bushy black eyebrows, a mustache, and a waist-long beard that his gray-as-stone eyes were almost invisible. The pointed steel helmet tucked under one arm had mashed his hair down more on his face, if that was possible. He wore a stained, grayish blue tunic over a chain mail shirt and stiff trousers that were tucked into hard leather boots, which had seen better days. They were covered in dirt, grass, and leaves, as if he'd walked through everything without discrimination.

Seeing their stares, Rognir scowled hard enough to split stone and gruffly barked, "Have you no manners? What are you staring at? Have you never seen a dwarf before?"

Matt was the first to recover. "Uh, actually, no."

"There are no dwarves on their home world," Lorian informed him, "or elves for that matter."

"What?" The dwarf was outraged, eyes afire. "No dwarves? Don't tell me it's all *humans*!"

"All humans," Ryan confirmed. "Not a bearded, short-tempered, hairy dwarf to be found."

"Short-tempered!" Rognir snapped, turning on the big man. "I'll show you short tempered." He reached over one shoulder as if for a weapon that wasn't there. Realizing this, he squared his shoulders and advanced all the same. "I don't need more than a fist to teach you a lesson anyway!"

Ryan remarked, "Careful, my knees can't take too much."

The dwarf sputtered as if struggling to think of a reply. Finally, he burst forth with a hearty laugh and slapped Ryan's arm. "Let's get some ale first, then we'll fight. My aim is better drunk." He turned toward the dining hall and headed off.

Ryan flashed a smile at the others. "I like him."

Eric nodded. So did he. Maybe having someone for Ryan to banter with would keep the knight from any dark moods, which seemed to come and go, a fact that struck him for how peculiar it was. Ryan had always had a sunny disposition, though Eric had noticed that there had always been something troubling behind it, though he could never figure it out. The sadness always surrounded Daniel, which wasn't surprising, but he got the impression there was more to it. But now Ryan clearly felt the weight of something on him, likely the man he'd accidentally killed. Eric wanted to talk to him about it but wasn't sure where to begin and had settled for just keeping an eye on the big guy, whose tendency to keep troubles to himself was more apparent now than ever. But maybe that wouldn't work, given their circumstances. They needed each other.

The group continued to a richly carved hall with a large oak tree growing out of one side. The sloping glass ceiling let fading daylight stream down while they feasted on wild boar, pheasant, fruits, spiced vegetables, steaming bread, spiced ale, and a rather strong elven wine. Rognir encouraged Ryan's drinking a little too much considering the quest before them, to Eric's unspoken disapproval. He exchanged a look with Anna, sensing she agreed. But they weren't going anywhere tomorrow and would instead focus on skill development and planning.

Rognir had been filled in on their imposter status, since he'd also known the true Ellorian Champions and wouldn't have been fooled. Lorian permitted no talk of this until after dinner, when they moved to a more private chamber, the doors locked. Eric surmised that even though elves were generally trustworthy and of good nature, the truth was a secret from the household staff. The oak-paneled room offered more privacy as they gathered around a long oak table with rounded corners and matching, high backed chairs with green cushions.

Getting right down to business, Lorian tried to bring the dwarf up to speed by remarking, "My understanding from Soliander and the scroll is that there is no way to free the dragons from the inside, so someone on Honyn had to do it."

"Who would do that, and why?" Anna asked, sipping her glass.

Rognir's grey eyes fell on her. "A better question is who *could* do that. The spells Soliander wove around the device were strong, and he was one of the most powerful wizards on any world. To dispel them and reach the gate would require equal skill, such as wielded by only three men on Honyn."

"Who?" Ryan interrupted, lifting his drink.

"Rohr of Marillon, Dieranon of Kianna, and Sonneri of Olliana," the dwarf replied.

Ryan's goblet stopped halfway to his mouth. "The queen's wizard?"

"Yes," answered Lorian. "Given the speed of the attacks on you after your arrival, he seems a likely suspect, for the others would not have learned of your arrival for days."

"But why would he summon us to stop the dragons if he's the one who freed them?" Ryan asked.

"Because they never meant the summons to work," Eric reminded him.

"Correct," agreed Morven, chiming in.

Rognir added, "You were attacked within hours, so whoever ordered it had to arrange it quickly, and know where you were staying. If it was not Sonneri, then it is possibly conspiracy from within the court, maybe someone secretly in league with the Dragon Cult."

"Great," muttered the knight, frowning, "we can't even trust those who brought us here. Maybe we should just tell everyone the truth."

Lorian shook his head. "I'm afraid that won't do any good. Whoever wants the champions dead would extend that to you now."

"Why?" Eric asked, not liking it.

"For any number of reasons, including an assumption you know their whereabouts. You have inherited their identities and now their enemies."

Great, the rogue thought. It had seemed a simple thing to play along until they knew what to say or do, but it was getting increasingly out of control. How many enemies did the real champions have after disrupting the world domination plans of countless evil bad guys on one world after another? Powerful people had powerful enemies.

As if thinking the same thing, Anna remarked faintly, "I hope we've inherited their friends, too."

Rognir winked at her. "You certainly have, my dear. You certainly have."

"You know," started Matt, "whoever stole the original scroll knows about this soclarin ore and has a motive to open the gate, to get the ore, so they can make strong magic items from it."

Ryan asked, "Yeah, but how would they open the gate unless they already have something made from soclarin?"

"Maybe they stole something of Soliander's first," the wizard answered. "You know, maybe someone stole the scroll, learned of the ore, stole something of Soliander's to access the gate, got past the spells at the castle, then opened the gate, and then went inside to get more ore."

"You might be on to something," Eric admitted. "Then again, if they can steal Soliander's stuff, why do they need to go through all the trouble to get to the raw ore when they've got his stash?"

"That's a good question," Matt admitted, frowning. "Maybe they wanted to make different items than what Soliander created."

Eric turned to Lorian. "Are all of these wizards able to travel between worlds? Maybe they went to Soliander's, uh, tower, or something, and tried to get in."

The elf nodded slowly. "Yes, they can."

"Sonneri had access to the scroll," observed Eric, "but no reason to steal it. He could've read it and just put it back, so in a way it suggests it wasn't him."

A brief silence followed before Anna observed, "Or that both he and another wizard know about it, so it could be either of them. He also could've arranged to have it stolen so he wouldn't be suspected."

"Very cunning," admitted Rognir, puffing on his pipe, "but not unreasonable."

Eric nodded but remarked, "We should focus on the most obvious explanation as being the likely one."

"The Dragon Cult was suspected in the theft," Lorian remarked, "since the scroll contains details on the gate and might presumably aid in opening it but does not."

"How many people knew about the scroll?" Eric asked. "That narrows the suspect list."

Morven replied, "We have no way of knowing."

"What about the other two wizards?" the rogue asked. "Have they been mysteriously absent or showing signs of powerful magic items that can't be explained?"

Lorian answered, "Not that we know of."

Frustrated, Ryan drained his goblet and said, "Okay, so we know the dragons are out but didn't release themselves, and there's one at Castle Darlonon. Has there been any word of some wizard walking around there? He'd be the one who did it."

Rognir cocked an eyebrow. "No, but we only know of Nir'lion because she was spotted flying. If the perpetrator is there, he has not revealed himself. It is possible that a wizard of great power is lying in wait for our arrival."

The four friends exchanged alarmed looks.

"Doesn't anyone have any *good* news?" Ryan asked in exasperation.

Lorian advised, "A complement of elves will take this quest with you, some quite well-versed in magic, and all skilled warriors. We also have a trained dragon slayer with us. You may not be the champions Olliana expected, but together we will fulfill this quest."

Eric wasn't so sure but was glad for the help. Otherwise they'd never see Earth again or return to their lives. All of this was far beyond intrusive, their lives put on hold in the meantime. It reminded him of something.

"I have a question," the rogue started, slouching. "The champions couldn't refuse a summons or a quest, but why would they put themselves in that position? How were they supposed to live their lives?"

Lorian nodded. "I have often wondered the same, but they did not discuss their reasons. I know they sometimes aren't happy with disruption caused by the timing of a given summons, but they put on a good face."

Ryan said, "It sounds like they didn't want to do it any more than we do."

Matt suggested, "Maybe someone forced them into the quests, just like us."

After a long pause, Lorian remarked with some surprise, "Four people of such power could not be easily compelled to do things they don't want to do."

Eric thought Matt was on to something. If they'd found a way out of it, that would explain why they weren't answering anymore. Maybe that was why he and the others had taken their place, but it didn't explain their disappearance, or the substitution really. More importantly, if they were true replacements, were they also now to be repeatedly summoned and unable to refuse? The idea alarmed him.

A soft knock turned their attention to the door and an elf discreetly opening it, carrying a pine tray of several wines and chopped fruits. Eric noticed that the intrusion surprised Lorian. He recognized the elf as the one who'd tried to take Matt's staff and magic books on arrival. The servant was unremarkable save for the white streaks in his otherwise black hair.

"Did they ever try to leave without completing a quest?" Eric asked, realizing too late that perhaps he should've waited until the newcomer left, but Lorian seemed unconcerned.

Watching the servant set the tray on the table, Morven replied, "Not to our knowledge. At the least, it would have looked quite unhero-like."

"I suppose so." Eric hadn't thought of that. "My point is that if they never tried, how did they know they couldn't?"

Lorian nodded as the servant began passing out the fruit bowls. "Assuming you're right and they were compelled against their will, it's possible that early in their adventures they tried and discovered it wouldn't work, but that is conjecture."

"I guess we'll never know," Anna remarked, sighing, "unless we find them and ask." Something seemed to occur to her. "Has anyone gone looking for them?"

"Yes," replied Morven. "But they have not been found."

Rognir said, "The fact remains that they disappeared altogether and have not returned to their home world. They have friends and family, of course. There have been no sightings of them anywhere."

"So they are missing," observed Ryan.

The dwarf nodded.

"Presumed dead?"

"No," answered Lorian, "it is not easy to presume such a thing about four such capable people."

"Imprisoned?"

"Also unlikely, but less so."

Ryan asked irritably, "Then what? What is most likely?"

Eric let the others do the talking, as the servant had caught his attention. He seemed to be taking his time. Something about the intensity of his eyes, the pointed way he looked at each of them as if noting their features, made Eric suspicious. As the elf reached him, their eyes met, and the servant's grey eyes reflected a quick and easy smile that exuded charisma and friendliness. Suddenly the rogue felt foolish. Maybe he was just letting things get to him when he shouldn't.

Matt broke his thought when he asked, "Could they be on a quest to a world where time moves at a different speed, so they've been there a short time but a hundred years has passed on other worlds?"

Rognir snorted. "I've never heard of such a world." His eyes sought confirmation from the elves and got it.

"Possibly because if anyone went to such a world, they'd be gone an awfully long time before you'd find out about the time difference," Eric noted. "Maybe they'll show up at home in fifty years."

Lorian nodded. "True, but before such a world could summon them, others would have traveled there and established contact, and when the extreme time difference was discovered, they would have warned people not to go there. Regardless, no one would tell such a world of the champions, build Quest Rings, and teach the summoning spell because once summoned to that world, the champions would be unable to help any other world for a long time."

"Good point," Matt admitted.

"How did different worlds find out about them?" Eric interrupted. Different lands on one world was one thing, but this interplanetary travel was quite another.

"Soliander sent an apprentice to most of the initial worlds," Morven replied, "instructing them on how to build the Quest Rings and use the spells. After that, other worlds shared the knowledge, as he had instructed them to do so freely. Also, it's accepted fact that Soliander sent the apprentice, so this assumption of the quests being involuntary is baseless." After a pause, he added, "In any case, no one would want them summoned to a world where they'd be for many years while only days passed everywhere else."

After a pause, Eric observed, "Unless someone wanted to get rid of them the easy way."

Lorian looked at him approvingly. "You are as clever as Andier himself. While they had many enemies who might wish that, they mostly earned those foes after the quests started."

"So it's not realistic?" Anna asked.

"No," Lorian replied, waving off the servant from pouring him wine, "for the simple reason that the four of you have taken their place."

"Why?" Eric asked. "Does that imply something?"

The elf answered, "Yes. If they were still on a quest, no one, them or you, could be summoned and you would not be here."

Anna summed up, "So regardless of where they went and for how long, the only current quest is ours."

"That is correct," replied Lorian.

They mulled that over in silence, picking at fruit, or in Ryan's case, enjoying more wine. Eric decided not to say anything.

"Does anyone know where the last quest was to, or what they had to do?" the knight asked.

The elves shook their heads. "Word tends to spread between worlds when they arrive somewhere," Morven answered, "unless the world has limited communication with other worlds, as is often the case. Some keep records of the champions' deeds, but their quests are often only related by the champions themselves when they return. Generally, no one knows where they go, only that they have vanished, sometimes before people's startled eyes."

"That's gotta take some getting used to." Ryan laughed.

Casting a sidelong look at him, Eric asked, "So they might not have been doing a quest when they went missing?"

Lorian nodded. "We don't know, but much investigation into their disappearance has been done and it was learned that each vanished at nearly the same time. The exact moment could not be determined for each, as they were apart when it happened and all but Eriana was alone at the time. She vanished in front of witnesses. The others did not."

"In other words," said Anna, "it was probably a quest they went on."

"Yes," the elf admitted.

Matt asked, "Okay, but the only quest is ours, right? Does this mean another quest was in effect all this time but recently completed, allowing us to be summoned?"

The elves and dwarf exchanged thoughtful looks.

"Possibly," answered Morven, stroking his long, brown hair.

"The important thing is how recently?" Eric asked, watching the servant finish up. The guy was certainly taking his time. "How often do people try to summon them despite this idea that they aren't answering anymore even though they can't refuse to?"

Lorian shrugged. "There is no way to tell."

"Guess," offered Ryan, and seeing the elf frown, suggested, "Once a week?"

"Possibly."

"Once a month?"

"Almost certainly."

"So then sometime in the last month, they completed a quest," Ryan offered.

"*They* completed a quest," repeated Eric, leaning forward. "If they completed it, where are they? There is no word of them returning home?" The servant was done, and Eric watched him head for the door, step out, and quietly close it behind him.

Morven answered, "No, all word is of them appearing here."

"Us," noted Ryan.

"They could've completed the last quest a long time ago, though," Anna disagreed, "and it was only now that we took their place."

"True," Eric agreed, "but then why did we take their place now, and why not someone else at another time?"

"Well," started Matt, "we were at the Quest Ring when a summoning happened."

"That should not have mattered," noted Morven, "for the Ring only summons champions to it, not away from it, though if your being there was connected with the previous quest, such as having just finished one, it might appear that the ring was involved in your summoning when it was not."

Lorian's eyebrows rose, clarifying, "If you were the real champions, and had completed a quest and returned to the Quest Ring, and another summoning happened at that moment, you would have come from there. The return spell, the one you witnessed, might have been triggered by the new summoning spell. However, on your way home, so to speak, you would have been diverted to the next quest. There were known instances when two quests happened in quick succession and they did not return home until the second was completed." Ryan began fidgeting with sudden energy as the elf concluded, "In your case, it would simply be coincidence to be standing at the Quest Ring, this Stonehenge, at that moment."

Ryan spoke up excitedly, slurring a few words. "Wait a minute. You said the return spell on Earth might have been triggered, so we might have been headed to *their* home world but came here for a new quest instead. Does that mean that if we complete this quest, we won't be sent to Earth on finishing it, but to their world?"

Anna gasped. "Oh my God! I never thought of that."

Neither had Eric. They might never see their families or friends again, their former lives over for good. The lack of response from the elves and dwarf suggested Ryan might be right. A sudden image filled Eric's head, of him returning to Andier's home only to meet the rogue's startled friends and family, likely demanding he explain what he'd done to Andier. He'd never get a moment's rest, especially when yet another summons took him away. And what if he and his friends were separated, living on different worlds, or in different cities, always far apart until a new quest thrust them headlong into danger? It begged a question.

"Did they all live on the same world? The same city?"

Morven nodded. "Same world, yes, but different cities, some on different continents."

"I suppose it could be worse. Did they have to be at a Quest Ring to be sent back?"

"No," replied Morven. "However, it made it much easier and required less spell casting power. The Ring bears some of this burden."

Probably smart, Eric realized. What if Soliander was exhausted and had to cast the spell without help, and with a bunch of monsters on their tail? He also realized there might be times when the quest was done but they couldn't reach the Quest Ring and yet still wanted to go home. It made sense.

"I have a better question," the knight started. "Can someone else satisfy the quest for them?"

Lorian nodded, studying Ryan's face so that Eric wondered if the elf also thought Ryan meant something by it. "Yes, though I don't think anyone ever did. Still, if the need goes away after they're summoned, they are free to return. Otherwise you could have a case where, say, they must kill a dragon, but the dragon dies of natural causes before they do so. The spell recognizes the quest is no longer valid, and releases them. Otherwise, they would be trapped forever on the summoning world."

Ryan frowned. "How could a spell possibly know something like that?"

"The Quest Ring acts a bit like an oracle," the elf answered, "due to the spells on it. It is like a living thing, watching for the outcome."

Matt looked impressed. "That's cool. Is that also why it knows if quest requirements are valid or not?"

Morven nodded. "Yes. It's also why a Quest Ring is needed for summoning. It performs necessary functions. What were you doing at the Ring on your world?"

That made Eric think of something else and he digressed. "Can there be more than one Quest Ring on a world?"

"Of course. There usually are."

"Okay. Well, we were just visiting it. The monument is of cultural significance even though no one knows what it's for, so people visit just to see it in person."

Anna clarified, "We were trying to find a pendant of mine that I had dropped earlier in the day."

The elves exchanged a look with Rognir, who asked, "What is this pendant you speak of?"

"Um, well, it was a family heirloom, hundreds of years old. It was passed down to me from an aunt."

"Is there anything special about it?" the dwarf asked, puffing on his pipe.

She opened her mouth to reply and then paused as if realizing something.

Eric figured out the reason and asked, "Didn't you say that the diamond had words written in it that no one could ever read?" She nodded. "What did the words look like?"

She shook her head. "I don't know. I never saw anything like it."

"Was it Norse Runes?" Ryan asked, "like the lettering of blue flames on Stonehenge?" Anna shook her head again. They'd all seen such writing before from playing Dungeons & Dragons.

Lorian eyed her closely, then went to a cabinet, pulling out a scroll, which he laid before her on the table and rolled out, watching her as the lettering appeared. "The words were like these?"

She nodded slowly as Matt leaned over to peek.

"Magic!" the wizard stood up excitedly. "The pendant had magic words inside it. No wonder no one could read it!"

Rognir scowled. "There is truly no magic on your world, and no one able to read it?"

"Yeah."

"But there must be. How else would the champions have been summoned there except by magic?" the dwarf asked. "It's obvious that they must have been, else you would not have come instead. You clearly have a Quest Ring."

"That's true," admitted Eric, "but if magic still exists, no one in modern society knows. I *think*."

Morven looked at them thoughtfully. "Perhaps this has been forgotten or turned to myth, just like your dragons, elves, and dwarves."

"Possibly," Ryan conceded, sighing.

"Getting back to this pendant," started Rognir, "it's possible that the champions' quest was to retrieve that pendant you speak of, and when you unwittingly brought it to the Quest Ring on your world, the quest was satisfied. Coincidentally, at that moment, a summoning attempt occurred and you were brought here instead of the champions because they were...indisposed in some way we do not understand. In any case, it allowed you to take their place for unknown reasons."

No one said anything as they mulled that over. Finally, Matt said, "So they could send themselves back, if they did the quest, and not need the Quest Ring? Soliander had a spell?"

"Yes" answered Lorian.

"Maybe that's the first thing I should learn," the wizard suggested.

"It's in your spell books," advised Lorian, "but it will take some time to master such a strong spell."

"All the more reason to get started," Matt replied.

Eric stifled a frown. They were at Sonneri's mercy, and he might be the one trying to kill them.

"My head is spinning," remarked Anna.

Eric gave her a smile. "Maybe you should lay off the wine."

"On the contrary," she replied, reaching for the decanter, "I think I need more."

The dwarf rumbled with laughter. "A lass after my own spirit. Drink up, my dear."

"Not too much," cautioned Lorian. "You have a long day tomorrow."

"All the more reason to forget about everything for tonight," said Ryan, agreeing with her. He took the wine and drained what was left.

Eric had to admit that maybe they had a point, but as safe as Arundell appeared, he decided that at least one of them should keep his wits about him.

CHAPTER TEN

ASPIRATIONS

The next morning started early for everyone, with a first day of training. They'd train all the way to the mountains as time and circumstance allowed. Ryan and Eric started at a grassy archery range just behind the main house, Morven instructing them in the cross bow – a bow mounted on a wooden block with a trigger like a gun, making it easier to use. Instead of an arrow with an arrowhead and feathers, it shot a bolt without either. To Eric, Ryan seemed unhappy about spending all day learning to use weapons, but they only fired at targets of straw, wooden blocks, or severed tree trunks. When he finally hit the latter, it nearly flew apart from the force.

Looking impressed, Ryan asked, "What's this bow made of?"

As Morven replied, Eric's eyes darted behind them toward the manor, seeing three elves watching them, one being the servant with white streaks in his hair.

"Ash wood, sinew, horn," Morven answered, "glued together with animal tendon. It is strong and resilient."

"A composite bow," observed Eric to Ryan. He'd heard of them but never seen one. More powerful than other bows, they could punch a hole through plate armor like Ryan's.

Their aim worsened with the long and short bows, though Eric was better than Ryan. Morven gave frequent guidance, criticism, and occasional displays of impressive skill, making them glad he would accompany them to Castle Darlonon. Otherwise they could only hope for bluffing cult members into laying down weapons before revealing how bad a shot they were.

⸺ ✦ ⋅ ✦ ⸺

"Leave the books," commanded Lorian from the doorway.

Matt reluctantly put down Soliander's bag and followed the elf for his first magic lesson, dying to know what he could do. Wouldn't it be great if he could fly, teleport, stop time, or best of all, make women fall for him not with a spell, but from admiration? A gleam appeared in his green eyes, excitement overcoming his caffeine withdrawal. Maybe he could make a cup of coffee appear, too.

"What's the plan?" he asked, carrying the staff.

"We will abide by the traditional approach, albeit accelerated," Lorian replied. "You will have my assistance on this quest, but if we are to assume your substitution for the true champions is perpetual, you must advance quickly but safely to perform on your own."

"Of course," Matt agreed. He had no desire to turn himself into a statistic, if such a thing existed for wizards who'd accidentally killed themselves. He wondered if a census bureau existed for that.

"I will explain the fundamentals of magic before you attempt to summon power from your staff."

"I thought magic items had the magic, not the person using it, so all you need to know is how to turn it on." He hadn't gotten any of his items to do anything yet, though he hadn't tried much, afraid to learn what they did the hard way and become that statistic. They hadn't come with owner's manuals.

Lorian nodded as they turned into another wing. "That is generally true, but wizards often make their own items more powerful, and if one fell into an untrained person's hands, it would be more dangerous, so for a staff like Soliander's, you must be able to summon the magic within or nothing will happen. This is true of most of his items, save those your friends have."

That surprised Matt. "They have magic items with them? Well, I guess I shouldn't be surprised. Hadn't thought of that. I wonder if there's a way to tell what the items are and what each does. But you say they can't use my staff?"

"Generally, no. However, it possesses simple spells anyone can access, such as casting light."

That made sense. The others hadn't been tested and Matt wondered if they'd show any promise, especially Anna, though Eriana's healing wasn't magic but a matter of faith and allowing the gods to use oneself as a vessel. She probably hated the idea.

"If work with the staff goes well," continued Lorian, "I'll teach you simple spells."

"Does that require me to read them?" Matt wondered. "I can't read elven or magic."

"When we reach that point, I'll cast spells to grant reading, writing, and speaking skill of those. The spell to do so for magic is very rarely cast because those who have earned the knowledge do not generally give it to those who have not."

"I bet," mused Matt, eager to reach that point. This was going to be cool.

While the boys received lessons, Anna contemplated their situation from a comfortable wooden chair in the ever-present garden. Today was training day and yet no one had plans for her. She wasn't expected to fight, thankfully, but healing hadn't come up either. Her friends not mentioning it didn't bother her, since they knew her inclinations, but the elves hadn't either. Had Eric told Lorian she was an atheist and not to bother with training her to channel gods she didn't believe in? She didn't want to be considered just baggage and unable to help. Worse, she'd be a distraction if they had to protect her all the time. Maybe she should just stay behind.

She sat biting her lip when the dwarf Rognir noisily approached, stomping on the loose gravel, metal items hanging from his belt clinking together. Judging from this dwarf, the race seemed as surly and grumpy as legend allowed. She'd picked up on an idea that elves and dwarves from different planets weren't the same, so she'd asked a few questions and learned that they preferred living underground beneath mountains, tunneling deep into them for pleasure and treasure, neither shared with outsiders. Humans often relied on the legendary stonecutting skills when building castles like Olliana.

"Mind if I join you, lass?" Rognir gruffly asked, voice so loud that he disturbed a flock of birds that took off en masse. He looked almost offended.

"Not at all," Anna replied, stifling a smile. Rognir hadn't been here long enough to know of her disposition on gods and healing, so she asked, "Do you know how people do healing here?"

Rognir pulled a pipe from a pouch. "The usual way, my dear. Pray to the gods and lay your hands on the person needing healing."

"Why does it work?"

He looked sideways at her. "Pardon me for asking, but shouldn't you know these things?"

"No, not really," she started, smoothing her priestess' robe and wishing once again she didn't have to wear it. "That sort of healing doesn't exist on Earth. We do it with medicine or surgery." He looked dubious.

"Why doesn't such healing work there?" Rognir asked. "Are your gods so displeased with your people that they do not answer?"

"No," Anna answered. "God doesn't exist."

He frowned. "Your gods don't exist? Why do people talk of them?"

She shrugged. "Mostly to make themselves feel better. People like to believe a divine being has a plan for them and that the bad things in their lives are not random, but will ultimately bear positive fruit. The idea gives them hope, but they're just reading what they want to believe into things and telling themselves it's God's will."

He nodded, the long beard rubbing across his plump belly. "Yes, humans are especially prone to interpreting everything. Sometimes a misfortune is just a misfortune, like a tree falling to block a road because it's old, not to thwart your travel plans."

"Exactly," she agreed emphatically, hazel eyes bright. It was always a relief to talk with someone rational about these things.

"But other times it is the will of a god," continued the dwarf. "It can be hard to tell when they act through intermediaries. How many gods are believed to exist on your world?"

"Just the one," she replied. "It wasn't always that way, though. The Greeks and Romans believed in many gods, but those religions have long since passed. What always strikes me is that once people stopped talking of them, the belief slowly died. Now most believe in one god, and talk about Him constantly, but if they stopped, down the road it would be accepted as fact that He never existed either. It's weird to me that more people don't see that."

He nodded sagely. "People often see what they want to see. Since these gods of yours are not real, they do not appear to people, I assume."

"Right. Sometimes people have what they call 'visions' of God, but there's no proof they aren't just delusional. Even so, it is exceptionally rare."

"Some gods keep to themselves," admitted Rognir, "so not appearing doesn't necessarily mean the god doesn't exist. Do you think that if people had more faith in this god of yours that he'd be more likely to appear?"

She shook her head. "No, because many people devoutly believe in God and yet He does not appear." She shrugged and added, "Mostly because he's not real."

"How are you so certain he is not real?"

Anna spread her hands. "There's no real unbiased proof He's any more real than any other notion of gods on Earth. See, the prevailing idea is that having *faith* in God's existence and plans for you is what's really important, so He purposely doesn't appear."

Rognir furrowed his brow. "What purpose does that serve?"

"I don't know. None, really, unless you consider that God isn't real at all and therefore faith in Him does indeed become everything."

The dwarf nodded, brow furrowed.

She continued, "Many religious leaders try to keep people from seeing this by discouraging such thoughts. They say things like people can't possibly understand the ways of a god, so we shouldn't ask such questions. If you're a humble person, you accept Him on faith, and to question is to be arrogant and therefore unworthy of God's benevolence. It's a social manipulation tactic, basically."

Warming up to her subject, she added, "If the priests were as benevolent as they pretend, they wouldn't need to use fear and coercion to make people believe. And why should belief be so important? Either God exists or He doesn't. Why does my belief matter? If I stop believing in Him, do I make Him disappear?"

Rognir grunted. "Fascinating. I've never heard of anything like that with gods, on this or any other world. Ours is a simpler scenario. Our gods simply show up as they desire."

That surprised her. "So then they really do exist?"

"Of course."

That set her back a bit. "How many are there?"

He puffed on his pipe. "On Honyn, the humans have fourteen, while we dwarves have nine. The elves have twenty-two. You'll find it is different on other worlds."

"Interesting. Are there any worlds where the gods never appear?"

"No," Rognir admitted. "I've never heard of that until you mentioned it, but there are worlds where they are quite fickle and only show up every thousand years or so, sometimes on cue."

Anna found that interesting but had trouble accepting people would expect her to call on the gods to heal them. A total lack of sincerity on her part would doom any attempts like a self-fulfilling prophecy. If she didn't believe, they wouldn't show, confirming her disbelief.

"How does a priest heal someone?" Anna asked again. "I know you said they call on the gods – a specific one, I assume – and touch the injured person, but what else can you tell me?"

He pursed his lips, thinking. "You must be familiar with the gods, their teachings, and personality, and have some affinity or love for what they represent. They can sense this when you call upon them and it influences their decision to help. If you only intend to call upon one god, that's the only one you must know intimately. It's best if you've spent some time speaking with this god first. Some gods, even benevolent ones, can be capricious. Have you been told the names of the gods here?"

Anna paused, realizing that was probably in the scroll she'd refused to look at. She confessed.

"You should read it," he advised, "if for no other reason than to make conversation with those wanting your advice. I can counsel you as we continue."

"You seem to know a lot about this."

He winked at her. "That's because I'm somewhat of a priest myself, lass, though my skills are meager."

Anna wished she'd known that before and wondered if she'd offended him at all, but she didn't think so. She'd been careful to discuss only God on Earth, not gods in general. She'd admitted her atheism in front of the wrong people before and had some turn on her rather nastily. Even less devout Christians could turn ugly over that. She called herself a "benevolent atheist," meaning she didn't go around denouncing believers. Sometimes she wondered if that was a mistake. If religions could crusade, maybe atheists should, too.

She decided to look at the religious scroll after all and left Rognir behind in a growing cloud of smoke from his pipe. On returning to their suite, she found Eric leaving for a swordsmanship lesson with Morven, Ryan sitting in a chair, looking bored.

"While everyone else is busy," she started, "can you give me a riding lesson?"

Eric spent the next hour learning to swing a short sword properly, focusing on defense, since avoiding death took precedence. To his surprise, the training included footwork that came easier with his background in martial arts, so the elf quickly focused on just the sword. Before long Eric's hand hurt from the grip twisting in his palm as the force of Morven's attack made it shift. He'd learned some basic skills that were in desperate need of refinement, and the elf had him work with his non-dominant hand, too. Morven dismissed him to give his hands a break. Eric left with his thanks and a promise to resume later.

As he neared the suite, he noticed the door was ajar and stopped short, the hackles on the back of his neck rising. Strange voices came from within. Something was wrong.

⸻ ◆ ◆ ⸻

Lorian led Matt to an octagonal room with tall granite walls, a domed ceiling with two open windows, and a single, thick, mahogany door, which he closed but did not lock; there was a thick beam that could be lowered to do so. This was the first fortified room Matt had seen here, most others having no locks at all. Arundell reminded him of simpler times in the U.S. when people didn't lock their front doors, the degree of trust refreshing.

"This room affords supernatural protection through magical wards," the elf remarked, leading him to the center, where two red cushions lay on the floor. "Most are denied entrance here, but today we will allow it, as your talents are unknown."

"So if I put us in danger," Matt surmised wryly, "you want people to get in and save us?"

"Something like that," replied Lorian lightly. They sat on the cushions as a robin flew in and landed on a ledge. "You must understand where magic comes from or you're no different from those using magic items, except more dangerous. Magic is inherently perilous, so we use pre-scribed means to perform it."

"Spells," Matt guessed.

"Correct. Spells can be fundamentally different on other worlds, but here a spell is a combination of words, gestures, and on rare occasions, physical matter. Not all are necessary. A spell's outcome is either failure or success. There's no accidental outcome unless only force of will is applied, which is why this is ill-advised. Magic draws energy from both living and inanimate objects nearby, another way people can be hurt, so spells control and reduce side effects. In addition, the wizard's strength, skill, and talent determine the power of a successful cast. A staff can assist and protect against catastrophe."

The elf said, "You must learn to draw on this magical energy to make Soliander's staff react. We'll start with bringing light to the orb. The staff's optional word of power will help and is needed for stronger effects."

"What's the word?"

"*Enumisar.*" At Lorian's indication, Matt stood the staff on one end, the orb above them.

Lorian advised, "Close your eyes. Reach out with your senses." The advice continued quietly as Matt searched, sensing nothing at first, but then like a light appearing in the darkness, a warmth glowed nearby. He yearned and it grew stronger, nearer, warmer. His heart pounded with a sudden desire and fear.

"Speak the word of power," Lorian whispered, watching in approval.

"Enumisar," Matt intoned. The word echoed in his mind, spreading outward to reach the force, from where a brief flicker washed back over him, making contact. He smiled like a boy getting his first kiss. He looked and saw a soft, yellow glow filling the orb, the faintest flame flickering there.

The elf looked pleased. "Few succeed on the first try. You have made contact, but not enough. Let your will flow. Embrace the touch."

With Lorian's endorsement, Matt closed his eyes and again reached into the power, immersing himself in a kind of spiritual energy bath. He grinned and let himself go, casting caution to the wind. "Enumisar!" Matt repeated lustily, his voice hoarse. Suddenly the force rushed into him. A huge fountain of fire erupted from the staff's crystal with a whoosh, a wave of heat blasting them from above and setting Lorian's cloak on fire. Matt yelped and rolled away, breaking contact and dropping the staff, the flames dying. Lorian snuffed out the fire on him.

Startled, Matt asked, "Did I do that?"

"You most certainly did." Lorian looked impressed but concerned. And slightly ruffled.

Awestruck, Matt said, "Wow. That was cool."

Lorian raised an eyebrow. "On the contrary it was quite hot."

Matt chuckled at the misunderstanding.

"We must work on your control," said the elf, sternly.

Chagrined, the young wizard said, "Sorry." His throat felt parched and his skin seemed dry. Either it was the heat or he'd drawn too much energy from himself.

Lorian licked his dry lips. "Now you understand the need for control, especially with your potential."

Matt nodded. "Please teach me."

The elf gestured to the cushion. "Resume your seat."

As Matt moved to do so, movement caught his eye and Lorian followed his gaze. Something lay smoldering on the floor. They approached to find the robin lying there, feathers singed and smoking. Lorian was about to say something when the robin abruptly turned into a raven. Matt's eyebrows rose. The bird moved slightly, not quite dead, and soon morphed into a falcon.

Lorian remarked in surprise, "A changeling spy! Your presence here is known."

Matt stared at the bird, concerned. "Maybe it's good that it won't live to tell anyone."

"An oversight on my part. I apologize."

"No harm done, I guess."

"Perhaps," answered Lorian as the bird stopped moving. "Someone still knows you're here."

"But now we know that someone knows, at least."

"True, but not who."

The elf called for a messenger to alert the staff but otherwise resumed the lesson as planned. Other elven wizards here could see to the manor's defense and the incident only strengthened Matt's resolve to achieve something today.

The instruction continued for several hours with Matt proving an apt and enthusiastic student. Years of analytical thinking from writing software code helped him grasp details and techniques. Finally, Lorian cast two spells on him so he could permanently read elven and magic languages. After Matt commented on wanting to read the spell books, with an eager gleam in his eyes, the elf doused some of the fun by instructing him to memorize two spells for their second session later that afternoon. It would keep him busy and out of trouble.

⸺ ✦ · ✦ ⸺

Eric stood quietly by the door to their rooms, hearing two strange voices just inside, one sounding somehow distant, as if farther away than was possible in their rooms. The other sounded quiet, respectful, but somehow unnerving. Silently stepping to the opening, the rogue cautiously peered inside. A figure in elven clothing stood with its back to him, gazing into a black orb it held aloft. Soliander's bag of books had been spread about on a table and rifled through. While Eric couldn't see the figure's face, the black hair streaked with white was unmistakable.

"I have found the spell books, master," said the elf respectfully to the orb, where a face hovered. "They appear exactly as you described. Do you wish me to return with them?"

After a pause, a voice replied from the orb. "No. Do not betray yourself. I will tend to them. What of the staff?"

"It is not here in the room," answered the intruder, "but I have seen it and it appears like your description."

"'Similar' and 'appearing' are not good enough," snapped the orb coldly. "You must be certain."

"Yes, master." The elf bowed.

"What of their identities?"

"None of them are who they claim to be, master, nor do they know the whereabouts of the true Ellorian Champions."

Eric cursed himself for letting them speak with this servant present, and it suddenly occurred to him to stop this communication, not listen to it for intel. He stepped forward and pushed open the door, hoping to catch the spy by surprise.

"Fool!" the orb snapped. "You are seen!"

The intruder whirled and threw a punch that knocked Eric back, a kick to the chest sending him to the floor. The elf leapt over him and started down the hall with surprising speed. Winded but undaunted, Eric pursued him.

The elf disappeared around first one corner and then another as they dashed by startled servants and house guests. Eric was losing ground and reached for a throwing knife to slow the intruder down as they neared an open archway, green fields beyond. Suddenly Lorian strode into view between the intruder and freedom, looking concerned at the commotion. Matt followed, a smile fading at the sight of Eric chasing someone.

"Stop him!" Eric shouted.

The spy threw a knife at Lorian, who leapt out of its path. He spoke a magic word and made a halting gesture. A brief flicker of light surrounded the intruder, but he didn't stop. Lorian's eyes registered surprise before he jumped forward, one leg arcing through the air violently. The intruder rolled under the kick, sprang to his feet, and took off, casting an intense look at the staff in Matt's hand.

Running across the grass toward the forest, the spy turned into a black buck with silver streaks, wicked black antlers thrashing through low branches as it dashed into the underbrush. Lorian transformed himself into an even larger brown buck and bounded after in pursuit. Eric and Matt exchanged startled looks.

Ryan suddenly cantered up with Anna lagging behind on her horse.

"Get on!" Ryan shouted, having clearly seen enough from where they'd been riding.

"Take Matt," Eric said, running up to Anna and leaping belly first onto her horse. He awkwardly managed to right himself behind her. Then he wrapped both arms around her and kicked the horse hard. Battle-trained and excited, it took off so fast he almost fell off. Ryan grabbed a half-willing Matt by the arm and hauled the wizard up behind him, then followed and overtook the others, his expert horsemanship paying off.

"Down!" Ryan called out as they raced into thin branches at a gallop. Matt scrunched down behind the knight's broad back as they leaned forward. Anna buried her face in her own horse's neck. Trying to shield her from the branches that slapped at him, Eric reached forward with one hand, feeling them sting his hands and face before they burst into daylight.

To one side, two bucks frantically raced through the thin forest, bounding over fallen trees and ducking low branches. The brown one had already halved the distance to the smaller black one. Ryan charged ahead and Eric realized he was looking for a good place to block the way. They soon slowed to a trot, moving into the woods ahead of the deer. Eric's horse followed more from training than from Anna's weak and confused commands.

"Everybody off," commanded the knight, "and spread out."

They clumsily complied before Eric realized this wasn't smart. The buck's antlers were fearsome weapons that suddenly appeared before them as the buck crashed into view. It came straight toward the undefended Ellorian Champions. The intruder saw the way blocked and an available horse, so he changed back into an elf and stepped toward it, something falling to the ground and rolling under some leaves as he did so. Ryan stood nearest that horse and slapped its rump so that it moved out of reach, the other horse following.

Seeing the false Lord Korrin, the elf sneered and stepped forward. Then the brown buck bounded up behind him and he turned to face Lorian, whose antlers were too close for the elf to transform before he'd be gored. With a snarl of irritation, the intruder turned back to Ryan but found Eric had replaced the knight. The rogue flashed an insincere smile of greeting and punched the elf in the face, knocking him down.

"Now we're even," the rogue remarked in satisfaction. To his surprise, the spy's nose had shattered, spraying blood everywhere. Eric didn't think he'd hit that hard.

Lorian morphed back into an elf and approached, hauling the spy up with Eric's help.

"Who are you?" Lorian demanded, receiving only a glare in response.

Matt stood watching the item that had fallen into the leaves, seeing its surface moving strangely. He went to where it lay and pushed aside the leaves to find an orb, which still swirled with colors as he looked into it. A partially hidden face stared back. At first he assumed it was his reflection, for it certainly stared with a curiosity bordering on his, but while his face shone with innocent wonder, nothing innocent existed in the cold, angry visage that appraised him.

"Lorian, I found something that guy dropped," he said, unnerved.

The elf's eyes widened on seeing the orb. "Bring it here, quickly."

The wizard did so, but as he neared the intruder, words of magic that he now recognized suddenly erupted from the orb.

"Rolinmor astorli nurarki a finta!" *Burning light, strike as fire!*

Crackling bolts of lightning arced from the orb to strike the spy in the head and chest, incinerating him. Eric and Lorian recoiled in surprise, letting the intruder fall as Matt dropped the orb in alarm. When the attack finally stopped, the smell of charred flesh filled the air. Anna choked and turned away to vomit. No one had to check the intruder's pulse to tell he was dead.

As they watched, the body shimmered briefly, and the countenance changed from beautiful to sinister. The skin turned black as night, the hair a dull silver. What had been pleasant elven features were now cold and foreboding. Even in death, a certain arrogance had seemingly come over the corpse's expression.

"A dark elf!" Lorian exclaimed.

Eric noted, "You're surprised? I thought dark elves were known to be up to no good."

The elf nodded. "Yes, what you've heard is true." He flicked a glance at the rogue. "Once again you seem to know all about a race that you believe does not exist on your world. In any case, dark elves live far from Alunia and have no business here." He cocked his head, examining the body.

"What is it?" Eric asked.

"I'm not sure," Lorian replied. "Something about this dark elf is different in a way I cannot ascertain. We will need to examine his remains."

"Lorian," Matt interrupted, getting his attention. "The orb?"

The elf retrieved it and Matt saw it had gone dark, looking like little more than a shiny black ball, and weighing several pounds. He told Lorian what he'd seen in it, getting a nod of recognition.

"It's a communication sphere," announced Lorian, slipping it into a pouch. "It is unfortunate we cannot learn what this elf was doing here or who he was communicating with."

"He was using it when I caught him," said Eric, watching Anna, who still looked pale. He related what happened prior to the pursuit.

"But I thought no one knew we were coming here," Ryan objected.

"No," disagreed Matt, "the queen's inner circle knew."

"Yeah, but she'd have no reason to stop us," observed Anna, grimacing, "unless it was Sonneri."

"Perhaps not," agreed Lorian, "but I have known Queen Lorella for years. She is trustworthy. But it is not unheard of for those close to a ruling body to have their own secret agenda." He went on to relate the bird spy Matt accidentally roasted. They absorbed that in silence.

Ryan remarked, "So two different spies. Does that mean someone was being cautious by making sure one spy succeeded if the other failed, or were two different people trying to get information about us?"

"I suspect the latter," Lorian replied, "based on what Andier has related."

Eric asked, "Is there any way to see who this spy was talking to last?"

"You mean like dialing star sixty-nine?" Matt asked, thinking of telephones and calling back the last number that called you.

Clearly not understanding the reference, the elf just said, "Not that I know of, no."

"We should warn the queen, for her own protection," Anna suggested weakly, "in case there *is* a spy in her midst."

"Agreed," said Lorian. "I will send someone."

Suddenly Matt noticed an elf silently step out from behind a nearby tree, then another and another. He'd heard of their legendary quiet in books but never witnessed it. They'd come right up on them without anyone noticing, save perhaps Lorian, who didn't look surprised. The elf directed the newcomers to take the body to the house as the rest of them followed, feeling like a funeral procession. The body count continued to climb and it was hard not to wonder if it would soon include them.

CHAPTER ELEVEN

The Ellorian Champions

Unable to stop his pacing, Ryan waited for Lorian to join him in a private meeting room. The time had come to get at least himself out of going to Castle Darlonon, as guilty as that made him feel about not helping his friends. He'd decided he could live with that, however, but not with causing another person's death. The scene of the dark elf's murder had shocked him, and though someone else had done it, even being on Honyn had led to that. It seemed that death would follow them until this quest ended, and he wanted his part done right now. He would not watch another man die.

When Lorian arrived with a questioning look on his face, Ryan turned to him almost angrily.

"Shut the door," he commanded, then realized his rudeness and softened his tone. "Please."

The elf nodded and did so, quietly watching Ryan continue pacing.

"How many elves are going to the castle?" Ryan finally asked, opting for small talk first.

"I haven't decided," Lorian began, "but sufficient numbers that the four of you should see little fighting or a need for magic and healing."

"Good." After a pause, he blurted out, "Because I don't intend to go with you at all."

Lorian's surprise shone on his face. "You will remain behind while your friends ride into danger?"

Ryan opened his mouth, then shut it. That wasn't fair. It made it sound like that was his goal. "Look, I can't do this. I'm not a knight and know nothing about sword fighting, and I don't like killing people! I want no part of it!"

Gesturing to a chair, the elf said, "Let us sit and talk. I understand your reluctance. You seem to know something of elves, but let me assure you we value life greatly and do not lightly end it or risk our own."

That sounded like elves, alright. Ryan reluctantly took a chair, trying to calm down.

"It is common among elves," Lorian continued, "to avoid a death strike and instead disable our opponents, but we also understand that death is sometimes the outcome of such violence. Even the gentlest among us must acknowledge that those who seek to do evil through violence are risking their own lives of their own volition. They must expect violent opposition, and it is foolishness for us to refuse self-defense."

"But I'm a Christian!" Ryan protested. "We're supposed to turn the other cheek because violence begets violence. The cycle will never end if we don't. There are whole regions of Earth that will forever be at war because they always retaliate."

Lorian held up a hand to calm him. "But what happens if you do not defend yourself? Are you not merely cut down, your life ended by those with an opposing view of what is right and just in the world? Is it right that your values cease to exist because you would not defend them? If they mean so little..." He trailed off.

Ryan sat at a loss for words, unsure where to start. Finally he said, "They mean a lot, but I don't want to have to kill for them."

"Understandable, but it is sometimes necessary. Something that you must understand, and this is of great importance, is that ending a life when that life is seeking to end yours, is wholly different from the aggressor trying to end the lives of others to further some cause of your fancy."

"Yes!" Ryan agreed, standing up in his passion. "But I'm going there to kill a dragon!"

Lorian shook his head as the knight paced. "No, you are not. That is not part of the quest. You are to *banish* the dragons, not harm them."

Ryan opened and then shut his mouth again, his emotions ahead of his mind. "But what if I have to kill this one in order to banish the others? Doesn't that make me the aggressor? This dragon hasn't hurt anyone since coming through, right?"

"On the contrary, it killed four men that we know of, but I'm afraid it is only a matter of time before it kills far more. It is the nature of these dragons."

"But preemptively killing this dragon before it kills someone else is hardly a justification. That's murder!"

"What if we are right about its intentions based on dragons' history? Would you prefer to wait until all the dragons are released and kill countless people before realizing they are indeed the killers history has proven them to be, and then act? Is that not a greater evil for all the lives lost while you waited for the dragons to prove their nature?"

Ryan's heart sank. The elf was right about that. He'd certainly feel worse. "The lesser of two evils," he muttered.

Rising and coming around the table to him, the elf put a hand on his arm. "Listen, Ryan," he started, using his real name for the first time, "I know this fight is not yours, but it is important that you accompany us. Your armor is protected against dragon fire. It is the only one of its kind available to us in the time allowed and it will not fit any of my elves. We are too slender. It might be needed to get at least you past the dragon and to the gate, or allow you to distract her while Soliander closes it. We need you. Honyn needs you. Your friends need you."

After a long pause, Ryan quietly said, "I wish they didn't and could just go without me."

Lorian shook his head. "I don't think you mean that. You say you cannot live with the thought of taking another life, but can you live with the thought of your friends dying while you remain safe here, especially when your presence might have prevented their deaths?"

Ryan hadn't thought of that and knew he would forever blame himself. His shoulders slumped in defeat.

The elf said, "I can teach you how to avoid delivering fatal strikes while defending yourself, and since this is your preference, I would like to see you enter into such training with vigor and not reluctance. You can do great good without causing death. We can also teach you how to use your lance to kill a dragon so that you will understand what not to do if you wish to only hurt it, or stop it."

Ryan looked up, seeing compassionate slanted eyes on him. He knew the elf was right, and while he didn't like it, there was no escaping it. He sensed a kind of kinship and suddenly felt grateful.

"So, if I stay behind, my friends might die," he said quietly, "and if I go, I might hurt or kill someone. It seems like no matter what I do, death is going to find someone."

"In all probability, yes. The important thing is that if you come along, you can help decide who survives, but if you remain here you are powerless to help anyone, including yourself."

Ryan looked up, realizing something. "With me separated, someone could attack me here while you're all gone, couldn't they?"

Lorian nodded. "Yes, though the estate is well protected."

The knight made a rueful expression, thinking of the day's events. "Not enough, apparently." He let out a big sigh. "I guess we had better get started."

— ♦·♦ —

Ryan wasn't the only one bothered by the spies. Both Anna and Matt found concentrating on their studies difficult, and the former finally went for a walk that didn't help because she no longer felt safe. She kept expecting someone to jump out from every corner or a staff member to suddenly become a threat. She finally secluded herself in Lorian's library with a few books on Honyn's religions and slowly became immersed in them, mostly out of curiosity.

For his part, Matt struggled to remain focused but more out of excitement than worry. He'd encountered two spies today and wanted to know how to detect them, and more importantly, put a stop to what they were doing. If he could cast a lightning bolt spell like the figure in the orb, someone would think twice about messing with him or his friends. He could now read every word of the spell books and couldn't believe the powerful spells in them. Only Lorian's expectations for him and the fear of something going wrong stopped him from working on them.

Lorian had taken the orb away and not discussed it with them beyond assuring them it wasn't something they wanted near. As Eric had observed, it was better not to have what amounted to a phone that someone could call you on and then kill you through. And people had once talked about cell phones emitting radiation.

As the day continued, both Eric and Ryan learned swordsmanship from Morven and Lorian respectively, and shortly before dinner, Matt succeeded in casting a spell under Lorian's watchful eye. The wizard could read the words on both his staff and Ryan's sword now, though he refused to tell anyone what the staff said, feeling some responsibility to keep it unknown as much for his sake as Soliander's. He discovered that even Lorian could not read it despite the words being in the language of magic. It seemed that only its true possessor could, which suggested Matt's ownership had more finality than he was comfortable with. The sword wasn't as complicated, however, and had the words "Brave is the Heart – True Flies the Steel" written on its two sides. The sentiment got a frown from Ryan, for the blade would never find its calling in his hands.

By nightfall they once again gathered in Lorian's private meeting room. Eric had finished reading the scroll Soliander had written and discovered no mention of how the Dragon Gate worked. There was probably good reason for that, but now their only hope lay in something being written on the gate itself. Otherwise they'd just have to wing it, and no one thought that would turn out well. Now he wanted more information on the Ellorians themselves.

The rogue asked, "What can you tell us about Andier and the others? If people think I'm him, some info on him would be nice."

Seeing four curious faces turned toward him, Lorian responded, "Andier comes from the kingdom of Roir on another world. Less is known about him than the others, even Soliander, because it's his desire to draw information from others, not reveal it about himself. Like all good men of his ilk, he knows that others' ignorance of him is to his advantage. Not only do they not know what to expect from him, but it makes his reputation larger than life, and such things go a long way in negotiations. Having details of your personality and past known can only be used against you, and the champions certainly have their enemies."

"From thwarting people's plans?" Anna asked.

"Yes," answered the elf. "For every group that sings songs of their deeds, there's another that curses their names. Each of the champions had enemies even before they started working together."

Before the elf could continue, Matt wondered aloud, "When did they meet? Why did they join forces?"

This time Morven answered. "Before that, each had done quests alone or with helpers who weren't up to the task, such as Korrin needing a wizard but finding only someone so unskilled that they became a second danger as a result. As the Ellorians started encountering each other and learned they shared a passion for solving the problems of various kingdoms, each realized the others were the competent comrades they desired."

Anna asked, "How many quests did they go on? How long were they doing this?"

"Several years, and hundreds of quests in that time."

"Wow. That doesn't leave a lot of personal time."

"Yes it is," agreed Rognir, puffing on a pipe that gave off a sweet scent. "This self-sacrifice is responsible for the respect in which they are held, and for the willingness of summoners to provide every comfort imaginable during their stay."

"What else can you tell me about Andier?" Eric asked, getting back on track. He noticed they spoke of the champions in the present tense, as if they still lived somewhere. Hopefully that was true, and it would be great if they showed up any time now to take over.

Lorian turned back to him. "Little. He is deadly with knives, swords, the bow and arrow, and with his hands and feet, much the way you are from what I saw in your suite. His balance is superb, and he's nearly as adept from horse-back, even dragon-back. He can scale any wall, get beyond any trap, and solve any riddle. His ability to get others to unwittingly reveal information is legendary, and it's said he often knows people better than they know themselves, and within minutes of meeting them. He is called the Sil-ver-Tongued Rogue with good reason. He is also rather charming with the ladies, as you might imagine."

"Well," Eric drawled, trying to make light of all that, "at least I have that last part taken care of." He glanced at An-na, who laughed a little too hard about that.

Morven added, "Andier is an only child and it is not known if any relatives live, though undoubtedly some do. He would not want anyone to know so threats to them cannot be used against him."

Eric nodded, thinking that being unaware of any living relatives was another thing he shared with Andier.

Morven turned to Anna, his face lighting up as he spoke so that Eric wondered if he had a crush on the subject of his words. "The Lady Eriana of Coreth is unusual in her peacefulness, which shines from her. Her presence alone lifts spirits, and she seems on first glance to have never known anguish, for many people assume such tranquility could not possibly lie on the far side of tragedy. They have never known it to be so, have never seen someone be at such peace after catastrophe, but Eriana has known deep pain.

"It is said she was shattered in her teenage years by a betrayal from someone close to her. It devastated her mind and spirit, causing great turmoil and leaving her desperate for kindness and care from others. Instead, she fell in with the wrong sort and received quite the opposite, making her confusion and anguish worse. It was in this darkness of the mind and soul that her power – and ultimately, her peace – were found. We do not know by what means she recovered herself, but the wisdom for which she became famous suggests deep introspection.

"Some time after this, she sought to help a gravely wounded friend and found herself begging the gods for aid, which was granted with vigor. So touched was she by this answer that she devoted herself to helping others, and the power she has wielded as a devotee of the gods is quite unusual. Her new calling gave her the serenity for which she is now well revered."

"We call it self-actualization on Earth," remarked Anna.

Eric thought she looked displeased, almost disapproving. Did she think she couldn't be that way herself? "How old was she?" he asked.

"Each was in their mid to upper twenties when they disappeared," answered Morven, "perhaps a few years older than each of you."

"However," started Lorian, "their experiences gave them gravity beyond their years so that they appeared older. You seem young by comparison, especially to an elf."

"So everyone should expect us to look a decade older," observed Eric.

"Yes," replied Lorian, "but few ever saw them for long. Casual encounters with you will leave most people fooled, and many will be too awestruck to question anything."

"That helps," remarked Eric. He noticed they spoke about this as if he and the others were permanent replacements, which he didn't like, but something else had his attention. "What can you tell us about Korrin?"

Morven set down his wine glass and looked at Ryan as he replied. "He received training as a knight from an early age and seems to excel with every weapon he touches. He even fights well with things that aren't intended to be weapons. His strength is impressive, and he's been known to shatter an opponent's sword or shield with a single-handed blow. The title Dragon Slayer is well-earned and initially caused his great reputation, for he was trained in killing them with both the lance and sword. You'll find that his armor there is fire-proof, to a degree."

"To a degree?" Ryan asked skeptically. He started to laugh. "What does that mean? I'll only get second degree burns?"

"It means you'll feel no effects from dragon fire the first few blasts within a short time," answered Morven. "Then the protection lessens until it has a chance to restore itself, which usually takes a day from what I remember. The magic is strong. It should be, as Soliander cast the spell."

"That was rather sporting of him," said Matt. "Do you know what magic items we all have?"

Morven replied. "Maybe not all, but many, yes." He went on to say that Soliander created various things for them. One was called the Trinity Ring, for it could heal someone three times before being spent, and all but Eriana wore one. Korrin bore another ring called the Dispersion Ring, which allowed the hand wearing it to pass through magical barriers and generally be unaffected by magic up to the shoulder. For Andier, another ring made his hand do more damage and act like a magical weapon, since some creatures could only be struck by one and he often fought with hand and foot. Lorian didn't know all their items, however, and remarked that all of them lost their power in certain areas where magic didn't work at all.

"What about Soliander?" Matt asked. "What can you tell us about him?"

This time Rognir replied. "For all Andier's silence about his life and wants, Soliander is the most mysterious of the four, not because the details of his life aren't known, but because they are. It is he who has had enough brushes with darkness to make some question his allegiance to matters of peaceful living, quietly of course.

"It has long been known that those of a dark disposition attain power more readily, due to the absence of a conscience to impede their progress. If their aspirations go awry and cause a death, for example, it is of no consequence to them, and while Soliander is not this way, he has always desired great power, and with good reason once the quests began in earnest. The champions are summoned to fight truly fearsome foes of often great magical power, and it is Soliander's own might that often defeats these opponents. Imagine needing to be the most powerful wizard on not only one world, but across many. As a result, he sometimes takes great chances with his soul, dancing a fine line between the light and darkness to achieve his goal."

"That said," interjected Lorian, "he is a good man, but one greatly preoccupied with other matters and not given to idle conversation. His reputation for being uninterested in social matters, to the point of rudeness, is well known." Looking at Matt, he remarked, "You are far more approachable so that some will be surprised by this, but you should expect to find yourself standing alone at social events. Soliander is a most intimidating man."

Matt nodded, and Eric remembered his account of Raith at the banquet and how nervous the young wizard had seemed. No one else had spoken to him all night.

"You had best turn in early tonight," advised Lorian, rising, "for the quest begins tomorrow and you will need your strength and energy in the days ahead."

— ✦ • ✦ —

The arch wizard Sonneri frowned at the black orb before him. A wizard of his power didn't fail to make such simple scrying devices work, so he knew it wasn't him. Something had happened, and while it stood to reason that the spy might be in an area of Lorian's estate where contact couldn't happen, he had a bad feeling that wasn't it. If Soliander had caught on, Sonneri didn't relish the ensuing discussion.

"Stupid bird," he muttered, throwing a black cloth over the orb and turning away. Queen Lorella expected a report on their progress to Castle Darlonon, and while he could still provide one, it would be the last. She had been rather demanding the last few weeks, which was unlike her, but she was under great stress after all. It affected all of them, but he'd noticed that no relief had come to the queen with the champions' arrival, which was odd. The last time they'd been here, the situation had been astronomically worse and the task far harder, so Lorella should've been as giddy as a girl. Not so. Wondering about that, Sonneri left the tower for her meeting rooms, something nagging at the back of his mind.

CHAPTER TWELVE

UNREST IN THE FOREST

The quest began in earnest the next morning as they departed Arundell in the company of Lorian, Morven, Rognir, and a dozen elves. They traveled light, with little more than grey, woolen bedrolls and long bows tied to battle-ready horses, the leather saddle packs easily carrying what little supplies they needed. The dirt trails offered few challenges, allowing them to ride side-by-side and talk idly, but everyone kept quiet. The apprehensive mood of the group made Ryan wonder if he'd cast a pall over them. His long face matched his melancholy heart, since he'd believed for days he wouldn't be going and yet here he sat. Since he agreed with Lorian's reasoning, there was no sense thinking about it, but it weighed on him anyway and he rode in resigned silence.

The quest wasn't anything like stories made them seem. He realized all those fantasy role-playing games were true foolishness and that there was nothing romantic about this. It hadn't seemed that way on arrival and when leaving Olliana amidst cheering crowds, but those people had no clue about death. Maybe it was always that way when people went to war. People who didn't do the fighting often had romantic visions of it while those doing the killing and watching friends die were scarred for life.

The thought strengthened his resolve to escape unharmed, for he had no intention of watching his friends die or spending any more of his life mourning those close to him – whether his actions contributed to it or not. And maybe that was the heart of the matter. He would fight to save himself and his friends, and that was about all. Never mind the quest. It was only important because they couldn't go home until it was done. He wasn't a hero and didn't want to be one now that he understood what it took.

Along the way, he decided to make sure they could find their way back if something happened to the elves or Rognir. When Lorian offered to teach him and Eric scouting tricks, he accepted, learning how to tell a footprint's age and subtle signs of passage, whether it be crushed grass, overturned leaves, disturbed branches, or the more obvious overturned stones and broken limbs. Deer, elk, rabbit, and elven prints lay on every trail, but eventually they came upon a print they hadn't seen before.

"What does *that* belong to?" Ryan asked, surprised by the print's size. Longer and wider than his by half, the single set of tracks lay half in the grass and half out. Even he could tell the creator wore two mismatched boots.

Lorian's eyes moved from one print to the next. "Nothing we have to worry about now," the elf answered, rising. He made a gesture to the other elves, who cast wary glances about their path. "I hadn't expected to see this so far from the mountains, but the marks are a week old."

"Okay, but what is it?" the knight persisted as the elf remounted. So many fantasy creatures were coming to life on Honyn that the footprints' size and spacing suggested names like giant, ogre, and troll. He wasn't looking forward to meeting anything like that.

"Let us ride." Lorian took the lead again and the others followed as the knight stood there frowning. It wasn't like the elf to be tightlipped, and he and Eric exchanged a look.

Anna took the opportunity to reposition herself away from Rognir, who had pressured her to choose a god to call on when the time came. The dwarf was a priest and her three friends each wore a ring with three healing spells, so they'd be fine and not need her to pretend. She'd find a way to be helpful when the action started, stopping short of any violence. Despite the run of films and TV shows with women kicking butt, she didn't have delusions of spinning kicks and the like. She'd leave that to Eric. Staying alert would be enough for now.

She pulled up beside Matt, who rode with his nose buried in a spell book. He'd long ago let the reins drop, prompting Morven to take them and lead the horse. The breadth of available spells amazed him into reading about all of them instead of focusing on a select few to learn. He'd expected restrictions on what he could learn, such as some spells reading like gibberish until he was powerful enough, but he understood all of it and began testing himself, reciting the words without looking at them, trying to get them right.

The first night, they'd camped in the elven forest, feeling vulnerable as darkness descended. They'd been attacked in a fortified, armed castle and in Lorian's estate, so being in the open seemed absurd even with the elves standing guard. Ryan lay awake for a long time, ears straining for any weird sounds, of which there were plenty in the alien forest. Most he recognized as bird calls or night insects, and while the howl of a wolf sounded familiar, a deeper growl far off caught his ear. Two elves exchanged a look and the knight lay back heavily. It was going to be a long night. His only consolation was the belief, however uninformed, that whatever made those big footprints would make enough noise to give him some warning if it showed up here. He'd never slept in armor before but felt more comfortable in it despite it being uncomfortable.

As the second day passed, the forest-covered mountains loomed larger through the treetops, the ground rising and falling as they entered the foothills. Tomorrow would see them at the castle, meaning one last day before seeing a dragon in person. Ryan had to admit the idea still excited him if he ignored everything else, but toward noon that became impossible. The big footprints had reappeared. This time the guides' unmistakable reaction prompted him to urge his horse up to Lorian.

"What is it?" Ryan asked. The elf rose from examining the tracks, one hand discreetly loosening his sword.

"Ogres," he replied, swinging into the saddle. "Three of them. One walks with a limp." He looked the knight in the eye. "The tracks were made yesterday."

Shit, Ryan swore to himself. Remembering the other footprints being older, he asked, "Did we catch up to them?"

Loran shook his head. "None of the prints match the other set exactly. Given the unrest in the Tarron Mountains from the Dragon Cult's activities, and those like Cirion trying to reach Castle Darlonon, and Olliana trying to stop them, the ogres have likely come down to the woods for sport and will not be returning soon." He indicated the prints and remarked, "These travel parallel to the mountains, not toward them or even away like the ones yesterday."

"So there's a good chance these three are still around here?" Ryan noticed the other elves quietly checking their weapons.

Lorian didn't answer, instead remarking, "We're a few hours from the elven outpost where we'll stay tonight. They can advise us on how things fare."

That surprised the knight. "Would the ogres have easily gotten by the outpost to reach here? Wouldn't the elves have stopped them?"

Lorian's knowing green eyes met his before the elf moved on. Ryan frowned, aware of the elves repositioning themselves to surround and protect them. If the ogres had made it by the elves, what would they find ahead? He didn't know how big a deal ogres were, but an elven guard station being overrun didn't seem like a minor event. Curiosity about the number of elves there and its fortifications ate away at him. They only had twelve with them.

Toward late afternoon they stopped on the trail, having twice seen more ogre prints at least a day old and moving in various directions, as if they wandered in search of something to do. An encounter seemed inevitable. Morven made a trilling bird call twice and they waited for a reply from somewhere ahead, but nothing came. Again he made the sound only to be greeted with silence. The elf looked at Lorian and, receiving a curt nod, dismounted. As he started forward, Eric decided to follow. He half expected Lorian to tell him not to, but instead he received words of caution.

"With stealth, Andier," Lorian advised quietly. "Learn from Morven, and be armed."

Ryan shifted in his saddle, indecisive about going, too, or telling Eric to stay, and when Morven gave the rogue a look of encouragement and they moved off, he felt a pang of jealousy. They knew Eric could play his part far better than Ryan could his. If he tried to go, their reaction would likely be different. In a way, they didn't trust him, or probably even Matt or Anna, to do their parts, but Eric seemed like the real thing. The idea of being a knight still appealed to Ryan despite the violence that came with it and he frowned at his hypocrisy. He couldn't want the admiration, respect, and celebrity without the killing and maiming that would earn it, and if death led to such esteem, how could he enjoy it anyway? And yet some desire for it remained, likely from his days at RenFest, which was fake, unlike this.

He looked down at the beautiful golden armor that made him feel so cool, even proud, every time he saw it. It wouldn't look so nice with someone's blood all over it, especially his, but that reminded him of its purpose, to keep his blood from being shed. That in turn reminded him what this was about – protecting people. This was the real reason knights received those accolades he apparently wanted. Maybe he should stop trying to be so noble and just accept that he wanted to be adulated. Was that so bad? Helping Daniel all these years had made him want to be a hero to his brother, despite his true nature: a coward. Perhaps he just had to find a way to help people without hurting someone else in the process. For now, he felt relieved to be out of it. Let Eric be Andier and find out what's going on ahead. He'd be Korrin another day.

Up the dirt trail, Morven quietly led Eric, careful not to disturb fallen leaves or snap a twig. The rogue had broken into enough places as a youth to know the craft of stealth, though the consequences here would be far worse than a stint in juvenile detention on Earth. He felt ready but nervous, especially when Morven pointed out several large footprints amidst smaller ones he recognized as elven. The pair moved off the trail into the woods, paralleling the path the others were on and stopping to listen every twenty paces. The faint sounds from the horses behind them faded as they advanced, no sound ahead.

After a hundred yards, they slowed and crouched. Morven peered up into the trees, looking for something the rogue's eyes couldn't find. "The watch post above us is vacant," he whispered, eyes searching the trees ahead, "and should not be. I see no sign of a body or struggle. Let us proceed."

Worried, Eric asked, "Should we get the others?"

Morven considered before answering. "No. You will climb the watch tree for a view into the camp while I scout ahead to make sure you have time to come down if trouble arises."

The rogue had mixed emotions about that and thought the elf ought to do that first. He'd be vulnerable up there. "What should I expect to see?"

"Into the camp, just beyond the tall hedge, with elves inside."

Dubious, Eric looked for any signs of an outpost ahead and saw none amidst the trees and bushes. He'd never have suspected a fortified position lay there.

Handing him a pair of horn-rimmed glasses, the elf said, "Take these. They will increase your sight."

Eric nodded and they crept to the watch tree, but as they neared Morven stopped him, sniffing the air. He slowly pulled a sword from its sheath.

"What is it?" the rogue whispered.

"Death," the elf replied. "Much of it. And ogres."

"Where? From inside the camp?"

The elf sniffed the air again. "Something is nearer."

Eric cocked an eyebrow. "Which is nearer? Ogres?" After a pause, he added, "Or Death?"

Morven glanced back. It was an important distinction. "Death."

There wasn't much to say about that and the elf gestured for him to start climbing. Somewhere above them was a hidden platform. The tree's hand and foot holds were carved from the trunk, a piece of bark-colored cloth concealing them from a distance. Eric went up smoothly, for he practiced parkour and could've climbed without the aids. He stayed alert for anything odd but saw no signs of a hasty exit from a wounded elf, and no blood, even at the three-foot square platform, where one branch functioned like a chair. To one side, the trail below peeked out through the foliage, winding over the hills for some distance, and in one clearing a glint of light caught the eye.

Ryan's armor, he realized, getting his bearings.

A closer view of the trail just outside the camp showed Morven wasn't kidding about death. Out on the road lay an elf, face down as if leaving the outpost for Arundell, three carrion birds picking away at the remains. While gruesome, it paled in comparison to the outpost itself. Through the leaves, Eric saw carnage amidst the wooden tower and walls, enough to realize no one lived. He counted seven dead elves and nine dead ogres, more birds pecking away at them, their distant squawks the only sound. More bodies undoubtedly lay out of sight within.

Eric looked and saw Morven patiently waiting. The elf moved his fingers at him.

What do you see? the fingers asked.

Surprised by that, the rogue answered and came down while Morven gave another bird call. This was one was answered from behind them, and soon they gathered near the body of the fallen elf on the trail. He had been bludgeoned from behind. Eric expected the grisly scene to appall Ryan in particular, but if so, the knight surprised him, gritting his teeth, looking away, and saying nothing. No one else did either.

They quietly advanced, the smell of death growing as they entered the camp with swords drawn and arrows nocked. Nothing inside moved save the birds, which took to the sky with loud protests, all pretenses of stealth going with them. Anything nearby now knew they were here.

Lorian ordered scouts into the woods while others searched the camp. Barracks large enough for a dozen people stood badly damaged and an open stone fire pit with charred embers lay in the center. A simple wooden tower provided a high archery point. A raised walkway encircled the wall's interior. Only one doorway allowed entrance, forcing any threat from the mountains to circle the camp before finding it. After the scouts returned, Lorian ordered the broken doors barricaded against roaming ogres, though none were found and all footprints were days old. Thirteen dead elves and nearly as many ogres lay both within and outside the walls. A large band had defeated these elves, and Lorian sent an elf back to Arundell to warn them and send replacements.

"We're still spending the night here?" Ryan asked, wrinkling his nose. Matt stood leaning against a wall, covering his nose with a sleeve, eyes closed.

"Yes," Lorian admitted, almost apologetically. "It is the only wise choice."

"What about the bodies?" Anna asked. "We can't stay here with them. There's a risk of infection."

"We will burn them tonight when the smoke will not attract attention."

The priestess nodded. That was safe and much faster than burial, but the smell would be awful. She already felt like it was never going to be out of her mind. Fortunately, when the time came, Lorian cast a simple spell to mute their sense of smell. It was especially welcome considering all of them were needed to move the corpses, though they spared Anna in a show of chivalry that came not only from her friends, but the elves and dwarf. She wasn't complaining.

The same couldn't be said for Matt, who clearly felt no need to hide his distaste, especially when they handled the large ogres. They were nine feet tall with an almost reddish skin, bulbous, crooked features, and soiled clothing. They exuded filth even before death. The number of wounds required to bring them down daunted him, and all but a few had arrows in them. Touching their clothing wasn't much better than their dirty bodies and everyone felt disgusted.

It seemed like forever before the funeral pyre burned in the darkness, black smoke curling into the night sky as everyone settled in for a long night. The horses were stabled inside with elves stationed at each watch post, in and outside the camp. Their owl-like calls came through the darkness every few minutes. Soon Anna found it comforting because it never changed and she hoped that would continue till dawn.

She sat staring into the funeral pyre's flames without seeing them. The scene of carnage had cast doubt on her ability to help anyone here like she did at the hospital, where she could diagnose and administer the proper aid. She was out in the field, not a cozy building waiting for the wounded to arrive, surrounded by all the latest equipment. Even if she were an EMT riding around in an ambulance, she'd be stocked up and ready to go with basic supplies.

As it was, she had nothing, just an amulet around her neck and a scroll full of gods she didn't believe existed. It hadn't mattered today, but what about tomorrow? Maybe wanting to believe it would all be better in an instant was why people had believed in witchcraft and all the other superstitions she'd scoffed at. Maybe people were still just being suckered into false hope even today. She shouldn't be so hard on them.

She needed to lighten the attitude she'd developed, but it was hard when someone like Ryan spouted religious stuff, taking it literally. She saw him up in the tower now, looking out at the Tarron Mountains as if hoping for a sight of the castle. He'd seemed melancholy since the estate but there hadn't been a chance to talk alone since. She was about to go to him when Eric dropped in beside her.

"Hello," he started quietly. She got the impression that he was trying not to disturb Matt, who sat nearby with his nose in spell books again. "How are you doing?"

Anna opened her mouth to say she was fine, but then closed it. She needn't keep up appearances about this whole thing with him. If they couldn't be honest with each other here, they were even worse off.

"Worried," she confessed, frowning.

He nodded. "About anything in particular?"

After a moment, she admitted, "Everything but you, really. You're the only one who can take care of yourself in this. The rest of us are hopeless."

His dubious expression suggested he didn't agree and she felt glad that he didn't contradict her. She needed to believe it.

"I take it you aren't planning to heal anyone with prayer," he remarked without judgment.

"I doubt I could," she admitted.

"Since you're in a new reality, can you pretend and go through the motions of communing with these gods in case it turns out to be real? It won't be the first surprise on this quest."

She looked into the pile of burning elves and ogres. He had a point there, and while the carnage had made her guard drop, she wasn't ready for that. "Maybe, but not yet," she admitted.

He leaned toward her, remarking, "Not to rush you, but you're a little short on time."

She knew what he meant, that they'd reach the castle and trouble tomorrow, but in looking at the pyre, she realized they might all be short on time in a different way if they were all killed. Companionship for her friends made her lean against him for comfort, missing the days when he would joke with her. Everything had become serious and it seemed like all of them were changing. Eric put one arm around her.

Up in the tower, Ryan happened to look down just then and felt an unexpected pang of jealousy. He turned back to his sword, which stood point down before him as he sat on a bench, the hilt in his hand. Tomorrow he'd have to use it and he reminded himself of the reason – to defend himself and his friends so *they* wouldn't end up in a funeral pyre on a strange world where friends and family would never know what became of them. He resigned himself to the coming violence and would pray for forgiveness tonight before it even started. Seeing the elves in mourning, he realized his second lesson with the lance wasn't going to happen tonight and he hoped to never need it.

As he sat lost in thought, he didn't notice Anna climbing up to him until she sat down beside him. They exchanged a look before both turned their attention over the dark forest, the looming mountains a darker black against the night sky, two of the three moons visible overhead. Not for the first time, Ryan stared at them bleakly for what they were – a reminder that they were far from home.

He seldom forgot to wonder what Daniel was doing back on Earth, but for the first time it occurred to him that Daniel was probably worried what had happened to him and the others. After all, it wasn't like Ryan to not check in. A search had likely started right away but not mattered. It wasn't like anyone would find them.

"Are you ready?" Anna asked quietly as he put away the sword.

He glanced at her, having wondered the same thing about her. "Are you?"

"Not really, no. I'm hoping I won't be needed."

He nodded slowly. "I couldn't agree more."

"There's nothing I can do to help anyone," said Anna, "so I feel kind of useless. I can't exactly heal people here."

He looked out over the woods. "Don't be so sure. Magic works here, and they believe in it. So do I, in fact. I've seen it now, and we've heard the stories Matt's been telling of his magic training. If magic works and people believe in it, it stands to reason that faith-based healing works, too, since they believe in that. No one's lied to us about anything. So far."

She nodded reluctantly. "Maybe, but that doesn't mean I'll be able to do it. And I'd have to believe it first, which I don't see happening anytime soon. I wish I had at least basic medical supplies like on Earth." After a moment, she added, "You know, there are people who believe in faith-based healing back home, too, but it doesn't work there."

Knowing they were tiptoeing around her atheism and politely avoiding an argument about that, he asked, "How can you be sure?"

She frowned. "Well, I suppose I can't be, but do you really believe that it works on Earth?"

He opened his mouth to say yes, then closed it. "I don't know. I've thought about taking Daniel to one of these guys, but they wanted a lot of money, which to me meant it was a scam."

"Right," she said.

Suddenly something occurred to him. "Wait a minute. If you could learn to heal people here, you could do it on Earth and heal Daniel!" He stood up in excitement. "Think about it. We know magic works there because the Quest Ring worked there, so it stands to reason that healing works, too. You just have to learn how and then you could heal Daniel!"

They stared at each other silently. "But Ryan–"

"No! No buts!" He grabbed her by the arms and lifted her to her feet. "It will work! I know it!" His excited shouts turned the attention of those in the camp to them. "How could I have not seen it earlier? *That's* the reason I'm here.

You're here. It all makes sense now. This is God's doing. He has given me a chance, a chance to save Daniel!" His bright eyes turned back to her. "He's given *you* a chance. You can do it. I know you can!"

Finally Anna found words to stop him from going any further. "Ryan, just wait a minute," she started gently. "I understand your hope but you're getting way ahead of yourself."

"No I'm not!"

"Yes you are, and you're putting way too much pressure on me."

That pierced his excitement some, but not much. "Okay, that's true, and I'm sorry, but you have to promise to try for me. For Daniel. Will you? Please? I know it's against your beliefs and everything and I'm sorry for that, but we have a different reality here and I would be sooo grateful if you would just give it a chance to see what can happen."

He stared into her eyes, dimly aware of them darting away from his and back, like a trapped deer. He opened his mouth to say more when she finally spoke.

"Okay, okay," she said gently, "just stop. I'll look into it. I already have. Just stop, okay?"

He was about to try to convince her more but then thought better of it. "You promise? Please?"

"Yes, I promise," she said, looking around hastily. "To look into it, not to succeed."

"Okay. Okay, that's fair. But you have to have faith, Anna, or nothing happens. Please open yourself to it."

She said nothing more, turning to the ladder as if to escape, and he wondered if he'd gone too far. Probably. For the first time since they'd left Stonehenge, he felt calm, and with a renewed purpose. Now he regretted any time avoiding learning things that might benefit them, and ultimately, his brother, who was going to be amazed when

Anna helped him. Ryan spent the rest of the night imagining it.

The night passed without incident from ogres or anything else and they left the outpost on horseback at dawn. As the day wore on, the foothills grew steeper, the trail narrowing to single file and the trees and underbrush growing denser. Anna kept her distance from Ryan, while Matt once again kept his nose buried in spell books. Morven and Eric rode ahead of the group, the latter in training for how to track and listen to the forest's sounds. Even his sense of smell received instruction.

"Ogres have a certain scent," advised the elf, long brown hair tightly braided. "You no doubt recall it from last night, though it was mixed with the smell of death."

"Yes, I remember," the rogue wryly admitted.

Toward noon they stopped in a small clearing for lunch consisting of elven bread smothered in fruit jam, downed with spring water that invigorated them more than Ryan would have expected. It tasted like sweet water. Both he and Matt had passed on breakfast due to nerves and nausea but both were able to eat this time.

Ryan hadn't stopped thinking about Anna healing Daniel since he'd thought of it. He felt renewed purpose and was chafing for something to get her motivated. He knew she liked his brother and would be happy to heal him once able. The trick was getting her to see that they lived in a new reality now and that she had to change her perspective. He wanted to talk to her more, but every time their eyes met, he saw her looking like she wanted to avoid him. A pang of regret filled him. Wouldn't it be ironic if his pressure became the reason she refused to open herself up to the gods of this world or of Earth? He wanted to laugh. Or cry. For now, he decided to bite his tongue, sitting over by Matt and studiously avoiding any hope-filled gazes at the medical student.

Ahead on the trail, a sharp shout preceded a hoarse bellow. Several thuds boomed ominously before a crack of stone striking stone and a scream split the air. Everyone rose and reached for weapons as Lorian issued commands, pointing up the trail where two elves ran with bows drawn. Rognir came to stand beside the champions, gesturing for Ryan to get out his sword. The dwarf's axe gleamed before them, its obvious wear and tear adding realism to their dread.

"What is it?" Anna asked, moving toward her horse. Ryan thought she looked ready to mount and go. The idea sounded better the second someone answered her.

"Ogres," replied Matt, able to understand elven thanks to Lorian's spell.

"Indeed." Rognir brandished his axe, taking warm up swings. "Battle is upon us. I suggest you remain behind me."

"No argument there," muttered Matt as angry sounds reached them.

He wiped both hands on his robe and Ryan suspected the wizard's palms were sweaty, like his. Ryan mentally reviewed what Lorian taught him about not hurting anyone much, though that now seemed less important than protecting himself. The assassin attack had happened so fast he never had time to think about it, but this time the waiting was awful and he eyed the horses. He would not be the first to run, but if someone else went for it, he was all in.

Suddenly a low rumbling began as the ogres charged around the bend, two elves retreating ahead of them. Morven and others stood at the trailhead with arrows nocked, and when the ogres came into view, he called out in elven. The elves let fly, all at the lead ogre, six arrows striking it in the head, neck, and chest. It tumbled in a heap, its huge, spiked club rolling ahead of it. Two other ogres tripped over it, slowing the pack and giving the elves time for one more volley. None of the remaining six or seven ogres fell.

Rognir moved a few steps ahead of the champions as if to bar the way to them and Ryan reluctantly joined him. An arrow soared overhead toward the ogres from behind the champions, via the other elf watching their rear. As the attackers reached the clearing, a line of elves tried to bottle them up on the path so that only one or two ogres could attack at once, but momentum carried four ogres into the clearing, their wooden clubs whooshing through the air, metal protrusions catching elven blades. They weren't kidding around and Ryan paled at the sickening crunch as an elf's shoulder shattered and he flew sideways. Lorian replaced the fallen one, sword bouncing right off a club that soon sent another elf to the ground with pulverized bones. Rognir clomped forward to drag the wounded elf back by the tunic before bending to heal him as Ryan watched curiously, but unable to see the result.

Suddenly Eric threw a knife over the heads of the elves, but the blade missed when the beast happened to move. The knife distracted the ogre long enough for Lorian to kill it. Eric's next knife flew true into another's throat, killing it instantly. As the corpse toppled backward, Ryan felt no regret, just relief. What did that mean about him?

A roar to one side startled him. An ogre had come around the thick brush and trees unseen. Its club hurtled toward his head and he barely ducked as it whooshed by. He retreated, eyes wide, forgetting everything Lorian had taught him. As the club came down like a hammer, he sidestepped and stumbled on a tree root. By the time he recovered, there was no dodging the coming blow. He raised the sword and met the club with a clang, nearly losing his grip. The ogre raised the club with both hands, lust for death on its face. Did it sense what Ryan did, that the knight stood dead center, too close to dodge, and had little idea how to use that sword? Realizing his peril, Ryan lunged and stabbed it through the stomach. The ogre squealed hideously and slid back off the blade, sickly red blood oozing out. Ryan blanched at what he'd done. His self-preservation instinct had overridden his dispositions as if they were nothing.

The ogre's expression promised such death and personal hatred that Ryan snapped out of it. It was still going to kill him, but he didn't have to do the same. With a grimace of resignation, he punched the ogre in the wound and it doubled over, screeching awfully. Then Ryan clobbered it in the jaw. The ogre toppled backwards and lay stunned and unmoving.

A moment passed before Ryan realized he'd done it. He'd stopped it, and without killing it. Or at least he thought so. Suddenly worried he ended a life, he looked at the Trinity Ring on one hand. Rognir had told him how to use it, so he put one hand on the ogre and focused his will on the middle stone. Tingling warmth spread from his hand, which glowed softly as the belly wound all but disappeared. He'd never seen magical healing or experienced it, feeling like an affirmation of God's power had occurred. Sighing in relief, he rose and moved over by Anna and Matt. Maybe he could do this champion stuff after all.

He saw that another three ogres lay dead, despite Lorian's comments that elves held all life sacred. Maybe elves weren't so pious after all. Or maybe they just understood something that he didn't. Rognir had meanwhile healed several elves and Ryan could tell that Anna hadn't moved from where he'd last seen her, far from the action. He couldn't blame her, but it meant she wasn't even trying. Even *he* was.

Anna had watched Rognir leaning over one injured elf after another as if helping them, but she hadn't seen anything happen. No glow of godly power. No wounds closing.

Nothing. She wasn't even sure he'd helped them in any way, not to mention by laying on hands. His back had been turned each time. Part of her felt annoyed by that, but part of her was relieved that no proof she was wrong about gods had shown up. The medical student in her couldn't help thinking of how one wound or another would be treated back on Earth.

Ryan's fight with the ogre had surprised her a little, that he could fight back so well despite the whole non-violence thing. If she wasn't so consumed by fear she might've almost felt proud of him. She had no idea why he'd leaned over the ogre after. Still waiting beside Matt, she now watched Eric standing ready for another knife throw, when something caught her eye. The ogre Ryan had fought rose to its feet. Her eyes darted to its belly, wondering how that could be, and she stared uncomprehending at the belly wound that was now gone. For a moment, this distracted her into not realizing it was raising its club and swinging at the nearest target.

"Eric!" she screamed as the club flew toward his shoulder.

The martial artist was already turning, but Anna saw it wouldn't be fast enough. With a sickening crunch of shattered bones, the blow flung him five feet away, where he landed screaming and writhing in pain, the knife from his other hand sticking out of his thigh. Without thinking, Anna ran over to him, putting herself in danger as she knelt and tried to stop him from rolling back in forth in agony. Behind her, she heard Matt's voice speaking words that sounded like magic.

"Kertemor iafiirlompu terteli, uapiiltoko nukoorkel naakli." *Shards of ice like darts be thrown, strike my foe down to the bone.*

Anna looked up at the ogre, only now realizing her peril. She'd seen enough men ogle her to be surprised by a similar expression on its disgusting face. If Matt's spell had worked, there was no sign of it. She heard him saying it again, faster, more nervously she thought, and realized it hadn't worked. Then another voice spoke similar yet different words and she glanced over to see Lorian crumbling a piece of stone in one outstretched hand, toward the ogre. She looked up again. The ogre's face twisted in surprise, its movement slowing to a stop and a grunt abruptly cutting off. Its skin turned a deep grey as it turned to stone, upraised club and all.

Suddenly the noisy Rognir stopped beside her, examining the still writhing Eric, who continuously moaned in such pain that Anna fought back tears. "How bad is it?"

Anna shook her head, unable to speak. His shoulder had shattered. He'd never use the arm again and modern hospitals back home would never get all the bone fragments out. Even his neck had twisted from the tortured angle of his shoulder and he'd never be pain free again. The dwarf laid a hand on the rogue and spoke a word. Eric relaxed into a stupor, his head lolling to one side as if he were delirious, no longer groaning.

"He will feel no pain for a few minutes," Rognir advised her, "but you must heal him quickly."

She'd forgotten all about that, but now was not the time for half-baked theories. She opened her mouth to say so but what came out was, "But I don't know how."

"Lay your hands on him," he advised gently, "and ask your chosen god for help with all your heart and soul. I know you care for him. The gods will answer you."

She looked down at the rogue, his glazed eyes on hers as if dimly aware. Placing both hands on him, she honestly wanted him healed, but the gods she'd read about all seemed jumbled to her, their names and what they stood for confused. There were too many and she longed for one god to make it simple like on Earth, which only reminded her that this was all nonsense. She looked down at her hands, tightly clenched on Eric's clothes. Nothing was happening. It didn't surprise her. Her pleading eyes sought the dwarf's.

Rognir took her hands away and placed his own on the rogue. In dwarven, he spoke quietly for almost a minute, sincerity on his bearded face. Anna wished she could understand him, gain some insight into what he was doing. Finally, a golden light spread from Rognir's hands over Eric's shoulder before fading, like all signs of Eric's injuries. Even his leg had healed. The rogue blinked and sat up, clear eyes on the dwarf.

"Thank you," Eric said emphatically. "Words cannot describe..."

Rognir patted him. "Then do not strain yourself. There is no need." He got to his feet wearily. From what Anna had heard, the power she'd finally just witnessed used the priest's body as a conduit, an act that was draining. The dwarf had healed multiple people just now. He took a long pull from a pouch that Anna knew wasn't water before stomping away past a dead elf. The skull damage had killed that one instantly. Anna realized it was the one who knew how to slay a dragon and hoped Ryan didn't notice that. Only now did Anna realize the battle was over.

She turned Eric. "Are you alright?"

He nodded slowly, as if lost in thought. Then he began to smile. "You've got to try that," he said, and she assumed he meant healing someone, until he added, "It feels great."

"You're sure?"

"Yeah." He sounded surprised, but then he looked away and she followed his gaze to Ryan. Even from here, the big guy looked pale and shaken. The knight had healed the ogre, which had then nearly killed Eric. Wondering what he was thinking, she turned to the rogue, and the quiet anger she now saw in his eyes left little to wonder about.

"Not now," she said quietly. "Not when you're mad."

"I'm never not going to be mad."

She leaned over to hug him and sudden tears spilled down her cheeks, he put both arms around her and they stayed there for several minutes.

Though the ogres – and one elf before them – were dead, Lorian maintained high alert, making everyone mount and continue down the trail still armed. He said that once the sounds of battle had rung out, other nearby ogres would've come hot for blood if around, but other things more cunning could now be watching and waiting. All seemed eerily quiet as they advanced to the scene of the initial attack, finding the lead elf's body.

While the elves tended to the remains, Eric went to talk to Ryan, who stood on the far side of his horse as if wanting to be alone and away from everyone. The rogue patted Ryan's horse on his way around the back so it wouldn't get startled and kick him. He'd had enough blunt-force trauma for one day. Stopping next to Ryan, he tried to mute his anger.

"What were you thinking healing that ogre?"

Ryan's face couldn't have gotten much longer. "I didn't want it to die." When Eric didn't say anything, the knight added, "Is that so wrong?"

"Well no, not in theory, but when the choice is us or them, then yes. It was already knocked out. You didn't have to make it recover. I mean, come on, Ryan, that was ridiculous. If it had swung higher and hit my head, I'd be dead."

Looking at his feet, the knight muttered, "I know. You don't have to remind me."

Frustration mounting, the rogue added, "What is it with you anyway? Why are you so afraid of hurting anyone? I mean most people don't *want* to, but they can at least be rational about it when something's trying to *kill* them. You make such a big deal of out this to the point of letting someone else get hurt anyway, so it's kind of a moot point, isn't it?" When the big man just looked away, Eric continued, "Did you hurt someone once or something? Is that it?" Again the knight said nothing, just turning his face away. "That's it, isn't it? You act like you're all traumatized by it or something. Why don't you just get over it and move on?"

Seeming startled, some fire appeared in Ryan's eyes as he turned back. "Because *he* can't," Ryan replied before turning his back, "so why should I?"

"Who?"

"It doesn't matter."

"Oh yes it does. I almost got killed today over it so I think I've just earned the right to know whose life is more important than mine."

"Would you stop it? It was an accident. I didn't mean for you to get hurt."

"So? I *did* get hurt. Was you hurting this other guy also an accident? I can't imagine you doing something on purpose."

"*Thanks.*"

Eric wasn't used to hearing sarcasm from Ryan. That was *his* domain. But when the knight didn't answer the question, he repeated it.

Ryan sighed irritably and admitted over his shoulder, "Yes."

"Okay great. Now we're getting somewhere. So it was an accident. Why don't you forgive yourself and forget about it? And get on with your life. And stop letting it cause other accidents?"

"Well what right do I have to get on with my life if he can't get on with his?" Ryan snapped. He didn't mention that there was no forgetting about it, not with a daily reminder, but he didn't want to let on too much. He didn't think he could stand them knowing the truth. It was better to let them wonder at his preoccupations – even if they thought less of him for it – than to see their knowing eyes on him all the time.

"Why, is he dead?" Eric asked.

"No, he's not dead," Ryan answered in annoyance.

"Then what? Paraly–" Eric stopped in mid word. It made all the sense in the world and he didn't know why he hadn't realized it before.

Ryan had stiffened and silence hung heavy in the air. Suddenly the rogue realized that everyone was listening to their conversation.

"Was it Daniel?" Eric asked quietly. Ryan turned his head away again, fists and jaw clenched. In the silence, Eric asked more pointedly, "Did you paralyze Daniel?"

He didn't mean it to sound like an accusation, but Ryan now whirled around, his face turning red with fury. He visibly struggled for words before finally responding.

"Yes!" he shouted. "It was Daniel, all right? I paralyzed my brother, God damn it. Is that what you wanted to know? Does *that* make you happy? *I'm* the one who put him in that fucking wheelchair for the rest of his life. *I* was the one who was fucking around and knocked him off the trampoline. It was *me*, God damn it!"

Eric was suddenly aware of Ryan's size, having seen big, angry men take out trained martial artists before. If he'd known his questions would lead to this revelation, he'd have gone about it differently. Now he tried to defuse the situation. "It was an accident," he started.

"So? What difference does that make? He's still *paralyzed*."

"Intent matters, and you know it does. It's why I'm not mad at you for healing the ogre desp–"

"Oh really? You sure sounded mad a minute ago. Don't you fucking pity me, God damn it. I don't need that shit from you."

Eric opened his mouth to reply but Anna's hand on his arm stopped him.

"Ryan," she started quietly.

He glanced at her. "Oh what do *you* want?"

She bit her lip. "To see you happy."

He seemed to swallow a retort before thinking of something else to say. "Good, then you can learn how to heal by magic or whatever it is, and when we get back home you can fix Daniel. *That* will make me happy, and nothing else."

Politely, she responded, "You know I'm going to try for your sake as much as your brother's, but you should prepare for the possibility that it won't work and find a way to accept what's happened. Otherwise you'll be miserable for the rest of your life. Is that really what you want?"

"As a matter of fact, it is," he said snidely. "Why do I deserve to be happy when Daniel isn't?"

"Why are you so sure he's unhappy?"

"How can he not be?" Ryan interrupted incredulously.

"He's moved on with his life, adapted to the injury, and found a purpose, just like everyone else does with their lives. He finished college, got a job, and has a life, but you quit school, won't work, and you won't do anything with your life so you're available to him all the time. That's great in spirit, but he doesn't need or even want that. He wants you to live your life, too, but you're the one who's held back by what happened."

He glared at her, wanting this conversation to end. "Well you're going to fix that by healing him, and since you're all so determined to help, I expect to see everyone doing just that."

CHAPTER THIRTEEN

A RUIN ALIVE

The dark silhouette of a castle stood out against the night sky, a handful of lights twinkling in its black windows like stars. The moonlight showed no details of it or the surrounding mountains, but the path to it had been easy enough to follow. Below, the dark tree tops of the forest swayed in the night breeze, hiding whatever lay underneath and suggesting the forest teemed with activity. The rustling leaves were audible all the way up here and gave them the creeps.

As Cirion's mercenaries watched the castle, a sight they weren't expecting caught their eyes. Another silhouette, this time of two giant wings attached to a thick body with four legs and a long tail, rose up from within. With powerful strokes, the dragon soared into a nearby cloud to disappear. Relaxing, they realized now might be a good time to get through the gate before it came back.

The winding road into the mountains had hidden them from the castle's inhabitants, since trees had claimed what Darlonon abandoned. Likely knowing nothing of fortifications and keeping lines of sight open, the cult members, hired mercenaries, and a handful of ogres, had unknowingly allowed Cirion's mercenaries to get up here without resistance, but they weren't the only ones here.

A young wizard leaned against a boulder to save his strength, not at all happy with how much he'd been relied upon to get past the guards from Olliana. Stationed along the road, the guards barred the way to Castle Darlonon in such a way as to prevent anyone from simply going around them. While the magic he'd used to do so anyway had drained his strength, the exercise had been worse. They'd been running along the road the last few hours, having left the noisy horses behind in a ravine. The others seemed to think his struggles were an annoyance and that he now slowed them down, but without Raith, they wouldn't have gotten this far, and certainly not before the Ellorians.

How quickly they forget, he thought to himself darkly.

He'd enchanted their horses to gallop across the land much faster than biology allowed, moving from Olliana to the ravine far below in record time. Cirion's surprise at the show of power had been clear, but the wizard had foreseen that. He'd been toting around a new spell book and told their leader that such superior spells came from its pages. That part was true, but he'd really mastered the whole book long ago. Sometimes it was wise to be more powerful than people expected. In fact, it *always* was.

Whether stopping time for a minute, making the guards forget them, turning themselves invisible, or some other spell, Raith had shuttled them past everyone so that only the guards at the gate remained. He now claimed he was out of such tricks. Let someone else expend their strength, like Cirion, whose fighting and stealth could lead them forward.

The rogue peered around a boulder at the open space before the castle. He'd been here before and it hadn't changed much except for no longer being deserted. Between the tree growth and small landslides that hadn't been cleared, enough cover existed to reach the closed gates unseen. A big hole in one would let them in, though someone undoubtedly watched it from inside. Through it they saw two ogres pacing back and forth, with more likely out of sight, but there was only one way to tell.

Cirion gave the signal and they moved ahead.

He hadn't really known what to expect, but when Ryan finally laid eyes on the ruined Castle Darlonon high above, his stomach twisted. This was it. They were here. It was real. Lights even shone in some of the windows, though nothing could be made out from here. Maybe that was good. He didn't want to think about who, or what, waited for them.

No one had said anything to him about the earlier incident and for that he'd been glad, until now. Part of him felt something was warranted from someone, maybe even himself for his outbursts, but he wasn't ready. He'd been emoting a "leave me alone" vibe ever since, too, but maybe tensions should have been resolved before they headed inside. Now that he sat there with true peril awaiting, he regretted not smoothing things over. He glanced over at Anna, and on seeing her blank gaze, which seemed unfriendly to him, he flashed a half smile. She nodded and looked away and he sighed.

Only his family had known who paralyzed Daniel because they'd decided long ago to shield him from others blaming or pitying him. The omission was meant to protect him when he felt undeserving of that anymore. After all, as Daniel's older brother, it was his job to protect him, and in this he had failed miserably. His parents' protection had only made him feel more ashamed of what he'd done. That shame drove him to hover over his brother constantly, to protect him, to provide anything he needed. To make amends. He couldn't help it, even though he knew Daniel didn't like it. He sighed again, almost relieved the secret was out.

From the saddle, he watched as the others dismounted, secured their horses, and took what they needed from their packs. The dwarves who'd built the castle had used this tunnel entrance until construction ended, when they magically sealed and concealed it. Even now there seemed to be nothing but yet another jagged rock wall in the cliff face, but that could've been just the darkness of night. He took Rognir's blunt announcement that they'd arrived on faith. No one else seemed perplexed, so Ryan dismounted, remembering to take his helmet and the lance, wondering if there'd be any corners too tight to get the lance around. Maybe he'd have to leave it behind.

Eric stood gazing up as if looking for a route to climb it, his rock-climbing experience likely making easy work of it, but unless the elves could do that, too, he'd be going alone. The rogue had a sealed pocket in his clothes, with climbing chalk that he'd arrived with. He also had lock picking tools and other devices like a glass cutter in hidden pockets in the leather pants and jacket.

Matt had been preoccupied since the ogre battle, trying to shrug off his failure to cast a spell. There could've been any number of reasons for it, but he knew nerves had been the only reason. The words had been right. He'd looked at them again since and confirmed it. He'd just felt their eyes on him, people wondering what he'd attempt, whether it would work or not, and his mouth had grown dry. His eyes had sought Lorian's for approval but seen only alarm that he was doing anything. He'd tried to shut it all out, waiting for the power to fill him, but nothing had come, especially not the icy darts he'd expected to shoot through the air. The pressure to do it before the ogre crushed Anna's head hadn't helped. Thank God for Lorian, who had since favored him with a smile or two that suggested compassion that Matt resented because it resembled pity. But he wasn't holding a grudge. The elf meant well.

Lorian summoned him to the rock wall. "Remember, your staff can detect magic," remarked Lorian to Matt, who'd learned more about Soliander's staff, including that it automatically protected him from many things, which was a relief. "Use it to discover the door's location. It is hidden by illusion."

The young wizard nodded. He'd practiced this trick on his magic items in front of his friends so he wasn't worried. After a moment's concentration, a rusty and stubborn looking iron door materialized nearby in the rock. Only he could see it until he pointed it out to the others, tracing its shape and describing it to them. Lorian started to approach it when Matt stopped him.

"Wait," he said, aware that the detection spell hadn't abated. "There's more."

The elf cocked an eyebrow. "Can you discern its nature?"

Matt pursed his lips, but he wasn't the one who could sense something and the staff wasn't passing along impressions. "Not really, no."

"There is a spell for it. It is called the Omni-Eye and reveals the details of an existing spell. Did you learn it?"

The wizard remembered seeing it but hadn't memorized it. He shook his head and the elf made him stand back. Matt watched eagerly, hoping to learn something from the guy he considered the master to his apprentice, but aside from a few gestures, there wasn't much to see.

"Interesting," Lorian remarked. "Anyone who touches the door will be transferred inside the castle to the dungeon and an alarm beacon will light in several guard rooms."

Matt grunted. "You got all that from that? That's pretty cool. Could we use it to get inside? It would certainly save time."

"You mean trigger the spell on purpose?" Lorian asked, eyebrow cocked. "Yes, but we can't risk the alarm, though it's unlikely anyone inside would know what it means. Still, being trapped in the dungeon is a real possibility."

"True," the wizard conceded, disappointed. Being teleported places seemed like fun, but that really depended on where you arrived and who was waiting for you. "Can you disarm it?"

Lorian nodded. "Can you?"

Matt made a face. "Somehow I knew you'd ask that."

The elf stepped aside and added, "Nothing will happen if you fail, so do not be concerned."

Except I'll look stupid, thought the wizard. He shook his head, trying to block out the thought. He had just succeeded a minute ago and still felt good, so he closed his eyes and reached out to the staff. He'd done this many times now but finding the right impulse to awaken required concentration. He searched with his will, blanking his mind and letting his desire guide the staff. At times like this it seemed his lack of concentration helped him, for his mind picked up on the staff's subtle responses. Images formed in his head and he couldn't resist focusing on them, which helped him grasp the staff's power. Opening his eyes, he reached forward with one hand and a ray of light snaked out to engulf the door with a slight flash before retreating into his hand. A twirling ball of light hovered there for just a moment before fading to black and puffing out, smoke curling into the air.

"Excellent," Lorian congratulated him. Anna and Eric gave a smattering of applause. Pleased but embarrassed, Matt indicated no other spells were on the door.

Rognir took the lead, remarking, "This will lead up a slope, through storage rooms, and by several hallways we can ignore, though we had best be wary of anything that's taken up residence since the castle was abandoned."

His comments reminded Matt of role-playing games where monsters lurked in every room and traps could lie anywhere.

"What about traps?" Ryan asked, watching an elf hand out unlit torches. He donned his golden helmet, leaving the visor raised.

The dwarf put on his own helmet. "There shouldn't be any in the lower areas, not from dwarves anyway. I can't say what the humans did after we built it." Eyeing the lance, he added, "That shouldn't be a problem."

"Where will we come out?" Eric asked.

Rognir gruffly answered, "Let us not waste time. You will see soon enough."

After heaving the door open, Rognir and Lorian led the way with lit torches, the champions in the middle with Morven right behind, other elves bringing up the rear. Matt remembered to light his staff, experimenting with changing its brightness, radius, and beam. He was starting to think this was all very cool when they soon found their path blocked once again.

Anna observed, "Somebody really wanted to keep people out."

"That somebody was Soliander," noted Lorian.

Matt thought that the bluish metal door looked quite new; it had been fused with the stone all around it, not just cut into place. The walls, ceiling, and floor had even bowed inward as if to grasp the door. He saw no handle or hinge. Only a fist-sized, circular hole lay in the center, with several notches cut into the otherwise smooth circle of it. The door looked familiar, though he'd never seen anything like it. Not even realizing why he did it, Matt lowered the staff, placing the lit crystal into the hole. It didn't fit at first because he hadn't lined up the prongs holding it, but once he did it slid right into place. The door gave a brief pulse before turning transparent and releasing the staff. He put one hand against it, but his flesh passed right through it because it was now only an illusion.

"How did you know to do that?" Ryan asked.

The wizard looked blank, but then a spark of realization lit his eyes. "A hunch. The symbol on the door looks like one I saw during the magic test Lorian gave me, though I don't understand why." After a moment, he added, "It also doesn't explain how I knew what to do."

"Something to ponder later," advised Lorian, gesturing for them to pass through before it closed. They stepped into an empty storage room beyond and the door turned solid behind them. As the others followed Rognir, Lorian quietly observed to Matt, "Only Soliander could make it past that."

"Or someone with his staff," corrected Matt, wondering if the elf was trying to tell him something.

Like any good medicine, it tasted awful to prevent misuse, and so Cirion choked down the foul tasting stuff with a grimace until the blue vial sat empty. As he lowered the vial, the slash on his forehead disappeared, as did the more troublesome, bloody gash on his sword arm and a smaller one on a leg. Most of those around him were doing the same, for few had escaped the battle unscathed.

They had made it past the five ogres and the mercenaries beyond the gate but with a terrible price. Four of his men were dead and most of the others were hurt, but the rogue regretted it not. They'd known what they were getting themselves into when they signed up with him and he wouldn't tolerate any whining about it now. Still, he'd expected better swordplay from several, who at least paid with their own lives, but they had risked his as well. Their ineptness also caused an alarmingly quick reduction in their healing potions. After using up most of what they'd brought, he'd looked to Raith to see if any were hidden in those robes, but the wizard shook his head. Hopefully no more would be needed, but he doubted that. He wasn't entirely certain the wizard was telling the truth about that, either.

They stood in the castle's entrance hall, doors closed behind them. No sounds of running feet came their way thanks to Nola's quick aim with the crossbow. A robed cult member had gone sprinting between the curving stairs on either side and straight into the castle's further reaches, but the crossbow bolt had slain him in mid stride. For now, no one knew they were here except the dead, and Cirion intended to keep it that way.

The flaming tiles he'd encountered last time hadn't been active in the courtyard, presumably done away with by the current occupants. The stairways, however, were still out of the question due to what was happening on them and had apparently been happening for a long time. With swords, knives, and bows in hand, men dressed much like them stood on the stairs in climbing positions, and yet they moved not at all. Each stood caught in time, alive but forever unmoving. They'd all been here the last time Cirion had, and in fact two of them were his men, and yet they hadn't moved more than an inch in all that time. The rogue looked longingly at an ornate dagger in one man's hand, for it was his and had been borrowed shortly before the man became ensnared. He'd resigned himself to never getting it back.

Cirion gestured toward the guy with a bolt in his back. "That way."

Nola and Raith followed, their hired men following, weapons drawn. Ahead stood an archway with two hallways leading right and left to the rest of the castle. The main wing stood straight ahead, but the rogue hadn't been lying to Anna when telling her a maze lay there. He suspected traps waited everywhere, and while he specialized in getting past them, many would be magical and beyond his skills. A glance showed the young wizard's lips silently moving as he tried to detect magic along each path. At the very least, they wouldn't be going straight into that room.

"Anything?" Cirion asked, realizing the ogre blood dripping from his sword to the floor would leave a trail. He wiped it on an ogre's shirt.

"Yes," the wizard answered. "There's something in every direction, but more directly ahead. Still, I think we should go forward, even if by another route. The gate is bound to be in a big room in the main wing."

Cirion frowned. "Wouldn't it be hidden in some out of the way place where no one would look for it."

"No," the wizard disagreed. "Remember, the dragons had to be pulled into it, so it must be enormous, and the only rooms that big are public places."

"He's right," agreed Nola.

And Cirion knew she did so reluctantly. Neither of them trusted the wizard. Well, they didn't trust *anyone*, but they both thought Raith was hiding something. The show of strength he'd put on to get them here had surprised him. To agree with Raith now probably made her feel like she was playing a part in some machination of his she didn't understand. That's how Cirion felt. Beyond the outrage of being duped by someone they'd held in contempt, he knew such things usually ended with the ignorant person dead. It was too bad Nola hadn't managed to drug Korrin with that sleeping potion after the banquet; that damn Andier ruined that. It would've given them a head start of a few days, but thanks to Raith, it seemed they'd arrived first anyway.

"All right," Cirion started, "let's avoid the big halls unless we can see into them before entering. That dragon will be back soon, so let's get on with our search before we find it sitting between us and the Dragon Gate." He gestured to a side hallway that hopefully led in the same general direction while providing cover. "This way."

He and Raith took the lead, each doing their part to detect traps as Nola and their hired henchman followed. The way seemed clear as they paralleled the big room on one side via a hallway leading further into the castle. Doorways spilled into other rooms, some with spells upon them, but all were empty of life. Down an adjacent corridor lay several skeletons and a more recent corpse with flesh still on it, all with charred clothing. From the next doorway beyond it, a sliver of golden light streamed into the hall. Cirion motioned Nola forward as he listened to men speaking without concern of being overheard.

"The dragon's out for her nightly feast," said a gruff voice, "but she'll be back soon."

"Good thing it's not one of us," remarked another, chuckling.

Only nervous laughter greeted that, and someone asked, "Your service to the dragons stops short of being dinner?"

Before anyone could answer, Cirion kicked in the door. The nearest guard turned to find Cirion's short sword slicing into his chest. The guard went down with a grunt and the three other men stared in shock as the intruders charged. Nola's crossbow found its target across the room, piercing through a man's belly and pinning him to his chair. She was already swinging her sword at another man who soon fell dead. The last guard ran toward another door. Seeing this, the guard bolted to his chair yelled out, "No! Not that way!"

It was too late. As he crossed the threshold, the man turned to solid ice, his momentum carrying him sliding across the floor toward the stairs across the room, a wide-eyed expression frozen on his face. As he tumbled down it, the ice – and him along with it – shattered, cascading downward like ice cubes made of body parts.

"Nasty use for a transmutation spell," muttered Raith, smirking. "Anywhere that's safe to go, the guards know and have been. Either the dragon cleared a path through the halls or a wizard working for them did it."

Nola looked at him flatly. "Or the wizard who opened the gate."

"Or that," he admitted.

"So how do we figure out which paths those are?" Cirion asked, noting his henchmen keeping alert in the hall.

In the silence, the wounded guard whimpered and the intruders exchanged a look. Soon they had pried him from the crossbow bolt and chair and were headed back down the corridor, the guard in front with Cirion's knife to his throat. Unless he wanted to be the first victim of a trap, he'd steer them clear all the way to the gate, but it proved more difficult than that.

"Wait, wait," said the guard, and they paused near a hall's end.

"What is it?" Cirion whispered.

"Guards," the man replied quickly, "around this corner. They're always here. The gate room is up the stairs beyond it."

Nola cautiously took a look to confirm it. "A lot of them on a wide staircase, looking bored," she reported, turning to Raith coldly. "You better have something good ready."

Cirion knocked out the guard and quietly laid him aside, and when the wizard gave the signal, they launched their attack. As they charged forward and startled guardsmen fumbled for weapons, the flapping of leathery wings accompanied a loud roar before the floor shook hard enough to knock them all off balance. Part of a wall nearby crumbled and an arrow intended for them missed wildly. A disturbed look passed between intruders and guardsmen alike.

The dragon had returned.

They stood quietly in the dark, their torches doused, the wizard's staff dark. Just ahead sat an open room full of dust, cobwebs, and scattered crates, but no signs of recent passage. On the far side, an open archway revealed a stone staircase rising toward the castle's main areas, dim firelight dancing down the stairwell from above. A nearby noise had inspired their caution, but it didn't compare to the deep thud that now shook the walls, loose mortar falling from the ceiling, a rotting board dropping with a muted clatter. Anna cringed at the sound. Only a dragon somewhere above them could've made that thud. As the elves unsheathed their swords, she eyed the lance. Such a slender weapon taking out something massive enough to make that loud a noise seemed improbable.

Eric crept up the stairs with Lorian. After peering around the corner, they motioned for the others to follow. Anna made it there first, eager to see why the light above was so much brighter than expected on the floor below, and why the sound of flames was so deep, loud, and unusual. She leaned around Eric's shoulder and saw why. Before them roared a superheated wall of crackling flames barring the way. No wonder the area below lay undisturbed. Nothing could get by this.

Except Soliander. When asked, the techie had no ideas, his staff not helping.

"Something's hanging in the air there, guys," Anna said quietly, squinting at the fire. "It's a cylinder of some sort."

After a moment, Lorian remarked, "Ah, I've heard of this from Soliander. This device of his sustains a spell without wavering and is nearly impossible to remove, unless…" He trailed off, turning to Ryan. "Korrin, do you still wear the Dispersion Ring? You can reach the device without getting burned. Just grab it and the spell will end."

Anna had seldom seen such a dubious expression on someone's face.

"Are you sure?" he asked

"Yes. Another item of Soliander's, especially a magic resistant one, is the only way. Remember your arm will be unaffected up to the shoulder. It is magical fire, not real."

"It seems real enough to me." He began pulling out a gauntlet to don. "Wait a minute, I thought the armor was fire proof."

Lorian shook his head. "Only against dragon fire."

"Great," he muttered. He held up one hand toward the fire, remarking, "Well, I feel the heat everywhere except on this arm. Maybe there's some truth to it."

Anna bit her lip. There had better be more than *some* truth to it.

Taking a deep breath, Ryan pulled the helmet's visor down to protect his face, donned the right gauntlet, and carefully reached through the fire. The flames vanished as his hand closed around the device. Visibly relieved, he pulled up the visor with the other, bare hand, but the metal had become hot in just seconds and burned his fingers.

"Ow!" He jerked his hand away, seeing red blisters already forming.

"Let me see," said Anna, the medical student in her taking control. "Second degree burns. We need to wrap this."

Rognir cleared his throat. "Why don't you just heal him, lass?"

She looked at the dwarf uncomfortably. Rognir's healing of Eric had deeply impressed but troubled her, weakening her resolute disbelief in gods. She'd reconsidered this whole business with more seriousness than the hollow promises she'd made Ryan. Following Eric's suggestion to start pretending, she'd chosen a goddess to call on, identifying with Goddess Kiarin's philosophies. She'd imagined a pretend conversation with her but gone no farther, feeling silly. She wasn't ready and couldn't open her heart to this.

"I have a better idea," started the knight, rescuing her. "I'll just use the Trinity Ring."

With mixed emotions, Anna watched as the wound disappeared even as another opened in her heart. She'd seen it twice now. The proof could not be denied. Her upset eyes met Rognir's disappointed gaze, which stung.

— ❖ · ❖ · ❖ —

Perndara the dragon beamed with pleasure. She'd resumed nightly flights after learning the Ellorian Champions were coming, since pretending she wasn't here made little sense now. The exercise kept her from feeling imprisoned yet again, this time in the ruin. She had to settle for sticking her head in a waterfall instead of a dip in an ocean or lake like on that other world. Of course she could have gone back through the gate for a while, but...

Never again! she thought.

Standing by the Dragon Gate, she snarled at it before overhearing the sounds of steel on steel. The Ellorians were here! Afire with excitement, she impatiently waited for them to get past those amateurish cult members. Her preparations were in order – both her own and those directed by Nir'lion. She bellowed a small spout of flames to get warmed up but didn't waste it. The bile that fueled their fire breathing only lasted so long. Days would pass before a full supply built up again.

Soon quiet descended and she waited expectantly for the door to open, but the minutes ticked by. Finally a familiar knocking preceded a cult member timidly entering. Behind him, two others dragged a man with fresh blood staining his leather tunic. They dropped him to his knees and walked out, shutting the door. It seemed that her legion of admirers – or at least, that's how she chose to think of them – had captured someone, but not a champion, just a mercenary.

The man gazed at her with suitable horror, the ghastly wound in his belly more than just oozing blood. She asked a few questions he seemed too terrified to answer, which was just as well, for she wasn't much in the mood for conversation herself. She was quite hungry and topped off her recent snack of mountain goat. Her fanged mouth engulfed him and his screams.

⸺ ✦ ⋅ ✦ ⸺

There had clearly been a battle, and recently. A rivulet of deep red blood still flowed across the floor from the nearest slain man, whose sightless eyes stared at them as they listened at an archway. Ryan stared just as unseeing, reminded of the lives at stake but surprised to feel little pity. Maybe he was getting used to death, however horrible that seemed, but his distaste for cults likely contributed. He only felt pity on realizing that some of these zealots might not be the ones who coerced others to their vision, but the ones who'd been coerced.

"What do you think happened?" he whispered, putting a comforting hand on Matt, who looked like he was going to throw up.

Rognir's eyes moved over the bodies. "We're not the only ones in the castle uninvited," he observed. The bodies were all human, but two looked like cult members from their matching attire while the rest were mercenaries, each dressed in his own unique fashion.

Lorian retrieved an arrow, noting its craftsmanship. "The fletching style is of Ormund. Cirion is here."

"How?" Anna asked. "We were supposed to get here first."

"When we find them," started Eric, frowning, "we can ask." Any chance at surprising the cult or dragon had vanished and there was no telling where Cirion's mercenaries were now.

"Good plan," Rognir gruffly approved, "except we'd better forget them and head for the dragon immediately."

"Wait," said Ryan, "one of them moved." He indicated which one and Lorian crept forward. The wounded cult member stirred when Lorian touched him but lay unconscious until Rognir healed the man enough to come out of it. Anna pursed her lips.

"What happened here?" Lorian sternly demanded.

His tunic torn and bloody, the young cult member glared back, no love lost for those whose allegiance didn't lie with dragons. "Why would I tell you that?"

"Because your future is in our hands," started the elf, "and we'll be more forgiving of what you've done here if you cooperate."

Sneering, the cult member muttered, "Unlikely. I would show *you* no mercy."

"Then how about because I'll bash your head in if you don't," barked Rognir, scowling and raising up his well-used axe.

The man blanched. "We fought intruders, some captured, some killed."

"Where were the captured taken?" Rognir demanded. "To the dragon?"

"No. Only one. The others went to the dungeon."

"And which way is that?"

Gesturing with his head, the cult member said, "Back that way."

"It had better be." Without warning, the dwarf slammed the butt of his axe into the man's forehead, knocking him out.

⸺ ✦ · ✦ ⸺

As they were shoved along a crumbling corridor, Cirion failed to hide a look of concern that convinced Nola how grave their situation was this time. They'd been captured on other exploits and gotten out of it, but not with a dragon involved. Taking one on wasn't why they were here. He suspected the most gravely wounded of their group had been taken to it moments ago and met a gruesome end. The rest were likely headed to a cell, at least for now.

Guards forced him, Nola, Raith, and another survivor down several flights of stairs through increasingly damp areas, the signs of disrepair mounting. Cirion hoped the dungeon locks were poorly kept and easily picked, or the bars were coming loose from the crumbling walls. He'd used that to his advantage before. Few torches lit the way and he suspected they'd be the dungeons' first inhabitants in a long time, his hopes rising. Unprepared jailors were the easiest to escape from.

Their weapons had been confiscated, but they might have less need of them if just fleeing. Too few of them had survived to reach the gate now unless the champions' arrival distracted the dragon, or it flew out of the castle again. The glory of closing it had vanished. Saving his own skin, and to a lesser extent, Nola's, was all that mattered. Everyone else, including that suddenly capable wizard, Raith, was expendable. It wasn't that Raith had done anything wrong, but people with unexpected strength were dangerous. He and Nola had shared a look or two of agreement. It was only a matter of time before one or the other stuck a knife in the wizard's back – maybe right after he helped get them out of here.

The guards rudely shoved them into a dank cell and Cirion expected Raith to follow, but the wizard was shoved into a cell across from them. A sign on the wall showed a broken wizard's staff and the rogue nodded to himself. Of course. A room with magic protection so that spells failed. The wizard wouldn't be helping them escape anywhere.

"What's this?" the guard grunted, yanking down the nape of Raith's robe far enough that even Cirion could see the symbol tattooed on the base of his neck from across the way. It hadn't been there before, the rogue was certain, having seen the wizard's nape more than once. Had Raith been using an illusion spell to hide it? The spell would've stopped working once in that cell. Most people would've recognized the symbol at once. The guard turned Raith around, and Cirion saw the wizard caught between a frown, a smirk, and a glare. With a knife to the throat, the guard led the wizard away again and this time Cirion suspected he knew where they were going.

CHAPTER FOURTEEN

CONFRONTATION

The shimmering portal that hung in the air before him differed from those that others used to travel across or even between worlds. He could, unassisted, make it appear anywhere, such was his power. This took great strength, so he sometimes used more mundane avenues, especially if he'd recently experienced battle to sap his energy, but years had passed since anyone had been foolish enough to challenge him. Most wizards used permanent portals created by someone else to travel to a fixed location, but he always chose his own destination and often visited places that few others dared. Fixed portals were usually guarded, though, like any skilled wizard, he could make people forget he'd arrived.

The black robed wizard looked over at the rosewood cabinet in one corner, now empty after years. He hefted the staff, its weight familiar, the crystal atop it held by a bluish steel few had ever seen. Memories of happier times returned, but so did painful ones best left forgotten. Companions long lost had once given his life greater dynamics if not pleasure, and his was a life devoid of trust since separating from them. Still, the choice had been his, and it wasn't one he consciously regretted.

He brushed aside the thought to focus on the task at hand. The time had come to learn who these champions-apparent were. His spy had learned enough before foolishly being caught, forcing him to incinerate the dark elf so Lorian couldn't learn anything. A corpse only revealed so much. He had blocked the communication orb from reaching any of his other orbs. Still, he had a secret to keep and to that end he'd planned how best to deal with these imposters. Death was of course the ultimate option, as always, and this time there'd be four bodies for people to mourn over, not just a memory of heroes vanished.

"So tell me," purred Perndara, her deep, husky voice rattling the loose stones nearby, "why is a member of my Dragon Cult sneaking into a castle guarded by the very same cult?"

Raith hadn't thought of a good reply for her question despite knowing it was coming. With a mixture of defiance and awe, he regarded the golden dragon silently. She loomed more massive than any depiction in literature and was far more beautiful than he'd imagined dragons could be. The foul scent of death on her breath had never been mentioned. Nor had the giant, smooth intakes of breath, or the hot exhale that carried the reminder of flames, or the floor rumbling with her shifting weight as dust fell from the ceiling, the ruin adjusting to her. Only the folded leathery wings, the barbed tail curled around a pillar, and the great fanged mouth were common features of every story, and they were enough to induce amazement. The dragon's piercing, malevolent gaze chilled him. Even without its other advantages, its intelligence and magic were fearsome. It was little wonder the champions banished them—

the dragons of Honyn weren't given to good deeds and peaceful living.

"Unless, of course," continued the dragon, "you are not a true member of the cult but an imposter. I wonder how best to determine your loyalty in the absence of an explanation."

The wizard's heart skipped a beat. Honyn's dragons had inventive and nasty ways of getting answers and demonstrations of devotion, sometimes resulting in a loyal but dead follower. Cirion would have thought lesser things would scare him, but Raith was quite a different man than Cirion knew and had faced far worse threats than his supposed leader would have imagined.

"The intruders I was with want to close the Dragon Gate and I needed to be certain they could not," he started, hoping this turned out well.

"Then why not simply kill them?" Perndara interrupted, unimpressed. "You needn't masquerade as one of them."

Thinking quickly, Raith said, "They have a scroll written by the Ellorians who imprisoned you. It describes how the gate works, or so I believe. They have not allowed me to see it or know its location. If I kill them it might fall into the wrong hands again."

"I see. Go on."

Realizing the dragon was baiting him, Raith stifled a sigh. Did she know better than to help people explain themselves? Getting them to say too much was always a goal, one he'd used himself. He chose his elaborations carefully. The dragons couldn't know why he'd really come here. Not only would they kill him, but they would do for themselves what he intended to do for himself, and that would be disastrous. His loyalty to the cult – to anyone but himself, really – had ended the moment he read the scroll's contents.

"I needed to locate and destroy the scroll," he began, "but before I could, they insisted on coming here in an attempt to seal the gate for their own idiotic glory. I came along, hoping to discover what they'd done with the scroll and stop them."

"And did you learn this thing?"

He feigned a frown. "No." He knew exactly where the scroll was and had been all along – in one of his robe's pockets. Cirion didn't even know it existed.

The dragon was disapproving. "And when were you planning to stop them? It was getting rather late."

Raith nodded, still feeling a bit charmed by the magnificent beast despite his new allegiance to himself. They saw you in the sky and thought to work the gate while you were gone. I thought that would be my opportunity."

"But they have failed," stated Perndara flatly, "as have you. How did you come to know they possessed the scroll?"

He paused and decided to bolster his lies with some honesty, since he wasn't coming off as well as he'd have liked. "Dragon Cult members stole it from Olliana at my direction long ago," he confessed, "so it could be destroyed, but it was lost through foolishness." He smiled slightly. The thieves had indeed been foolish, for if a man won't reveal his identity when he hires you, you should expect your death instead of gratitude for a job well done. "When I heard this group had paid a huge sum for a scroll, I surmised they had it and convinced them I could help them here. They soon admitted to the possession but that was all."

He didn't admit to hearing rumors of Cirion's mercenaries having come before but encountered all manner of traps, which was a principal reason he'd used Cirion to get here. Better his men get killed than Raith. Every wizard needed warriors to do grunt work. Even Soliander paraded around with those other champions.

Perndara contemplated and he knew she wasn't entirely convinced. A long pause followed and he projected a desire to be helpful and pleasing, mixed with fear and awe.

"I sense magic power in you," observed Perndara approvingly. "You can be of service to me."

The wizard bowed, wondering where this was headed and flattered despite himself. *Stop it, you fool.*

"My sources tell me the Ellorians are on their way. I want you to challenge Soliander and keep him occupied."

Raith hesitated. He might be far stronger than Cirion's group knew, but he'd not win a direct challenge against *that* wizard. He only sought a way to achieve his goal before anyone knew what he was doing. He just hoped that whoever had opened the gate hadn't beaten him to that goal. It clearly wasn't Soliander and he was ready to fight whoever had done it to the death to get what he wanted. There was no graceful way to refuse this request, however, and he'd long ago learned the immense value in making empty promises to gain trust.

"Certainly," he replied, bowing as if honored, and with some annoyance he realized he wasn't entirely faking it. "I will keep him from disturbing you."

"See that you do." She then instructed him on where to be and what to do and he moved to the far end of the hall, so near the open gate that he struggled to keep from staring at it. Once the champions distracted Perndara and he had a moment alone with the gate, he would seize his destiny.

***

"Are we going to rescue them?" Anna asked, dubiously.

Eric frowned at the idea. Across the hall from the unlit room they stood in, a descending stairway led to the dungeon, the faint sounds of men talking and laughing drifting up from below. No one was looking forward to visiting it. If they weren't careful, they might get to visit anyway. A patrol of guards had already passed by once. Enough torches and lanterns flickered along the stone walls that they knew company lurked everywhere, and they had doused their own.

"I think they can wait," remarked Eric. "I don't want them along while we're facing the dragon. It's like having another enemy in our midst."

"Easy for you to say," muttered Ryan, gripping the lance. "You don't have to do much."

"I don't know," started Matt, "they've got another wizard with them and he could be a big help."

"I agree with Soliander," said Lorian. "Though we will have to fight our way to them and it might arouse guards elsewhere, the addition of another wizard is worth the risk."

Rognir grunted as a loud clatter rose up the stairs. Shouting followed. "No one will think twice about a commotion down there, as long as we are quick."

"True," agreed the elf, "the mercenaries are typically amateurish. Let us proceed before someone comes." With that he peeked into the hallway and then ventured across and down the stairs, other elves and Rognir following. Before joining them, Eric frowned at his friends.

"Keep an eye on Cirion and the others when we get them out," he suggested. "I expect nothing but trouble from them and am surprised Lorian wants them along."

"Maybe he doubts our ability to help," remarked Matt.

"Probably," Eric admitted ruefully. "Just don't trust them with anything, especially our safety."

"Agreed," said Ryan, wondering what Nola really had planned for him that night.

Eric peeked into the hallway and quickly leaned back. Guards were coming, this time from another direction that provided full view of them. He ushered the others back, but the empty room provided no cover and wasn't nearly dark enough. He tried the only door, which opened to reveal a large, empty room, two torches burning. Motioning for everyone to go in, he barely followed as the guards reached the opening. Shutting the door quietly, he turned to the others and stopped short. They were gone. So was the large hall, a much smaller one in its place, brightly lit by lanterns. Confused, he turned to the door and discovered it was gone, too.

* * *

Ryan blinked in the bright light, which, along with the lack of dust and cobwebs, suggested a well-used room they had better leave. Suits of armor and weapons lined the walls, gleaming as if new. He turned to the others and found himself alone. Maybe they hadn't come through the door after him, but then he saw that even that was gone, too. In its place stood a solid wall.

Maybe the door is camouflaged, he thought, pulled off a glove to feel for a seam, but his fingertips felt only the natural pits and chips in the limestone. He was about to call out to see if they could hear him on the other side when a door creaked behind him.

He turned as a warrior in dusky black armor strode in, malice in every step, a short plume of white feathers atop its helmeted head. The raised visor revealed a dark elf's cruel features. The elf unsheathed a black sword, metal ringing with the motion as it advanced on him, its metal-shod feet clanging with every step like the tolling of a bell. Death had come for him at last.

Ryan fumbled for his own sword, stepping forward to avoid being cornered and looking for an escape, but he saw only the door beyond his attacker. As if reacting to his thoughts, it slammed shut, locks clanking furiously on the far side. The elf struck at him, their blades clanging once, twice, three times. Ryan's defenses steadily pulled his sword to one side, exposing his front, and the dark blade struck at his chest, bouncing off the armor.

Stepping back and regrouping, Ryan parried several blows imperfectly. He got the impression the elf was testing his defenses, for the elf didn't take every opening, instead looking for all the faults to form an overall strategy. Lorian had taught Ryan how to do it and now he knew the ploy was being used on him.

And so Ryan went on the offensive to disrupt him. At first the elf seemed surprised, but a few strokes later Ryan stepped back with a gasp, holding his side, where a deep cut oozed blood. His poor assault had let the elf's blade slip between the plates.

No more attacks unless something comes up, he decided, sobering up. It's my turn to test and evaluate.

Time after time the swords crossed, the elf faster, the knight better protected, Korrin's armor impervious to the elf's sword unless a stabbing blow made it through the chainmail. Ryan's strikes badly dented the other's armor but happened too infrequently. The elf's blade stabbed him again and again, a half dozen cuts oozing blood, and yet the elf had only one meaningful wound to his unused arm. Ryan was losing and not getting more blows to land.

As if realizing this, the elf began striking the same wounds over and over but not making them worse, just causing more pain. Being tortured to death wasn't on Ryan's agenda and he grew angry. He suddenly realized the elf had become predictable. Sacrificing his left leg to the next attack, he didn't bother with the expected defense, already swinging hard at the surprised elf instead.

Both blows struck home, Ryan's only stinging while the elf received a deep gash that likely cracked ribs. Wild relief and anger surged within Ryan and he pressed forward, hammering down at the retreating elf's sword arm. And suddenly he realized his strength made up for his skill. He'd been afraid to use that strength since hurting Daniel so long ago, but now rage set him free and he slammed the sword down again and again. It forced the elf to hold his blade with both hands, eliminating any one-handed maneuverability. Still using only one arm himself, Ryan punched the elf in the face with the other, feeling grim satisfaction as he knocked the elf backward.

It was a mistake, for the elf regrouped and returned to the fight meaning business but seeming wary as they circled each other. A flurry of quick strikes kept Ryan from delivering a big swing. Cuts began to appear on him, a terrible wound causing him to limp and poorly support his weight, another making his left hand unresponsive. He grew lightheaded from blood loss, his judgment slipping.

Maybe that's why his sword arm dropped suddenly. The elf lunged and Ryan hauled the sword upward, blades crashing together and rising above their heads. With a crash he head-butted the elf's face with his helmet, knocking him back and then slamming the sword into the elf's thigh, down to the bone.

With a shriek, the elf fell to one knee but still tried to stab the knight through the belly. Seeing it coming, Ryan brought his sword down on his foe's neck, cutting deep through armor, bone, and sinew, nearly beheading him. Blood sprayed all over Ryan, whose anger abruptly vanished at what he'd done, the ghastly mortal wound spurting blood with each heartbeat. The elf would be dead in a minute, but not if Ryan used the last and most powerful healing spell in the Trinity Ring. He bent to use the ring but then stopped short.

The last time he healed an enemy, Eric nearly got killed. This time it would be himself. His wounds weren't life threatening but he'd lose another fight if not healed. His friends, Daniel, and everyone on this world were depending on him. Besides, he wasn't ready to die. And Lorian was right. An aggressor brought death upon themselves. The choice had been made. Seeing the dark elf's still angry eyes on him, Ryan snapped out of his particular brand of foolishness after a lifetime of it. With a coldness that surprised him, he brought the sword down one more time, finishing the elf.

On stepping through the door, Anna spied an elaborate mural and turned to examine the depiction of a battle winding down and priests kneeling among the wounded, helping, caring, and healing them. The looks of gratitude made her realize patients didn't care how you made them better, just that you did. All of this healing stuff wasn't about her, and she blushed at her selfishness. If appealing to a god was the only means to heal such terrible wounds, then wasn't she obligated to try?

But then why her? Surely not just anyone could convince a god to heal someone through them. She wasn't a logical choice and knew that pretending to be Eriana wouldn't convince anyone of her merits. Rognir must have gone through some training or somehow been found worthy. Having not done either, Anna didn't expect a god to answer her even if she tried. One never had before, since the god of Earth wasn't real, at least to her.

She became so engrossed in her thoughts and the mural that she lost all sense of time and only slowly became aware of the clanging of metal behind her. She turned to see Ryan fighting a warrior in black and the others were gone. On trying the door she came through to get help, she discovered it wouldn't open no matter how hard she pulled.

Helplessly, Anna turned to watch, wincing at every wound inflicted on Ryan, her medical training helping her assess each. His fierce expression convinced her this was a fight to the death, but the sight of Ryan beheading his opponent shocked her. For a moment she was too startled to move, but then she rushed to him.

"My God, Ryan, are you alright?"

Dazed, he looked right through her, woozy and disoriented. Then he crashed to the ground with a clatter.

"Ryan, stay with me," she begged, kneeling beside him. She had to stop the bleeding but saw nothing to use as a tourniquet except her robe's hem. Struggling to tear off a piece, she finally used his dagger to do so. She tried to bind the worst wound on his leg, but the thigh plate stood in the way until she got it off, remembering how from their night at the inn. She pulled tight but knew it wasn't enough, the chain mail that was covering his leg making it too hard to stop the bleeding.

"Ryan." She leaned over him, patting his face to wake him, getting blood all over his cheek. "Ryan, please stay with me. I need your strength." Even as she said it, she knew he was too weak to pull the tourniquet any tighter than she had. She desperately tried again, pulling with all her might to no avail. He was going to die right here in front of her if she didn't find another way.

Feeling like a fool, she remembered Eriana's method, and only a moment passed before she brushed aside her disposition about it. She placed one hand on his forehead and another on his chest, trying to remember what Rognir had told her. She didn't know the words he used but surely the Goddess Kiarin would answer to save Ryan.

"Lady Kiarin," she began, struggling for words, "please spare this man's life. He does not deserve to die here today. He shouldn't even be here and – " She stopped herself. That probably wasn't a good line of thought to follow. Maybe if she admitted how important he was to her. Surely her personal connection mattered.

"Please Kiarin. I don't want to lose him. He is a good man, the best I've known, and such men are rare and deserve long lives. Please spare him." Shaking her head in uncertainty, she continued, "I don't know what else to say to you. Please forgive my methods and look into my heart instead, to see my words are true. Please answer my call."

Even as she said it, from somewhere deep within her the memory of unanswered pleas to God surfaced and along with them anger about never being answered. She tried to snuff the resentment and uttered another plea to Kiarin, but her heart also carried something akin to an insistence that she get a reply. She'd never have expressed the sentiment aloud but it lived on in her still, and that was enough. Nothing was happening.

Ryan's head rolled to one side and she gasped, checking his pulse with a trembling hand, begging Kiarin for help. She found no heartbeat and the flow of blood from his wounds faded, his skin white.

"Oh my God, no. Please no."

She begged Kiarin again but it was too late. Ryan lay dead. Several minutes of desperate CPR followed with nothing changing. Tears poured down her face as she clung to his body, a blur of emotions raging in her. Looking heavenward, she screamed, "Why won't you answer me?"

But there was no response. Unable to look at Ryan's pale face any longer, she staggered to her feet and stumbled into a corridor she hadn't noticed before, not knowing or caring where it led.

—— • · • ——

Even as the wizard stepped across the door's threshold, he knew something was up. The staff sent a pulse up his arm and he found himself standing somewhere other than the large hall he'd briefly seen. Either he'd been transported or he now saw an illusion. Since the staff no longer alerted him to magic, he suspected the former. It still looked like Darlonon, but he easily could've been teleported anywhere on Honyn – or even off world. It wasn't a pleasant thought.

Matt stood in a ten by ten room with a corridor to one side. It offered the only way out, though he wasn't sure he wanted to go wherever it led. The teleportation had undoubtedly been Soliander's doing like all the magic they'd encountered inside. He wondered if something similar had happened to the others or if he'd been treated differently on account of the staff. So far Soliander's spells had recognized it, so perhaps only the arch wizard himself would have been transferred to where Matt stood now. The idea piqued his curiosity but stood little chance of being verified.

The room stood bare save for an oval mirror that hung in space across from him. Aside from its lack of support, it was unremarkable. He examined his reflection, not having seen himself in the Majestic Majus' black garb yet. The overall impression was intimidating and made worse by the black hood obscuring his face, its shadows suggesting something sinister. With a start, he realized he wasn't wearing the hood, and no sooner had that difference registered than the reflection stepped from within the apparent mirror and into the room, the portal vanishing. Matt gasped and stepped back, but it was too late. With a curt gesture, the figure spoke a word and Matt could no longer move. It grabbed him by the robe.

"Who are you?" the figure demanded, piercing eyes glaring.

"Uh, Soliander," Matt stammered, frightened.

The glare hardened. "No, you are not. What is your *name*?"

Unsure what to say, Matt repeated with more confidence, "Soliander."

The man's eyes flashed. "*Soranumirae*," he intoned, and sudden pressure crushed Matt's chest. His eyes bulged as he struggled to breathe, his face turning red. Merciless eyes stared back and only when Matt started to black out did the figure speak again. "*Earimunaros*." The pressure released and Matt gasped for air, dizzy and weak. Before he'd finished recovering, the figure looked ready to do it again.

"Matt!" he blurted between gasps, in over his head and wanting out. "My name's Matt. Sorenson, from Earth."

The figure's eyes intensified as if recognizing the name, surprised by it, or both. "Earth?"

"Yes. My planet. Where I came from." Matt squirmed as the figure stared at him silently. Maybe he'd said something wrong.

"And who travels with you?"

Matt figured little harm could come from giving their real names, since this man clearly knew he wasn't Soliander. "Eric, Anna, and Ryan, all from Earth, too."

The man cocked an eyebrow, eyes boring into his. "Not Andier, Eriana, or that lumbering idiot Korrin?"

"No. We're not really them, just pretending to be."

The man seemed satisfied and thoughtful before returning attention to his captive. "Who sent you?"

"Uh, Queen Lorella."

The figure scowled. "Not to this castle, to this world."

Matt wasn't sure how to answer that. "We were summoned by Sonneri."

The man frowned and paused, rephrasing his question. "Did Andier, Eriana, or Korrin somehow arrange for you to arrive in their place during the next summoning?"

"No, I don't think so. I don't know." Matt noticed he didn't ask about Soliander, and with a start the significance of their identical possessions registered, right down to the supposedly one of a kind staff each held. His eyes widened in excitement and fear, but he dared not ask the question, instead focusing on how he was going to get out of this. He couldn't move his arms but wondered if his magic items might work. His eyes turned to the staff.

"It is no use," the figure said, seeing his gaze. "You cannot cast a spell. I have seen to that. Your magic devices will also not work." Suddenly the figure paused, wide eyes on Matt's staff. "You...you have a copy of the staff! This should not be." Suspicious eyes turned on the techie, a glint of new menace appearing. "Well, no matter. You won't live to use it. You will remain until I am done with you, and you will reveal what I want to know."

With that, the man put one hand on Matt's forehead and spoke magic words he understood. "Be open and true, your mind laid bare, safe and secure, your secrets treasured, honored, and shared. Let all be revealed in the comfort of benevolence, kindness, and trust, for to free yourself of your fear is to free your heart's woes. Be open to me, in all your beautiful glory."

Despite the soothing words, Matt resisted as the man probed his mind, control of his thoughts wrested away. As if his memories were television stations and this man held the remote, his thoughts leapt from one thing to another, randomly and without regard for Matt's privacy. He flushed at being violated, embarrassing moments mixing with what anyone knew about him, secrets of no value to this man devoured as readily as their time on Honyn. Matt's life flashed before his eyes, anger building as he sensed amusement and scorn about his life and identity from the man.

He could still think for himself, it seemed, and in the back of his mind an idea lay hidden, his eyes on the identical staves. If he could control his staff, then in theory he could control the other one, too. Matt's staff might have been disabled by the wizard, but the other one likely hadn't been.

In desperation, Matt focused his will on the figure's staff, reaching out to it with all his might. At first it wouldn't recognize him as if uncertain that two people could connect to it at once, but then Matt felt it react. So, too, did the figure, realizing Matt's intent and surprised it was working, which Matt sensed due to their connection. But it was too late. With a burst of hope, Matt embraced the energy and spoke the word, "Enumisar." Flames erupted from it to engulf the man and in an instant Matt fell free of his grasp and the spell binding him. Scorching heat washed over him as he turned and ran, screams of pain and rage mixing with the crackle and whoosh of fire behind him.

⸻ ◆ ∙ ◆ ⸻

Standing with a knife in each hand, the rogue looked around warily. He'd come through the door last and seen his friends in the room before him, but now they and the room itself were gone. The knives had come out when he realized he wasn't alone. Across the room stood a tall woman in a silky, golden robe, voluptuous curves tempting his eyes away from her striking face. A vision of loveliness, she looked at him expectantly if not pleasantly, hands folded behind her back. The room stood otherwise empty of even an exit. All four walls, the ceiling, and the floor were solid, unless the way lay hidden. Searching might yield something, but he suspected the woman held the answer and stepped a little closer. They stared at each other silently and when she finally cocked an inquisitive eyebrow at him, he spoke.

"Greetings," Eric said, deciding on diplomacy. "I don't mean to be rude, and would love to stay and chat, but I need to get out of this room and back to where I was."

"That you may do," she replied in a vibrant, alto voice.

"How?"

In response she simply smiled. He got the impression that she was amused by the possibility that he thought it would be that easy. He paused to get his bearings. Since rooms normally didn't behave this way, he had to assume this was Soliander's doing and not something the former inhabitants had left behind. Then again, assumptions were never good, especially now. He needed to know who and what she was and why she was here. Then he could figure out how to get out of here.

"Are you real?"

She paused. "Yes."

He looked at her shrewdly, knowing the hesitation meant something. It had been a bad question. She could be a real illusion.

"Are you a being of flesh and blood?"

"No."

So she was real but not physical. He realized these questions weren't really getting him anywhere and changed subjects. "Did Soliander summon you?"

She smirked. "No."

Again her demeanor tipped him off that she wasn't entirely honest because that hadn't been a good question either. Technically the wizard was nowhere to be found and yet the spell had still gone off. In a way, Eric had caused her to be here. "Is Soliander responsible for you being summoned to this room when I entered it?"

"Yes."

He nodded, satisfied. This could take a while if he wasn't specific. He wondered if there was a limit on the number of questions he could ask, or a time limit, like many of the computer games he'd played. How was he supposed to know? He could ask, but she hadn't been forthcoming and only given yes or no answers. Still, Soliander must have meant this as a test, not an execution or imprisonment, so there had to be rules and it wasn't sportsmanlike to prevent him from knowing them. She hadn't answered his general question on how to get out, however, so he thought long and hard before opening his mouth again.

"What are the limitations imposed upon our interaction?"

She beamed as if pleased at the leap in his logic. "You may ask ten questions."

His eyes widened. How many had he already asked? Five or six, at least.

Seeing his reaction, she winked knowingly. "You have four left."

What? Shit. If he'd known that he wouldn't have asked half of them. Maybe he should be grateful he found out now. He wanted to ask what happened after that but of course that would waste a question. He muttered, "After that I guess I'll be stuck here."

A glint of steel appeared in her eyes as her arms slid out from behind her back, a short sword gleaming in each hand. A shiver ran over him. She might have looked like a woman, but she was clearly something more deadly – if that were possible – and her motion suggested great skill and willingness, both of which he lacked. He was no match with the sword, and he suspected a knife or two wouldn't take her out before she – or it – reached him. He had to say something to get out of this, but it could have been anything. Asking a question probably wasn't going to do it. That would just allow him to figure out what to say. He knew what he wanted to know but thought about how to phrase it for several minutes before finally asking.

"How can I convince you to let me gain my freedom from this room?"

"You must prove your freedom is wise."

Finally, he thought, *a real clue. Okay, so why is my freedom wise? I'm here to reset the gate, but this spell predates the gate being open again, so that can't be it. The spell was created by Soliander, probably to stop people from reaching the gate, but not himself, of course. So I could say I just want to leave and maybe it would let me go, but if I was Soliander, I wouldn't fall for a lie because I could just try to get in some other way.*

The rogue stopped there, biting his lip. He wondered who Soliander would let reach the gate but drew a blank, since only the other champions were likely, but maybe that was it. The only people who could be trusted were those who'd been involved from the start, and they were probably the only ones Soliander thought would try to reach the gate with good intentions. That had to be it. Now Eric might be pretending to be Andier, but that wasn't enough. Maybe he had to prove he was one of the other three. It warranted a question.

"If I can prove I am Andier, Korrin, or Eriana, will you let me escape?"

"Yes."

Eric sighed in relief. He had two questions left and felt close now. There were only two ways he could think of to prove it. Either he had an item of Andier's he could show, and he should have everything with him, or he had to know something only they would know. He hoped for the former and thought about what he wore. None of the items were that unique, aside from being well made, but then he remembered the short sword and Ryan's observation that both of their swords might have been made of soclarin ore. His eyes lit up. That was something only the Ellorians had. He slowly pulled out the sword and held it up for her to see.

"This is made of soclarin ore," he began, "as only they would...." He didn't finish the statement, for the woman leapt at him with swords slicing through the air, a frenzy of slashing motion. Startled, the rogue barely had time to launch one knife, which she casually caught on a blade and flung aside. Then she was on him like a whirlwind of steel and he knew he was going to die. Their swords met only once before a blade slashed his arm, another his chest, and finally both plunged to the hilt into his belly. In agony, he bent forward over her fists, her sinister eyes looking into his with contempt. She then shoved him back and off the twin blades. He fell on his back, his abdomen a bloody mess.

It occurred to him too late that Soliander had described the ore in the scroll so anyone could have known about it, and that it was the worst thing he could've said. After all, that's probably why someone had opened the gate and Soliander certainly didn't want the ore falling into the wrong hands. Feeling like a fool, he looked up at his killer without blame as she straddled him with both swords raised above her head, ready to finish him. He suddenly remembered the Trinity Ring and that Soliander had made it and Eric knew the voice commands – something only the champions knew.

"Oonurarki," he choked out, and the woman vanished as the ring's strongest spell healed him. He sat up, finding himself in the room he'd seen before stepping through the door. An *illusion*, he observed without surprise, noting his injuries had been real enough.

Taking stock, he rose and decided not to open the door he'd come through yet. It had obviously triggered a trap and once had been enough. Maybe the others were dealing with something, too, and so he moved off to one side to wait. Not long after, a distraught Anna ran through another door, covered in blood. Seeing him, she buried her face in his shoulder before he knew it.

Momentarily speechless, he finally asked, "Are you hurt?" Her head shook. "Then whose blood? Matt?" Again she shook her head. "Ryan?" She nodded and he put her at arm's length. "Where?" He started for the door.

"No!" Anna said, grabbing him again. "No, it's too late."

"What? What do you...?" He trailed off, her distress answering the question.

Lone, steel-shod footsteps sounded from a hallway to one side and he moved to guard her, pulling out two throwing knives. A figure in golden armor stepped into sight, bloodied sword in one hand and a lance in the other. Blood covered much of the knight, who gave no indication of being in pain as he flashed a relieved smile.

"Ryan!" Eric let out a sigh of relief. Anna's head snapped up and her mouth fell open. The big man came forward, eyes looking for the wizard.

"Where's Matt?" he asked, putting away the sword. Anna suddenly rushed into his arms.

"I don't know about you," started the rogue, glancing around warily, "but I just dealt with an illusion that dumped me here when it was done. I think Anna did, too. She saw you die, I think."

"Oh," said Ryan, turning serious. "Well, I'm fine, Anna," he said to her, putting a hand on her awkwardly. "It's okay. I mean I did get hurt but I was able to heal myself with the ring."

She nodded and pulled herself together to step back. "So maybe you dealt with an illusion, too," she suggested, wiping tears from her face.

"Maybe," he agreed. They heard feet running toward them from another hallway and Matt ran into view, looking terrified.

"We've got to get out of here!" Matt yelled, looking back.

"What's the matter?" Ryan asked.

"There's a powerful wizard not far behind me. He's pissed!" He stopped to catch his breath. "I set him on fire."

"That would do it." Eric smirked.

The knight shrugged. "It's probably an illusion. We all just experienced one, separately, it seems. Yours is probably over just like the rest of ours."

A scream of rage sounded from behind Matt. "Did that sound like an illusion?"

"Actually, no," Ryan admitted. He looked at Eric. "Do you think we'd experience each other's illusions? We didn't before."

Eric took Anna's arm and started for a door across from the one that triggered everything. "Let's not find out."

With trouble coming from behind, they didn't wonder what lay behind the door as they jerked it open and stepped through, but only an ascending stairway greeted them. The others started up as Ryan bolted the door behind him. It wasn't until he saw them standing at the top and not moving that alarm bells went off in his head. He crept up quietly, hoping to get a peek without letting himself be seen by whatever had arrested their attention, but all thoughts of that vanished when a tremendous roar shook the walls. It was deafening and shocking in its massiveness and could only mean one thing.

As he watched, a sinuous golden neck rose high into the air, pulling an enormous head with it. Two gigantic, baleful eyes swept over his friends and then picked him out from down below them, not missing a thing as its prey arrived. Ryan heard a slow rushing of air he didn't understand until the dragon opened its fanged mouth and the sound reversed, accompanied by a huge spout of searing flames racing toward them.

———— • • • ————

"They did not follow?" Lorian asked, worried. He, the dwarf, and the other, remaining eight elves stood on a landing halfway down to the dungeon. The guards could still be heard laughing and joking below, unaware of the impending attack, but now the rescue of Cirion's mercenaries might have to wait. The absence of the champions didn't bode well. Lorian cursed himself for letting them come last. Something must have happened.

"We'd better check on them," Rognir muttered, starting toward the stair with a muted clatter of metal.

"No," started Lorian, fearing the dwarf would be heard. "I'll go. Continue on to Cirion. You should still outnumber whoever's down here."

The dwarf frowned. "This fellow isn't nearly as important."

"Yes, but the wizard can help us. The cult likely didn't expect prisoners and probably only diverted a few guards for this. Nine of you likely outnumbers them and one more won't make a difference."

"You underestimate yourself."

Lorian nodded thanks and hefted his sword as he cautiously retraced his steps. No fighting had been heard, which suggested the four had taken to hiding. While only Andier had skill in the role he played, Lorian doubted the group would give in easily. They'd shown a willingness to defend themselves at least.

Atop the stairs, he saw and heard nothing, their last known location empty. The far door seemed the most likely place they'd have gone, so he opened it, peered in, but saw no signs of them in a room with several doors and corridors. He pursed his lips, considering. They'd probably gone that way, but there were too many options to investigate. They could be quite far removed from here by now. Perhaps he had better look anyway.

He took one step in when a scream split the air. It came not from below where he expected fighting but off to one side and behind. He shut the door and returned to the hall, seeing no one but hearing rushed footsteps and a staff thumping on the floor, moving away, so he followed. At the first corner, he caught the scent of burned flesh and saw a figure in smoldering black robes moving away. Assuming it was Matt, he hurried after to help the wounded wizard, but the figure's aggressive gait was quite unlike the techie's, so he slowed in suspicion.

Around corners and down stairways, he discreetly followed the figure until suspecting he knew how to intercept it. The dust had been disturbed along the route, so any traps had likely been cleared. He descended stairs into the darkness, no torches burning along the way, and ducked behind a marble statue at the bottom, in a dark room adorned with pillars. Across the room, a dim light grew brighter and footsteps louder along with the thumping staff as the figure stalked into the room from a hallway. Despite the face being turned away, Lorian stared in recognition, questions swirling as he followed, wondering what to do or say. Something wasn't right.

Always waiting until the figure vanished around a corner, Lorian followed quietly until hearing magic words. He peered around it to see the robed figure standing before an ornate golden frame covered in dust, shimmering rays of light pouring from it to cast dancing shadows around the room. The figure took one step toward the portal and Lorian stepped out into the room.

"Soliander!"

The figure turned with such fierceness that the elf knew something was coming. He dove behind the wall as a blast of lightning scorched the hall and blew stones all over him, a dust cloud obscuring the air, a deafening rumbling all around. When it stopped, he couldn't hear anything and worried the figure would be standing above him when he turned, but it was not. A gash on one leg made it hard to stand, and on peering around the corner that, he felt no surprise that all signs of the wizard were gone.

⁓ ✦ ⁕ ✦ ⁓

Now that Cirion had inspected the jail, he felt confident of a quick escape. These cult members knew little about imprisoning someone and it had seemed an afterthought to take their weapons. Well, most of their weapons. They knew even less about searching a man of his talents, apparently. More importantly, he had enough tools of his trade to do the deed with little trouble. He picked at the new lock on the rusting bars as Nola chipped away at the crumbling mortar holding them to the stone.

As he glanced over at her, looking fetching as always in her leather armor, the sound of fighting erupted out of sight but didn't last long. Elves and a dwarf soon appeared with weapons drawn.

Noting the missing champions, Cirion wryly asked, "Lose someone?"

The leading elf replied flatly, "Yes, one elf."

"You had better be worth it," barked the dwarf, who continued by the cell, leading several elves further into the dungeon looking for other threats.

Watching him go, Cirion turned to the elf and observed, "You look familiar."

"Morven," came the reply as he unlocked the gate and pulled it open with a screech.

"Ah, Lorian's friend. He is here then? With the Ellorians?"

"Yes. We had best return to them. I assume you are still interested in helping seal the Dragon Gate."

Cirion cocked an eyebrow. "They would let me?"

"Provided you are well behaved. Come along. Your weapons are this way." Morven turned to go as the dwarf returned without further struggle.

Cirion stopped him. "Wait. What of our wizard?"

The dwarf replied, "The dungeon is otherwise empty."

"I'd like to look for him."

Frowning, Morven replied, "No. Another wizard would be helpful and is the only reason we came for you, but we'll not further risk giving away our presence."

The walls shook from a tremendous roar that could only come from one thing.

Cirion smirked. "I think it's too late for that."

CHAPTER FIFTEEN

DESTINY SEIZED

As the wall of flames rushed toward them, Ryan waited in horror. This would be far worse than that little burn he'd gotten at the wall of fire. He couldn't bear to watch as it reached his friends and engulfed them, but when nothing got to him, he looked up in surprise, which only grew at the sight before him. Matt stood with one hand before him as if to stop traffic, the other holding the staff, its crystal shining brightly. The oncoming flames were striking an invisible barrier Matt had erected. Ryan could hardly believe it and almost yelled excited encouragement to the techie before realizing that doing so might distract him.

When the flames stopped, Ryan joined the others atop the stairs, catching his first sight of a dragon. The sight filled him with awe that would've had him gawking were it not for the terror of it having just tried to kill them for what was undoubtedly only the first time. Tendrils of smoke drifted up from her nostrils, two baleful, malicious golden eyes turned from the others to him, with what looked like recognition and renewed fury. Her torso was tall as a two-story house, golden scales flashing with reflected firelight. The giant wings lay folded, her tail uncoiling from a pillar behind her, four giant, clawed feet and fang-filled mouth formidable weapons. The floor rumbled with her every move and it was a wonder the whole place didn't come down around them. Behind her, where thrones had likely once stood, he at last saw the Dragon Gate.

It nearly filled the hall at that end, standing on a waist high platform with three steps. A giant oval, it was wider than it was tall to accommodate the outstretched wings of dragons in flight as it pulled them in. It lay almost flat, tilted up toward the gaping hole in the roof, its lowest point at the steps. And it was on. Like a still lake in the black of night, it reflected torchlight and the tapestries above it, wisps of smoke curling along its misty surface. Waiting near it stood Raith, lips moving in what Ryan assumed was a spell with them as its target. How could they fight off both a dragon and a wizard?

He tore his eyes away to Matt, who still stood with arms outstretched, breathing hard. The knight wondered if the barrier would remain up and how long Matt could do that. The dragon had similar ideas, it seemed, for with one foot she casually flung a bench at them. All but the wizard took cover but it bounced harmlessly off the barrier. Matt flinched as if the blow weakened him. His arm sagged and his breathing deepened. They needed cover and the knight looked around.

The wide hall stretched to either side in a long rectangle, for they hadn't entered from the nearby main doors at one end, though they were close. Along this wall and the one opposite stood other stairwells, a long row of balconies overhead. Tattered, faded tapestries hung in ruins everywhere while scattered torches and lanterns dimly lit the dark room. An enormous gaping hole in the ceiling revealed the starry sky overhead, with piles of rubble from the half-ruined roof lying shoved to one side.

Ryan ushered the others behind a nearby fountain with a low wall around it as Matt indicated his spell had ended. The dragon would come after all of them, but only he could withstand her fire if Matt felt too tired to do that again. Seeing the dragon moving toward them, he stepped out before he could think it through any further, lance in one hand and sword in the other. He had to at least lure it away from his friends, not only to keep them alive, but to distract it so they could reach the gate. He still didn't want to kill it and doubted he even could.

"Ryan!" Anna called out.

Eric said, "No, he's fireproof, remember?"

"So what?" she asked incredulously. "It's not claw or tooth-proof!"

"We're not going to let that happen," Matt put in, still catching his breath, "but I agree on not following him out there."

"You've got to reach the gate," Eric reminded him.

Matt eyed the distance to the gate. "How am I supposed to get over there?"

"I don't know," Eric admitted. "Ryan's probably trying to distract it. Stay ready for an opportunity and I'll do everything I can to help."

Ryan approached and the dragon reared up near the ceiling and slammed both front claws into the floor, the boom thundering deep into the castle, loose mortar cascading down around the room and a balcony tumbling to the floor with a crash.

"Dragon Slayer!" Perndara roared. "This is one dragon who will slay you instead!"

One giant foot swept toward him from the right and he swung the sword at it, though it was bigger than his whole body and he braced for the impact. Instead, red blood sprayed all over him as the sword cleanly severed all three toes and the dragon shrieked, the toes tumbling across the floor instead of Ryan. The dragon's roar of pain shook the walls and she shifted weight to avoid standing on the maimed foot. Then she turned on Ryan and unleashed a torrent of flames. At the last second, he slammed shut the helmet visor. Fire blasted him, the force making him step back. The others stared, looking for a sign that Ryan still lived among the flames, but all they could see was his planted feet still upright.

Eric pulled his arm away from Anna, who clung to him, and rose. He took two steps and hurled a knife at one of the dragon's enormous eyes. The blade twirled through the air and struck home, the fire stream abruptly ending in another shriek of pain. Perndara raised the injured foot to nudge out the blade but couldn't, finally shaking her head furiously until it went flying. Something yellow oozed from the eye as she turned to see Eric throwing another. This she deflected with a turn of her head, but the blade still sliced into her golden scales. She spoke a few words and the eye healed itself, her foot no longer bleeding but not growing back. Ryan began to advance on her and the dragon retreated.

"Matt," said Eric, "if she starts to cast a spell, you have to help distract her. Ryan won't stand a chance if she does magic on him."

"She's moving too far away."

The rogue looked at the archers now arriving on the balcony, most waiting for a good shot at them, some repositioning themselves to get one. This hiding place wouldn't last long. Before they could react well, he ran along the wall under the balcony on one side. The archers let their arrows fly at him as Anna yelled out a warning, but the archers were neither accurate nor well organized and he avoided the haphazard volley, diving behind a rubble pile nearer the gate, where the wizard there locked eyes with him. Raith began gesturing, his lips moving. Eric raised up and quickly threw a knife that ricocheted off Raith's bony hands, disrupting the spell and causing a shout of pain. He didn't get back down fast enough, for two arrows struck the wall overhead while another lodged into his left arm. He fell back with a groan and glared at the arrow there. Working himself up to pulling it out and using the Trinity Ring on himself, he saw Matt watching him.

Are you okay? the wizard's fingers asked.

Yeah. Good enough.

As Perndara retreated from the knight, her long barbed tail struck the Dragon Gate's shimmering surface and momentarily turned to smoke like anything about to pass through it would. She glanced back at it as Korrin called out to her.

"Back through the gate, dragon," Ryan hollered, "or you will die here today!"

Her head whipped back around to him, furious eyes flashing. "Never! Never again!" Her giant jaws thrust at him, snapping, but he kept the lance between them. She retreated and Ryan lunged with the lance, stabbing her deeply in the neck. Perndara yanked backwards off of it and roared while blood spurted out.

The main doors behind Anna and Matt flew outward with a loud bang as two cult members arrived with a dozen mercenaries. Matt turned and a wall of crackling flames erupted from the floor between them, stretching to each wall. A tapestry caught fire on one end and quickly spread to the second floor, igniting another.

"How long can you do that?" Anna asked.

"I don't know. I'm surprised I did it at all."

Another commotion broke out to one side. "Focus on the fire," Anna advised Matt, who didn't follow her advice, looking over to see the next threat. The flame wall began to lower, then vanished altogether as men leapt over it with swords at the ready. Fortunately, the new commotion was the elves, Rognir, Nola, Cirion, and Cirion's remaining henchman arriving to take on the mercenaries. Rognir and Morven stopped beside them.

"You all right, lass?" the dwarf asked, seeming relieved to see them.

"Yeah we're okay."

"Soliander," Rognir started, giving Matt a pat, "assist Korrin while I show these elves how to fight." He charged away with a clatter.

Morven had already let an arrow fly at the dragon's head, but it bounced harmlessly off the golden scales as Perndara moved. A second arrow flew true but also ricocheted. The elf turned to the archers and began picking them off one by one.

As an arrow killed their lone henchman, Cirion and Nola ducked into a stairway to take in the scene. He spied Raith standing by the Dragon Gate, eyeing it hungrily, unmolested and apparently trusted by the dragon, but as Cirion watched, the wizard ascended the gate's steps and cast a final look at the suddenly chaotic hall, making brief eye contact with the rogue. A flash of recognition preceded a condescending smirk before the wizard stepped onto the gleaming surface of the Dragon Gate. At once he turned to smoke, which retained his shape an instant before slowly dissipating across the portal, twisting around and down until it vanished. He was gone.

Nola cursed and fired her crossbow at the archers, picking off one before seeing movement from another balcony. She trained her bow on the lone figure but didn't fire. Lorian had finally made it to the hall, his leg healed with a potion, his position on the balcony letting him assess the situation.

"Ryan," he called, "it is Lorian. Do not take your eyes from the dragon. You have done well, but you must pierce her heart with the lance."

"I don't want to kill her," Ryan replied.

"You have no choice. She will never let you near the gate alive."

"I'm already closer to it," the knight disagreed, advancing again, but then he stopped as a hail of arrows suddenly rained down on him. They bounced off harmlessly, but they distracted him enough that Perndara's jaws snapped toward him and clamped down on the lance, yanking it from his grasp. She tossed it behind her where it clattered to the floor behind the Dragon Gate, with a triumphant glare returning to the knight.

"Shit!" Ryan cursed.

Eric saw this and began creeping along the wall. The archers didn't react to his motion, but Perndara had sucked in a breath to roast him when a crackling bolt of lightning filled the room. A charred black wound, oozing dark blood, appeared in the dragon's chest. Roaring in pain, the dragon changed her target and sent flames at the source of the lightning. Lorian saw the retaliation coming and ran back through the balcony door, diving to the floor and around a corner as scorching heat washed over him. The door and benches burst into flames as the former flew off its hinges and crashed against the wall nearby. He quickly patted his cloak to make sure he wasn't on fire, too, then got to his feet to find another view point. This one stood blocked with flaming benches.

Ryan ran forward and swung hard at her good front leg before she could get her weight off it. The blade sliced into it easily, flinging blood out the other side as the sword passed through. She reared up on her hind legs to get away from the blade, spewing more fire over him instinctively, like a cat hissing at a threat.

"The charred spot on her chest," Lorian yelled, "is where you must strike."

Ryan couldn't reach it without the lance, even if the dragon came down from her reared-up position, which she couldn't do without landing on his sword. She swung first one front foot and then the other at him, narrowly missing, but then she swiftly turned and slammed him hard with a back foot, sending him tumbling across the hall. The sword fell with a clatter and he didn't stop rolling until he was all the way back by the fountain, dazed and groaning. Anna ran to him as the dragon advanced. Eric crept toward the lance.

At the hall's main doors, one elf went down in a heap, fatally wounded. Morven and the other elves had nearly finished killing the remaining mercenaries, but one leapt over the body, charging ahead to strike down the legendary Soliander, who recoiled and fumbled for words or items to block the raised sword about to end him. The blow somehow stopped just inches from Matt as if striking an invisible barrier. With a shriek, the man fell over dead, bearing a wound just like the one he would've inflicted. The wizard gaped in disbelief.

Anna knelt beside the fallen knight. "Ryan," she started, hands on him, "where are you hurt?"

"Everywhere," he moaned.

Anna tried to block out the approaching dragon and laid her hands on him, trying to call to Kiarin. The blood from Ryan's illusionary death still darkened her robe.

Perndara saw the white-robed figure trying to heal the Dragon Slayer and swept her claws through the air. Anna never saw them coming, but Lorian did. He shouted words and thrust out his hand, sending shards of ice into the dragon's neck. Perndara flinched, the motion changing her claw's path so that it struck only a glancing blow that still nearly ripped Anna's arm off, sending her tumbling into a heap where she lay unmoving.

Ryan saw the flash of golden scales remove Anna from above him, a shower of awful red blood splattering his visor. He bolted up despite the pain, screaming her name and seeing a pile of white robes stained with fresh blood. He rose, favoring one leg, and started for her when an enormous growl made him turn, for the limping dragon loomed overhead, triumphant, ferocious eyes ablaze. He stood defenseless.

Watching this, a visibly livid Matt gripped Soliander's staff in both hands and closed his eyes. Moments later, a forked tongue of lightning burst from the crystal to strike each of the dragon's eyes, boring into them. The enraged dragon flung her head side to side, trying to escape, but the twin beams followed her every move. When they stopped, only two scorched holes remained of Perndara's orbs, and no amount of magical healing would ever bring them back.

A deafening howl shook the walls, drowning out the sound of the lance sliding under Perndara and across the dusty floor. Eric had retrieved it and now sent it right up to Ryan, who stopped it with his foot. The knight lifted the lance, concentrating on the black scorch mark on the dragon's chest. Perndara never even knew he had it back when the Dragon Slayer took two quick steps and slammed the lance's tip into the bull's eye Lorian had given him.

The blow went deep into the dragon's chest. She reared up as if startled, a small puff of smoke curling up from her nostrils, jaws agape. She paused there as if to collapse would acknowledge Death had come for her, but finally she crashed to the floor with a great rumble that knocked loose stones from the broken ceiling. The body twitched and slowly the weight of her giant corpse settled. After a moment of silence, the great lungs expelled a final breath that washed over him.

Ryan let out a deep sigh, unsure how to feel, but the dragon didn't matter now. His reluctance to do harm had gotten yet another person hurt, and worst of all, she was the one person who could save Daniel. The dragon wasn't the only thing that had just died, for something in Ryan had, too, and yet it set him free like he hadn't been since the day of the accident so long ago. The man who had recently stood in horror over the body of the slain assassin was gone, replaced by a man who could look at something he'd just purposely killed with little regret.

Ryan looked about the room, so preoccupied with the dragon that he only just now saw the bodies everywhere, most behind the fountain and some on the balconies. Many survivors bore blood. Everything about this mission was so important to everyone that they were willing to risk their lives either to keep the dragons away or assist in their return.

He went to Anna, seeing Rognir leaning over her, soft light fading from his hands as the priest finished healing her. "How is she?" the knight asked the dwarf, seeing her eyes opening.

"She'll be fine, lad," replied the dwarf, watching as Nola and Cirion emerged from hiding to take aim at the remaining archers, who'd been standing in shock. Now they fell lifeless one by one until some realized the battle was lost and fled. "A better question," began Rognir, "is how are you? You took a mighty blow."

Ryan had almost forgotten, the adrenaline having kept the pain at bay. He was about to reply when Morven came up to them, looking grim. Two elves had died and another lay badly wounded. The dwarf started to rise sluggishly, weakened by all the healing he'd done. He could only do so much before his own strength gave out.

"Maybe I can help," began Eric, having clambered over the dragon to reach them. He gently pushed the dwarf back down and went over to the wounded, using the last of his ring's spells on the more gravely hurt. One elf still had a broken leg, so the rogue had Matt come over and do the same. Ryan gathered his sword and lance, Eric retrieved his knives, and Lorian slid down from the balcony on a tattered tapestry. The sounds of men fleeing echoed from all corners of the ruin. Aside from a few dead, everyone was accounted for, with one exception.

CHAPTER SIXTEEN

A Hero's Welcome

Matt felt good as he watched the battle's aftermath. While he seemed a one-trick pony, fire erupting from the staff was a fearsome trick, and he had cast a few spells aside from that. Only now could he look at the dragon with the awe and fascination it deserved.

"Has anyone seen Raith?" Morven asked, interrupting his thoughts.

"I saw him go through the gate," Cirion admitted angrily. "I'm going after him."

"Not so fast," said Ryan coldly, clamping a big hand on Cirion's arm. "You've already caused enough trouble."

The rogue tried to pull free but got nowhere. He was no match for Korrin and knew it. He stepped back, eyes hard, while Ryan moved to stand between the gate and everyone else. If they wanted to get to it, they'd have to go through him, and for the first time in ages he was willing to use his strength to get his point across.

"Should we go after him?" Anna asked dubiously. "There's no telling what's on the other side."

Eric shook his head. "Too risky. There are thousands of dragons there, and whoever opened the gate can appear and lock it behind us."

Images suddenly flashed inside Matt's head; of the black-robed figure that attacked him standing here just weeks ago with his identical staff inserted into the gate's base; of that wizard fashioning the gate from soclarin ore; of a knight, rogue, and priestess in his company on a quest, dressed just like Matt's friends were now; of the figure's hand penning the original scroll describing their time here; of a rosewood cabinet opening to reveal the staff and robe locked within; of his own face as seen by the figure through the orb just before lightning flashed from it to electrocute the dark elf spy.

Matt's mouth fell open and he just stopped himself from blurting out his realization. He'd known it earlier but had forgotten during the fight. Now Nola and Cirion stood here and this was none of their business.

"You two," he said with such a commanding voice that he startled his friends, "get over there behind the fountain." When the pair hesitated, he barked, "Now!"

Lorian nodded at his elves and a few escorted a glowering Cirion and Nola out of earshot. The others gathered around Matt more closely, perplexed.

"Soliander did it," the wizard said in a quiet voice, amazed by the truth of it. "The real Soliander. He's the one who opened the gate, and he attacked me downstairs. That's who you heard screaming before."

Expressions of disbelief surrounded him except from Lorian.

The elf nodded, looking grim. "I suspected as much myself." Inquisitive eyes turned on him and he added, "When you did not join us in the dungeon I went looking for you and saw what I thought was you walking away, so I followed. It soon became apparent that it was someone else despite the identical staff, which was impossible. Or so I thought. It would seem that you each have a copy of it, presumably a result of the summoning spell always equipping the champions with whatever they need for the quest. I am not sure how that works, but since they could be summoned from anywhere at any time, they cannot expect to be dressed appropriately and the spell resolves this for them. I suspected the truth as I followed the figure, and when he opened a portal to depart through, he nearly killed me. I did not confirm his identity. You are sure?"

"Positive," Matt answered. "He attacked me downstairs and tried to pull information from my mind with a spell of some kind." He flushed at the memory. "He wasn't very nice about it. I noticed our staves were the same, too. In fact, that was how I got away. He made my staff stop working but I was able to reach out to his and make it burn him, so I did. I don't think he was expecting that. Anyway, I think I somehow got some of the info in his head by mistake," he concluded, realizing he now knew what the real champions looked like.

Lorian made a sound. "Interesting. It is a two-way spell unless the one controlling it prevents that, as was undoubtedly his intention. His control would likely have slipped given the injuries he sustained."

"So you learned things from him beyond his identity?" Eric asked intently. "Now we know at least one of the real champions is alive, which raises a ton of questions. What else can you tell us? Did you sense anything about the others?"

Matt thought for a moment and frowned, shaking his head. "I don't know. It's not like that, I don't think. I don't even know what I know. I just know for certain it was him that attacked me, and when you wondered who'd opened the gate, I just knew that, too, as if his memory was mine."

Eric asked, "Can you tell why he opened the gate?"

Matt paused but again shook his head. "I don't know. I'm not getting anything."

"Maybe because you're trying on purpose now," suggested Anna, laying a comforting hand on him.

Lorian nodded, looking concerned about the revelations. "Yes, that could be. Since the transfer was involuntary, the memories and knowledge may be difficult to retrieve. We have more pressing issues, however, and can talk more of this later."

Wondering if hypnosis might work, Matt brushed that aside and asked, "So we'll leave Raith on the other side of the gate with the dragons?" As he wondered what was over there, images of a thick forest covering a mountain range popped into his head, but that was all.

"Yes," said Lorian, indicating Cirion and Nola could return to them now. "We can discuss his motives later, but he'll be unable to cause trouble once you seal the gate. We should act fast."

Matt took the hint and started for the gate with everyone following, which made him a bit nervous. He may have struck at the dragon with people watching, but that had been emotional. This was different – everything depended on it. He glanced over his shoulder at the small crowd, prompting Ryan to make all but his friends and Lorian stay back. The image of Soliander standing here at least gave Matt some idea what to do. The staff sent a pulse up his arm, letting him know magic was afoot, though he assumed that was the gate itself.

He mounted the steps, looking at the gate's misty surface in awe and tempted to touch it, but then the thought of dragons rising up through it banished that idea. He could daydream later. Flipping the staff upside down, he inserted the crystal into a hole. At once, a cone of blue light shot up into the sky from the gate before extinguishing, the gate's glistening surface turning to smoke with a slight whoosh, tendrils drifting upward. He could now see through the empty oval to the floor beneath.

Matt sighed in relief and came down the steps. "I guess that was it."

The staff sent another pulse up his arm, but he didn't know what it meant. Maybe something else was causing that. With the gate off, he decided he didn't care what else lay around here. Besides, maybe the gate always gave off that reaction. Once again he lamented the lack of owner's manuals or general knowledge of how things were supposed to work. Maybe if he meditated or something, he could learn such ideas from Soliander's memories.

"Now we can go home!" Ryan gripped his shoulder in congratulations. He sighed in relief. "I can't wait to see Daniel." His bright eyes turned to Anna and she frowned, looking away.

"We should return to my estate," remarked Lorian, "on the way to Olliana. Let us depart."

As Matt left with the others, he suddenly realized Cirion and Nola were gone and remarked on this.

"Damn those two!" Rognir spat, unhooking his axe. "I bet I know just what they'll be up to when we leave, too. Looting this corpse!" He gestured at the dragon, which surprised Matt.

"Why?" he asked.

"These scales, teeth, and claws are worth a fortune," the dwarf answered gruffly. "Lorian, as much as I love Arundell, I will stay behind. I have two heads to bust open." With that, he quickly said his goodbyes and stomped off through a doorway, clanking all the way. He stood little chance of sneaking up on Cirion. Matt noticed Anna looking after him regretfully. Was she regretting not learning more from him?

Ryan sighed. "It's just as well. I don't trust those two and don't want them with us anyway."

"Agreed," said Eric and Lorian in unison.

They left Castle Darlonon, making an uneventful return to Lorian's estate, a group of thirty elves meeting the weary travelers along the way. The forest teemed with them as they hunted down ogres and restored peace below the mountains. Since many an elf stopped to offer kind words. The quest had finally become almost fun now that it was over, and their worries were largely forgotten as they gathered with Lorian in Arundell's meeting room one last time.

In discussing Raith's involvement, they concluded someone might have to return one day to deal with the wizard, assuming the dragons or any traps left by Soliander didn't get him first. If he learned to use the ore, he could lie in wait for someone to open the gate and spring a trap of his own, so coming back sooner rather than later was agreed upon. With the real Soliander on the loose, the gate could be reopened again, and were a duel to happen between the two wizards, with dragons eager to destroy them both, the consequences could be terrible for Honyn. They assumed Soliander had opened the gate to get more soclarin but had no answers for why he'd left it that way.

Due to his questioning of Matt, they surmised Soliander knew nothing of where the other champions were and wasn't involved in the substitution. It was now apparent that the summoning had been altered in some fundamental way, since Soliander lived and yet Matt had come in his place. The real Ellorians could refuse or were spared, but their replacements could not, which suggested they might be summoned again and again, which no one wanted to think about.

Soliander's behavior concerned Lorian most, for it was quite unlike the man he'd known, raising serious questions. What had he been doing all this time? Where had he been? Did anyone know he still lived? It seemed unlikely, but then why was he hiding his existence? Did he have a new identity and a new life to go with it somewhere? Why was he acting this way? If the other champions lived, were their personalities so distorted as well? Soliander seemed to think they existed somewhere. Was he looking for them? And why? His actions suggested sinister intent, not a man searching for his friends, so finding them might spell trouble for the others.

Matt hoped answers would come soon so they could also escape the quests, but Soliander didn't seem amenable to polite conversation. It seemed likely that the Ellorian Champions were free as well, and despite no reports of them appearing home, perhaps they had done so secretly so they'd be left alone. A chance to speak with them might come sooner than they wanted because the real possibility existed that, instead of returning to Earth, they would be returned to their counterparts' homes instead if the spell couldn't tell the difference between them and the real champions. If so, Lorian promised to visit. He recommended telling the truth of their masquerade to the elven court, which had the power to send him across worlds as needed. Such aid would be invaluable and the elves would certainly keep the secret.

They decided to keep the truth about Soliander from Queen Lorella and the rest of Honyn, however. It would raise too many questions about not only the real arch wizard but the four new champions, though this did pose one problem.

"There's one more thing," started Matt, "the queen will want to know who opened the gate and we can't very well tell her it was Soliander if she thinks I'm him."

"True," agreed Anna, frowning. "So what do we tell her? I'd rather not lie, so can we just say we don't know? Is learning the truth part of the quest?"

"No, it is not," replied Lorian.

"Failing to admit it is still a lie, by the way," Eric interjected, "but I think we just go with a better lie than not knowing. Let's blame it on Raith. We think he's a cult member and involved in the stolen scroll anyway, so this isn't a stretch. As a cult member, he would have wanted to open the gate anyway but it was already open."

"The queen might not know a soclarin item is needed to open the gate, but if she asks if he had one, we'll just duck the question," added Matt. "He went through the gate before we could have asked him that."

Ryan nodded. "I think that is the way to go."

"There's something I should mention," began Matt. "When Soliander did his mind meld spell on me, he learned our real names and that we're from Earth, a name he seemed to recognize. I'm concerned he might track us down there and finish what he started."

Everyone's expressions became sober and serious.

Eric observed, "He could go after our families."

"Daniel," Ryan whispered, paling. Looking at Matt, he remarked, "I sure hope you can cast spells back home because if he shows up, you're our only real chance."

Matt exchanged a concerned look with the others.

They soon turned to drinking the night away in the safety of the elven estate, trying to forget the worst parts of the quest or what might lie ahead. On their way back to Olliana, each had their own preoccupation.

With help from Lorian, Matt practiced spells every day, hoping they still worked on Earth. He didn't know what to expect but suspected he wouldn't have the staff or books. He tried to memorize everything and spent all day with his nose buried in books to the point of rudeness. The others understood and left him alone.

Eric and Ryan both learned tracking from the elves and took seriously elements of horsemanship and wilderness survival that might be needed if they ever did another quest. Both expressed an interest in learning elven, so Lorian just cast the spell on all of them, then dwarven. Learning other languages like ogre came up but the elf said with a smile that they needed to absorb what they had already gained. There would be time enough for more later.

Anna had lapsed into quietness that prompted more than one to ask if she was feeling okay. She would nod and smile serenely but not say much about her inner world. She didn't understand what she was feeling and had something to sort through on her own. When Rognir had healed her, she'd felt the powerful effect of a god's compassionate touch in her. Part of her felt deeply shaken by it, but this was mostly psychological, her mind struggling to accept what had happened. Emotionally, she had never felt more at peace. She sensed that she'd been changed forever by it, and while that scared her a little, she felt eager to leave behind her old disposition and embrace something new. She been reading everything she could about the gods here, face buried in a scroll almost as much as Matt.

As they neared Olliana, people emerged from roadside homes and inns to offer congratulations, flowers, and even their chastity. Ryan exchanged knowing looks with Eric and Matt about the bounty of female flesh offering itself up, and how unfortunate it was that they had to be going.

"It's good to be the champions," remarked Eric, pulling up beside Ryan.

Ryan laughed, his banner snapping in the breeze atop his lance. "Yes, if only we had time to enjoy it."

Chiding them, Anna remarked, "Just think how many diseases you could bring back with you."

Undaunted, Ryan suggested, "You could always cure us." The boys laughed aloud while she failed to suppress a grin. The return to joking was nice.

They trotted through Olliana's main crowded cobblestone streets with Lorian and surrounded by elves, though

Morven had remained behind at the estate. The escort Queen Lorella had sent out to meet them led the way, steel-clad knights riding in formation. The crowd's roar of appreciation greeted the champions and flowers flew, gifts were given, and ribbons were strewn around their necks.

From a balcony, the queen gave a suitable speech, declaring the day a holiday and that a festival of celebration was to begin immediately. Yet another banquet in their honor would be held that night, but first the champions gathered in the War Room to tell the queen, her wizard Sonneri, and the Prime Minister the details of the quest.

"I understand you were successful in sealing the Dragon Gate," the queen observed, smiling from her seat behind the hexagonal table. "Please tell us precisely what happened."

With a look at Eric to see which of them would speak for them, Ryan received an encouraging nod and replied, "Certainly, Your Majesty. When we arrived at the castle, we discovered that Cirion's group had arrived ahead of us, but they were captured with some loss of life. We freed those remaining and set about dealing with the dragon."

Queen Lorella asked, "And were you able to chase her back through the gate before sealing it?"

Resignation on his face, the knight replied, "No, my queen. We had hoped to subdue her, but her hostility was too great, and in the course of battle she was killed."

The queen's eyes widened in shock, a flash of anger appearing before she relaxed and assumed a look of resigned acceptance. "While I don't agree with the Dragon Cult's methods," she explained, "I do understand their desire to see the dragons live well and prosper. I had hoped bloodshed could be avoided and the dragon spared, but I'm sure you only did what was necessary."

Ryan hadn't realized she had a preference but wasn't surprised. He responded warmly and genuinely. "I can assure you I made every attempt to spare the dragon's life and avoid her death. It was very regrettable."

The look she gave him made it clear she didn't believe a word of it, her knuckles white from clenching the arms of the chair. "What happened when you sealed the gate?"

Matt responded, "Very little. No dragons were pulled into it, so Nir'lion was the only one here."

The queen nodded. "But you're certain the gate is now closed?"

"Yes."

One hand on his big belly, Sonneri asked, "What did you learn about who opened the gate?"

Ryan replied, "We believe that a wizard named Raith opened it. He is the one who stole the scroll and learned its contents, which gave him motive."

Queen Lorella asked, "What motive is that? I thought simply freeing the dragons was the reason."

Realizing his mistake, Ryan admitted, "Yes, it was, since Raith was a Dragon Cult member, but in reading the scroll he discovered the existence of soclarin ore on the world where the dragons are imprisoned."

Seeming satisfied, she asked, "Will this wizard be able to open the gate again?"

"No," Matt answered. "He was present during the battle and stepped through the gate before we shut it. He is now trapped on the other side."

With arched eyebrows, the queen considered that in silence.

The next morning, the champions made their final preparations for leaving, saying goodbye to Lorian. Word of their success had spread so that those armies threatening war against Kingdom Alunia had stood down. Castle Darlonon and the forest had been cleared out by the elves and Alunia's forces. Everything was returning to normal here and they hoped their own lives were next on the list. They suspected they'd been reported missing.

It was standing room only as they ascended the steps to the dais and turned to face those they'd saved from destruction. As before, only the rich and privileged attended, but many more such people gathered now. The queen bade them farewell with a last speech, and in the applause that followed, Sonneri cast a stern look at the crowd to be quiet. Turning to the book before him on a podium, he began to speak so quietly none could hear, but Matt tried to read his lips, another skill he'd picked up for his deaf mother because she often read his. He tried to memorize the words and gestures, realizing he'd lost the opportunity to learn that spell and should've thought of that, but hopefully he'd never need it.

The stone pillars around them began to glow with words of blue fire, the decorative markings on the floor turning white beneath their feet. Soliander's staff sent a continuous pulse up Matt's arm, letting him know magic was afoot, and the wizard knew he'd miss the power he'd come to wield here. Of the four, he'd done the most amazing things and would return to a life far more ordinary, and only his eyes were sad as the pillars burst into flames with a loud whoosh and the room around them disappeared.

CHAPTER SEVENTEEN

RESOLUTIONS

Jack Riley stood just inside the door of Anna's condo in Gaithersburg Maryland, not sure where to begin but sure he didn't want to start at all. No friend would want the task before him and it felt premature. It certainly didn't offer hope. Packing Anna's things as if she was never returning just felt wrong. He wasn't ready to let go and didn't understand her father's decision. Maybe he just wanted some action to break the frustration of getting no answers, no resolution, nothing to change, even if this particular action suggested an abandonment of hope. The weeks of waiting and wondering were unpleasant, certainly, but this wasn't the way to go. What would Anna say if she returned? You waited just weeks before deciding I was gone forever? Gee, thanks.

He smiled at the thought. They went back a long way – he and Matt, too – growing up in the same neighborhood. Unlike with many friendships, time had not forced them apart, and while he wasn't part of the foursome, he certainly knew the others, too. It was hard to know one but not all, they did so much together, but Jack had a life elsewhere. A less secure guy might have felt he was a fifth wheel with all the inside jokes and you-had-to-be-there references, but he was fine with that. They had shared adventures with him as well, but for weeks he'd been wondering if they were now sharing some nightmare instead.

More than two weeks had passed since Anna Lynn Sumner, Eric Foster, Matt Sorenson, and Ryan LaRue had disappeared in England, their van found abandoned by the side of the road. A motive for their return to the monoliths after hours remained unknown. No security cameras existed at Stonehenge and the British authorities had found little to help their investigation. No witnesses or signs of foul play turned up and the volume of footprints nearby eliminated any signs of theirs. Only the digital camera found in the car, with its few pictures of the happy friends in their last moments, proved they had really been here, but they shed no light on the situation. The best guess – and that was all they had – was that they had been abducted and taken away in another car.

A ransom had first been suspected, with the wealthy Ryan the target and the others just bystanders, but one never appeared. Nor had any bodies, thankfully. No terrorist organization or anti-American group had claimed responsibility, and no signs of mental instability or unhappiness existed among the four. There had been nothing to go on and nothing had changed since finding the abandoned SUV.

The mystery had captured not only England's imagination, but the world's, due in no small part to Ryan's family. The considerable wealth of the LaRue estate had been brought to bear on the investigation and broadcasting of each police report, but it had aided them little. Scores of press conferences and both television and radio appeals had resulted in only false leads. The offered reward money had simply swamped the resources available to handle those leads. Daniel had personally appeared on TV to appeal for help, remarking on how much his brother looked after him and would never disappear this way. That situation had added to the world's sympathy that yet another tragedy of some kind had befallen the family.

Candlelight vigils had been held both in England and the United States with speeches by friends and tearful pleas from parents. A prime time TV special had even detailed their lives, disappearance, media storm, and the international investigation, with the typical stock footage of friends in happier times and how bright their futures were – or had been. The four lost friends had become famous for the wrong reason, and if they were ever to turn up alive, a worldwide media storm would greet them, questions flying. Everyone wanted answers, but those closest to them really just wanted them back.

With the apparent exception of Anna's father, thought Jack.

He stepped further into the condo, seeing the cats come out from hiding in expectation of food. He'd been taking care of them and was supposed to take them home soon, once he cleared out the place. Anna's father hadn't put it on the market yet, but it couldn't be far off. It seemed he wanted to put the whole mess behind him and move on. Still feeling like this was a terrible mistake, Jack picked up a cat and headed for the kitchen. He would start tomorrow.

— ⁘ —

Autumn leaves rustled under the horse's hooves as the elf cantered along the road from Olliana. After much toil and danger, he rode with less alertness than usual, for there was little to worry about so close to the city. He needed to relax anyway after all the recent fighting and stress. It was why he'd freed the other elves with him to stay or go on alone, for he wanted some time to himself. He breathed in the fresh air and scents of the forest as he entered a wooded stretch of road. It reminded Lorian of home, his destination.

He could enjoy the comforts of Arundell for the first time in months, a crate of rare wine waiting for such an august occasion as the second banishment of the dragons and, even better, the death of Nir'lion. While elves valued life, some lives were bent on the destruction of all others and were best extinguished for the greater good. She wouldn't be causing such trouble again even on the uninhabited Soclarin, a thought which reminded him of the ore.

It was just as well that the gate had been sealed and that ore locked away. The ore was a dangerous thing for anyone to learn the existence of, and it pleased him that Queen Lorella, her Prime Minister, and Sonneri had agreed to destroy the scroll copy. No one else would learn its contents, and it could be safely forgotten. Hopefully Soliander would never open the gate again, or if he did, the new champions could lock it swiftly next time. They had done very well, very well indeed.

Thoughts of Soliander troubled him. The wizard he'd known would never have let the dragons loose to cause such damage or been so careless about leaving the gate unguarded. Where he had gone to and what he'd been doing all this time troubled Lorian as much as the attempts on both his and Matt's lives. It raised fears about what had become of the real Andier, Eriana, and Korrin. Something told him the wizard had something to do with their disappearance and he rode along thinking of every detail he could remember from their time together, looking for clues into this destructive behavior. Lost in thought, he never saw the net falling until it was too late. It swept him from the horse's back to the ground, where someone delivered a blow that knocked him out.

⸺ ❖ ⸺

Queen Lorella strode into her private chambers, leaving her guards outside and breathing a sigh of relief that this whole affair with the Ellorians was over, at least publicly. There were reconciliation meetings to occur between kingdoms via messengers and other intermediaries, but she'd leave those details to others as befitting a ruler of her stature. Now the armies threatening war had backed down, their warriors going back to their regular lives, unmindful of any danger that might turn up in the next days. Everyone's guard would drop and no one would think to watch the skies any longer.

She smiled. This was perfect, even better than she had planned. For a time, there she'd been rather angry, and more importantly, at a loss for how to salvage the situation. Then the champions had come against all odds and a new plan was born, one that left Honyn even more unsuspecting than before. It had unfortunately cost the life of the same foolish dragon that had caused the problem by being spotted, and there would be a hefty price to pay for her death, but in the end, disaster had not only been averted but turned to her advantage.

She turned to a map of Honyn on a table, eyeing the nearby kingdoms and recalling what Olliana's generals had told her about troop movements and battle tactics in the event a dragon horde emerged from the gate. No one had been willing to share plans due to suspicion about which kingdom's wizard had unleashed them, but knowing they wouldn't cooperate with each other was worth knowing, too. The fools didn't deserve the peace they now enjoyed, but sometimes fools got what they deserved. Their lack of loyalty to each other and to the kingdom that had now twice saved them would cost them.

A sound behind her indicated someone had entered through the secret entrance and now waited quietly, obediently, like a respectful servant should. Unlike some, she commanded authority and didn't tolerate abuses to respect, though one had disobeyed her recently and caused no end of trouble.

Irritated by the memory, the queen asked sharply, "Have you received word from the castle?"

"Yes, my queen. They arrived safely just as you intended."

"And what of the elf?"

"He will join them shortly."

She turned toward him menacingly, eyes turning to red fire as a glint of her power surged. "See that he does...or I will devour you alive."

A feeble, "My queen", was all he could muster as he bowed and backed out of the room.

Heading for a tall shape covered by a golden cloth in one corner, she decided to see for herself, for these spies couldn't be trusted despite their sincerity. She pulled the cloth to the floor, revealing a shimmering portal that seemed to show a portrait of herself. Her depiction wore a soiled gown that had known better days. Time had a way of changing such finery for the worse without good care. The woman's body had fared only slightly better, dirt smudging each cheek, her hair dirty and matted. Some might have thought the queen gazed upon some impending future reality, but she wasn't even really looking at herself at all. Smiling grimly, she put one hand to the mirror's edge, spoke a magic word, and stepped through, vanishing from Olliana.

— ⁑ —

After a moment of flashing colors and whooshing air, he stepped onto blackened and charred earth, blinking in the sunlight. Mountains loomed all around and deep green forest covered everything but the area just before him, which looked to have been blasted with fire so severely that nothing grew here anymore. His eyes searched the sky for threats, but nothing appeared. No signs of movement came from the slopes' craggy shadows and cave openings, but that didn't mean he wasn't being watched. He'd maintain a constant vigil lest his death appear on wings, but for now everything seemed fine. He was alone.

As he glanced about to get his bearings, he noticed a faint trail leading away from the Dragon Gate behind him. Raith's eyes lit up and he set off at a jog, his distaste for such exertions forgotten. Time was short, for the champions wouldn't take long to kill that stupid dragon. While he'd long admired the creatures, he'd never met one before the banishment. He knew some dragons were smarter than others and was certain that this dragon hadn't been the famed Nir'lion. He'd probably not have gotten past that one. Curiosity as to her whereabouts lingered, though it occurred to him that perhaps she had died here somehow. It was something to ponder later.

Now he had to get to the soclarin ore, retrieve a healthy supply, evade the Ellorians when they arrived, and get back through the gate. Then he'd find his way back to the horses and eventually reach his secret tower in the crags of the Naken Peaks. He would learn to fashion magic items from the ore as Soliander had done, and once ready, would bring all of Honyn to its knees.

With lust for power distracting him, he made quick progress up the winding path, shadowed by the thick canopy of trees. The dragons wouldn't see him now unless one shape shifted to human form and followed, but he doubted they would. Dragons didn't care to remain in that form long and had little reason to suspect anything was here. Soliander had undoubtedly not told them of the ore, and unless they'd discovered it on their own, they were none the wiser.

The trail ended in a thicket that only someone in armor could pass without getting shredded, and while it looked natural, he suspected otherwise. He murmured a quick incantation, but nothing happened. Gripping his staff for more power, he tried again. This time the brush parted to reveal a short path. He smirked and set off.

The winding trail soon deposited Raith in a narrow, sloping ravine of rough stone that rose sharply toward a natural cave. Feeling clever for getting this far, he started for the mine opening, pulling a fist-sized bag from a pocket. It would hold far more than it appeared, being enchanted to be nearly bottomless and hold tons of weight without burdening the one who carried it. It neatly eliminated the need for help, which was just as well. He'd never have gotten assistants here anyway and it spared him the trouble of killing his hired help yet again, not that he really cared.

He'd taken no more than a few steps when the rock wall beside the entrance broke apart. It didn't fall to the ground as expected, instead forming itself into a humanoid shape taller than him, two powerful arms and legs attached to a muscular torso. The menacing head turned to him with a sound of grating stone, two hollow eyes narrowing as it stepped in his direction.

"A stone golem," he muttered, disappointed. "I should've known." Only blunt force could defeat one but his staff would snap like kindling. Magical power was his forte anyway. His eyes on the heavens, he focused his will on a cloud and spoke.

"Uusrolinip, uusrarkitor!" *Two arcs of fire, two blasts of light!*

With a loud boom that echoed off the mountains, a forked shaft of lightning struck the golem in the head and leg, but it continued forward as if nothing had happened.

Raith realized too late that it wasn't the force of lightning that blew things apart, but the effect on the material's composition. Earth was largely immune to it. He had wasted energy and had only so much time before it reached him.

The stone golem stopped to touch the rock wall and a large boulder rolled out of seemingly nowhere. The golem lifted it and then hurled it at Raith with startling speed. Thinking fast, he continued to cast the next spell on his mind – levitation – but changed targets from the golem to another boulder, which he lifted into the path of the one hurtling toward him. They collided with a horrible crack, showering the ravine with jagged fragments. One struck him hard enough to dislocate his shoulder and he gasped at the pain, blood running down his arm. Quickly he pulled out a vial and tore the stopper off with his teeth, draining it in one gulp. The injury healed like it had never been, and when he looked up again, movement behind the golem startled him.

A figure dressed in black robes sat upon a rock, a staff in one hand. For a moment, an unexpected and yet likely name came to mind, but it couldn't be. Even great wizards couldn't be two places at once. Then all thought of the black figure vanished as the golem lifted another boulder, this one smaller and more easily targeted than before.

Raith barely dodged it before another followed. He wasn't the most agile fellow and couldn't keep this up, so he tilted his staff forward and focused. With a loud bang, the next head-sized boulder shattered two paces from him on an invisible barrier, the shards scattering. Dust cascaded around him as Raith trembled from the impact. Another rock did the same, then another and another, each one testing his strength, each one pushing the barrier closer to him.

The golem advanced, still hurling boulders as it came, pulling stone from its own chest and throwing it. As if made of liquid rock, it filled the hole in its chest from its own body as it absorbed more stone from the ground while walking, reforming itself spontaneously. The distance between them quickly shortened and a surge of panic struck Raith. He had one chance to drop the barrier and destroy this thing and then run for his life, for the robed figure would go next and his strength was spent.

Suddenly an idea hit him as the golem loomed overhead. He dropped the shield and again used the levitation spell, hurling the golem backward straight at the robed figure, hoping to kill two birds with one stone. The figure never even moved as the golem shattered on him and fragments flew everywhere. A cloud of dust obscured the result, but the golem's head rolled straight toward him, between his legs, and came to rest a few feet behind. He had done it!

Then movement caught his eye. The cloud faded to reveal the robed figure without a mark upon it, for it had erected its own barrier. It rose to its feet and as Raith fumbled for a magic item, the sound of stone moving came from behind. He turned and saw in horror that the golem had reformed and was swinging a crushing fist at him. Ribs snapped like twigs as he was flung to the ground, the last healing vial breaking with the impact. The golem took one step and hurled another rock down at him, smashing his pelvis to bits. He would have screamed but for the stabbing pain in his lungs that left him gasping at his murderer.

The golem raised a final boulder.

"Stop."

The golem halted.

Soft footsteps signaled the approaching figure, which wore a badly singed robe but walked without pain. The figure stopped and gestured for the golem to move aside.

"You," Raith wheezed, more certain of the identity now that he recognized something he'd seen at the banquet in Olliana. He'd seen drawings of it many times before and would know it anywhere.

"You no doubt recognize my staff," answered the figure in calm approval, "as all serious wizards should. And of course, you're presence here is a great sign of your seriousness. You have come for the soclarin."

Raith didn't bother to confirm it. The voice sounded different than he remembered, but then his senses were beginning to fail him. He'd already lost feeling in his legs.

"It was you who stole the scroll," observed the figure.

"Yes," Raith confessed, seeing little reason to hide his secrets anymore. He would soon have no need of them.

"Personally, or did you hire someone?"

"Hired."

"And then killed them upon delivery?"

Raith nodded slightly, suddenly overcome with sorrow for what was happening to him. The figure could heal him but clearly wasn't going to despite this going against everything Raith knew about the man whose voice he heard. Then again, so did allowing a golem to bludgeon him to death.

"Excellent. And you have the scroll with you?"

Again Raith nodded, but the figure made no move to retrieve it.

"Did you not wonder why I left the gate open?" the figure asked. "Or did you, like everyone else, assume I had gone forever and perhaps someone else had done it?"

Raith struggled to acquit himself well but relinquished his pride as a spasm shook him and blood trickled out his mouth. "I don't know," he confessed.

"That's because you are a fool," replied the figure coldly, watching without compassion as the young wizard slumped further. "You, my dear boy, are the reason the gate is open. I needed to know who had the stolen scroll, who outside the court knew about soclarin, as the individual would come looking for it. You triggered the spell I put on the gate to alert me when you stepped through, and you have met your end via the golem I left waiting for you. For all your ambition, you are, like so many, blinded by it, and therefore come to the pathetic end that is your destiny." The figure chuckled. "And in the process, your ambition has caused the dragons to be free to doom your world."

Feeling a haze overtake him, Raith said quietly, "But I *want* the dragons free."

"And so shall they be."

Surprised, Raith asked, "You won't close..." His breath failed him.

"No. Only you knew of the ore, and you'll not leave here alive. No one else knew to come looking for it, but I suspect others may know now. The trap must remain." He cast a glance toward the gate, visible beyond the tree tops. "And I care nothing for what becomes of Honyn."

The figure pulled back the hood, revealing black hair and a cold expression. The face was similar to the one Raith anticipated but not the same. His surprise was plain.

"I am not who you expected?" the figure asked.

"S-s-s," stuttered Raith, confused as blackness overtook him. "Soliander?"

"Indeed," confirmed the wizard, "the *real* Soliander."

CHAPTER EIGHTEEN

END GAME

Right from the start Eric had his suspicions. He'd only traveled via worm hole – or whatever it was – once before, but the vivid memory remained. There had been lots of flashing lights, roaring sounds, wardrobe changes, that sort of thing, but none of that happened this time. Maybe the spell sending them home was different, but they still needed their clothes back. Granted, all this magic stuff was rather new to him, but something didn't seem right. It wasn't just his lingering fear that they weren't really headed home either. His suspicions only deepened when the spell stopped almost as soon as it began.

His first thought was that something had gone wrong. For one, he still wore the leather armor and weapons, Matt still looked like a wizard, and Ryan and Anna hadn't changed either. They also weren't standing in a field surrounded by the stone monoliths of Stonehenge, but in the center of a dusty chamber with cobwebs on the walls. The stone work, general disrepair, and odor of decay seemed familiar. Through a dirty, stained-glass window off to one side, forest-covered foothills sloped away for miles. A nearby wooden door stood closed, but another was open enough to reveal a tall, swiveling mirror with the looking glass removed. The room was sparsely furnished, but what little remained lay covered in filth and mold, mildew having rotted cushions and curtains. The only newer items were a wooden tray with an empty plate and drinking cup on the center table, and a rough cot in one corner. Upon this sat a woman about twice their age. She looked to have seen better days, for the dirtiness of the room had clung to her gown, face, and hands, as if the room's disrepair were slowly consuming her, making her a part of itself.

Anna turned to him. "Where are we?"

It was the woman who answered. "Castle Darlonon. I assume from your astonished expressions that you did not come here to rescue me?"

"No," Anna answered. She peered curiously at the woman. "You look a lot like Queen Lorella."

"That's because I *am* Queen Lorella," she replied, rising with a natural air of authority her surroundings hadn't changed.

"You do look a lot like her," Ryan admitted, stepping closer, "enough to be her sister maybe, but we just came from where she is."

"Olliana? That is an imposter and has been for some time."

"How do we know you're not the illusion?" Eric asked.

"The staff isn't telling me there's anything," Matt observed. Suddenly he looked surprised and opened his mouth to say something when Anna spoke.

Anna asked, "Why would someone impersonate the queen?"

"Because the queen learns all," said a bold female voice from the other room, "and that's just the sort of information I need."

They stared as another Queen Lorella stepped into view wearing a smug sneer and a tight-fitting leather outfit showing a dragon's head emblazoned on the breast, every tone and movement hinting at danger and cunning, not elegant benevolence. Behind her stood a swivel mirror shimmering with light. Eric noticed that Matt looked less surprised than the others. Had the staff warned him that magic mirror was on?

"You have no doubt noticed," continued the new arrival, stalking into the room in black, heeled boots, "that you have not been safely delivered to your precious home world, wherever that may be – and I intend to know. A visit there seems only fitting once I have terrorized Honyn, a joy for which I will wait no longer. When done I will return to tear answers from your hearts, one by one, until there is nothing left of you. And what I want most to know is where the real champions are."

Looking back and forth between the two queens, Ryan objected, "But the spell was supposed to send us back. We finished the quest."

"Did you now?" the imposter interrupted, snidely amused. "You accomplished nothing more than what I let you believe, fool! The gate stands open even now. Its closing was an illusion, as was Sonneri's attempt to send you home, though he thought it was real, but he saw what I wanted him to see while another spell of mine brought you here." She laughed cruelly.

"Nir'lion," Eric said in realization. *Two* dragons had come through. Who had they killed?

"But we killed Nir'lion," Ryan protested.

"No!" the dragon snarled, slapping him so hard that he crashed to the floor with three bloody gashes on his cheek. "You killed my daughter," Nir'lion growled as Anna bent down to him, "and for that I will roast you alive!" Tendrils of smoke drifted up from her nostrils, a reek of power from her engulfing the room like a smothering weight.

"What now?" asked Eric, hoping to distract her from more violence.

"Oh, I want a great many things. My brethren will be arriving in minutes to take back this world that belongs to *us*."

Hoping for answers and to stall, he asked, "Why didn't all of you come back before? Why just you and your daughter?"

She gave him a withering look. "What point lay there in that? Unless I found and killed every wizard able to close the gate, someone could just send us back. I had to find and execute them all first, before anyone knew we'd returned. Perndara ruined that by being seen."

"You didn't know only Soliander can do it. Or someone with the ore."

"Yes, not until I replaced the queen here and read the scroll, but then I learned someone had stolen a copy. I had to kill them. I cannot allow knowledge of how to close the gate become commonplace."

"Why did you summon the champions? It wasn't supposed to work."

She rolled her eyes. "That's *why* I had them summoned. Empty gesture to silence the kingdoms threatening war, which could interfere with finding out who could close the gate."

"You knew we weren't them at once, didn't you?"

"Of course. I would never forget *those* four. The question now is how you came to be here in their stead and where they are. Giving me the answer is the only reason you're still alive."

Eric wasn't looking forward to being tortured, however she was planning to do it. He had to stall for time. "Why didn't you just do something to us then? Why let us complete the quest, or appear to?"

"I wanted to know who you were. My spies soon assured me that you were not up to the quest's challenge, which meant that by fooling you into believing the gate had been closed, I could undo the damage that Perndara had done to my plans. And it worked. Armies have already stood down. You even found out for me who stole the scroll."

They had indeed. But Raith was on the other side of the gate, still alive, unless the dragons over there had gotten him, which seemed likely. "What of Perndara? She fought us and if we'd done the spell to close the gate, she would've been pulled through. Since we weren't doing it for real, we would've known it didn't work."

"She was supposed to pretend she couldn't handle you and fly back through it before you tried. As it turns out, she couldn't handle you for real."

The dragon looked at him as if realizing he was a bigger threat than believed. Maybe they could use that to their advantage, but he had no idea how. The entire quest had been a trap. They'd achieved nothing, would not be going home, and Honyn would be destroyed. They had snatched defeat from the jaws of victory.

"So now what?" Ryan asked from where he still sat on the floor.

Nir'lion sneered. "Now you will wait for my return, when I will learn from you and your elven friend in the dungeon how you have come to be here instead of the Ellorians."

"Wait for your return?" the rogue asked, relieved she was leaving.

Nir'lion turned to the window, smashing it and sending shards of glass to the floor. "The armies of Honyn are unsuspecting once more, and the time has come."

She climbed onto the window ledge and leapt into the sky as storm clouds rolled in. She dropped out of sight at once. Eric raced to the window to see her morph into an enormous golden dragon bigger than the one they'd killed, her wings snapping out to catch the wind. As she soared away, a great rumbling shook the room, sending loose mortar falling from the ceiling and dislodging blocks from the walls. From the gate room, dragon upon dragon soared into the sky, some slamming claws into the ruin in a first swipe at the world they would destroy. The darkening sky filled with death on wings, silver, blue, red, green, golden, and black dragons headed in every direction and roaring with bloodlust. As if at one with the impending dragon storm, the sky unleashed a crack of lightning and torrents of rain began to lash the tower.

Eric turned around, glad to see Ryan rising now that Matt had used the Trinity Ring on him. It now had only one spell left and the other rings were spent, so if Anna didn't start healing people soon, someone might stay hurt next time.

Anna interrupted his thoughts on asking, "How did you come to be here, Your Majesty?"

The queen sighed. "She came to me in human form as an emissary from Nurinor, bearing the gift of a golden mirror she placed in the royal suite. One moment I stood alone with it, and the next something invisible wrenched me through it. I've been trapped here since. I heard the fight with the other dragon and had hoped to be rescued, but no one came."

Eric said, "I assume you heard the part where we're not the real champions and have somehow been substituted for them. Before you ask, we don't know how or what's going on. We've learned a lot and done okay on the quest, aside from being fooled by Nir'lion."

"Yes, I've known for some time. And there's no shame in being fooled by her. I was. The magic of dragons is very powerful."

"So what do we do now?" Matt asked, eyeing the portal mirror in the other room.

Eric saw his gaze and said, "I doubt she would have left us here with that if we could use it."

"We've got to get out of here," answered Ryan. "She made a mistake bringing us here because the Dragon Gate is downstairs. We just have to get to it."

"Right," agreed Eric, surprised by that, "but that means it's probably really hard to get out of here or to it." He listened at the door but heard nothing. "I'm not sure where we are, though it seems like a tower from the view."

"The northwest corner," offered the queen, looking skeptical. "There are guards outside and at the bottom of the tower."

"Okay," said Ryan, lowering his voice, "assuming we can get out of here, let's plan what we're doing. Do we just close the gate or go get Raith, too?"

Eric said, "It's been a week since he went through. Do we have any reason to believe he's still there? He could've come back. The gate has been unsealed all this time. Or the dragons could've killed him."

They looked at Matt to see if he was getting any images in his head. "He might still be there," the wizard admitted, "but there's no way to tell. Soliander has an earth golem guarding the place."

"I think we have to be sure," said Anna, "because if he's *here* with soclarin then it's our fault and we need to go after him. If he's there we need to stop him."

Eric frowned. She was right. "Okay, let's go through the gate, but we have to hurry. Nir'lion probably won't be back soon, but there's only so much time before she knows we're gone." He started examining the door's lock, pulling tools from various pockets in his black leather pants.

Ryan observed, "She'll never suspect we went through the gate unless someone sees us."

"What about Lorian, or whoever she's got downstairs?" Matt asked. "Should we get him now? He could help us."

"I think we just run the risk of being caught," answered Eric, inserting a tool into the door and fumbling around with it. It had been years since he did this and it brought back bad memories. "Let's get Lorian when we come back."

Anna interjected, "Okay, but what about the queen? She can't come with us. It's too dangerous."

Ryan exchanged a look with Lorella. "Yeah, but leaving her here isn't wise, especially once we take out the guards. Who knows what else is still in this place? The guards are keeping her in here but also protecting her in a way."

That was a good point that no one had an answer for until Matt reached for his spell book. "I have an idea," he started. "There's a spell of invisibility in here somewhere. She can just stay here until we return and no one will realize she's still here."

Ryan remarked, "That might work. Do you know how to cast it?"

The wizard made a face. "No. I have to find it first. Ah, here it is. It doesn't look too bad." He spent a few moments practicing the words and gestures. Then he gave the staff and book to Ryan before approaching the queen, who arched an eyebrow at the idea of him casting a spell on her. He faltered.

"I, uh, beg your pardon, your honor," Matt started, and Eric smiled at the title, "but I need to, uh, cast this spell on you, if you don't mind."

At that, Eric chuckled, prompting Anna to smack his arm. It jostled the tool in the lock, which clicked. In surprise, the rogue pulled on the door and it opened with a creak. He waited before going any further.

"Your Majesty," Anna started confidently, "we're certain this is the best way to protect you while we're gone."

"If I didn't agree I wouldn't still be standing here," the queen replied with muted humor. Turning to Matt, she asked pointedly, "Are you sure you know what you're doing?"

Projecting confidence, he replied, "Yes."

Queen Lorella held his gaze a moment. Eric watched, knowing she was judging Matt, who managed to hold her gaze without flinching. "Then proceed."

He nodded and went over the words and motions again, but just when he was about to do the spell, he paused. "Um, would you mind closing your eyes?" She complied without comment and he visibly relaxed and began the spell. One moment the queen stood there and the next she had vanished.

"Good work," said Anna approvingly.

"I think you four had better be going," remarked the invisible queen.

"Right," Eric agreed.

Ryan and Eric unsheathed their swords before opening the door a crack. Golden torch light filled the hall. The rogue opened it wider, ready for anything, but nothing happened. He stuck his head out a bit further, but his forehead bumped into something invisible.

"Ouch," he said, rubbing it. Then he reached out to feel the opening, discovering it was blocked from top to bottom with an invisible wall. Two guards to one side stepped into view, smug grins mocking him. Frowning, he turned to Matt and gestured for the wizard to do his thing, even though the guards would be ready. Matt focused his will on the staff and blockage but didn't have any luck dispelling it.

Disappointed, the wizard remarked, "I can't get rid of it. The other ones I did were by Soliander, and his staff helped a lot with his own spells, I guess. These are by the dragon, I bet, and they're supposed to be very strong in magic. I guess I'm not much of a wizard," he concluded.

Eric sighed and closed the door so they could talk in private. He wondered why the queen hadn't mentioned it, but she had likely assumed Matt could get around it. Or maybe she hadn't known. The dragon had known they were coming, clearly. Looking around the room, his eyes fell on the shards of glass.

"The window," he said, starting for it. "She probably didn't plan to bust through it like that so maybe it's not protected." He stuck a hand through it without trouble, then his head, peering down into the dark gulf, gusts of wind tearing at his black hair. The courtyard stood to one side far below, dense treetops to the other, and nothing but boulders directly beneath him and a window thirty feet straight down. Descending that would be tricky even for him, despite his years of rock climbing. He had none of the usual safety gear except chalk, but if he could make it to the window, he could come back up and take out the unsuspecting guards.

After hearing the plan, Ryan asked, "Even if that works, how are the rest of us going to get out? The door will still be blocked."

"They can turn it off," said the queen. "One of the guards has a little device that removes it and puts it back. It's how they bring me food."

"Great," said Eric, projecting confidence he didn't really feel. "See you in a few minutes."

As the others exchanged worried looks, he clambered onto the window ledge, dangling his legs over the side. Rain soaked them quickly as he put chalk on his hands. The rain might wash it off, but it was better than nothing. He rolled onto his stomach and eased both legs out and down, searching with the leather boots for a foothold. The castle's disrepair proved a boon, for chips and holes had been left unrepaired and he soon disappeared over the side, making his way down. Despite the rain and wind lashing at him, the rogue descending steadily until the ruin revealed its dangers. As he lifted one foot, the other foothold suddenly gave way, blocks of stones tumbling into the darkness and leaving him swinging by one wet hand.

"Eric!" Ryan called out, wanting to help, but there was nothing he could do. Then Matt appeared beside him, lance in hand. The knight extended it down to the rogue, who grabbed it in relief, able to trust it more than the castle. There seemed nowhere to hold onto the tower anymore except the one handhold he already had. Water dripped down the lance and over his hand as wind tore at him, but he was halfway to the other window.

"Hold on tight!" Eric yelled up to Ryan. "I'm gonna let go of the tower for a second!"

Ryan swore in protest and Eric had to just hope the big guy was as strong as he always seemed. This was a bad idea that wasn't getting any better. Eric reluctantly let go of the wall, all of his weight on the slippery lance. He moved down the lance as fast as he dared, slipping once before finding the next handhold. He was past the trouble spot and soon made it to the window ledge without further incident.

Unfortunately the window was closed, with no handle on the outside for the obvious reason. Breaking the window might make too much noise, but among Andier's tools he'd found a small glass cutter in one pocket. In short order he'd cut a hole big enough for his hand, unlocked the window, and climbed in, shutting it behind him.

He paused on the musty carpet, taking stock. He was alone, drenched, but free, and thankful to be alive. He reached a wooden door that seemed to lead into the castle and tried the handle, but it was locked. Out came the lock-picking tools once more, but this one was jammed, which might have accounted for why the room was still furnished. Fortunately he knew how to get around that and soon creaked open the door carefully. The dimly lit stairwell on the other side was empty and quiet.

——— ✦ · ✦ ———

The moons had glistened on the smooth surface of Lake Isinia when Joril and Siarra first rowed out into the beautiful, calm night. Their parents wouldn't let them be together for reasons youths often chose to ignore, and this seemed the only way to consummate their love in private. No one on shore could see what they were doing and so it was that they lay together under the peaceful sky, not noticing the storm clouds gather overheard until the first drops roused them from a dreamy, post-coitus sleep. Joril sat up, realizing how far they'd drifted and that they had to get moving, and fast. And yet he sat still, for the first flash of lightning revealed something he thought impossible. He stared into the sky so intensely that Siarra asked what was the matter, but then another flash revealed their fate and his reply turned into a scream. A black dragon swooped down upon them, an ear splitting shriek accompanying the giant boulder it let fly. The stone smashed the boat to kindling and dragged them deep down to the lake's depths, burying them together in death.

Not too distant, the trees rustled quietly as Morven rode along, eyeing the sky above the next ridge when he could. The stars seemed to fade in and out strangely when the tree tops parted. The elven village of Yulin lay over that ridge, and on cresting its top, he stopped in amazement at the sight below. The village stood ablaze, black smoke curling into the sky to obscure the stars, the smell of death and charred flesh heavy in the air. The cause made itself apparent when a red dragon landed before him with a thud, two hostile eyes afire with malice. Only instinct saved him as the dragon's head snapped forward. Teeth covered in blood clamped down on the horse just as he rolled off. The dragon couldn't spit it out fast enough to reach Morven, who fled into the woods as fast as mortal legs would fly.

In the kingdom of Nurinor, Lord Neelim sat astride his horse, watching the battle unfold below as his knights crushed ogres and trolls in a rampage to rid the region of them. His domain held no place for such uncivilized creatures. And so it was that suitable horror filled him on seeing another nightmare soaring across the plains below his cliff-top vantage point. Not one but a full score of death on wings came toward his realm. First one and then another roared from a distance until a chorus filled the air and all those below stopped to stare. Some dragons descended among the melee to roast men and beast alive while others soared past the carnage to his kingdom's heart. Among them, one silver dragon headed straight for him, his armor catching the light and its attention. It plucked him from the horse and flew onward, crushing his bones with the force. His scream ended when the dragon bit him in half and swallowed him, armor and all.

A cargo ship on the Lisen Ocean found fire raining down upon it, setting it ablaze so that it burned to the waterline, all hands lost. A wizard's tower on the Peaks of Normin toppled to the crags below, shattering into as many pieces as the dragons tore the wizard within. On the walls of Castle Roinin, men sounded the alarm to no avail, weapons of war unready for the onslaught of tooth and nail, fire and malevolence, might and magic. All of Honyn burned in disillusionment and despair. The Ellorians had failed them and hope disappeared as fast as life.

The mastermind of it all, Nir'lion flew over the still pristine city that was surely on everyone's mind, for Kingdom Alunia had claimed the dragons were gone. That deception demanded the worst revenge humans could muster, but when she was through there'd be nothing left for humanity to destroy. She had warned the dragons to leave this gleaming city untouched, that had so prospered from their banishment. Its destruction was hers to enjoy, and relish it she would. The time had come. With a shriek that put other dragons to shame, she swept down from the sky, blasting the royal tower with fire before landing atop its battlements. Let all those below see her, know her, and fear her. This world belonged to her now.

In another castle not far away, Ryan figured he'd given the rogue enough time, having seen him disappear through the window below. His turn to help with their escape had come. He opened the door to see two men grinning as if particularly amused by his captivity. He'd seen looks of jealousy flung at Lord Korrin before and used it to his advantage, hoping to distract them for Eric. The bigger, blond guard seemed in charge from the way he carried himself.

Giving his own smirk, Ryan poured on the cockiness and said, "Why don't the two of you and I settle this like men? Let me out of here and you can both take me on. Neither of you could hope to beat me by yourself, of course, but together you have nothing to lose except your pride."

The blond guard spat on the floor. "I don't need help to beat you, Korrin. You're no champion. If it weren't for all that magical armor, you'd be nothing more than a dandy."

The other guard laughed as if to ingratiate himself with the other one and Ryan replied, "A fist fight, then. I should've known better than to expect something more sophisticated from you. Let's get started, unless you're afraid a dandy will beat you." When the guard didn't take the bait, he added, "Maybe when I'm done mopping the floor with you, I'll enjoy your women, too, assuming you're man enough to get any."

The guard came closer, scowling. "I have more women than I know what to do with and—"

"Or do you prefer men?" Ryan interrupted with suggestive look at the other guard. "This one seems willing to please you."

"You son of a bitch!" the guard yelled, coming up to the opening. "I know what you're trying to do and I'm not pulling down this wall just to have a go at you."

"You don't need to," replied Ryan before punching the unsuspecting man's face, sending him flying backward into a crumpled, unmoving heap. Amazed silence followed and no one moved. Suddenly the other guard fell to the floor and lay still. A dripping Eric stood behind him, the blow to the back of the head having done its job.

"How did you hit the guard through the barrier?" Anna asked, looking shocked.

"I've got that magic ring, remember?" Ryan replied, holding up the hand with the Dispersion Ring, which made his arm unaffected by magic. "I forgot about it."

"You seem to be getting past your aversion to violence," Eric noted, using a small rod he found on the blond guard to disable the spell. Ryan frowned at the sense of approval but didn't say anything as they filed out of the room, leaving the queen behind and giving her the rod so she could manipulate the barrier herself.

Matt and Eric quietly led the way down the stone steps, the wizard saying the staff should warn them of spells, and the rogue looking for more traps, though they doubted any existed, since the guards went up and down. They might have known to avoid a certain step or two, though footprints indicated they put their feet everywhere in the dust and dirt. He motioned for the others to follow the path just to be sure. Everyone kept quiet and Ryan in particular once again appreciated how quiet his armor was.

Halfway down the curling tower stairs, the rogue stopped, motioning for the others to remain still. He began a sign language conversation with Matt, and not for the first time, Ryan wished he knew what they were discussing. If this summoning thing became a real issue, with them being sent on quests again and again, both he and Anna had to learn this valuable skill.

The conversation finally stopped, and the wizard reached into a pocket, pulling out a small bag he stuck one hand into as he crept forward, Eric retreating to give him room. Finally, the wizard seemed to whisper something before throwing sand from the bag forward. The sound of someone falling with a small clatter reached his ears, but then Eric and Matt rushed forward.

"Stop him! Stop him!" Matt fiercely whispered, alarming Ryan, who made it to the corner just as the sound of something metal bouncing down stone stairs began. The guard that Matt had made fall asleep had collapsed and was now starting down the steps, his dislodged helmet already disappearing around the corner. Eric just missed grabbing an arm as the man followed with a horrible racket that just kept going and going as he went seemingly all the way to the bottom. Ryan exchanged a look of alarm with the others and shot Matt a glance.

"The whole castle probably heard that!"

"Sorry. I didn't think of that."

"I think we had better be going," said Eric, who was still dripping with water and leaving a trail.

On reaching the tower's bottom, they discovered the still sleeping guard. Eric hid the man's weapons in case they encountered him again. Then he and Ryan dragged the man around a corner and left him there.

"Let's keep moving," Eric suggested, eyes assessing which way to go. "Remember we have to stay in halls that look like they've been used."

They continued through the castle with only one minor fight, Eric's flying feet and fists taking care of it quickly. Again they hid the unconscious men to avoid leaving a trail of bodies. Soon they stood at the gate room's main entrance, hesitating. The huge carcass of Perndara still lay where it had fallen, the smell overpowering them, its teeth and scales harvested by Cirion or someone else. It sickened all of them.

"It's too bad we didn't find another door," Ryan quietly remarked, eyeing the room. "We have to walk the entire length of the hall to reach the gate."

"True," agreed Eric, watching the rain fall in through the roof, "but finding another door might cause more problems than just heading across. I don't see anyone, do you guys?" Aside from some sort of guard, it stood to reason another dragon might be here, but there wasn't, at least not in dragon form.

"No," replied the wizard, "but the staff feels something. I just don't know what."

"Then you go first," suggested the rogue.

"Very funny."

"I wasn't joking."

"Let's head along the side where we came in before," suggested Ryan, "since we know what's over there. Hopefully no one is hiding in here somewhere, but there's bound to be something guarding the gate."

They headed off, Matt and Eric in the lead again as they skirted the dragon. Anna pursed her lips on stepping by the place where a god had first touched her. Why had it needed to be at a scene of such pain and death? Was that just the way of it? She'd long known people found god when in their darkest moments. Until now, she'd never realized she'd revisit the place where it happened again, but it hardly felt like a special moment given the rotting corpse overpowering her nose and the fear of more death being imminent. She found herself whispering a prayer to the goddess Kiarin as they went.

They soon came around to the gate, which no longer looked as if it was off. Smoke curled along its surface just like when they'd first seen it, and it seemed unguarded. Together they mounted the steps but didn't get far. Something began to form in the air above the top step. The shimmering figure of light and darkness resembled the ghost of a dead knight that had decayed in the ground for years. A wicked sword appeared in one hand as two hollow eyes swept over them, stopping on Anna. Before anyone else could react, it leapt from the steps to land before her, one ghostly hand grabbing her by the throat.

"You will be mine!" it said in a hollow voice. She stared in horror, drawn into its eyes and unable to look away. What she saw in them she couldn't name, but she knew death would only be the beginning of a new existence beside this thing for eternity. And yet a longing overcame her, one so deep and urgent that she whimpered in terror, her will to live fading as a will to be its bride came over her. She heard the others shouting but their voices seemed far away as if she'd already left her body behind.

She became dimly aware of Ryan's hand trying to grasp the spirit by its own neck, but his hand passed through it. The eyes that had bored into hers turned toward the knight and the mesmerizing lure of them left Anna. Ryan was gasping in pain as she reached for the medallion at her own neck, seeing the spirit's head turning back toward her. As her fingers closed around it, urgency compelled her to scream out in her mind to Kiarin for help, all doubts or hesitation gone.

The goddess' face appeared in her mind at once, a brief look of outrage preceding a wave of strength that filled Anna. Still gripping the medallion with one hand, she grasped the death knight by the forehead with the other.

Bright light engulfed the ghost, which screamed as the darkness within it exploded with light. When Anna could next see her surroundings, nothing of the figure remained and her friends stood staring at her. Ryan's arm was covered in frost and he stood wincing in obvious pain. She took it in both hands and thought to Kiarin with genuine thankfulness, Just a little more please, for *Ryan*. The touch came again and the frost melted away, leaving the knight's hand warm and refreshed.

Ryan lifted the hand before him, flexing the fingers and turning to her with a smile. She suspected she knew what he was thinking. They had argued so many times about the existence of God and now she had used the power of one to heal him. She couldn't deny it now, not after this, not that she felt much inclined to. This time she hadn't just seen it, or been on the receiving end of it, but both, asking a god for help and being answered. She felt jubilant, but when Ryan swept her into a bear hug, she knew he'd expect her to do it back on Earth and there was no telling whether it would work.

Eric pulled them apart, casting a sharp look at Ryan as he asked Anna, "Are you alright?" She only nodded, and he wondered aloud, "I wonder why it went for you."

"The medallion," she said. "It saw the medallion. Something about it attracted its attention."

"What was that you did there?" Ryan asked.

"Talk about it later."

Eric said, "Yeah, we don't have time for this." He took her by the arm and they mounted the steps. "Then let's go before something else shows up."

Anna gazed at the whirls of smoke on the Dragon Gate's surface. They were already one world removed from Earth and now it would be two. Aside from Matt's assurances that little probably awaited them on the other side, no one wanted to go through. The gate's lock lay right there and all they had to do was seal it and this would all be over, which caused a brief argument. Ryan just wanted to go home to Daniel. He and Matt tried to persuade Eric to forget about Raith, but it was Anna who finally made them do it. Whether they wanted it or not, they had a responsibility despite the risk of Soliander appearing and locking them on Soclarin forever.

"I guess I'll go first," Matt volunteered despite his concerns, "just in case the staff wards off anything over there." Even as he said it, something seemed to occur to him. "I know what's over there," said the wizard, looking surprised, "and why Soliander opened the gate in the first place. He did it to lure whoever stole the scroll there, not to get more soclarin. The gate being open is a trap, and stepping through it sounds an alarm, but as long as the staff is present, it doesn't do anything. That's how he sets up spells to affect everyone but him. He obviously wasn't expecting a duplicate of his staff to exist." The wizard indicated that the staff no longer alerted him to the presence of magic, which meant what he'd felt last time had been Nir'lion's traps, not the gate itself.

Anna cast a final glance about the room and noticed the tower from which they'd come was visible through the hole in the ceiling. Hopefully, Queen Lorella would be fine up there. "I think we should all go through at once," she suggested, taking Ryan and Eric's hands so they were all touching. They agreed, steeling themselves for the unknown as they stepped onto the surface.

⸻ ❖ · ❖ ⸻

Nir'lion reveled in the destruction she had wrought. Buildings lay in ruins around her, towers had collapsed like dominoes, and only shattered windows remained in castle walls. Amidst the inferno ran screaming people frantic to save their lives. Their desperation healed the wound in her heart. Their suffering had only begun. She'd eaten the Prime Minister who had so often gotten on her nerves, but so far Sonneri had eluded her. He could run, but he'd not be able to hide forever. Now she had other things to attend to, however, and rose back into the sky, signaling other dragons to continue with their onslaught now that she'd taken the best prizes for herself.

The smoke disappeared behind her as she glided to Castle Darlonon on powerful wings, other fires raging on the horizon, where her kin soared in the rain-filled sky. All of Honyn must tremble, she knew, and the fear that preceded her arrival anywhere was like a red carpet thrown before a gala affair. She had missed that terribly, for her only joy came in the anguish of others, and as the mountains grew larger before her, the anticipation of tormenting those false champions grew and grew.

On arriving at the ruin, she roared to the heavens and dug her claws into the tower, sending blocks tumbling to the ground while she held onto her perch. One great eye looked in through the windows but saw no sign of champions or queen. The door stood open, the guards unconscious on the floor. Her nostrils flared in anger, and that's when the fresh scent of fear caught her senses. Someone was still here.

A spoken magic word later and the truth stood revealed, a frightened Queen Lorella flattened against the far wall and edging toward the open door. Nir'lion snarled and sent one razor sharp claw smashing into the room, grabbing the screaming queen and pulling her from the now crumbling prison, blocks of stone tumbling into the trees below. The dragon pushed off into the sky, sending the tower swaying dangerously as the top collapsed in on itself, half burying the room Lorella had been in.

"Where are they?" the dragon demanded, tossing her through the rain-drenched sky like a rag doll. Lorella screamed as the jagged peaks rushed up to meet her, but Nir'lion snatched her from the air, baring bloody teeth as she snarled the question again.

"The gate!" Lorella cried out. "They are at the gate!"

Nir'lion had suspected that. "How long ago?"

"An hour," the queen blurted, slipping.

Nir'lion snorted a puff of smoke as she turned toward the tower. An hour was enough time to have closed the gate, so either they were unable to do it, or they'd gone through for the ore. In either case, she knew what to do.

"I'll deal with you later," Nir'lion warned as she deposited the queen in the crumbling room. Then she leapt away and soared up, giant golden wings beating the air as Queen Lorella lost sight of her. Moments later a great rush of air signaled the dragon hurtling toward the gate.

⚬ ◆ ⚬ ◆ ⚬

The crumbling walls of Castle Darlonon disappeared into blackness that slowly faded, revealing forest-covered mountain slopes all around the champions. In a small valley, another Dragon Gate sat alone, tilted up at a sky where two suns shone. Many of the trees stood burnt to cinders, some long ago, some so recent they smoldered even now, as if the dragons had taken one last vengeful blast at their prison on the way out. Scorched and blackened earth surrounded the gate and nothing moved anywhere. It looked both new and familiar to Matt, who eyed the sky for dragons but saw none.

Ryan hefted his lance and stepped off to the top step first, nudging the wizard. "Which way?"

Matt looked for the faint path where he expected it to be. "There."

Like Raith before them, they followed the trail to the ravine, the sight of the young wizard's broken and battered body greeting them. Matt suspected he knew why and the golem that emerged from the rock wall confirmed it. As it approached, he went forward, unsure what to do but sensing this was his battle. He held the staff before him, intending to summon fire, but the golem abruptly stopped and bowed.

They stared in silence for a moment.

"It thinks you're..." Eric started before stopping himself. "Soliander, why don't you ask your servant here to recount what happened for us?"

Mat nodded. This impersonation thing had its advantages. "Of course. Golem, tell us what happened to this man."

The golem straightened, looking at him and ignoring the others. "But master saw," it said. Its voice sounded like stones grinding together.

Matt felt his skin crawl at the confirmation that the arch wizard had been here recently, their encounter still fresh. "Tell me."

"Him came," it said, indicating Raith. "You said so. Hurt him. You said so. Left him alive! You said so!"

Digesting that, Matt quietly muttered to the others, "When he comes, hurt him but don't kill him so he can be questioned. Those were the orders." Turning to the golem, he said, "Very good. You have done well," he reassured the monster. "What happened next?"

Looking confused, it replied, "You saw. You spoke."

The wizard glanced at Raith's body but didn't see any obvious signs of spell craft. If Soliander's words had been magic, the golem likely wouldn't have understood, but that didn't seem to be the case. "What did I say? What did we discuss?"

"Scroll. Ore. Stealing!"

They exchanged looks before Eric said, "Raith stole the scroll and came here to steal the ore, as we suspected."

"No surprise there," remarked Ryan.

Matt turned to them, eyes narrowed. "So if he opened the gate and left it that way to lure whoever stole the scroll here, why is it still open? He could've closed it."

"He could close it with us inside, so we should go," Ryan said, looking toward the trail.

Anna put a hand on his arm. "That's true, but Raith's been dead about a week, I'd say, so Soliander got what he wanted and could've closed the gate by now and didn't. I don't think he's intending to."

Matt frowned, unable to scrounge up a motive from his connection with Soliander. Maybe the decision to leave the gate open had come after their encounter.

Ryan asked, "When do you think Soliander came here? It had to be after the fight with the dragon because Raith went through during that and that would've set off the alarm, but we didn't see Soliander go through after him, so he had to do it after we left."

"Right," said Eric. "He must've known the gate wasn't really closed despite the illusion that it was."

Anna observed, "Which means he knows we never completed the quest and are therefore still on Honyn, or were until coming here."

Ryan asked, "Do you think that's why he left it open? To keep us from leaving?"

Eric looked at him pointedly. "Or is it to keep us from returning to Earth?"

Matt grunted. "I suspect you're right. All of you. Because he wanted to know how we took the champions' place and that obviously happened on Earth. We could be there now but we're stuck here."

Ryan said, "That's got to be it then. He's trapped us here, not on Soclarin, but on Honyn, by leaving the gate open. We have to get home."

Eric nodded. "And quickly, though I'm not sure how much we could do back on Earth."

"True," said Matt, turning to the golem. "What else happened?"

It shrugged. "You take. You leave."

"What did I take?"

"Scroll."

"Ah," said the wizard. "Of course. He wanted the scroll back so no one would know of the ore. He probably doesn't know there's a copy."

"Let's keep it that way," suggested Ryan.

"Right," said Matt, not intending to communicate with the arch wizard again. Once had been bad enough. "Maybe we should get some of this ore while we're here. We can't take it to Earth, I don't think, because we can't bring anything back with us, I assume, but the elves can hold onto some. Items made from it have already proven useful."

The others weren't so sure about that and a brief conversation led to a compromise. They took no more than a few pounds of soclarin, putting it into the magic bag Matt found on Raith's body. Like all magic items, the bag had continued giving off a magical vibe after its possessor's death, alerting him to this and other items left on the dead wizard. He didn't know what the other things did but would give them to Lorian or Sonneri. It was too bad he couldn't take them to Earth or start creating his own private stash.

They made their way back toward the gate, intending to end this quest for real, but as they left the trees to see the gate gleaming in the sun, a golden dragon burst through it and spread its wings, soaring up and arcing to view the ground. Nir'lion turned sharply. They had been seen.

"Run for the gate!" Ryan yelled, running with the lance. "We don't have to fight her, just seal it!"

Eric ran after him. "No! We'll never make it!"

Matt yelled, "No, Eric! Stay with me! Ryan is fireproof and I can block her fire and anything she throws at us at least once."

Eric swore and came back to stand behind him with Anna. Ryan stopped a dozen strides from them, looked back, and then stayed where he was, hefting the lance and loosening his sword. Matt nodded to himself. It gave the dragon two targets instead of one. Three problems for her was even better.

"Eric, get a knife to throw, even if you miss. She might, too, because of it. Ryan!" he yelled, seeing Nir'lion closing fast, "be ready with the lance. Even if you can't hit her, make her think you can."

The dragon opened her mouth. So did Matt, words of magic, and fire, erupting with equal fury. He saw Eric's knife fly over their heads from behind and heard the rogue get closer to him after throwing it. Nir'lion rolled slightly to evade the blade as she neared. The shield went up around them moments before the flames arrived and blinded Matt to everything else. A roar of flames. A loud shriek of pain. A whoosh of air buffeting them. The dragon breath stopped, Nir'lion having passed them. Matt glanced in concern at the knight, who stood unmolested, the lance on the ground ten paces from him. The dragon rose back into the sky and banked, blood dropping from a gash in her side. Ryan picked up the source of her wound, red on the end. His eyes met the wizard's.

"*Got* her," he yelled in satisfaction.

"How bad?" asked Anna.

"Not enough. Just pissed her off, I bet."

"She's coming after you this time," predicted Eric. He ran for the tree line.

"What's the plan?" Ryan yelled to them.

"The same," said Matt, wondering what the rogue was doing but trusting him, "but expect her to go for you. She knows about the armor. It will be a blow, not the fire. Dodge to the ground."

Ryan nodded. They all looked for Eric and saw him keeping out of sight, two throwing knives ready. Nir'lion was approaching lower this time, as Matt expected if she intended to physically strike any of them. Would she use more than her fire on Ryan?

"Watch for the claws and tail!" he yelled.

The knight didn't react, the dragon headed straight for him. As she reached the clearing, mouth agape with flames swirling within, first one and then another knife from Eric flew toward her. The first bounced off into the trees. The other pierced her side. The dragon breathed fire all over Ryan, but at the speed of her passage, it didn't last long. A claw didn't lash at him. Neither did the tail as she passed, but suddenly it slammed into Matt's shield as Anna cried out. The shield held firm.

"Didn't expect that," Matt observed, feeling weaker. Did Nir'lion know that every blow took some of his strength away? Probably. And every spout of fire at Ryan weakened his armor's fireproofing. Eric changed positions near the trees, closer to Ryan.

"We have to attack, not just defend," he yelled.

The knight threw his lance to the rogue and drew his sword. Eric moved to the tree line as if to hide from the dragon, who was circling again.

Matt asked, "Anna, does the goddess have any ability to protect us with a shield of some kind?"

"I don't know," she admitted. "I think so."

"Eric's right. We need to attack. I can't as long as I'm protecting us. If you could do it, that frees me to do a spell."

"Okay, let me try. I need to concentrate."

"Right. I'll shut up. Maybe close your eyes. Hold on to me. You don't need to watch."

"Easier said than done, closing my eyes to this." But she put one hand on his shoulder.

Nir'lion appeared to be focused squarely on the knight again. Had she realized Matt was no danger with his shield up? They needed Anna to succeed in shielding Matt herself so the wizard could nail the unsuspecting dragon with *something.*

As she soared just above the low trees and reached the clearing, Ryan yelled, "Now!"

With one hand on the butt and another on the shaft to guide his aim, Eric threw the lance upward at Nir'lion's unprotected belly, his entire body behind the motion. Matt thought it couldn't possibly reach or do much, but it must've been lighter than he thought for how high it went. Even as Nir'lion blasted fire toward Ryan, the thrown lance flew high enough to strike, the angle causing it to puncture her belly. The fire abruptly stopped as Nir'lion grasped it with a hind leg and yanked it out. Her tail fell low enough as it passed Ryan that the knight slashed with the sword and cut a gash near the tip. Nir'lion roared as she rose into the sky, throwing Ryan's lance far into the trees, blood cascading from belly and tail. She spoke a few words and the bleeding stopped.

"Lower your shield," said Anna.

Matt turned in surprised. "You're sure?" She nodded. "Because if you're wrong – "'

"I'm not. Trust me."

Their eyes met and he saw only strength and clarity in them. He turned toward the dragon. This time Nir'lion seemed focused on him. What could he cast that didn't involve gestures until the last second? He mentally flipped through Soliander's spell book, a choice surfacing. As the dragon neared, he didn't see the telltale fire swirling in her mouth. Claws? The tail? Her magic? Trusting in Anna, he began his own spell, the words coming easily as he relied on the trusty staff and his most fearsome trick. He hardly saw Eric throw a knife. Then the dragon's spell sent a hail of large boulders raining down on Matt and Anna even as flames blasted them. One rocked the ground next to them, half buried in earth. Another bounced off Anna's shield as she grunted. A third slammed into the ground before them and bounced over, a cascade of dirt showering them but ricocheting off the shield. Another struck a glancing blow as dragon fire obscured the rest, though from Anna's moan it seemed that another scored a direct hit before deflection.

When the flames vanished, Matt retaliated as the dragon soared away, a focused beam of fire bursting from the staff's crystal to burn deep wounds in the dragon's back and one wing. She roared and nearly flipped over in the air to plummet toward the clearing, rolling in the sky to land on all fours with an incredible thud. Nir'lion took a few steps forward, swung her backside around, and then kicked out at Ryan, clobbering the knight so that he flew into a nearby tree and didn't move again. She looked back and sucked in a breath. Flames appeared in her open mouth, eyes on Matt and ablaze with fury. Even as the fire began to rush forward, a knife from Eric struck her neck and she swung the tail across the ground at him. He leapt over it. The flames hung in her mouth. The tail came back and he rolled under it, then threw another knife that bounced off her head. Mouth agape, she brought forth the flames toward the rogue, who ran for the trees.

"Saarilmor nukal o nusaak taasili kuniase mu'unia a rolinmor purta!" *Flying metal, hot as fire, seek head and heart as I desire!*

The words from Matt caused a hail of metal shards to pelt Nir'lion, whose head swiveled from Eric to him, a blast of flames roaring around him and Anna again. When her flames stopped, Matt conjured his own from the staff. Even as the fire raced toward the dragon, she kicked out at the priestess and sent Anna tumbling across the ground. Matt's spell faltered, but then fury tore through him and the flames strengthened. The dragon leapt into the air, wings beating furiously as she escaped his attack. Eric ran across the ground to reach Anna, who wasn't moving. Looking for blood, Matt saw none on her white robes and wondered just how badly she was hurt. Ryan hadn't moved from where he lay. A growing anger grew within. The dragon flew over the nearby peaks and disappeared, but he knew it wouldn't last.

Matt heard Eric quietly calling Anna's name while holding her. That meant she was unconscious. "Get her out of sight," he called, watching for Nir'lion. Eric seemed to agree, for he carefully picked her up over one shoulder and made for the tree line. Matt raised his shield.

Where is she? he thought, eyes scanning the sky. He looked at his friends and all of them were seemingly out of harm's way. Matt was the lone target remaining and felt confident his shield would hold. He stood alone in the clearing, the Dragon Gate off to one side. If Nir'lion had been smart, she would've brought help, for they'd never have beaten two dragons at once. It didn't look like they were going to beat *one.*

A subtle sound of a wing flapping caught his ears, but he still saw nothing. He checked each mountain around them, wondering which one she'd come out from behind. He gazed straight up. Nothing. A sound of rustling leaves caught his ears to one side, but there was nothing there. The wind? He felt no motion. The sound grew louder and he turned to the direction, suddenly seeing the treetops sway violently right at the clearing's edge.

Invisible! he realized. A blow of some kind. That had to be the reason.

He ran to one side as a whoosh of air reached him, the snapping shut of giant jaws just feet away. The dragon appeared to him now, for the illusion of invisibility only worked if he didn't know of her spell. The sight of her golden body passing overhead, claws haphazardly swiping at him, stunned him. As she passed him, the staff in one of his hands violently flew away. He watched in horror as it tumbled end over end, up and above the trees for a hundred yards before falling among the boles. The dragon's tail had struck it. The way to close the gate was gone. The way to shield himself was gone. The source of aid he needed for every spell that stood a chance of stopping Nir'lion was gone. Matt watched in terror as the golden dragon turned, a whorl of fire already brewing in her opening mouth, a look of triumph dawning in the golden eyes.

"Time to die," she growled, banking toward him.

Matt eyed the distance. Ten seconds, if that, before he died. Then Anna, Eric, and Ryan died. Then everyone on Honyn. And maybe everyone back on Earth if the dragons figured out that's where they came from. Or thought that's where the Ellorians were hiding. Andier. Eriana. Korrin.

Soliander.

Before he understood why, his hand reached into a pocket and pulled out a dagger, images of a spell he'd never seen before popping into his head. As if he'd cast it before, the words came to his mind and out his mouth, the hand with the blade held up, pointing toward the dragon that was hurtling at him. He saw her lungs expand. He saw the words on the page of a spell book. He saw what was supposed to happen when he finished the words. Matt searched around him for every source of energy to draw from. With the staff gone, that meant everything that lived. As if the staff had blinded him to other sources of power before, he suddenly saw and felt them all, trees, plants, insects, birds, mammals. With a rush of ecstasy mixed with fury, the power roared into him.

"Kuniali mu'unia a narosmor likaa a rarkimor kiapan. Mu'oste aatsum!" *Fly true this steel, as light as air, as fast as light, a fate you seal/steal!*

The dagger in his hand erupted into flames and leapt from his outstretched hand. Leaving a trail of fire behind it, the blade arced through the air at Nir'lion, who began spraying her own fire toward Matt. She turned to evade the flaming dagger, but it moved with her like a heat seeking missile, slamming into her chest and passing right through the golden scales. With a look of shock, surprise, and horror, Nir'lion stopped flapping her wings. The flames in her mouth drew back in as if she'd inhaled them. Matt began to topple backwards, his last sight an enormous golden dragon that appeared to be dead in the air slamming into the clearing with a thunderous crash and tumbling into the trees, where she burst into flames.

CHAPTER NINETEEN

FIRESTORM

Eric shielded himself and the unconscious Anna from the roaring flames as Nir'lion burned. He finally tore his eyes away to see Matt on his back. None of his friends were moving. He ran to the wizard, stopping above him in shock. Matt's hair had gone grey. Deep lines creased his face like he'd aged forty years. His breath came in ragged gasps. Thinking quickly, he knelt and looked at the wizard's Trinity Ring. It had one spell left. He knew that his and Ryan's were spent. Rather than healing Matt, he removed the item and ran to Anna, whom he used it on. Her eyes fluttered open and he quickly filled her in, noting that her protective spell must have shielded her quite a bit from the dragon's blow. She nodded and felt strong enough to stand. He helped over to Matt.

"Oh my God!" Anna said, kneeling and laying her hands on the wizard. "What happened to him?"

"You've got to do something," Eric urged her.

She closed her eyes. While Eric waited, he looked over at Ryan, the dragon, and then finally noticed several dead birds on the ground. The grass that hadn't long since been burnt by dragon fire had withered and died. So had all the trees near the clearing's edge. Everything nearby but them appeared to be dead. The mostly untrained wizard had drained the energy from everything, killing it all. What had kept him from drawing energy from them, too?

His gaze returned to Matt. The lines in the wizard's face disappeared as his features returned to normal and his eyes opened. Anna looked fatigued. Being a vessel of a god's power was not without its drawbacks.

"You're getting better at this," Eric remarked.

"It's getting easier to reach her each time."

Eric helped her up.

Matt sat up slowly, eyes on the nearby flaming dragon, then the knight. "What about Ryan? Is he okay?"

Eric extended a hand and helped him to his feet. "Time to find out."

They headed over and found the knight on his back, awake, and in tremendous pain.

"Can you tell us what's wrong?" Eric asked him.

"I'll be able to tell," said Anna, closing her eyes as she knelt beside him. It started sooner this time, Eric thought, but took longer, for Ryan had been more badly hurt. Several bones had been broken and the armor had to be loosened to prevent the dents from digging into him. Anna was so fatigued that she refused to get up. Knowing she needed rest, Eric suggested the others remain together while he went in search of Soliander's staff and Korrin's less important lance. It took more than an hour to retrieve them, and by then, Anna felt well enough to walk with assistance. They headed for the Dragon Gate, eager to put all of this behind them.

Matt couldn't help eyeing the dragon. The dagger spell wasn't supposed to include fire. It just should've sent the dagger at his target and followed any evasion until the blade pierced the heart. He had clearly overdone the drawing of power and nearly killed himself. If he ever had the chance to do magic again, he really needed to learn control. But he'd killed Nir'lion. He'd outsmarted her, too, much of that improvised battle plan being his. He'd never felt so formidable and proud, the memory of that power coursing through him and its utter destruction on someone trying kill him and his friends bringing a smile to his face.

Burn, bitch, burn.

With a final look at the scene, the champions left Soclarin, disappearing through the Dragon Gate to find the great hall of Castle Darlonon on Honyn empty, rain still pouring through the roof. Matt wasted no time putting the staff into the gate, having no idea how to close it for real, but then words formed in his mind as if he'd said them all before. His arm gestured before he understood what he was doing, the gate reacting like a finely tuned instrument. A rainbow of colors swirled across its surface, a ray of light shooting into the rainy sky. As if striking an invisible layer in the stratosphere, it burst into a ring that spread outward as if to encircle the planet.

For a few moments, nothing else happened and they stood exchanging glances at each other and back at the sky. Then the first dragon came into view, being pulled backward by an invisible force, its wings beating uselessly. It looked back then, the motion making it tumble over so that it now appeared to be flying forward, but all four legs and its wings showed signs of fighting the inevitable. With a roar of defiance, hatred, and anger, it hurtled down toward the gate and then disappeared with a whoosh and a puff, air buffeting the amazed champions. Eric suggested everyone but Matt step away in case a stray wing, claw, or tail managed to hit one of them. That's when Matt realized a shield protected him, so he felt safe, having a front row seat to the spectacle.

Dragon after dragon lost control as the gate wrested them from whatever act of destruction they were engaged in. Pulled across the sky, they shrieked in defiant outrage as they plummeted into the castle and through the Dragon Gate, a blur of silvers, reds, blues, and other colors. Matt lost count of how many as the numbers rose to the thousands, the champions their last sight as they were violently flung from Honyn once more. No sooner had the last of their kind gone through than the gate closed with a flash. The champions stood breathless, eyeing each other wordlessly until Matt pulled the staff free.

"Wow," said the wizard. "That was the most incredible thing I've ever seen." He turned away and saw the queen's collapsed tower through the ceiling's hole. The others followed his gaze as he added, "We'd better get up there."

"Let's get Lorian first," suggested Eric.

And so they did, finding an empty prison, the elf abandoned inside by mercenaries and cult members who'd already fled, no one wanting to face those who'd closed the Dragon Gate. They gave him the bag of soclarin ore for safe keeping and wasted no time climbing the queen's tower, giant cracks in it raising fears that worsened on seeing blocks of dislodged stone on the stairs. The fallen guard had disappeared, but the two unconscious guards remained at the top. Anna knelt beside each and with a quick prayer brought them awake, Ryan's sword point indicating they ought to flee down the steps as fast as their legs would allow. They quickly disappeared.

As Matt watched, Eric and Lorian clambered over the loose stone blocking the doorway, the outside wall of the tower in ruins, a gaping hole revealing the quieting storm outside and wind tearing at the walls. The fallen ceiling had buried almost everything but the adjacent room with the mirror. As Eric stepped into the opening there, a wooden table leg came straight at his head. He barely blocked it with his hand.

Queen Lorella, no longer invisible, gasped. "Oh! I thought you were..."

"I know," he replied, relaxing. "It's over. Let's get out of here."

"Gladly."

Lorian saw the portal the dragon had used to visit her captive. "An elven Mirror of Sulinae," he said in surprise, moving toward it. "Do you know where it leads?"

"Yes," answered Matt from the doorway, "to Castle Olliana somewhere."

"Good. Then let's use it." The elf stroked its edge and spoke magic words as the others joined them. It had never occurred to Matt that Lorian might know how to use it. In moments, the frame filled with an image of the queen's royal chambers, empty. The elf gestured for them to go through, Eric first, then Anna, the queen, and Ryan, all disappearing from Castle Darlonon in relief. Even as Matt left the ruin, the tower began to tremble ominously. Lorian shoved him through and leapt after as the tower collapsed in a shower of debris, taking the other mirror with it. This one shut off abruptly. A moment of silence followed before everyone realized they were safe.

—— ❖ · ❖ ——

The next day, Ryan felt a mixture of relief and regret that they were going home. For the most part, he was eager, but he'd finally had time to think about the reality of this quest, for the first time since arriving. Dragons. Elves. Magic. It was all real. It seemed almost strange to finally marvel now, but danger, fear, and the unknown had taken any potential fun or amusement right out of this whole thing. He'd heard himself sighing repeatedly since arriving back in Olliana, where they'd taken care of various issues, including a good bath, warm meal, and a little too much wine and mead, followed by a long sleep.

They reached an agreement with Sonneri and the queen on how to deal with Honyn's questions about why the dragons had appeared after the quest's apparent completion. The story was that the Ellorians needed to spring Nir'lion's trap on purpose as the only way to discover and rescue the queen, held prisoner in an unknown location with the dragon taking her place. Revealing this also helped Queen Lorella avoid explaining some questionable decisions Nir'lion had made while posing as her, even as she quickly reversed those orders. Since they couldn't admit the real Soliander opened the gate, they claimed Raith had done it without giving his name so that neither Cirion nor Nola would counter this. The pair hadn't been seen and couldn't be trusted to keep secrets either way. To prevent further trouble with the Dragon Gate, a protective force would guard what remained of Castle Darlonon indefinitely.

Most of Honyn had seen the dramatic display of dragons pulled across the sky, knowing what it meant, but few cheers had erupted due to the devastation. Months, even years of rebuilding and burying the dead lay ahead. This time no fanfare accompanied their quiet departure, everyone feeling it was inappropriate. It almost seemed like they'd failed Honyn and were skulking off in secret, their accomplishment diminished by destruction.

Now Matt stood in the throne room with the others, atop the dais, the Quest Ring around them beginning to light up with words of blue fire. They hadn't seen the ring since arriving and hadn't previously noticed the hole on one pillar, for the top of Soliander's staff, which would trigger the return spell if the quest was done. In the back of his mind, he prayed they were truly headed home, not to the home worlds of the four champions they'd replaced. It would be especially bad in Matt's case, arriving right into Soliander's grip. They hadn't spoken of it, but Eric had quietly told him not to speculate aloud about it so as not to worry the techie. If it happened, it happened, and there wouldn't be much they could do about it. There was only one way to tell what was going to happen.

Hoping for the best, Ryan let his thoughts turn to home. Were people looking for them? What should they say about their absence when asked? More importantly, what, if anything, had Soliander done to their friends and family while they'd remained here?

Moments later, the vortex of light and sound ended and the four friends stood in the dark countryside, a black sky above, a familiar moon to one side, and giant stone monoliths beside them. Stonehenge looked just like it had when they left and caused an audible sigh of relief from all of them, which made them start to laugh.

"We're home!" Ryan said, noticing that Eric was not only dressed as before, but holding the SUV's flashlight in his hands. It was on, too.

"Thank God," said Anna.

"It's cold," Matt observed.

Ryan nodded. The air seemed a bit too cool for what they wore – the same Earth clothes they'd been wearing several weeks earlier. "I don't think we're dressed for the weather anymore."

Eric remarked, "I guess the spell just returns you to how you were before the quest, not change your clothes to something appropriate like it does when you're summoned."

"I hope we're never summoned while naked," Matt joked. "That could be awkward on returning."

"Let's hope we're never summoned again," said Anna.

"I'm just glad to be back in my own clothes," remarked Ryan. He pulled out his iPhone but still had no signal. Checking in on Daniel, or giving him the good news that they were back, would have to wait.

"It's good we didn't return in those outfits we had on," said Matt. "That might've been hard to explain. I wish I had the spell books, though."

"Speaking of explanations," started Ryan, "we need to get our story straight."

"Can we get out of here first?" Anna asked, shivering. "I'm freezing."

Ryan gestured to where the SUV had been parked. It was gone. "Yeah, but how? We need to start walking, I guess."

"Then let's go," she replied, starting off and looking at the pendant in her hand, unable to put it on because the necklace clasp had broken. "I'll guess we'll never know if this pendant had anything to do with the quest. Matt, maybe you can look at the words within it to see what they say."

He agreed to do it once they had a chance. They compared suggestions on a story about their disappearance as they walked, from alien abduction to getting lost in the countryside, but each invited more questions and lies they all had to keep straight. It wasn't going to work and they knew it.

Finally Eric suggested, "Maybe we should just say we don't know. We came back for the necklace, found it, and when we turned back to the SUV, it was gone. We didn't hear it leave and just don't know what happened. We still had the keys." He looked at Ryan. "You still have them?"

The big man felt in his pockets and pulled them out. "Yes."

"Okay," Eric continued, "so we started walking back, hitched a ride or whatever, and only when we got to your aunt's house and your aunt freaked out did we know something was wrong, besides the SUV being stolen, I mean. That's when we heard we'd been gone however many days it turns out to be. I think I lost track."

"That might be a good idea," Ryan conceded. "It keeps us from getting into a bunch of lies."

Matt agreed but added, "The only problem is people will want some sort of answer."

Anna offered, "We can just say, 'so do we'."

Eric nodded. "The best lie is a simple one."

After a few minutes, Ryan stopped. In the excitement of returning he'd forgotten something. "Anna, let's see if you can heal me here."

The others stopped, exchanging a dubious look. Before they could talk him out of it, Ryan used his keys to scratch a cut into his palm. It wasn't much, but it would have to do. Grimacing, he held it out to her as she sighed.

"This really could have waited for a better time. Don't get your hopes up," she reminded him.

"C'mon," he replied, "think positively. You have to believe in it. You've done it before. You can do it."

She sighed and he suspected she wasn't really into it. Did he have to be dying before she tried? Apparently not, for she took his hand in hers and closed her eyes. She appeared to be making an effort, but nothing was happening. She opened her eyes.

"I'm sorry, Ryan," she said. "It's not working. I don't know why."

"Try again!"

"I did. I don't know what's the matter. Maybe none of that works here for some reason." Seeing him about to protest, she added, "Look, you know I would love to heal Daniel as much as you. You believe that, don't you?"

He opened his mouth to urge her to try again, but then stopped himself. "Yes, I do, but–"

"No buts," she replied. "It isn't working. Maybe it will work some other time, but not today. Okay? Can we just leave it at that?"

He sighed heavily. It couldn't have all been for nothing. There was no way God would do that to him. To Daniel. He'd try again with her later and see what could be done, but he couldn't just give up. Maybe they could somehow take Daniel with them on another quest, if it came to that, and she could heal him there. Surely that would work and if he came back with them, he wouldn't return to being injured. That would just be cruel.

As they continued, Eric kept the flashlight shining, hoping a car would soon stop for them, and one finally did. The friendly driver asked too many questions about what they were doing out in the middle of nowhere, and Anna, seated in the front, did her best to fend them off. She spied a newspaper folded up between seats and read the date aloud. Two weeks had passed. Desperate to get away from the questions, she asked for the nearest place to catch a taxi and they soon had a quieter ride, suspecting the questions would get a lot worse, and they were right.

*   *   *

A covered lanai was the ideal place to wait out an afternoon thunderstorm, and warming her bones was another reason Erin Jennings had moved to Florida. Once one past a certain age, such things made the hours easier. She chuckled to herself. She hadn't aged all *that* much since learning to call this world home, even though it sometimes felt like it inside. She had other ways to make the signs of time's passage vanish, but there was a limit on how much she could do before people started talking, and so here she was.

She put her legs up on the recliner and watched the rain fall over her screened-in pool, sipping a favorite zinfandel, for wine was one of the few things of her youth available here, everything else having been modernized into oblivion. The ornate wine glass was etched with an armored knight atop a charging steed, a sight that reminded her of a friend long lost. She hadn't seen him in many years and didn't know his whereabouts despite many fruitless searches. These days it seemed everyone could learn anything about anyone, thanks in large part to the internet, but try as one might, some people simply never surfaced. She didn't know if she'd recognize him anyway, for nearly twenty years had passed since they and two other friends had last been together.

They might not recognize her, either, especially with a different name and a new life as a banker's wife. Despite starting over, she was a student of history and spent time researching medieval times, becoming something of an expert, albeit unknown. She was a private person and chose not to advertise her scholarly findings lest it attract attention, but had anyone known the truth, she'd have been known as one of the foremost scholars on the period. At times she wondered if she should come forward, for that might draw forth these old friends if they were still around, but it would also raise scrutiny. She hadn't covered her own tracks as much as she probably should.

With her mind so much in the past, she often missed the news and so hadn't heard anything about the four friends who'd disappeared from Stonehenge. It wasn't until just now that she caught the early afternoon telecast of the frantic rush to bring the story to the world. She frowned at that, as always, not pleased with the speed of modern living. They knew nothing of a quiet day without television. She was tempted to turn it off until a pretty young woman appeared onscreen, talking about their reasons for visiting the monoliths. Around her neck hung a pendant she kept playing with, drawing the eye as the camera zoomed in on it.

"By the gods," Erin whispered, staring at the recognized stone, her wine glass slipping unnoticed to shatter on the lanai, the wine draining away like a rivulet of blood. Her face grew paler as the girl spoke of visiting the monument, vanishing for weeks, then returning as if nothing happened. She professed to have no recollection of the missing time, but Erin had been reading people in tough situations far longer than this pretty girl had and she knew a lie when she heard it. The spark of untold adventure in the girl's eyes said it all and Erin rose from her chair with a light in her own.

"What have they done?"

⬤ ◆ ◆ ⬤

A week after the firestorm started, it quieted to a dull roar as the media moved on to other stories and the flow of interviews trickled off, but all was not well with their lives. On the surface, little had changed for Ryan, whose parents had displayed more affection for him in a few days than in his whole life before that. In theory that was good, but the departure from their regular indifference and established lack of attention made him uncomfortable and didn't seem to be letting up. In fact, it got worse, as they wanted to know his every move and even suggested assigning a 24/7 bodyguard. Their monitoring of where he drove the GPS-equipped car made him disable that and the tracking app on his phone. He was starting to feel like a prisoner in his own life and didn't know what to do. When Daniel remarked on how annoying such hovering can be, the big guy finally understood his brother's need for space.

Their reunion had been the happiest moment of his life, and seeing that Daniel had survived without him the greatest relief. While he'd come to grips with the violence he'd experienced on Honyn, the first sight of Daniel had made him flush with renewed guilt he couldn't explain. He had to lie about his whereabouts to the one person who most deserved the truth, and since Ryan had never lied to Daniel before, he wasn't good at it. His brother didn't believe him, some awkward moments following. His friends watched with more understanding than ever and Ryan was glad he'd told them the truth about the accident.

Ryan's initial call to Daniel had led to his parents knowing of their return and soon, the world did, too, via a press conference they arranged. Amidst police reports and interviews, they'd finally flown home to meet their relieved families and friends. The question dodging had become painful, but the four friends stuck together, their ordeal creating a bond.

Things hadn't turned out quite so well for the others. All of Eric's martial arts students had moved on to another teacher in his absence, and the guy who had first been a temporary replacement during his "vacation" had taken his job. The owner, Kim Jung, was less than kind, asserting that Eric had abandoned his position and students and wasn't welcome back. The students and even his replacement were more forgiving and understanding, but ultimately it didn't matter. He had lost his job, a fact that made headlines. The backlash on Jung worsened after he stupidly aired his opinion on camera. Many of the school's roster went elsewhere, a move that both pleased and embarrassed Eric, who wasn't used to such shows of loyalty. He received a dozen offers from other schools, and many of his former student's parents withdrew their children to follow Eric to his new job.

Matt took a few days off and then reported to work as usual, though he got little done the first week with geek coworkers jokingly asking what being abducted by aliens felt like, or similar half-baked theories. Being at work dealing with irritating tech problems felt wildly uninspiring and he increasingly longed for more in his life. Not an hour passed without dreams of the power that was once his. He could be a different man with it, and life just wasn't the same without that energy coursing through him, like his black-and-white life had been infused with color only to cast him back to greyness. He'd tried to perform magic here without success despite his clear memory of the spells, which he'd written down in his own book. He hadn't yet been hypnotized to see what of Soliander's memories he retained and wasn't sure if it would matter now anyway. Besides, he'd need someone he trusted to do that.

Perhaps the biggest change had been for Anna, whose position at the hospital had been filled by necessity, though a similar one had become available. Jack Riley had never packed her things despite her father's request, but she learned of the intent anyway and was quite upset with being written off so quickly. Her father's lukewarm response to her return, not even offering her a hug, had surprised her. A few pointed questions later had revealed he'd investigated collecting her life insurance policy, too, and now she wasn't speaking to him, to her mother's consternation. She was starting to feel lost, her world so different from before. When she saw a patient near death or in agony that no medicine could alleviate, she wanted to reach out and heal them, but it was impossible. *God doesn't exist here. He isn't real*, she told herself, but the same assertion lacked the strength it once had, though her failures to reach Him had kept her atheism intact. She didn't want to think about any of it but it was always in the back of her mind now, her job a constant reminder. She felt relieved when the next weekend came.

The four friends gathered in Anna's condo Saturday night, enjoying some quiet and privacy. They hadn't been alone for long since their return, but they'd invited Jack to let him in on the truth. They had discussed the idea at length, the deciding factor being that someone needed to look after their interests if they were summoned again and he was the only one they could trust. The threat of Soliander's appearance was another reason to tell someone. If he showed up while they were on a quest, they wanted at least someone to be aware of who and what he was.

Now Jack sat quietly, trying to digest what they'd told him. He had laughed at the start, assuming it a joke, but the more details they'd revealed, the less funny it had become. Efforts to ask a question they couldn't answer had proven fruitless. The details were sobering in their complexity, and he'd tried catching them in lies to no avail. It had become clear that the level of planning needed for them to get all their stories straight, if they were lying, would have been a flattering amount of time to waste just to play a trick on him, and he had never known them to possess such imaginations as this.

But the pendant was the thing that got him. They'd acquired a loupe and taken turns looking at the words inside, but only Matt could understand them. They were indeed in the language of magic and read:

Within the jewel magic resides
Creatures, too, and all abide
To keep Earth safe from she who lies
The prison here keeps hope alive
The henge of stone shall set them free
Good and evil, equal be
Undo what's done and come what may
Risk the price all life could pay

They'd discussed this privately and now let Jack see for himself, and though he couldn't verify what it said, he'd never seen script like it and thought it would've been going awfully far to get that inscribed in there just to fool him.

And there was no escaping the reality that they'd disappeared and returned weeks later

As for the pendant, no one knew who "she who lies" was but they assumed that bringing the pendant to Stonehenge had set something unpredictable in motion. This had been one reason to tell someone the truth, for if anything odd began happening on Earth, like dragons appearing over Manhattan, they wanted someone besides them to know. It was possible they'd be off-world on another quest. They wanted Jack to be their eyes and ears while they were gone.

"So you haven't seen any sign of this Soliander on Earth?" Jack asked, focusing on what they wanted, though he didn't know what he could do against such a wizard if one appeared.

Ryan shook his head, his hand diving into a bag of Chex Mix. "No, thank God. We all asked our families if anyone strange had been hanging out around the houses or neighborhood, but they said only reporters."

"What do you think he might do if he shows up?" Jack asked.

They exchanged a look before Eric stopped himself from swiveling back and forth in an office chair. "Go after Matt, first, unless he tries to be sneakier by going after a less obvious target, for bait or something."

"What can you do to protect yourselves from this guy?" Jack asked, shaking his head.

"Move," suggested Matt, looking up from the laptop before him on the table. "I've already been looking into apartments. There's no sense in any of us staying where we are except maybe Anna, since you can't sell your condo as easily."

"That's actually not a bad idea," admitted Eric, "especially for you and me. We should get an apartment together."

"Absolutely," the techie agreed. "I don't want to be alone when he shows up."

"When?" Jack asked. "Not if?"

Matt shook his head. "I think it's only a matter of time."

Ryan said, "Maybe I can join you. My parents are driving me nuts. The only drawback is leaving Daniel, but my presence might bring Soliander to our doorstep and that's certainly worse. I can't let that wizard get to Daniel."

"Even better," said Matt.

Looking at Anna, Ryan added, "I don't think we should leave Anna alone, though."

Anna nodded, sipping a glass of zinfandel. "I agree, though I'm not sure I want to share an apartment with three guys, especially you three."

Eric replied, "You already shared space with us in far less modest circumstances."

"True," she admitted, playing with her pendant.

"Ryan," Jack started, "if the apartment is registered in your name, people may be able to find you. Maybe you should do it in mine."

Eric perked up. "Great idea. I knew it was smart to tell you. None of us should do a forwarding address for mail, either."

As talk turned to arranging such details, Jack took the opportunity to get another beer and excused himself for the kitchen. His head spun with crazy thoughts and he needed a moment alone to get a grip. They had never lied to him before but all of this suggested the world was a far different place than he knew. He wouldn't truly accept any of it unless he witnessed something with his own eyes. In the fridge sat the remains of a welcome back cake, and he dipped a finger in the icing before grabbing a drink and shutting the door. As he licked off his finger, a bright flash came from the room behind him, followed by a glass breaking, and sudden silence. He popped the beer can open and started back, saying, "Did a light burn out or...something." He stopped in the doorway, staring.

Matt's laptop still lay open and unlocked, when the techie was paranoid about not signing out if he stepped away. Anna's wineglass had broken on the floor, red wine spilling across it. Ryan's bag of Chex-mix had fallen over on the couch. And the office chair Eric had been sitting in was slowly spinning, empty.

They were gone.

———◆·◆———

Continue the adventure in *The Light Bringer (The Dragon Gate Series, #2)* at https://amzn.to/3dAmdAE or use the QR code below:

The Ever Fiend
Talon Stormbringer 1

ACKNOWLEDGEMENTS

Special thanks to Jean Hall, Clayton Clement, and
Christopher Candice for their input

Edited by Niyati Joshi and JJ Henke

Maps by Randy Ellefson

Cover design by Miblart

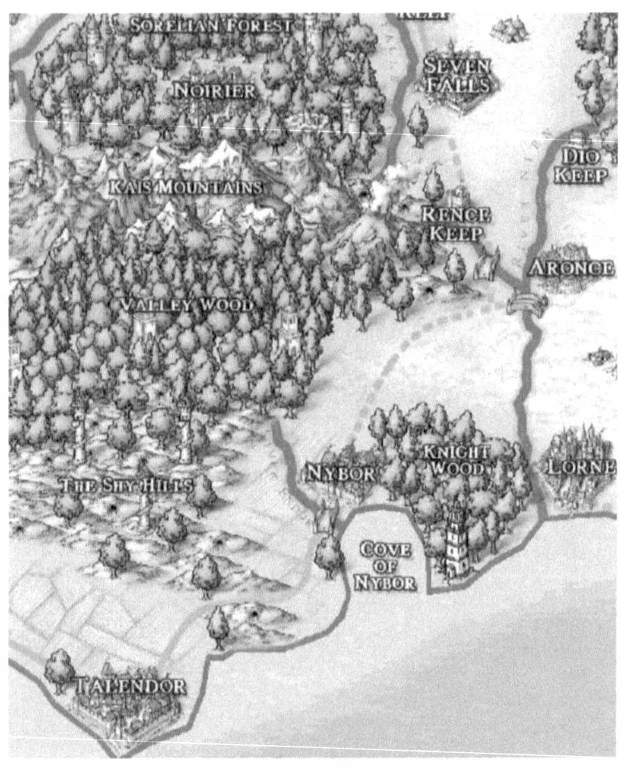

Partial Map of the Kingdom of Illiandor, continent Antaria,
on the world of Llurien
http://www.llurien.com/continents/antaria/

CHAPTER ONE

THE WHITE TOWER

While most in Talendor slumbered, Talon Storm-bringer crept through a hallway dark with moving shadows, his human ears and eyes alert. He'd already slipped undetected past a jhaikan and a mynx, undeterred by their ferocity and taste for man-flesh. Even the dozen sleeping riven in the courtyard hadn't given him pause, though fully armored knights would have turned away. The little monsters were infamous for stirring at the slightest sound, waking to become a whirling dervish of steel. Talon had been known to unleash the same from the sword gripped in one hand.

Now he heard nothing, not even his own passage, the supple black leather pants and tunic he wore never squeaking as he crept toward the doorway and his prize. The gold figurine of a great bird of prey, said to be magical and worth a fortune, awaited. Stories in taverns had piqued his interest but had also warned him of the dangers. The greatest of those was the wizard whose white tower he now prowled. Some said Viland Shadowbreaker enjoyed unsavory habits when few were looking, his public persona of benevolent charm masking a dark truth.

Talon reached the open doorway at the hall's end and peered in. Four torches cast their light along the walls. He shook his head at the obvious trap. No one would light so many torches for a room that held nothing but a pedestal, upon which sat the figurine, light glinting off its golden curves. A room without a lock much less a door could ensnare only a fool. And each of the earlier dangers he'd passed had offered an easy way around for a skilled thief like himself. The question was why Viland wanted to capture someone. Talon didn't intend to find out.

He sheathed his sword, then slipped a light rope from his waist, fashioning a loop on one end. Lassoing wasn't a skill he had spent much time mastering, but at the fourth attempt he managed to get it around the statue. A gentle tug, and the loop tightened. With a quick jerk he brought the figurine flying through the air to him. He deftly caught it and deposited it into a cloth sack. He hefted his sword, and with a smirk, turned back the way he had come.

"Astiana mer," said the silky, sophisticated voice behind him.

Talon froze more at the magic words than at the realization that a man was there. He tried to turn again but found that he could not. For all his strength, he could neither move his arms nor the powerful muscles of his legs. Like a statue he stood, imposing in his might, steel-gray eyes smoldering with indignation. The breeze from a nearby open window did not stir the golden hair around his broad shoulders, even though he felt the wind on his face and heard it crackle the torches that sent his shadow down the hall. Joining that shadow were two others—one tall, one short—as quiet footsteps approached from behind.

"Don't worry," said the man. "It's temporary. And you can still talk." When Talon didn't speak, the wizard sighed and said, "Mer astiana."

Suddenly freed, Talon squeezed his sword, flexed his limbs, and weighed some options. Quick as he was, his blade would never reach the wizard before another spell stopped him, for no sword could fly faster than words. And while the taller shadow was likely the wizard, he had no idea to whom or what the other shadow belonged. He had to know before launching an attack. Besides, he could hardly assess foes with his back to them. He slowly turned around, scowling.

A black-robed, balding man stood beside the empty pedestal, a reassuring smile on his swarthy face. Perhaps he was a Marulan from across the Antaran Sea. But Marulans were thought to be mostly savages, their skins as black as their deeds, and not wizards with an air of sophistication and opulence. The man did not have an accent that Talon could hear. The long face, nose, and limbs matched what Talon had heard from stories. The dark eyes of Viland Shadowbreaker observed him coolly.

Beside Viland stood a karelia, all four and a half feet of him covered in dusky black plate armor, the sigil of a flaming sword emblazoned on his chest. Black hair swept back into a tight ponytail and pointed ears accentuated the impression of efficient speed, which drew Talon's eyes to the sheathed, curved sword at the karelia's hip. For a pleasant species, he seemed uncommonly sinister, the delicate features at odds with the cocky menace upon them. The translucent lorenia lines, which all karelia were born with, streaked across his cheeks as if fleeing the blue eyes toward his jugular. That the lines faintly glowed blue told Talon that something supernatural was still at play here, or he would have been unable to see the lines from five paces.

"You are brave to release your hold on me," Talon said, testing Viland's grasp of the situation.

"No games, warrior. You were smart enough to use that lasso, and you're smart enough to know I can kill you long before you reach me."

No kerr shit, thought Talon approvingly. He had little patience for fools. "So what now?"

"You've passed my test and—"

"How is being caught a success?"

"That figurine is only a lure to test the bravery of the ambitious. Few will attempt the perils to reach it."

The swordsman shrugged. "Your dangers weren't that dangerous."

"I don't need heroes, just uncommon men. You'll do nicely."

Talon's eyes narrowed in annoyance. He didn't care for being someone's pawn. That he had fallen into a trap, despite knowing it existed, also grated on his nerves. "For what?"

Viland raised a hand, palm outward. "In a moment. I am no threat to you. I give you my word that, if you refuse my offer, I will blank your memory of this night and drop you on a ship bound for Llorus, rather than kill you."

"Sounds like a lot of trouble."

"It's less trouble dragging your living body from my home than your dead one. I would rather avoid attention. Besides, I am not a murderer. And I assume you'd prefer not being killed or seeing a Solon Judge after your theft. Now, if you'll accept my offer?"

"Let's hear it."

From his pocket, the wizard pulled a small vial of brightly glowing, silver liquid that cast dancing shadows around the room. "This is silver elixir, one of the most potent elements on Llurien. I need more. You will get it for me."

Talon suspected the dangers of doing so were far worse than losing his memory, but he'd never heard of the stuff and wasn't sure he wanted to know what people did with it. "From where?"

"The Ever Pathways."

Talon snorted. "They don't exist. I may be young but I don't believe in children's tales."

"Yes, you are young. Eighteen winters?"

"Not even that." Even years earlier, his size and bearing had often inspired assumptions that he was a man already. If that meant making his own way and being no stranger to the finer delights of women, he qualified.

"Maybe that accounts for your bravery. You'll have need of it. I assure you, Everland is real."

"And so is the Ever Fiend?" Talon laughed. "I conquered my fear of him at three."

Now the karelia spoke with condescension that was clear despite the almost child-like pitch of his voice. "Your fear will return if you catch sight of him."

Seeing that Talon was unimpressed, and unconvinced, the wizard said, "Being prepared means knowing the truth. Lies and illusion raise your risk of failure. I don't want more damned souls wandering the Ever Pathways. They're an obstacle to my designs."

He spoke words of magic and stretched out one hand toward Talon as if to grasp his forehead from afar. Talon took one step back before the room disappeared and his mind's eye filled with visions. A dark landscape with stormy clouds and eerie light. A black tower precariously perched beside the crumbling edge of an enormous crevasse, mist rising from its depths. Stunted trees with bone white trunks beside a pool of shining liquid. Shadowy figures furtively moving just out of sight. And a robed, hooded figure that suddenly appeared between them, sending them fleeing with shrieks of terror.

The visions stopped and Talon realized he'd raised his sword. The karelia's lorenia lines glowed brighter than before but faded as he watched. Talon lowered the blade and asked, "How do I know that these visions are not an illusion?"

Viland replied, "Once you enter the paths, you will see."

Realizing he would get no further, Talon asked, "And what do I get out of this, aside from keeping my memories?" Nothing of great importance had happened recently so that he was desperate to recall it, but allowing a wizard to tamper with his mind didn't sit well with him. That Viland had already done so without his permission strengthened Talon's resolve to prevent it from happening again.

"Anything you find on the Everway is yours to keep," said Viland, watching Talon's eyes drop to the vial, "but you may not take some of the elixir for yourself."

"What's to stop me?"

"It can only be contained in vials made from Ever Sand, and you will return the ones I give you. And then there's my sorelia." He nodded at the karelia beside him and any trace of amusement fell from Talon's face.

The sorelian race, though physically identical to the karelian species to which it belongs, is malevolent whereas the karelia are benevolent. Sorelia use the supernatural skills granted by the gods for dark purposes. They keep to themselves apart from the rest of Llurien, holed up in the Sorelian Forest not too far north of Talendor. Talon had never seen a sorelia before, at least that he knew of. Perhaps the sneer should've made him realize.

That Viland had a sorelia working with him suggested that the stories of his nefarious living were true. Sending a sorelia into the Ever Pathways could only bring evil on the world. Maybe Talon needed to ensure that this mission failed and that he escaped with his life. There was no telling what this wizard would do with the silver elixir once he had it. Having his memory wiped now almost seemed like the better alternative than getting involved with this, but then Viland would just get another man for the job. Talon didn't want someone with far fewer scruples than himself helping these two. He might've been a thief of late, but he only stole from those who could afford to lose what he took. That reminded him of something.

"You want me to risk my life," Talon began, "for the chance to find discarded baubles on the Pathways?"

"A bauble here is a prize there," Viland answered smoothly. "Anything magical left inside for too long becomes enhanced, and even ordinary items can become special."

Talon's eyes narrowed. "The place is chaos, the rumors say, as is everything from there."

The sorelia grinned without humor. "He is smarter than he looks," he said. "Indeed, warrior, Everland is chaos. Do not put on any armor or clothing found inside or you might never remove it. Weapons, however, are often advantageous, albeit hard to predict. Still, the danger is to the one struck, not to the wielder."

"I don't need the help."

"Suit yourself. He's Nyborian," the sorelia remarked to Viland, referring to Talon's hometown a week's ride northeast. "The accent is subtle, but I hear the influence of the wagon peoples of Lorne to the east."

Talon pursed his lips. He didn't like anyone knowing too much about him, though little could come of that. The wizard seemed to feel the same way, having shrugged indifferently until he noticed the claw on a leather cord around Talon's neck. Then he perked up and remarked in surprise, "Talon Stormbringer. I should've recognized you sooner. I'm delighted. Your reputation precedes you."

"As does yours, Viland Shadowbreaker."

Talon had hoped to keep his name to himself while in Talendor, a city that was twin to the kingdom's capital,

Illiandor, across the bay. Beyond that lay Nybor, where he'd lived with his parents until a jhaikan killed them; Talon had killed the beast and taken a claw to remember them by, then fled the memories. Someone had since seen the claw around his neck and called him Talon. The name had stuck, but he should've dropped the surname. Too late now. He had no family left in Nybor, and the brotherhood of knights to which his father had belonged didn't need to know about the dishonor he had brought upon his father by stealing for a living. Hopefully they'd never find out.

He asked the wizard, "If you need someone brave, why not send your pet jhaikan from the courtyard?"

"It's not real, for one," Viland replied, "but the Ever Fiend has a special hatred for jhaikan and that would invite trouble."

"As if this whole mission doesn't."

The legendary Ever Pathways could transport people from one place on Llurien to another in days instead of weeks, but few travelers made it out alive, and those who did had often gone insane. The karelia had eventually invented the Moon Gates to use the Ever Pathways at such speeds that one could traverse Llurien in an instant and bypass the dangers, but some still used Everland and the Ever Gates, such as the wizard standing before Talon now, black eyes glittering with forbidden knowledge.

Viland smiled. "The riven were also an illusion, but the mynx was not and will accompany you."

Talon raised an eyebrow, unsure the large feline could handle the terrors of Everland. "Battle trained?"

"Yes. Few animals have the courage to enter the pathways, but this one is unique. Noren here is his master." Viland nodded at the sorelia, who smirked.

Taking an animal, however tested, into a land of chaos didn't seem smart, but he had killed a rabid jaegar once and didn't doubt he could do the same to this mynx if it got out of control.

"You accept?" Viland asked, eyes gleaming.

Talon sighed. "When do we leave?"

EVERLAND

An hour later, Talon stood in the wide courtyard, the limestone wall he had climbed earlier surrounding him. Beyond that stood the few towers and homes tall enough to look down on him, though he couldn't see them anymore. To keep prying eyes away, the wizard had summoned a thick mist that hung above their heads, a breeze from the nearby Antaran Sea tugging at it. The cover wouldn't last long. On the stones around them were a wagon, empty crates, bulging sacks, and whatever mundane items Viland needed to run his home.

A stand of Siaran oaks and white Talana trees filled one corner, leaves trembling. Viland had assured him that the entrance to the Ever Pathways stood hidden behind them, invisible until it was opened. Only a spell could reveal the presence of a closed entrance. Karelia, who saw all manner of things few others could or would want to see, could even see one without trying to.

The sorelia, Noren, stood dressed as before, seemingly unmindful of the enormous sable mynx lying at his diminutive feet. Dark green patches dotted the cat's fur, visible only where it wasn't covered by plate armor on its back and sides. The half-green, half-black face, with a straight line down the center, made the maneless feline look distinctive. So did its unusual size—nearly as big as a horse—that indicated it was a male. Talon knew he would have to mind his tongue around the cat, for once bonded to a master, a mynx was fiercely loyal. If Talon spoke rudely to Noren, the sorelia wouldn't have to issue a command for the mynx to kill Talon; the mynx might do it on its own. And if Noren died in there, the cat could become trouble.

The others accompanying them were less impressive. One seemed to be an ordinary swordsman save for the cockiness in his stance and eyes, as if he wanted to dare Talon to swordplay but had thought better of it for the latter's size. Beside him and looking regal in gray plate mail stood a knight whose dour expression suggested little interest in this affair. His haunted eyes lingered instead on a dark-haired woman, who wore black leather and two short swords at her hips. She stood with more confidence than the knight or the swordsman. Surpassing them all in nonchalance was a male kryll, a species known for their mastery of physical combat, whether by hand or with weapons. He lounged catlike against the wall, a jhaikan-staff resting in the crook of his arm. Six of them, plus the cat, would enter Everland.

Talon knew nothing about them except that none were Ever Walkers–a group of individuals who voluntarily walked the Ever Pathways to seek fortune. He'd asked Viland about this only to be informed that Ever Walkers had been banned in the Kingdom of Illiandor and were hard to come by as a result. Besides, the wizard preferred not relying on people with an allegiance to someone other than himself, even if the Ever Walkers were more qualified for the risks involved. Not for the first time, Talon wondered what had happened to the man he was likely replacing, for he sensed this wasn't their first foray into Everland.

"How do we get to this silver elixir?" he asked Viland, who handed him a sash to wear from one shoulder to the opposite hip. It held six black vials, each corked but empty and with small handles.

"Noren will find the Poison Pond," the wizard answered, "where the waters are the elixir. He has been there before. You are to follow his lead."

"Poison Pond?"

Viland smiled without humor. "No one knows if it's truly poison, but riven were found floating in it once and it was assumed they'd died from drinking the enchanted waters. I suspect they merely drowned."

"Riven can't swim," Talon remarked. The diminutive species was too lazy to learn much of anything. With bodies consumed by one disease or another, it was entirely possible that their decaying flesh had poisoned the waters.

"Indeed. The question then is why would they enter the pool? The Ever Fiend is believed to sip from it and might have approached, frightening them into fleeing straight into it. We'll never know, but don't let the water touch you. Strange things have happened to flesh when contacted. Use the handles on the vials." Seeing Talon looking dubious, he added, "Now you know why I need someone brave."

"Or foolish."

"Or that."

Talon noticed Noren smirking, while the swordsman sneered, the knight looked nauseated, and the woman grinned. The kryll yawned. Talon only trusted him and the knight, if anyone. And maybe the cat.

Viland strode around the grove's edge while the others trailed along, stopping between the trees and the wall. As they watched, the wizard stretched out both hands and spoke in tones that Talon recognized. The trees began to lean sideways as a whorl of darkness filled the space between them; birds squawked furiously as they fled into the night sky. The mynx growled low in its throat and Noren said nothing to calm it, the lorenia lines on his face glowing bright blue at the magic afoot. Light seemed to disappear into the haphazardly shaped opening, as if the chaos beyond it hungered for the life out here. The Ever Gate looked nothing like a doorway, and its edges continued to ebb and flow as it became more substantial. Viland stopped speaking and dropped both arms to his sides.

"Quickly now," he said, gesturing toward it as the others began shuffling forward.

Talon cocked an eyebrow, realizing that he was ignorant of things that hadn't even occurred to him yet. "If you aren't coming with us, how do we open it to return?"

"A spell is only needed to open it from outside. The challenge of escaping is finding the door again. Noren will do that. Only karelia can find their way."

Talon gripped his sword harder, not caring for relying on a sorelia's sense of direction. All karelia are excellent navigators, thanks to the goddess of intuition who had been one of their creators. But sorelia are a corrupted version of the karelian species and there is no telling how they differ. Besides, the Ever Pathways distorted everything that went into them. "What about the cat? Does it know the way back?"

Noren smirked at him for the implication that he wouldn't survive, the blue lorenia glow reflecting in his unfriendly eyes. The sorelia turned to the Ever Gate and gazed intently as if he could see something in the blackness beyond it that the others could not. Without a word, he stepped into it with the mynx. Against his better judgment, Talon followed. As if reacting to some energy he couldn't see, the blond hair on his arms rose as he passed through, a brief wave of severe cold rushed over him, and an acrid smell accompanied a wave of nausea. His vision went black for an instant, but that only spurred him forward, his feet coming to rest on firm turf. He paused to look around, the others joining and moving past him as if already familiar with the experience.

The Ever Gate, still open, appeared more like a doorway from this side, roughly rectangular, an edge of shimmering blackness surrounding a window of lighter darkness. Around it and in every direction lay a landscape not unlike Llurien itself, save that a twilight without end seemed to permeate the air. Mustiness filled his nostrils. Turbulent, dark clouds swirled overhead. Stands of unfamiliar trees randomly grew atop rolling hills and flat land alike, a thick forest standing some miles to one side, with steep mountain peaks farther beyond. Nearer trees blocked other views.

Noren and the mynx advanced in parallel toward the mountains with purpose. The lorenia lines on the sorelia's face were dimmer now, which surprised Talon, for he thought this land was so magical that the karelia's senses would've been almost overloaded here.

Talon's gaze fell on the young knight, whose chest plate bore the symbol of his rank—a sword crossed with a shield. He was a Knight of the Sword, the first rank out of training. That the shield icon had a halo around it surprised Talon, for while all knighthood rank symbols included the shield, if it was depicted glowing, that meant he had already earned the prestigious Knight of Coiryn honor for bravery. And yet he scanned their surroundings with troubled, fearful eyes. Talon glanced about once more only to discover that the Ever Gate had seemingly vanished. The mountains now ran behind them, too.

Seeing his startled reaction, the knight remarked, "It is of no use. *We* were lost within twenty paces. Only the sorelia can lead us out. Protect him with your life, for your soul depends on it."

Talon nodded. What good were the senses if one could not trust them? Was it only his eyes that deceived him, or would his ears, too? The worst aspect of the disorientation was that he felt certain he was not, in fact, disoriented. He asked, "Why is a Knight of Coiryn working for a wizard?"

The knight frowned, scratching at two days of black stubble. "I must repay a debt, and no other reason. The name is Dal."

"Talon. A debt for what?"

"My own affair."

"Fair enough. You've been here before?"

"Once."

"And how many times until your debt is paid?"

"I do not know."

Talon stifled a grunt. No man should enter into a bargain without knowing the terms. "The knighthood doesn't know, I assume."

Dal glanced suspiciously at him but then relaxed. "It'd be my head or my honor."

"One as good as the other," commented Talon, though he didn't agree. But he knew knights believed that and wanted at least one person on his side while in this place. The knight gave him an appraising look. Talon asked, "What does Viland do with this silver elixir?"

"That I do not know, nor do I wish to."

"What if he's doing something the knighthood would disapprove of?"

The knight smirked. "Now you know why I don't ask."

Talon stifled a frown. "Ignorance won't save you from a Solon Judge's sentence should the truth be awful."

Dal sighed. "I know, but I have no choice in the matter and would rather not know. Sleep is hard to come by as it is."

Talon wondered what kept the man awake at night. Was it his conscience? He knew better than to ask personal details and instead inquired, "What can you tell me about this place?"

"Be on your guard. And there is no shame in running from that which cannot be predicted, in behavior or otherwise." Despite his words, an expression of great bitterness swept over Dal's rugged features.

Talon suspected that this admission of fleeing bothered him. "Have you fought anything here?"

"No."

"Run from anything?"

This time a spark of anger lit Dal's eyes and he appeared to choose his words carefully. "A Knight of Coiryn does not run from anything lightly, you can be sure of that."

"I am. What did you run from?"

"Pray to Coiryn you don't find out."

Sensing an end to their talk, Talon wondered if the god of courage, or any of the other gods, held dominion in this place. Had they created it along with Llurien? It seemed likely, as his world and Everland were connected, but for what purpose? Maybe the gods used it to travel, but from what Talon knew, they could appear anywhere in an instant, so why would they need the paths?

Maybe the City of the Gods lay here. That would explain why getting lost was so easy, for it was said that the gods didn't want visitors; if they wanted you, they'd appear before you. Or you'd suddenly appear before *them*.

Seeing the woman admiring him from the corner of her dark, mysterious eyes, Talon moved closer. "Why are you here?"

"Enchanting my blades," she said, gripping the twin swords in their scabbards. Her curious gaze held his without flinching and he decided he liked her.

"Cold steel is all you need."

Talon's mother had been a valend wizard—one who creates magic items for a living—but his knight father had instilled in him the value of not relying on anything but skill to win the day. This swordswoman cut a fine figure in the black leather. Many a man had likely been nicked by one of her blades for an improper advance, but he felt undeterred.

She replied, "An advantage gained is an advantage earned."

He nodded. "How will you do it?"

"Dip them in the Poison Pond. The silver elixir will give them powers."

"Powers you can't control," he observed. "Chaos Blades, they're called in the stories. It is foolish."

She laughed, the sound taking an eerie tone in this disturbed land, and her mirth quickly vanished on hearing it. "It will be foolish for anyone to cross blades with me again! The chaos will be theirs to fear, not mine."

"So you hope."

"And what of you?" the woman asked, eyeing his muscled physique so intently that the other swordsman, who'd been observing them, scowled darkly. "Are you just a thief, or is there more to you?"

He smiled. "When I unsheathe my sword, you'll have your answer."

"Jenar Darkfire isn't the only one who wishes to know this," observed the kryll, falling in beside them, his smooth gait at once suggestive of relaxed ease and great might, as if the latter caused the former. Like many kryll, he gave the impression of being unconcerned by the prospect of danger—their legendary mastery of weapons was no doubt one reason for this. His leather armor differed little from Talon's except in style and brown color. Kryll were acrobatic and preferred nimbleness to the encumbrance of heavier armor. Besides, why be struck and trust your armor to save you when you can avoid the blow altogether? He had a strong brow and straight nose typical of the species, black hair in a tight braid, red eyes regarding Talon calmly.

"Who are you, Talon the Nyborian?" the kryll asked.

Talon shrugged, noting that the kryll was as tall as he and almost as muscular, though slimmer and more refined, his agility easily apparent in the smooth walk. Talon had little interest in relating his past, for it didn't matter. "I'm a man with a sword."

Appraising him, the kryll asked, "Trained by kryll?"

"My father. A knight."

"To become one? And yet you are not."

Hearing a question he would rather not answer, Talon asked, "What brings you here?"

"I come for the elixir as well, to study it." He nodded his head as if bowing. "Mikolyn of House Rivermoon."

Talon nodded his understanding. Every kryll has a subject to which he devotes considerable research, becoming an expert. "Then you're not here to study men with swords."

Mikolyn laughed. "Indeed. May your blade fly as true as your wit, Stormbringer. We shall have need of both ere long."

"You couldn't find silver elixir on Lluricn? Someone must have it."

"It is illegal to possess in most places. And those with it do not admit to it, or part with it lightly, since it is so hard to acquire. Besides, how can I truly understand it if I have not seen its source?"

"There wasn't anything less dangerous to study?"

Mikolyn smiled. "How am I to make a name for myself studying things as ordinary as men with swords?"

Talon appreciated a turn of phrase but remarked, "Everyone here wants attention. I want to avoid it."

"Perhaps you should change your name. It is rather striking."

"What makes you think I haven't already?"

The kryll smiled. "We must share a drink of kryllan wine upon our return, you and I. Perhaps there's much to learn from you after all."

Talon was about to respond when his ears caught a dull thudding that he recognized as hooves, but there was something strangely heavy about the sound. It seemed like a single horse but somehow not, but then far away sounds traveled differently here, seeming muted or coming from the wrong direction instead of from the source. A glance at the kryll and Noren showed that they were aware of it, too. So was the mynx, its ears up. The noise grew louder and the sorelia gestured to a crop of bushes that they hurried to get behind.

Staring toward the source, Talon sensed something unnatural when two dozen horses crested a hill at a gallop and charged toward them. Black to the last, they moved in four rows of six, tightly bunched, like a military formation. Nothing could explain that, unless invisible riders were guiding them. They turned to one side in unison, then turned again moments later.

"They're moving together," Talon observed, "hooves landing as one."

"That's just wrong," muttered the knight in distaste.

"The Ever Fiend is controlling them," Noren explained with certainty, causing the woman to murmur in concern.

"He's searching for us?" Jenar asked, looking around nervously.

"Not us specifically," the sorelia replied, and the others seemed to relax.

"How do you know this?" Talon asked. That Talon knew nothing of this land except stories from his youth made him feel uncomfortably unprepared.

"Do you have a better explanation?"

Talon had to admit he did not. Part of him still did not accept that this children's bogeyman existed, even though other things about this realm were confirmed. The horde of horses wheeled away, disappearing over another rise until the sound of their hooves faded away and the group could carry on.

The Nyborian found the swordsman striding beside him, chainmail-covered chest puffed up. A thin black mustache seemed designed to bolster his manliness while the cocky gaze had the opposite effect of making him seem weak. "The man you replaced is dead," Orin said, amused, "in case you were wondering."

Talon had already sized up this fellow and asked, "Your doing?"

The man snorted. "No. Why? Worried I'll stick my sword in you?"

"Only if I turn my back."

Jenar laughed and Orin turned red. "Shut your mouth, Jenar!"

"So what happened to your friend?" Talon asked, hiding his amusement.

"Wasn't my friend, but maybe you'll run into him here and he'll tell you."

"You said he's dead."

For an answer, Orin grinned and boasted, "Been here three times already. Doubt you'll last that long."

"If I have to do it with you, certainly not."

Jenar laughed again and Orin angrily retorted, "None of my friends are brave enough to come."

Talon observed. "Or foolish enough. You come for vanity?"

Orin scowled as if to deny it and then glared. "Don't act like you're better than me, Stormbringer. You got caught stealing to earn your place here."

"Same as you? I don't see you getting past a jhaikan, mynx, or riven."

"I could if I wanted to! Didn't need to."

"Then how did you earn your place?"

When Orin didn't answer, Noren remarked over one shoulder, "He has inclinations Viland helps him satisfy, in exchange for his aid."

Talon cocked an eyebrow. He didn't really want to know, didn't care, and decided their conversation was over. The man's demeanor stifled Talon's temptation to ask if he knew what Viland did with the elixir, for he would likely get a boastful answer that wasn't well informed. The sorelia was far likelier to know, though perhaps unwilling to tell. Talon quickened his pace slightly and soon fell in beside Noren and the mynx, who strode casually, suggesting no danger neared them just now.

The sorelia looked at him shrewdly. "You have gray eyes, Nyborian."

Talon sensed the sorelia was suggesting something. Those damn karelia saw too many things. "What of it?"

"You have a karelian ancestor."

He failed to hide a surprised reaction that Noren had figured that out. He had learned on the streets that eyes can betray a man, just not in this particular way. Someone on his mother's side had been karelian. "How you can tell that?"

"Humans are most often brown-eyed. Most karelia are green. Gray eyes can appear to be green and in a human it's one indication of a potential karelian ancestor."

"*Potential*," Talon stressed. "The Iris Myth is kerr shit."

Each of the seven groups of gods associates itself with a color in the spectrum, and since each group created a species, their species usually has that color eyes. The traits of the gods also dominate that species' outlook. Since all seven groups created humans together, mixing their traits, the colors mixed, too, causing most humans to have brown eyes—and a temperament far more variable than any other species. Since humans are forever trying to decide what each other is really like, and often resort to superficial means of assessing another human's character, the Iris Myth was born. Any human without brown eyes is thought to have another species as an ancestor, and since each species is associated with certain character traits, that suggests which traits dominate the human, too.

Talon added, "Gray eyes can also appear blue, which would suggest I had a jhaikan ancestor instead. Boys used to taunt me with that, but no one ever said it to me twice."

Noren grinned. "Why? Did you assault them?

"Something like that," he admitted.

"Do you see nothing amusing about this, considering the gods of wrath, cruelty, cunning, and domination created jhaikan?"

Behind them, Olin snorted.

Noren continued, "If it's wrong, then why do most karelia have green eyes like the four gods who created them? Or jhaikan blue like their gods?"

"My gray eyes don't mean I have a jhaikan ancestor, any more than your blue eyes do."

"We sorelia are an accident of mischief, and so our irises are more random in color, like you humans."

"*Random*," Talon stressed.

Noren smiled at Talon without friendliness. "Do your eyes see things other humans don't?"

"No," he lied, then changed the subject. "You seem in league with this wizard. What does he do with this elixir?"

"You must get it regardless, Stormbringer."

Talon sensed the sorelia understood his intent to refuse this quest depending on what he learned. Those damn karelia were too smart sometimes. He decided not to pretend that Noren was wrong, and replied, "I prefer a clear conscience."

"Strange, for a thief."

He let that pass. "You're avoiding the question."

"You can ask him yourself."

"He's unlikely to tell me."

"And you think I'm more likely?"

"No, it's just that you're with me at the moment. Is the answer so terrible that you fear to tell, or are you afraid of what I'll do with the knowledge?"

Noren smiled. "No on both counts. I fear little, and certainly not just a man with a sword, however impressive he may appear. And what could you do? Viland is respected. You are not."

Apparently sorelia lacked karelian tact, but Talon wasn't one for hurt feelings. He sensed no answers were coming and decided to ask the wizard before handing over the vials. He changed the subject again. "What do you gain from all this?"

"Access to this land. Unguarded Ever Gates are hard to find."

Wondering how awful the answer would be, Talon asked, "What does a sorelia want here?"

Noren gave his first unreserved smile. "Nyborian, where some see horrors, others see treasures unimaginable, and that is what I've come for. I have the same deal with the wizard as you. I keep whatever I find, and since the pathways keep changing, the path I tread is never the same twice. It always brings me something new, no matter how many times I walk it."

"And how many times is that?" For an answer, Talon received only a smile. "What do you do with the things you find?"

Noren looked away with a smirk. "Sell or give them to the unsuspecting. Weapons are seldom fun for that, as they don't inflict something on the wielder. But anything that can be worn, like magical armor, is typically cursed. And the wearer often cannot remove it."

Talon glowered. This sorelia was the evil one, it seemed, not the wizard. Or maybe Noren was just worse. Stopping him from returning cursed items might be more important than returning without the elixir. "Why do this to people? For the sake of evil?"

"Perhaps. Maybe I have a different sense of justice than you."

"Undoubtedly. How is it justice to sell cursed items to unsuspecting people?"

"Those who seek an advantage over others through magic ought to pay the price for their ambition."

Thinking of Jenar, Talon glanced back to see her scowling intensely at the sorelia, who seemed to know it as if he had eyes in the back of his head, for the way he grinned. "What of your wizard?" Talon asked. "He seeks advantage through this elixir."

"He will destroy himself sooner or later, probably with it."

"You care nothing for him."

"I'm sorelian. And he is not a friend, just a business partner. I'm sure you understand."

Talon did indeed and hadn't expected much more. "You've kept nothing you've found here? Not even one thing?"

"I never said that."

"What was it?"

The karelia gazed at him as if trying to decide how much impact a revelation could have. "The sword," Noren admitted, hand on the hilt.

"What does it do?"

"Pray you never find out from me swinging it at you."

Normally Talon ignored such warnings, but a Chaos Blade was not something to face knowingly. If the stories were true, one didn't have to strike you to wreak havoc of unnatural kinds.

The group continued in silence, scanning for trouble as they skirted forests at a distance. Woods offered a place to hide but might be the place from where a threat emerged. Even the plants were a danger. They moved as if controlled by a mind. One tree held a humanoid skeleton it seemed to be playing with. An entire grove briefly marched along the horizon like a herd of animals before disappearing toward some unseen goal.

Some grass fields they trod had clearly been grazed by something, while others were tall and showed signs of recent passage by someone. In one instance, Noren indicated the tracks were their own; they had not lost their way, but the landscape had shifted as if sections of land floated like islands on an unseen sea. Even distinctive mountains changed location, suggesting that the land masses rotated, too.

Talon couldn't understand how Noren knew where they were going. When asked, the sorelia admitted that his gods-given sixth sense allowed him to feel where the Poison Pond was, no matter what happened. It explained why he sometimes changed direction abruptly. Though a sorelia couldn't be trusted, they had no choice but to do so. The feeling of vulnerability that this introduced rankled Talon.

That feeling worsened when they reached an uncovered, dark stone bridge that spanned a river of black water a hundred yards wide. Three boats with paddles were moored to each side and, a short distance away, the waters emptied into a wide expanse that Noren called the Lake of Souls. Talon, Noren, and the mynx took the lead, with Dal and Mikolyn on rear guard while Jenar and Orin took the middle. The span showed signs of being ancient and unfamiliar in some way Talon couldn't place. The low walls had crumbled in places, archaic words and symbols appearing there at even intervals, some resembling magic words and others indecipherable.

"What do the words say?" the knight asked, booted feet thudding on the bridge.

"Don't read them aloud," cautioned Noren, eyes stern.

"Why?" Talon asked, curious what would happen but not interested in finding out the hard way. He supposed that he did trust the sorelia with certain things.

"If you have talent for magic," Noren replied, "there's no telling what might happen."

Mockingly, Jenar said, "Then I guess I shouldn't read them."

Talon arched an eyebrow. "You have the gift?"

"If you want to call it that. Never cared for the studying, so talent is all I have. No skill."

Noren eyed her dismissively. "You come here for power and yet refuse to master that which you were born with. Fool."

She bristled until Talon laid a hand on her arm. "Ignore him. I know some of these words but not the others."

Jenar asked, "You have the talent, too?"

He nodded. Like most people with the gift of magic, he knew valenders—beginner spells to help get by in life and which generally acted on objects, not people. He didn't use them often, but some had proven invaluable more than once. "I prefer the sword."

"Another fool." Noren looked about to say more when the mynx's ears shot forward and the cat put both front paws on a wall to raise himself higher. He stared intently in the direction they were going and growled low. "Jhaikan," Noren announced, as if recognizing the cat's tone. Talon knew the cats were trained to give different vocalizations. "Quickly, we must hide."

CHAPTER THREE

THE SHADOW RIDERS

Talon drew his kryllan sword. "We'll engage here. The bridge is only wide enough for three to fight, which favors us." They might not get off in time to hide, which he didn't care much for anyway.

"There." Mikolyn pointed to half a dozen figures that emerged from behind a copse, running in their direction. He began swinging his nine-foot staff of Siaran oak in a twirling blur, the foot-long, steel endcaps whistling as his hands expertly moved between three leather-wrapped grips spaced inches apart. The jhaikan-staff resembled normal quarterstaffs with two exceptions—it could be dismantled into smaller pieces for travel and then reassembled, and, with a spoken word, the wielder could make blades protrude from either end like a spear or scythe. Mikolyn did this now to one end, giving himself slicing death there and bludgeoning power on the other side.

They outnumbered the jhaikan by one due to the battle mynx. A lone jhaikan could easily kill a half dozen normal opponents like Jenar or Orin, but with himself, a kryll, the mynx, and Noren, they stood a good chance. After a glance back, as if searching for a hiding place, Noren seemed to agree, issuing a command to the cat, who moved ahead of them to stand guard.

Talon strode to the bridge's apex and motioned for the kryll and sorelia to flank him, which they did. The knight grumbled that he should take Talon's place, but the Nyborian's commanding demeanor silenced him. Dal pulled a long sword from a scabbard and stood between Jenar, her twin swords ready, and the worried-looking Orin.

"Is there anything supernatural about these jhaikan?" Talon asked, looking at Noren to see if the lorenia lines on his face were lighting up. But then they could react to anything of that sort, and onlookers had no way of knowing what a karelia was sensing.

"Not that I see." As Noren spoke, he unsheathed a karelian longsword, the blade evenly curved with a single cutting edge. A soft green light shone around the black metal and in the magic lettering on the blade, the emerald alight in the pommel beneath his small hands.

Talon remarked, "You must not fight in the dark much, carrying a glowing sword like that."

Noren smirked. "I thought you said your eyes don't see things others can't."

Talon didn't respond, as all time for chatter ended when the six jhaikan reached the bridge at a run. Each stood over nine feet and moved fast on two powerful legs, their clawed hands empty. Sinuous tails swayed with agitation behind them, the spike on the end a formidable weapon. From their wide mouths, rows of serrated teeth were another danger. Their keen sense of smell in a snout-like muzzle could help them hone in on someone, but instead they seemed intent on listening intensely, their ears rapidly swiveling independently of each other.

Their reptilian skin changed colors haphazardly, as if they'd lost all control of their camouflaging abilities. They often glanced backward as they approached, an uncommon sight for a violent species known for stalking and hunting prey. Their obvious flight was a powerful sight, for jhaikan were the thing from which all others on Llurien fled. That disturbed Talon more than the sight of each of them wearing plate armor, for the species normally eschewed such protection, opting for just forearm bracers and mailed gloves with the fingertips removed.

But worst of all was the damage that armor had taken. There were gashes from swords that might've been afire for the scorch marks left behind. White frost covered dents. And wiggling arrows seemed to be trying to bore their way deeper. Talon sensed their numbers were reduced and wondered if challenging the leader to single combat would earn them safe passage if he emerged victorious, as that was the jhaikan custom.

"Should we challenge them?" he asked of Mikolyn. Kryll were traditional enemies of jhaikan, more so than any other species, and read their moods better, which became easier as their foe advanced up the bridge, their haste even more apparent.

"No," answered Orin a little too emphatically.

Mikolyn seemed to agree. "They may not acknowledge. Something is amiss among them."

Talon nodded, sensing the same. Jhaikan were masters of strategy, but he felt certain they just wanted to get past them. Maybe he and the others should've just stepped aside, but now it was too late. With a snarl, the center jhaikan ignored the mynx, who leapt at one of the others, and came straight for Talon.

A steel-gloved hand swung for his sword as if to grasp it, but instead of blocking, Talon turned his weapon's point so the other's hand would impale itself. The jhaikan's glove prevented penetration and its other clawed hand flew toward him. Talon ducked and slashed at its forward leg, the blade coming away red. The jhaikan feigned another swing but Talon sensed the intent and severed the limb. His jhaikan howled and Talon stabbed it through the chest before decapitating it with one tremendous blow.

He stole a glance at the others. Noren seemed unable to get past his mynx, who swiped low at another jhaikan, which had bites and claw wounds to both legs and arms. The cat's armor had been dented in two places. Mikolyn's jhaikan had one arm hanging uselessly but the kryll had been slashed across the chest. He seemed unaffected, jhaikan-staff still whistling through the air, this time crushing the jhaikan's collarbone. The remaining jhaikan hanging back seemed ready to charge when not looking nervously over their shoulders. Talon risked a look but couldn't see what they were so afraid of.

The mynx clamped down on a jhaikan's arm, which the jhaikan raised high, exposing the cat's unprotected belly. Talon leapt forward and sliced off the limb, the jhaikan roaring in fury but unable to stop Talon's sword from cutting its torso nearly in half. At the same moment, Mikolyn let out a battle cry and smashed his opponent's skull in so hard that the jhaikan tumbled over the bridge's low wall. A splash below led to a sickening sizzling sound so odd that both kryll and Nyborian looked over the edge to see what was happening. The body turned red as if boiling, the water around it seething with bubbles, before it sank.

Seeing the way clearer, the remaining three jhaikan charged. Noren stepped aside, as did Jenar and Orin, but Dal stood his ground, swinging hard at the lead jhaikan, who blocked the blow and slashed his chest so hard that it flung him onto his back. The three jhaikan ran straight over him and away, soon disappearing.

Talon helped the knight up, noticing that his destroyed breastplate hung poorly, the straps holding it on partially severed. With a yank, he pulled it off and tossed it aside.

"We need to get off this bridge before whatever they're running from gets here."

"It must be fearsome," observed the kryll, wincing in pain. "We would've had a worse time had they not been so determined to get past us."

Noren spent a moment tending to his mynx and saying words in sorelian that Talon didn't recognize. He turned to Talon. "My cat's name," he began, "is Nightwish. Should you desire it, he will follow your commands from here onward."

"Why?"

"You saved his life. I've seen to it that he will obey you."

Talon wondered if any trickery was afoot, but the sorelia seemed genuine. Did he have a sense of honor after all? Talon hadn't expected that. But he couldn't trust someone who wanted to loose cursed items on the unsuspecting. The cat, being an animal, wouldn't have duplicity, so perhaps the beast could be trusted. Talon would take care not to do the same with the sorelia.

The sound of horses galloping stopped further conversation. Talon motioned for everyone to run back the way they'd come. The rowboats beside the bridge offered the only hiding place. Talon lifted one from the black water and flipped it over as Dal and the swordsman took another and everyone crawled under, careful not to let the oozing liquid dripping from the bottoms touch them. No sooner had they gotten out of sight than a nightmare came into view.

The two dozen horses they'd seen earlier crested a hill in apparent pursuit of the jhaikan, heading straight for the bridge. Like before, they moved in unison and in formation, but this time, they bore visible riders, all shimmering blackness like shadows that rippled, glowing armor and weapons further masking their forms. Their dress and the curved blades in their hands reminded Talon of Coiryn Riders, but the god of courage they were named after would've been appalled by this sight. Talon repositioned himself to peer out from under the curved edge of the upside down rowboat, unable to determine what species the riders resembled, had they ever existed in flesh and blood. One held a lance upright, a black-and-white pennant flying from it, the symbol hard to see.

The hooves struck the stone bridge with a clatter that slowed as the riders neared and finally stopped, to Talon's dismay. Had the dead jhaikan been thrown into the river, the ghostly riders might've continued, but he couldn't blame them for investigating the corpses at their feet. He would have done the same. How often did they run across fresh bodies in this cursed place? That someone had done it meant they'd be on the lookout for the culprits. Talon and the others would not remain undetected for long.

Two riders dismounted and walked among the jhaikan bodies. Through the cold breath escaping their mouths, Talon saw their lips move. At the same moment, an eerie breeze seemed to stir up. But then he realized the wind was carrying words, and the breeze he felt was actually their voices slithering through the air. Chills raced down his spine. That he couldn't understand what was said seemed a blessing.

"They're trying to raise the jhaikan," whispered Noren beside him.

"Perfect," Talon replied. "Undead jhaikan is just what this place needs."

"Quiet! Both of you!" Jenar fiercely whispered.

A rider turned in their direction but returned his gaze to the dead before him. With a groan, two jhaikan slowly rose, one missing an arm and the other its head, and soon they entered into unholy conversation with their new masters, who sent them shuffling down the bridge toward Talon and the others. On reaching the end, they headed straight toward Talon's hiding place.

"Be ready," the Nyborian whispered, gripping his sword.

"By the gods," Jenar said, eyes wide.

Talon laid a hand on her, feeling protective. The undead jhaikan came perilously close, but from their gait he sensed they'd pass by. And they did, following the river. Meanwhile, the mounted horsemen dashed from the bridge with a racket that included the blowing of a horn, its clarion call dissonant and grating in the surreal atmosphere. If the horn had any effect, he couldn't tell. Staying behind were the two dismounted riders and their black horses, for what purpose Talon couldn't tell, but they seemed intent on remaining.

"Now we can be worried," he remarked.

"Indeed," whispered Noren. "Fortunately, those with the horn have left, or else we'd emerge only to have them all return, for I suspect it is used to call other riders to them."

Talon observed, "My blade is not magical."

The sorelia nodded. "Only mine is, so this fight will be mine. It is unlikely that normal weapons will hurt them. You and Nightwish will come. They will not know that only I am a danger to them."

Talon understood his role but hoped the sorelia wasn't being overconfident. "Surprise is impossible. We must get to the bridge before they can mount and ride past us."

"What if they ride the other way?" Jenar whispered.

He looked back at her silently, his flat gaze indicating that wouldn't be good. He said to Noren, "Nightwish should run to the bridge. He'll get there faster than either of us."

"Are you sure this is a good idea?" the knight whispered from the other rowboat.

Talon shook his head. "Follow, but do not get in the way of the charge."

"Agreed."

With a final look at the sorelia, who nodded consent, Talon thrust the rowboat up and off. The two riders whirled in their direction as Nightwish sprinted toward them, the Nyborian and Noren close behind, Jenar taking her time to follow. The other rowboat lifted up hastily as the kryll and knight emerged and followed them, Orin bringing up the rear.

Just as Talon feared, the riders mounted their horses to drive toward them, but the mynx was faster, reaching the bridge's end just as the first rider tried to jump past. The cat leapt at steed and rider, bearing both to the ground with a growl and then springing free. Still running, Talon pulled a dagger from his waist and hurled it at the fallen rider, who rose with surprising speed and swung a flaming sword at Nightwish. Despite hitting point first, Talon's blade bounced harmlessly away but distracted the rider, who missed the mynx. The cat jumped free and pounced on the fallen horse, which was trying to rise but now found a battle-trained mynx clawing its throat out.

Talon saw that the second rider would get by them, but suddenly a spear flew past his head from behind and impaled the horse, which staggered and fell to its front knees, throwing its rider to the ground. Talon leapt at the horse and sliced deep through its neck even as the beast fell dead, felled by what Talon only new realized was Mikolyn's jhaikan-staff.

In an instant, its rider was on him, swinging a frost-rimed flail. Talon ducked and the spiked ball flew past his head before circling again at a lower arc. The flail's chain wrapped around his upraised sword, yanking it from his suddenly frost-covered hand, but now the rider's weapon was useless until Talon's blade was removed from the ball and chain.

Talon glanced at Noren, whose black sword, glowing green, clashed with his opponent's flaming steel. Despite being shorter by a foot, the sorelia easily held his own and began pressing the rider backward before plunging the sword into its chest. Clutching Noren's blade with both black hands, the rider screamed as the black blade burst into green fire. The rider crumbled to dust, the flames on its dropped sword extinguishing.

"Talon! Here!" Jenar yelled.

He turned to see one of her swords flying through the air. With a quick roll toward it, he caught the hilt and turned, just in time to see his opponent throw a knife that he narrowly dodged. A grunt of pain behind sounded like Mikolyn and Talon suspected the kryll had been hit by it. He engaged the shadowy rider, luring it away from Noren, who quietly approached it from behind. The sorelia stabbed the glowing blade through the rider's back with the same results as on the previous opponent. Noren promptly scooped the ashes into a pouch before returning to the other pile to do the same. Talon didn't want to know what he intended to do with the ashes.

"We don't have time for souvenirs," he said, retrieving his sword and returning Jenar's. As their eyes met, another thing they didn't have time for came to mind. Though she hadn't participated in the battle much, Jenar looked invigorated and excited, lips parted, eyes alight. A sudden desire to kiss those lips surprised him with its strength, but he settled for an intense look of gratitude that made her blush and look away.

The sorelia didn't respond to Talon but took both the riders' weapons. He pulled a folded sack from within his armor and dropped them in, then slung it over one shoulder. "We must go, and quickly. The others are bound to return."

"Noren," the knight called from where he stood beside Mikolyn, who held one red hand to his side, a bloody dagger at his feet. "A potion healed his chest but had no effect on this new wound."

The sorelia approached and looked at the dagger that had caused the wound. "A Chaos Blade. The wound will not heal here."

"What can we do?"

Noren shrugged. "Magic is unpredictable until we're back on Llurien. The wound doesn't appear serious."

Mikolyn nodded grimly and pulled a bandage from a pouch at his waist, binding the wound as he could. As the others prepared to leave, Talon noticed Jenar pick up the Chaos Dagger and put it in her belt. He noticed Orin hanging back and stifled a frown, for Orin had made no secret of being willing to let others do the fighting while he kept himself safe. The swordsman was a liability and might get them killed if depended on.

Talon went to the rowboats and shoved two into the black water to suggest to anyone who came looking for them that they'd headed downriver toward the Lake of Souls.

As they crossed the bridge and continued on the other side, Dal remarked, "Those riders were from Avalends."

Talon nodded, having also recognized their tunic's insignia of a castle astride a river. The city lay to the east of Nybor beyond the plains of Lorne. Not expecting an answer, he asked, "What are they doing here?"

Noren pursed his lips. "Those were the Royal Riders of Avalends, I suspect. They haven't been seen in hundreds of years, since they entered Everland in search of their queen."

"The one who disappeared?" asked Talon, recalling the story from his schooling.

"Yes. She was kidnapped and thought to have been brought here by jhaikan, so the riders followed."

Jenar asked, "Why would they have brought her here?"

"They wouldn't have, and didn't."

"Then what happened to her?"

Noren grinned. "They ate her.

CHAPTER FOUR

THE POISON POND

A quarter hour later, Talon still felt that there was too much risk of the other Shadow Riders finding them. At his suggestion, they'd followed the riders' trail through swaying, tall grass in the hope of not leaving behind a trail of their own. To one side rolled hills. A vast plain stretched away on the other. Ahead lay a thick forest that seemed like a bad idea to enter.

"Do we intend to go in?" Talon asked Noren.

The sorelia shook his head. "We are near. I anticipate the scenery changing before we reach the woods, and being more like what surrounds the pond."

"How can you expect that?"

Noren eyed him, as if considering. "Do you not feel it? Search your senses."

"For what?"

"A sense of foreboding more acute than the rest, and in a specific direction from where you're facing. Once aware of it, you can feel its strength ebb and flow with your proximity to the source."

Behind them, Orin grunted. "And you karelia walk *toward* these things."

"Who else but us? Certainly not the likes of you." Noren paid no attention to the scowl his words caused.

Mikolyn let out a gasp and leaned hard on his jhaikanstaff for support. The others gathered around as Talon pulled the kryll's hand from his wound, noticing the frigid skin. The knife wound had turned black, tinged with blue frost that seemed to be encroaching from the edges as if working its way deeper.

"What is it?" Mikolyn asked, straining to see. "What's happening?"

Noren shook his head. "You're infected."

"With what?" Talon asked.

The sorelia shrugged. "If we do not hurry and get him back to Llurien, we shall find out."

"Then we return now," urged Talon, putting one of the kryll's arms around his shoulders and turning back toward the trail through the grass.

"No," disagreed Noren. "We are too close. It will take a short time to complete our task."

"You can't do it without me," Talon bluffed, for he saw no reason why the others couldn't get the silver elixir, unless something about this Poison Pond was so terrifying that the others wouldn't approach and he would. Certainly the kryll had the courage, but now this was a moot point. Perhaps he was the only one. The sorelia had admitted, when asked, that he needed to suppress supernatural life forms near the pond while Talon collected the prize, or else he would have done it himself.

"And you cannot return without me," Noren answered.

"You just told me how."

"No, I told you how to sense the Poison Pond, not an Ever Gate, much less the right one, and I doubt if you have the capability either way."

"You said yourself that I have karelian blood."

"But not karelian refinement. You do not know the art, have not been trained, and any talent you have will be diluted by your human ancestry. Don't be a fool. You're wasting time. If you really want to save him, then continue with us."

Without waiting to see if Talon was following, the sorelia led Nightwish toward what had just been a green canopy of trees ahead but which was now rolling hills with sparse underbrush. The sight sobered Talon. Used to finding his way with the sun or stars, or knowledge of an area, with landmarks like mountains that weren't moving, he felt no hope of escaping this land without the cursed sorelia, who clearly had little respect for anyone's life.

"Do as he asks," said Mikolyn, watching everyone follow Noren, "for he is right."

With the kryll's arm still around his shoulders, Talon grimaced but said nothing as they joined the others, who glanced back with a mixture of relief and regret, as if afraid of what Mikolyn might turn into. If someone suggested leaving the kryll behind so they wouldn't be around to find out, Talon would run them through. He exchanged a few quiet words of support and thanks with Mikolyn, who professed to not wanting to be a burden, before realizing aloud that the big Nyborian showed no signs of being burdened at all.

Miles later, Noren motioned for everyone to stop and sent Nightwish scampering up a hill before them, the cat moving with its tail low as if spooked. It slunk near the crest of the hill and slowly inched forward, ears alert and head snapping back and forth quickly. With a flick of its tail, it inched backward and then finally rose and came trotting back.

"We are there?" Talon surmised, sensing something even before the mynx's actions.

The sorelia patted the cat's head. "Yes, and something is near the water, as suspected. You may draw your weapons if you feel comforted by doing so, but none of you have one that will help you, save the girl."

Jenar looked surprised until the karelia eyed the Chaos Dagger tucked into her waistband. Her cheeks turned red. "Maybe I should go to the pond and enchant my swords first. Then we'll have two more."

Noren replied, "You won't make it there alive, or sane anyway, if I do not becalm that which lurks here." He gazed at her silently, as if impressed. Then he turned to Talon. "Perhaps I don't need you after all. It seems we have one with the courage to do what you're here for."

The woman beamed and Orin snickered while Talon frowned. "What about the Shadow Riders' weapons?"

"Unless you brought a glove to handle them," the sorelia answered, "you're better off not touching one."

Talon couldn't argue that.

Noren led them around the hill, everyone alert. He didn't need to tell them to keep quiet, but Talon suspected that whatever was guarding the pond already knew they were here. The lorenia lines on the sorelia's face had been growing brighter, though that could've meant anything magical. Still, he sensed something menacing just out of sight and all around, an impression of invisible forces swirling in anticipation of a meal consisting of their souls. Nightwish's back was arched and the cat's fur stood on end.

Rounding the hill, they came upon the Poison Pond. Roughly oblong, it lay fifty yards across, half again as wide. The silver waters rippled from an unseen wind that didn't strike the onlookers, an occasional circle of waves spreading outward as if something under the surface had moved. The liquid was thick enough to obscure whatever lay beneath and radiated light that cast dancing shadows on several boulders near its edge. Jet black, knee-high reeds swayed at one end, rising from the pool. Across the way, two Asyander trees, their trunks stark white, stood rooted near the edge but leaned sharply away as if desperate to escape the water.

All around the pond were the footprints of animals, humanoid species, and other beings whose mark Talon couldn't identify for all his years of tracking in the wild. The area immediately before them had trampled grass as if it was the preferred area to consume the sinister toxin. Aside from plants, no other sign of life existed, and Talon had the distinct impression that only death awaited those who came here. He glanced at the others; all but Noren and Mikolyn had wide, staring eyes. The sorelia had been right—had Talon known the growing sense of foreboding that he had been feeling had come from here, he would have been able to follow it without error to its source, just as Noren had. The realization made his stomach knot. He couldn't help putting one hand on his sword hilt and looking over each shoulder warily.

As the sorelia began gesturing and whispering words of magic, some of which Talon recognized, the feeling of dread began to fade. Was the danger afraid of them now? Repulsed? Intimidated? Or just realizing that the conquest was not that easy after all? He felt glad for Noren's skills, as creepy as the karelian species could sometimes be. Sometimes having one with you proved a boon, but sorelia lacked the honor that karelia exuded.

"It is time," Noren said in Antarian, the language common to all. He continued moving his arms in a pattern as if tracing something in the air. Talon had the impression that as long as the sorelia did this, his spell remained in effect. "We will wait here, Stormbringer, while you retrieve the elixir. Be careful not to touch it. If you think the Shadow

Rider's dagger caused a nasty wound in that kryll, it is nothing compared to the elixir's touch."

Before he could set off, Jenar appeared beside him, one hand on his bicep. She was so close that the faint scent of lluvien perfume, which he had not noticed before, filled his nostrils. She seemed somehow smaller, her eyes wide and head tilted down despite being shorter than him.

"Talon," she whispered. She seemed intent on saying more but didn't, as if inhibited by fear.

"Stay here with the others," he said reassuringly, trying to appear more unfazed than he was. "Nightwish will protect you while I'm at the water's edge. It will only be a minute."

"Stay wary," she advised.

He gripped her hand and then turned away, brushing her from his mind with an effort.

Drawing and raising his sword because instinct demanded it, Talon crept across the short green grass, which seemed unnaturally lush. He wondered if the nearby waters somehow invigorated it despite their name. He felt and sensed spirits hovering at the edge of his consciousness as if trying to probe him, his skin prickling. What good was a sword here? His fingers itched for the Chaos Blade that Jenar wore, but he didn't look back.

Now just strides from the Poison Pond, Talon turned his attention more fully to it. He had been aware of a hissing sound growing louder, and it seemed to come from the water itself. If something lurked just under it, ready to spring for him, he would never know until it did so, but he liked to think that Noren or even Viland would've told him if that was the case. They could've killed him long before now if his death was all they wanted. But then, maybe death wasn't what happened to those who fell in.

At the water's edge, Talon slowly crouched to one knee, ready to jump back if needed. Without looking, he unfastened one vial from the sash and popped the cork into the grass, which grew right to the water's edge. If the pool ever shrank and expanded, there was no sign of it, unless it was now at its fullest. Talon turned his sword so the point faced the water, to impale anything leaping from within. With his other hand, he lowered the vial to the surface, his eyes finally dropping to the task so as to avoid dipping too far and touching the dreaded liquid.

The vial's edge slipped into the pond, the viscous silver elixir oozing into the opening with a hiss like steam. Soon the flow stopped and he slowly lifted the bottle out, seeing the liquid fall away from its sides, none of it remaining on the vial. Until now, Talon hadn't considered the need to wipe excess elixir from a vial's exterior, but the question was moot. The falling droplets struck the surface as if striking a solid, expanding outward in a splash mark before slowly sinking. Talon stood the vial on the ground, stoppered it tightly with one hand, and put it back in his sash. In due time, he had completed the other vials and returned to the still-gesturing Noren as quickly as he dared, never turning his back to the Poison Pond. Jenar looked noticeably more relaxed than before, but then nothing had happened to him.

"It is done."

"Not quite," said Jenar, drawing her swords. She advanced with more bravado than Talon, whether because he had been unmolested or because she was intent to get this over with. Striding quickly, she made it to the shoreline and slid both blades into the silver elixir. She held them there for a dozen heartbeats and Talon wondered if she thought the amount of time submerged would impact what became of the now enchanted blades. Finally, she lifted both out, holding them point down so any liquid would pour off, which it did in twin streams. With a nervous little laugh, she held the blades up, and only then could Talon see that both glowed silver, illuminated from within.

Talon was about to urge her to return when something echoed her laughter, but wickedly. The direction from which it came could not be easily determined, and as Talon scanned back and forth, even behind, he saw the others doing so, too. Nightwish had risen to all fours, his tail bushy with fright for the only time Talon had seen. Suddenly Noren let out a gasp and fell back, his hands no longer moving, and the Nyborian knew that whatever he had been doing to suppress the supernatural here was over.

"It is here," the sorelia said, lorenia lines blazing anew as he pointed.

Beyond Jenar and across the shimmering waters, a cowled, black-robed figure floated toward them, no feet or hands visible. Within the hood lay only darkness that seemed to pull any light inward as if to devour it. At its approach, a chorus of terrified shrieks erupted from a horde of invisible beings near the pond. Orin cried out in fear. Dal uttered a prayer to Coiryn for strength. Jenar visibly trembled, the swords in both her hands shaking, drawing Talon's eyes, for only her blades were likely to kill the nightmare before them. Maybe it wasn't too late to risk touching the Shadow Riders' weapons in Noren's bag.

On reaching the silver water, the Ever Fiend stopped, and no one moved for long, tense moments. Talon stared into the hood and found himself unable to look away until the Fiend leaned down over the water, invisible hands seeming to support itself. The fabric never touched the silver surface while the Ever Fiend drank from the Poison Pond, which hissed and popped as its lips touched the surface.

After all the sorelia's warnings not to touch the stuff, Talon hadn't expected this. Did the silver elixir nourish the Ever Fiend when the liquid could destroy all others, rotting their bodies or soul? As Talon watched, the silhouette of arms began to appear as if the water replenished the foul creature, making it more substantial. The forearms and then hands materialized in black laced with silver, like veins on charred flesh. A white glow lit the inside of the hood so that Talon wasn't looking forward to the Ever Fiend rising.

"Why is it doing this?" Talon asked Noren, who stood beside him.

"I do not know," came the reply. "I have not seen it before."

"You've seen nothing drink from the pond?"

"No. It is death."

"How do you know if you've never seen it happen?"

"A fair question, but that is usually what's reported on Llurien."

"Usually?"

"Yes. A few have gone mad instead, mostly magic-users, and some have disappeared shortly after."

"Gone where?"

"No one knows."

When the sickening sizzle stopped, the pond's surface never moving, the Fiend straightened and raised its head. Talon caught a brief glimpse of a face that seemed human, the skin black, white eyes gleaming intensely, before darkness was again all that filled the hood. In that instant, he recognized an expression of strain and horror, as if the Ever Fiend was no better than the other tortured beings in this cursed land, merely the most powerful of them.

As everyone stood frozen, wondering what would come next, the Fiend spread both black arms and gestured downward toward the damned pond. Moaning in fear or despair, dozens of creatures emerged from between the nearby trees and from behind hills and boulders. Representing every species and quite a few animals, they ranged from skeletons and undead with rotting flesh and tattered clothes to those that seemed in the prime of their life. Scores of spirits, having lurked here all the while, materialized and flowed between them, their translucent bodies no less horrific. Two startled Talon as they brushed past him from behind, a wave of cold chilling his skin. A handful of ghosts waited on this side of the waters, all the others having been repelled to the far side by Noren's magic.

All wore an enthralled expression of subservience as they bent and drank the silver elixir, which coated the lips and chins of those with bodies. They otherwise showed no immediate effect, save for one that fell forward into the water and stopped moving, as if instantly killed. The spirits, by contrast, glowed more brightly, starting at their heads and spreading downward. One rose and shrieked uncontrollably, darting this way and that before rushing madly over a hill and out of sight, its hideous screaming audible for long moments until finally fading away. The Ever Fiend's laughter erupted from the cowl, darker than the blackness from which it emerged. At the sound, an undead kryll straightened and then fell face first into the Poison Pond, where it stopped moving.

As one, all of them stopped drinking and rose. Talon braced himself for some sort of assault, though it might take a minute for the horde to reach them. The ghosts nearest them stood with backs turned as if ignoring them, the two closest being just ten strides from a terrified Jenar. He scanned for an advantageous battleground, eyes returning to Jenar's swords. Then the Ever Fiend raised its arms once more and spoke a thickly accented line of archaic sounding words, which sounded like nothing Talen had ever heard.

Involuntarily, Talon took a step toward the Poison Pond before he strained to resist and stopped moving. Orin strode past him toward the water. Mikolyn and the knight did so more slowly, each sounding agonized as if fighting the movement as the Nyborian did. Only Noren remained still, but Talon saw the blaze of blue light from his lorenia lines and the visible effort on the karelia's face. Nightwish growled deep and turned to face his master, using both front paws to force Noren to the ground and hold him there. At the water's edge, Jenar dropped both swords and fell to her knees, hands on the grass, head bowing to the surface.

"No!" she cried, voice strangled.

And then her lips touched the silver elixir, the now familiar sizzling sound of someone drinking it reaching Talon's ears.

"By the gods," he said, heart pounding in fear for her. He reached for his dagger, arms easier to control than his feet, which took another step forward. By now, Orin had joined Jenar, whimpering in terror and pleading for mercy but to no avail. He, too, began to drink, but no sooner had he started than his body began to shake violently before falling into the Poison Pond, motionless. Jenar continued to drink beside him.

Wanting to save Jenar before she met the same fate, Talon surrendered to the compulsion to walk, two quick steps giving him the momentum to hurl a dagger at the Ever Fiend. As it flew, he again stopped his forward progress, which took all his strength. Whether through arrogance or something else, his target made no attempt to dodge. The weapon struck it in the chest but vanished in a burst of flame. The Ever Fiend stood unaffected.

At the water, the knight dropped to his knees with a clatter of plate mail and leaned over. As he began to drink, Mikolyn joined him. The Ever Fiend's minions stood vigil in eerie silence.

"Talon!" Noren called from beneath the mynx, voice strained. "The Chaos Blade. It is our only chance."

The Nyborian didn't respond but eyed the dagger on Jenar's belt. Getting that close when struggling to control his body seemed unwise, but the sorelia was right. Either that would work or they'd all be dead. Or worse.

He let himself be pulled forward more quickly, tongue straining for a taste of the elixir like a parched man. One failure of will and he would be fervently drinking. The compulsion strengthened as he neared, the Ever Fiend's hood turning toward him. Did it enjoy the challenge Talon posed? Did it consider him a strong member for its legions of the damned?

Talon reached Jenar's side and began to crouch, aware that he might not get up if either knee struck the ground. The sinister dagger hung within easy reach and he seized it and straightened, the move taking all his leg strength. With a twist of desperation, he wrenched his arm back and then hurled the dagger. The motion caused him to fall to both hands and knees, his head bowing to the dreadful liquid beside Jenar. He strained to lift his head and see the dagger's flight. Like before, the Ever Fiend didn't move, apparently unaware that this blade had advantages over the last. This time, when the blade struck, it sank deep into its heart. Talon heard a gasp from not only the Fiend, but also every other creature on the shore. Then, as one, they shrieked.

CHAPTER FIVE

A New Talent

Suddenly freed from the compulsion he had strained against, Talon nearly fell onto his backside in surprise. Across the silvery waters, the Ever Fiend writhed in agony, both black hands clutching at the dagger in its heart. A flash of white light lit the inside of the hood before darkness consumed it and the foul thing fell, head first, into the silver elixir, its upper body in the water. Each of its minions collapsed, as if dead. The ghosts vanished or fled. And Talon's companions lifted themselves up from the Poison Pond.

Talon grabbed Jenar by the shoulders and turned her to him. Her pupils had gone silver, like the elixir that ran down her chin from her drenched lips, a spot of it on her nose. She stared wide-eyed for a moment before scampering away and then sitting down, gasping. Talon leaned over Orin and ripped a rag from his tunic, then wiped Jenar's face with it. As he did so, the color of her eyes slowly returned to normal. Behind him, the knight and kryll were spitting, gagging, and cleaning themselves up. The cat had released its protective hold on its master Noren, who now approached them.

"Everyone come to me," the sorelia said, "quickly. I need to examine you."

"What for?" Jenar croaked, her breathing frantic, her knees pulled to her chest as if hugging them. "We are dead."

"Not yet," he replied. "You'd be face down if you were dead."

Taking the hint, Talon pulled Orin from the Poison Pond and turned him over, finding a look of horror on his face. He shoved the corpse into the waters, where it drifted for ten feet. Then several pairs of hands appeared from beneath the surface and pulled the body under, startling the onlookers.

"We should've decapitated him first," observed Noren, eyes scrutinizing Jenar. He seemed satisfied.

Unnerved and outraged by the suggestion, the knight spat silver into the grass. "What in Coiryn's name for? To desecrate the dead?"

Unmoved by the criticism, Noren replied, "To keep him dead, unless you're keen on meeting him again, maybe with supernatural powers that you will not be able to overcome."

Talon frowned. "Enough with speculation. We have what we came for. Back to Llurien, now."

The sorelia shook his head and turned from examining the knight's face and eyes. "If the Ever Fiend is truly dead, we must know. And it appears that killing him has killed all those under his control. This is revolutionary news, for the Ever Pathway may be safer than ever before. And you, Talon Stormbringer, will be famous across Llurien for having destroyed the dreaded Ever Fiend."

The Nyborian snorted. "I care nothing for fame, just my life. Mikolyn still needs help."

"I'm not sure that's true," the kryll admitted. The others turned to see that the ghastly wound in his side had turned silver, all signs of the blackened skin and frost gone.

"That looks worse, not better," Talon remarked, alarmed.

"Perhaps, but it doesn't hurt as before, or at all. I feel good, in fact."

Jenar nodded slowly, seeming much calmer, almost casual as she sat crossed legged now. "So do I. How can that be?" she asked Noren.

"I do not know," he admitted, "but on our return to Llurien, you can be examined. What of you, knight?"

Dal hesitated. "I feel fine but somehow sick inside all the same."

"Well enough to continue?"

The knight only frowned and Noren took it for acquiescence. Taking his sack of weapons, he started skirting the pond's edge, Nightwish walking beside him. The others looked to Talon and he reluctantly nodded. They still needed the karelia and examining the Fiend wouldn't take long. As he watched Jenar retrieve her swords, he saw the wisdom in doing something distasteful—he unsheathed his kryllan sword and quickly dipped it into the Poison Pond before following, the silver liquid dripping off its downward pointing tip as he walked. The knight and kryll exchanged a look and did the same with their sword and staff, respectively. Now they were armed for battle, should it come.

Talon kept alert as they approached the field of apparently dead-again minions. The spirits were still out there, though going by the diminished glow of lorenia lines on Noren's face, they might've been long gone. Nightwish showed few signs of wariness as he stepped around bodies with the sorelia, a sharply flicking tail revealing his distaste. Talon saw that every corpse had the same wound—a scorched and blackened cavity where a heart was, or in some cases, where it should've been. Some bore the distinct mark of a knife blade despite the absence of an actual dagger.

By silent agreement, the group stopped five paces from the seemingly dead Ever Fiend. Talon glanced at Noren, noticing no change to the lorenia lines. The sorelia met his gaze and nodded, so the Nyborian did what none of the others had the nerve to, though three of them had drunk from the sinister waters. That none of them wanted to go near the stuff again wasn't lost on him.

He approached the shrouded figure with sword at the ready, but it didn't move. To turn it over, he wasn't sure what to grab, for no limbs were apparent anymore, and he wondered if the cloak was enchanted in some way, but Noren likely would've told him if it was. As he hesitated, Nightwish brushed past him, grabbed the robe in his mouth, and pulled the Ever Fiend out to the pond's edge. Talon scratched the beast's black and green head a moment before leaning down to flip the carcass over. A sudden growl from the cat was his only warning as two pairs of silver coated hands burst from under the shimmering surface and roughly grabbed the Ever Fiend by the shoulders. With a violent jerk, the arms hauled the remains under the waters.

"It's time to leave this cursed place," Talon said, gray eyes stern.

"Yes," said Jenar, her voice sounding hollow to Talon's ears. She turned and began stepping over the bodies, leading them confidently. "This way."

Noren arched an eyebrow at her decisiveness as they followed. Talon kept scanning the bodies for some signs of movement but didn't see any. Even after they disappeared over a hill, he repeatedly glanced back, having taken rear guard with the knight. They walked in silence for some time, passing fallen bodies here and there as if everyone who had been tied to the Ever Fiend in some way had perished along with it. All bore a wound similar to those found collapsed by the pond.

Noren remarked that he was eager to return to the Poison Pond in the coming days because all those corpses would soon turn silver in decay. Soil enriched with this matter was called Ever Earth back on Llurien. Wizards used it for spells, but even common folk could plant something in it and achieve an unusual yield, not only in volume, but often in properties as well. It depended on what one planted in the stuff. The Nyborian thought this place was a source of too much that was evil in the world, more so than his childhood fairy tales had led him to believe.

"I feel unwell," the knight murmured to Talon, who eyed him. "I cannot place it. My mind is filled with regret."

Talon wasn't given much to introspection at his age. "I'd suggest a strong drink, but you've probably just consumed the strongest thing there is."

"No sooner had I drank it than this feeling came over me. I am ashamed."

Not understanding, Talon replied, "There's no shame in failing to resist the Ever Fiend's will."

"But you did. That is not what I mean. I am ashamed of my rank, and how I earned it." He sneered.

Talon's eyebrows rose. "You're a Knight of Coiryn!"

"I should not be," Dal admitted. "I have kept the secret for months but now I cannot bear it any longer. Stormbringer, you seem a man of honor and strength."

"As do you," he interrupted, only to hear Dal snort.

"Bards have even sung of my false deed. The hollowness of it all has grown on me."

Talon sensed that the knight was determined to unburden himself. He invoked the goddess of empathy. "I'm no

Priest of Darra to absolve you so you can enter Leisiran in death, if that is your worry."

"I know. Just hear my confession. You wished to know why I come to this place. I struck a bargain with the wizard. He cast an illusion that allowed me to seem brave as I fought and then chased off jhaikan, who seemingly fled through a Moon Gate to vanish. This happened before the Queen of Talendor so that I appeared to have saved her. For this I was promoted from Knight of the Valend to that of the Sword, and given the honorary Knight of Coiryn title."

Talon observed, "And these journeys into the Ever Pathways are the price you pay."

"You do not ask why I did it?"

"You don't strike me as a complicated man. It is self-evident."

The knight snorted bitterly. "I suppose so. And what am I now? A damned man lost on the Ever Pathways where he likely belongs."

"We are not lost or damned."

"I am. My shame grows with every accolade, and my honor is gone."

Talon did not disagree. "Some men have never had it."

The knight's face darkened. "Is it worse to have lost it?"

The Nyborian hadn't given it much thought but replied, "Lost honor can be regained by those who desire it. Those who never had it care nothing for acquiring it."

The knight gave him a long look. "Thank you, Talon Stormbringer. You have given me purpose. I will not die dishonored, if given the chance to redeem myself."

Talon noted that Dal's irises were turning silver and suspected that the knight's opportunities would be few. He seemed a decent man and Talon felt that he deserved a clean death, not whatever now awaited him. If it came to it, Talon would drive a sword straight through his heart rather than let him become one of the wretched denizens of this place. But even that might not put an end to him. Decapitation. That's what Noren had recommended. So be it.

The group ran across more bodies, this time a herd of harts. The woodland animals must've bounded through an open Ever Gate on their long legs by accident, for Talon couldn't imagine a scenario where such easily frightened game would pass through one on purpose. Surely no one brought them here as food, for this land corrupted anything that remained in it for too long; there was no telling what effect eating them would have. Every hart had an unexplained wound in its chest.

"It seems clear," began Mikolyn, "that by killing the Ever Fiend we have killed everything under his control."

Noren nodded. "The feel of this place is different now."

"How so?" Talon asked, though he sensed it himself.

"An oppressive weight has been lifted. Perhaps we have an opportunity."

Talon fixed a hard glare on him. "For what?"

"To reach the Black Tower and acquire its contents before anyone else does."

"The Ever Fiend's lair?" Mikolyn asked, looking intrigued. "It is said no one comes out alive."

"That's because of who lived there," replied the sorelia.

"You don't know that's the reason," Talon observed. "Anything could be guarding it."

"True, but it's plausible that with the Fiend and his minions dead, the way should be safer than at any other time. He could have set magical traps or something else still in effect, but the risk is worth taking."

The Nyborian asked, "Haven't you seen enough horror for today?"

Noren smiled. "I'm sorelian, the source of horror, according to some."

"What's inside this Black Tower?" the knight asked skeptically.

"No one knows," admitted Noren, "but if you were the Ever Fiend, ruling a vast land that's capable of turning any magic item into something more powerful, and even able to turn ordinary items into something special, would you not create and stockpile a vast supply of them?"

Jenar's eyes lit up. "I agree the risk is worth it. Come, Talon, we can have the most powerful weapons and armor known to exist."

He removed the hand she had laid on his arm, noting that it felt oddly cool to the touch and his skin remained cold where she had touched him. "Being forced to drink that terrible elixir taught you nothing?"

She shrugged. "I have cheated death."

"You do not know that. Something worse than death could be brewing inside you even now."

Jenar laughed vibrantly. "I feel fantastic. And if death, or worse, is already coming for me, then I must see this place first. Won't you come?"

"Entering a seemingly safe wizard's tower landed me in this mess. I'd rather not repeat the mistake."

"Stormbringer has a point," Dal admitted. "I say we return to Llurien."

Talon turned to the kryll. "Mikolyn?"

Sighing, Mikolyn's eyed Talon's sash full of silver elixir vials. "I do not have what I came for, the elixir. In all the chaos at the pond, I had forgotten. Regardless, this opportunity is unprecedented. It is worth investigating."

Noren smiled triumphantly. "Then it's settled. Even you, Stormbringer, cannot argue against majority rule. I have a general idea where the Black Tower is. We will have to search for it."

"No need. I know where it is," said Jenar. Seeing surprised expressions, she added apologetically, "Don't ask me how I know. I don't know myself."

The sorelia pursed his lips. "It appears that drinking the silver elixir has given you some ability to navigate the Ever Pathways."

Scowling, Talon observed, "Which means she can lead us out and we don't need you. Come, Jenar. Back to Llurien."

"Talon," she said, putting a caressing hand on his chest this time, gazing up at him through long lashes, "do this for me. Your strength can keep us safe, if that is truly what you desire."

"My strength would not be needed if we left this place."

She took his hand, squeezing it affectionately while she led them toward the Ever Fiend's Black Tower. Only the knight showed his reservations. No one had commented on his increasingly silver eyes. They seemingly knew the elixir's effect on Jenar. Mikolyn showed no ill effects, but his wound glowed faintly as if light shone from within. To Talon, all three of them had been poisoned. Orin might have been the luckiest of them, dead as he was. The Nyborian glanced back, but no one seemed to be behind them.

As they walked through field and forest, over hill and along another black river, Jenar commented on what lay before them and that each should be avoided for one reason or another. One forest had the dreaded kona leech plant, known for capturing people and keeping them alive while slowly drinking their blood for decades, except that here they fed on a victim's soul. On the horizon at another point stood the Jhaikan Grave, a vast, haunted battlefield where thousands of the vicious species had been slaughtered, though accounts differed on just who, or what, had done the killing. And finally they saw a small town with guard towers, a wall, and something humanoid milling about the lone entrance.

"That's one of the places we should avoid," Jenar remarked.

"I thought everyone is dead?" the knight asked, squinting. "Maybe there's something of use there."

She advised, "That's not a place for the Fiend's creatures. Those people you see over there are not under his control, which is why they're still alive. We are not alone."

"Then we should avoid them," Talon agreed.

"Indeed," said Noren, adding, "it's unlikely that anyone but us few realize what's happened and make for the Black Tower."

"It shouldn't be much longer," Jenar said, striding eagerly.

"That you know all of these things is troubling," Talon remarked. "How can we trust that you truly know the way?"

"Stormbringer has a point," remarked Dal, worry creasing his brow.

"Perhaps," began Mikolyn, "but she has identified places we've passed. Accurately, it seems."

"Indeed," Noren said. "I see no reason to doubt her."

"You're hardly without bias," Talon observed. "I doubt you'd care where we end up next as long as we stay in Everland. You seem to have no desire to return to Llurien."

"Nonsense," the sorelia replied. "I want the Black Tower's contents more than any bauble, as you'd once described items I can find on the Pathways. If I thought Jenar could not do it, I would not follow."

"But what makes you so sure she's leading us correctly?"

The karelia shrugged. "Nothing. But I have no reason to believe she is not. Do you?"

When the Nyborian only frowned, Jenar grinned, not taking offense at his questioning. "Have faith, Talon. I'm indebted to you and wouldn't risk your safety for nothing. You saved us all today."

"I wouldn't be so sure of that. Three of you drank and are already showing signs of something happening to you. And Orin is dead."

"Yes," agreed Mikolyn. "I've been wondering why he simply perished and we did not."

Noren shrugged. "His cowardice likely killed him."

Dal flushed and replied defensively, as if the remark had been about him, "I doubt that was the reason."

The sorelia gave him a knowing look and grinned hugely, and Talon wondered. Did Noren know of Dal's deal with the wizard? It seemed likely. He was Viland's partner in some way that Talon didn't understand. There was no telling what information he was privy to, but since the wizard and sorelia could choose who they sent into this place, it made sense that they chose together, using shared knowledge of the people they selected and whether they could be counted on or not. Or compelled to act one way or another. Noren probably knew things about each that the others wished he didn't.

The behavior of his companions had earned some of Talon's trust, but given that three of them had been tainted, and the sorelia had been born that way, Talon now trusted none of them. Relying on only himself was probably best, but then there was the troubling reality that either Noren or Jenar had to lead him from this place. Now that the sorelia had what he had come for originally, he had no need of Talon. Maybe Jenar's good graces were something Talon needed and he shouldn't show too much concern for her loyalties, at the risk of offending her.

Taking her bicep in one hand, and noticing how cold it was, he remarked casually, "I'm only concerned that you haven't had much chance to test the reliability of your new sense. You seem confident, which is good, but maybe you're being influenced by things we don't understand yet."

"You still have faith in me?" she asked playfully, leaning against him.

He smiled reassuringly and let the matter drop. "Of course."

They resumed walking, a rolling evergreen forest standing to one side for a time. The trees soon ended in a grassland, where a tower of gray limestone soared into the stormy air. It seemed out of place, no trails nearby and no reason for it to be here, but then everything here was peculiar. A low stone wall surrounded it, a broken wooden gate swinging freely on the side closest to them. They stopped and looked to Jenar, who indicated they had to pass by it to continue on their way. By silent agreement, they intended to steer clear.

As they approached, Talon saw the sorelia eyeing it curiously. "What is it?" he asked, hand on his sword hilt.

Noren began, "I think this is the—"

A woman's scream made them stop. All eyes turned to the tower's windows, from where it had come. After a glance at Talon that suggested this was a chance to redeem himself, the knight rushed forward while drawing his sword, shouting at them to help him save the woman, but no one else followed until the Nyborian took a step, too.

"No!" the sorelia urged him, grabbing his arm.

Scowling, Talon jerked free. "He can't go in there alone."

"No one should go in there."

"Too late," said Mikolyn ruefully, also advancing, his jhaikan-staff beginning to twirl casually as if he was warming up. Another scream split the air, sounding more terrified. Nightwish growled low in his throat.

Noren yelled at the knight, "Do not pass beyond the wall!" But Dal ignored the warning and charged by the broken gate onto the charred grass surrounding the tower.

"I think he might be right," said Jenar to Talon, following him. "It's better to steer clear, unless one of you can operate a Moon Gate."

That stopped the Nyborian. "A Moon Gate? What do you mean?"

Nodding at the building before them, she remarked, "It's the only way to enter the Vanishing Tower without waiting for it to appear before you. There's one inside so that we can use another to arrive there if we had it. But if we enter, we could use it to reach the Black Tower's Moon Gate in seconds."

Talon arched an eyebrow at the sorelia, who nodded.

"Yes, I can control one, of course. We'd have to hurry before the tower disappears." He began running for it, the sack of weapons he had been carrying making a racket. Jenar smirked and ran, too, with a scowling Talon bringing up the rear, the great cat loping beside him.

"Why would the tower disappear?" he yelled, seeing the knight bash open the door and fearlessly enter.

But no sooner had he said it than the whole building, grass, and wall surrounding it began to shimmer. The kryll nearly stepped over the perimeter but stopped himself. Moments later, the place had vanished, with the knight inside.

CHAPTER SIX

THE BLACK TOWER

Talon's knuckles were white on the sword hilt in its scabbard, his grim glare keeping the others from talking to him. Noren had explained that the infamous Vanishing Tower was unlikely to appear in the same place any time soon and that the knight was probably lost forever. He might escape the building, but if he did, he could be anywhere in Everland. They'd never see him again, it seemed, assuming he even survived. That glow in Dal's eyes had Talon certain that the knight would never leave this place regardless. Still, he had wanted to help the doomed man, and even Jenar's assurances that it was really Dal's own fault for charging in there did nothing to cheer him. He wanted out of this place.

Instead, they were headed for the Black Tower. If Talon could reach the Moon Gate there, he might still rescue the knight. He strode with greater purpose, nearly leaving the others behind.

Along the way, they passed an Ever Gate—one of several they'd seen, light or dark depending on whether it was day or night on the other side. They steered clear, both Noren and Jenar saying it wasn't the one which led back to the wizard who'd sent them here. Talon approached anyway and gazed out, seeing a seemingly impassable jungle lit by the sun, suggesting they must've been on the far side of the world.

Within an hour, they crested a hill to see the Black Tower in the distance, obsidian walls glistening as if wet and oozing. Before it stood the Black Grove, which stretched toward them and from right to left a great distance, the trees still as death, not a leaf rippling. Beyond it all rose a wall of mist that Noren said came from the Misty Cliff on the far side. No one knew what lay at its bottom, and the fog obscured whatever stood beyond it, if anything. Talon remembered it from the vision Viland had given him. Aside from lights twinkling in just one of the tower's windows, there were no signs of life.

Or death.

"Should we be worried that nothing appears to guard it?" Talon asked.

Jenar said, "No. The trees do that." At his dubious look, she smiled. "You'll see."

He reached for his sword but she stayed his hand and led them onward. A glance at Nightwish showed the cat's ears mostly forward but sometimes swiveling back or to the sides. The cat was on high alert and Talon had long ago learned to trust the instincts of animals. This one was made of stern stuff, for rumor had it that even battle-trained horses could not lightly be made to enter the pathways.

They followed a path that led straight toward the grove, where Talon detected the faint smell of blood. Nightwish growled and the Nyborian pulled out his sword, noticing the lorenia lines on Noren's face glowing softly. With the tall evergreens looming over them, all but Jenar stopped. The trees had black trunks and dark red leaves, which Noren eyed greedily. The karelia approached a tree as if to pull a leaf, but Jenar spoke like she had eyes in the back of her head.

"Don't."

The sorelia paused. "Explain."

"Take a leaf from the ground if you want, but unless you want to provoke the Linganore trees, I wouldn't pluck one."

Noren watched her step on the path through the forest and sighed, following with the others. The turbulent sky disappeared behind the thick canopy as they entered the Black Grove, but they'd only gone twenty paces when the path abruptly ended. Jenar walked forward anyway, and as she neared the boles, they rose on their roots and shuffled aside, letting her through. She calmly suggested that her companions hurry and they closed the gap with her, none of them failing to notice the trees gathering behind them as if to cut off escape. The trees continued to part ahead and close behind so that the travelers walked in a perpetual circle of foliage. No one spoke, their wary eyes saying all that was needed.

And those eyes widened when the trees parted once more to reveal a sickening sight. A thick, black branch hung over the path. A pulsating kona leech plant had entwined itself there, and in its grip lay a wide-eyed and staring man, his horrified eyes imploring them for help as the plant crushed him against the branch lengthwise. He appeared to be hugging it from beneath. One arm dangled toward the ground, the hand twitching toward them. The plant's green leaves shone with luster, a pod-like nest enveloping its victim as tentacled vines gripped the Linganore tree. A few unoccupied vines sensed the newcomers. They unwound and poised like snakes, one lashing out toward them.

Talon had seen this before during an excursion into Valley Wood. He severed a vine, which fell past him, oozing black ichor instead of the expected blood the plant usually drained from its prey. Not waiting for further attacks, he leapt forward with steel flashing and severed first one vine, then another. Striving to save itself, the plant tried to disgorge its victim, but it was too slow, allowing Talon to shear off a hunk perilously close to the man. The plant seemed to shriek as if alive. Unnerved, Talon waited a precious second for the victim to fall helplessly to the ground, giving him a free swing at the kona leech. With a clean stroke, careful not to strike the tree in case it, too, should join in attacking him, Talon cut the bloodsucking plant in half. As it landed, he made short work of the dying plant until a dozen pieces lay scattered around.

Mikolyn went to the fallen man to help him up, but the plant's victim shrank back, staring in horror toward the group.

"Ever...Ever...F-f-f-Fiend!" he stammered.

The Nyborian looked back in alarm but saw no one but his companions. "The Fiend is dead." He faced the man again but saw sightless eyes gazing into oblivion.

"And so is he," remarked Noren. "We were too late. That plant was feeding on his soul, not his blood as they do on Llurien. I wonder how long he's been here."

"Long enough to go insane," remarked Jenar quietly.

"What should we do?" Mikolyn asked.

"Behead him," answered Noren. "And not dawdle."

Talon grimaced at the butchery he was about to do, but with a clean stroke he severed the head from the body. He wiped his blade on the man's shirt and rose. Then he approached the trees, expecting them to part, but they did not. Then Jenar approached the boles, which shuffled aside while she flashed a grin at him.

Nothing more happened within the grove. They escaped to the far side where the wide Black Tower soared a thousand feet into the stormy sky. An additional twenty-eight small towers rose a hundred feet up from the main tower's side, each topped with a colored minaret. Their number matched that of the gods. That couldn't be a coincidence.

"There appears to be no way in," remarked the kryll.

Jenar nodded. "Not to most, but I know the way. There's no ground floor entrance unless you know what to do."

Talon followed with his sword drawn as they strode up to the Ever Fiend's home. He wondered what had happened to the companions of the kona leech plant's victim. They hadn't seen another such plant. Like some denizens of this place, did it, too, get here by accident? A grove of such creatures might be advantageous to the Ever Fiend, but then no one knew what the Fiend wanted, despite all the stories about it appearing on Llurien to steal this or that—often a living person, or so the bedtime stories said. Maybe the kryllan species knew, for they had an expert on almost everything in their ranks.

Jenar stopped before the Black Tower and appeared to carefully choose a blank spot, where she traced a vertical rectangle with a small circle at each corner. Then she drew a line from one corner of the rectangle to the opposite corner, and another line connecting the remaining two corners. Inside the rectangle she drew a triangle, and where its three points touched the rectangle, she again drew a small circle. In the center of the rectangle, she drew a large circle. Once this part was complete, the pattern glowed silver, the invisible door on which she had drawn this diagram sliding upward to reveal only blackness beyond.

Talon recognized the symbol as one associated with the gods. Was the Black Tower a doorway to their realm? The key to this place? A meeting spot? Or a place where horrible people were banished instead of tortured forever in Lochiare, damned to eternal boredom in Maeryndor, or their soul ripped apart in E'Kainum? Some had wondered if

Everland was yet another afterlife for the evil, but the gods would confirm nothing.

"I'm surprised it's that easy to enter such a formidable place," said Noren.

Jenar smiled wanly. "It only works because I drank from the Poison Pond and have the elixir in my system. That, and I have some magic talent."

"Interesting, albeit a steep price to pay."

"Hopefully there's no other price," remarked Talon, concerned for Jenar. Her skin seemed darker than before, but then that could've just been the lighting conditions. He spoke the word of magic which triggered the Ball of Light valender and a fist-sized orb appeared, bobbing in the air a few feet above and in front of his head. He had no doubt about it now—Jenar's skin had darkened as if she had gotten tanned by the sun in the last hour. He moved toward the opening as the light kept ahead of him, the others following.

As light filled the interior, Talon scanned for indications of danger that didn't appear. The smell of decay seemed to permeate the dank air, the source undetected. No sound came from anywhere. To the left and right stood hallways and before them descended a wide staircase. Another rose beside it into blackness.

"Where are these items we're risking our lives for?" he asked with disdain. He had made a living as a thief of late, but there was a limit to how much risk he took for that, and they'd far exceeded it.

"This way." Jenar brushed by him.

Talon had expected them to go up, but instead they descended deeper and deeper, through empty corridors and abandoned rooms. Nothing seemed to have been there in forever, thick cobwebs in corners and undisturbed dust everywhere. One large room bore a huge table with the symbol Jenar had traced earlier carved into its surface.

Twenty-eight chairs surrounded it. The furniture looked as if it had not been used in eons and had been styled in ways he found bizarre and unsettling, though he couldn't pinpoint why.

They reached a set of closed but unlocked double doors, both carved with a scene of wizards and warriors who bore features unlike any they'd seen. But then perhaps they were from other continents on Llurien. Jenar grinned at him before shoving open the doors. Beyond lay a room large enough to obscure the far side. Close to them, down a short flight of steps, were piles of weapons, organized by type. Swords, knives, and daggers lay in one, axes in another, hammers, flails, and maces farther away, spears and lances elsewhere, and great piles of arrows, crossbows, and both long and short bows. Along the walls stood suits of armor, and above the armor, more weapons occupied all the available wall space.

With a word, Noren took command of Talon's ball of light and split it into a dozen orbs that flew outward to positions near and far in the hall, illuminating its entirety. A murmur of appreciation escaped Mikolyn's lips, for the piles nearest them were duplicated several times across the vast sweep of the room, in the center of which stood a large dais as if a speaker would address a crowd from there. A Moon Gate stood at its center, the lack of a shimmering vista through its frame indicating it was off. Talon sighed in relief at its presence, wanting to head straight for it and find Dal.

The group descended to the weapon-strewn floor. Talon continued to the gate, though Noren was the only one who could cast the spell to activate it. With the tower deserted, they could have the time to get Dal and return, and then be done with this place.

Jenar joined him, as did Noren, each looking around and enjoying the vantage point. Nightwish roamed among the piles, pawing at odd items, while Mikolyn went to a pile of jhaikan-staffs, which he began looking through.

"I guess there's no way to tell," he began, "what any of these items do."

"Not until you use it, no," agreed the sorelia, who dropped the sack he had been carrying, eyes on the treasures before them.

The kryll asked, "Any chance that this Moon Gate is the kind that can be made to go to any other Moon Gate? Imagine taking all of this to Llurien."

Noren put his hands on the metal gate's rectangular frame and began examining it. Talon hoped the answer was no. The last thing Llurien needed was such a treasure trove of cursed items being let loose, and the sorelia had already admitted that was exactly what he wanted. Noren indicated the gate only went to one place, as far as he knew, so Talon suggested activating it so they could go find the knight. The sorelia frowned, Jenar seemed indifferent, but the kryll nodded his agreement, so Noren cast the spell and the gate shimmered to life, a glistening wall of silver offering an occasional glimpse of the destination—another room devoid of significance to them.

They gathered on the dais, calling Nightwish over, and were about to step through when the room lights dimmed. The mynx growled and backed away from the room's entrance, where a black robed and cowled figure drifted down the stairs. It looked just like the limbless Ever Fiend that Talon had killed at the Poison Pond, though it seemed somehow bigger, more intimidating. Only darkness filled the hood, but Talon could sense when their eyes met, a jolt of menace striking him.

"We killed you!" said Mikolyn, reaching for his jhaikan-staff. One hand went to the wound in his side, where the silver light began to grow brighter while he gasped in pain.

The figure glided to a stop not far from the dais, surrounded by weapons, the deadliest of which was itself. "No," it said, hollow voice echoing whereas theirs did not, "you killed Aeonyn, an apprentice."

A murmur escaped the sorelia. "More than one Ever Fiend? By the gods. We must tell Llurien."

Talon agreed but doubted they'd get the chance unless they went through the Moon Gate and somehow destroyed it so they couldn't be followed. Stalling, he asked the Fiend, "How many of you?"

"You will learn soon enough when you join them. All but you." The Ever Fiend raised a ghostly hand at the kryll. Mikolyn lifted from the floor with the motion, a burst of light erupting from his wound as he screamed in agony. Then the Fiend jerked its wrist and Mikolyn flew off the dais and into a suit of plate armor on a stand, which fell atop him, pinning him to the floor. When he lost consciousness, the wound's light began to fade and Talon feared he was dead.

"Why not the kryll?" Talon asked, one hand discreetly drawing the Chaos Blade at his waist.

"He had no magic talent," came the answer. "I can sense magic in all of you. One drink from the—"

Talon didn't wait for him to finish, hurling the enchanted blade. The Ever Fiend let the blade slam into its heart. It remained standing, calmly, and didn't even glance down while the weapon slowly exited the wound as if pulled out by an invisible hand. It clattered to the floor, steaming black ichor covering its length. Thinking like Noren for a moment, Talon briefly wondered what the stuff would be worth to a wizard, but as he watched, it boiled off the dagger and dissipated. From the hole in the Ever Fiend's chest, silver light gleamed until the wound closed as if it had never been there, even the robe mending itself.

Behind him, the Nyborian noticed Nightwish dragging Mikolyn from under the armor. The cat had little trouble, strong as he was, and the kryll began to stir. Jenar hadn't even drawn a sword; her lips were moving silently as if praying to some god. Beside the Moon Gate, Noren began to quietly speak strange words in karelian, the lorenia lines on his face glowing brighter.

Hoping to distract the Ever Fiend from Noren's actions, Talon descended the dais to a pile of spears and took one. "Something in here must kill you."

The Fiend laughed. "You are welcome to try, Stormbringer. Nothing in here has ever worked."

Talon arched an eyebrow. The Fiend sounded disappointed. Perhaps he could lend assistance. "Maybe the right person hasn't attacked you."

The Ever Fiend gestured at the piles. "Every weapon is different. Perhaps I'll let you try them all."

Talon hurled the weapon with all his might. The Fiend never moved as the spear struck it full in the face, the momentum throwing it backward to the floor.

CHAPTER SEVEN

AN OLD TALENT

Jenar gasped, and when Talon looked at her, she seemed aghast. Had *she* wanted to strike the Ever Fiend down? He ascended the dais again to speak to her when movement brought his gaze back to the Ever Fiend. The spear pushed up by itself and fell to one side. Then the Fiend silently rose to its previous position, seemingly unharmed. Talon felt that the only smart move was to rush through the Moon Gate and run for their lives. But Noren had another idea.

"You must go while I delay the Fiend," said the sorelia to him, the lorenia lines on his face and neck glowing so intensely that Talon almost couldn't see his eyes. "Take Nightwish. The world must learn there's more than one Fiend."

"You can tell just as well as I," responded Talon, surprised the karelia was willing to sacrifice himself, especially to such a fate. Who knew for how many eons Noren would be the Ever Fiend's slave?

Noren smiled without humor. "Who would believe a sorelia? Take my sword. You will need it more than I."

"The Fiend will destroy your soul." Talon reluctantly took the offered blade.

"You forget I'm karelian. I have already separated it from my body, which will battle the Fiend, and when it falls, my soul shall escape."

Talon remembered the words of magic the karelia had spoken. Karelia could willfully separate their souls from their bodies and still control both, a feat usually done when death is certain and there's some chance the soul won't reach an afterlife if it's still in the body at death. As gods-appointed caretakers of all spiritual matters on Llurien, the karelia tracked down ghosts and sent them to the afterlife. They blasted undead back to the grave. They communicated with the dead when necessary. Noren had done the dreaded spell—his spirit hovered nearby, ready to flee from the Ever Fiend's grasp the moment his body died.

Talon hesitated to leave him behind, but as Mikolyn staggered to the top of the dais beside the still open Moon Gate, Noren gave a sharply spoken command to Nightwish and the big cat reared up, pushing the kryll through the gate's opening with both paws before leaping into Talon and Jenar, propelling all three of them through and leaving Noren behind. Just before they vanished from one tower to arrive in the other, words of magic from both sorelia and Ever Fiend filled the air, accompanied by a whoosh, a boom of thunder, and a scream. The sound cut off as they left the treasure room into what looked like a throne room. Three gilded chairs stood at one end, faded banners and tapestries hanging from the gray limestone walls. Talon stopped himself from stumbling to the floor, one hand in Nightwish's dark fur and the other around Jenar's arm. Behind them, the Moon Gate remained on.

"We must go back," said Jenar, turning toward it. Talon shoved her forward and away.

"No. We must honor Noren's sacrifice. Hurry, away from this gate and out of this tower."

"But we are far from Talendor," Mikolyn protested weakly, rising to his feet with a grimace.

Talon helped him up. "It doesn't matter. The first chance to escape to Llurien, we take it, wrong Ever Gate or not."

With the cat and the kryll following, he forced a still protesting Jenar from the room. The Moon Gate continued shimmering as they escaped into a hall with a stairway curling down the tower. The Nyborian peered through a window on their way and saw the familiar stone wall around the Vanishing Tower, confirming their location. That meant Dal was around here somewhere, if he still lived, and Talon felt eager to find and save the knight.

As they descended from the building's pinnacle, Jenar's resistance faded and she began to lead the way, remarking that there was a way to know their whereabouts. On reaching the second floor, having passed all other rooms and doorways without stopping, she pushed into a central, circular room where a glowing orb four feet in diameter had been set into a circular, waist-high table of obsidian, where it floated. An image of blue covered much of the orb's surface, but a number of large, irregular shapes of brown and green did, too, and only on nearing it did Talon recognize one as the continent Antaria, from whence they'd come.

"A map," he said, watching in fascination as the orb suddenly swirled several seconds before stopping.

"The tower just changed locations," observed Jenar. "That's what the Orb of Vessyn does."

"It shows where on Llurien we are near?"

"It's actually what's causing the tower to change locations. It's supposed to stay in one place unless someone makes it move, but this place corrupts everything magical, so it does whatever it wants now. It has for centuries."

"Fascinating," Mikolyn said, sounding weak and clutching his side. "I've heard of the orb. It's legendary. No one's known what happened to it."

Talon didn't share his amazement. He gazed at it and didn't recognize the continent they were on now, but Jenar touched the shining surface and the word "Llorus" appeared in white letters. She pressed a small mountain range and the words "Tissan Peaks" shown atop them. She placed both hands on it, causing the view to get much closer so that a walled town appeared, the word "Nieve" above it when she touched it. Letting her hand linger, the orb emitted a short burst of light.

"We just moved to there, in the Kingdom of Baeshor," Jenar remarked.

"We can control it?" Talon asked, excited by the chance to go where they needed so quickly.

"Seems like it."

"Good. Back to Talendor!"

So engrossed in the display was Talon that he didn't hear a metal-shod foot strike the stone floor behind them until nearly too late, a growl from Nightwish confirming that an enemy approached. Two more steps sounded, nearing him, as he turned and began to raise Noren's sword to ward off the gleaming long sword that slashed down at him. Mikolyn was faster, or had heard the knight sooner, for the jhaikan-staff flashed upward to block the blade and turn it aside.

"Dal!" Talon yelled, relieved but confused by the attack—until he saw the silver light shining from the man's eyes and a look of wrath twisting his features. The knight wasted no time, sword swinging again, but this time for Mikolyn, who'd seemingly spent his last bit of strength in saving the Nyborian. The blade sheared through the kryll's shoulder and halfway through his torso, killing him. Dal tried to pull the blade free but it was stuck in bone and sinew. Talon hesitated, remembering his vow to decapitate the now undead knight rather than leave him to this fate.

Jenar leapt forward, twin swords ripping through Dal's armor like it was no more than cloth. Both weapons now revealed the awful power granted by the Poison Pond: one left a trail of sizzling silver liquid in its wake, flesh charring at the touch, while the other caused everything within six inches of the wound it left to freeze solid. Nightwish bore the knight to the stone floor only to have the frozen half of Dal's torso shatter on impact, the eerie light quickly fading from his staring eyes.

For a moment no one moved, as Talon stood wondering what had happened to the knight and the woman he had come to rescue. Then a voice spoke near the door.

"Stormbringer, you must escape the tower now!"

Talon's eyes scanned for the source, which began to coalesce before him as Nightwish rose to all fours alertly but not indicating danger. The familiar sight of Noren materialized, but only as a ghostly phantasm, a soft white glow surrounding him.

"You are dead?" Talon asked in concern.

"No, but I am defeated and held in thrall so he can take me to the Poison Pond. He comes here now for you. Flee before he reaches this room and sees where you —"

Suddenly Noren let out a shriek, his face and body contorting in pain, eyes bulging in horror. The screaming continued as his spirit flew backwards from the room as if hauled away by an invisible force. They could hear the sound of his fast passage up and away to the tower's top before the anguished cries abruptly cut off.

Talon turned back to the orb and Jenar said, "We're on Namaera now, on the other side of the world."

"Not for long." He moved the orb until it showed the southern edge of Antaria, then zoomed in near Talendor, but he didn't have Jenar's expertise with the device and accidentally made the tower stop near, but not near enough, to their target. The orb gave a flash.

Jenar glanced upward. "He's here. I can sense him."

Talon grabbed her arm and fled with Nightwish from the room, down a flight of stairs, and out into the grass surrounding the Vanishing Tower. He had never thought to be happy to see the landscape of Everland. They ran through the broken wooden gate and escaped into an open field, sprinting for some distance before stopping. When they looked behind, the tower was gone again. There was no sign of the Ever Fiend.

"Which way?" Talon asked.

Jenar pointed and the three survivors began a fast walk, having a few hours to go, and only now did Talon begin to realize his fatigue, having lost all sense of time and space. As before, the landscape sometimes changed without warning, making Talon swear he would never enter this place again. He hadn't realized how much comfort there lay in a mountain that stayed put, or a forest that didn't come alive, or even a river of thirst-quenching water instead of black ichor.

Nightwish suddenly went alert beside them and they moved behind a bush to peer over the crest of a hill. Before them were the Shadow Riders who'd left the bridge before their fight. Only six of them remained and they no longer moved in a tight formation. Instead they milled about, as if uncertain of what to do or where to go. Their leader, he with the Shadow Horn and lance with pennant, sat still atop his steed, eyes staring vacantly, but at times he seemed to perk up as if hearing something in the distance, his black horse moving restlessly beneath him.

"We must get by them," said Jenar, fingering her cursed swords.

"They seem lost."

She nodded. "Maybe the Ever Fiend we killed controlled them and they are without a master."

"For now. This might make it easier to destroy them."

She smiled at him, the first time she had shown humor in a while. "Let's find out."

CHAPTER EIGHT

THE CURSE OF POWER

Talon and Jenar spent a few moments planning an attack that relied on Nightwish. He made use of the riders being in a small valley, taller hills on each side of them. Their poor positioning would've surprised him were it not for their general disorientation.

Leaving Jenar where she was, he and Nightwish crouched low and skirted the riders' position until they were on the opposite side of them. With his years of sneaking around, the Nyborian was nearly as silent as the beast, his supple leather never creaking. Once in position, Talon sent the cat over the hill with a command to be at ease and only counterattack, for he hoped that no battle frenzy would start immediately. As expected, the horsemen turned toward Nightwish, their attention on the cat, and as he had hoped, they'd come alert but not charged the seemingly unthreatening animal. Talon moved back toward Jenar but stopped halfway so that they surrounded their prey on three sides, but neither human showed themselves.

That changed when Jenar quietly rose with twin swords in hand and began advancing on the riders from behind. Nightwish's presence provided the distraction

Jenar needed to approach them. Talon watched for the right moment, which came when one of the rear horses whinnied and began to turn as if having sensed the danger from behind. With a battle cry, Talon rose and ran over the hill's crest into view, plunging toward the nearest rider, who swiveled in his direction. Talon's rush carried him past Nightwish, to whom he shouted an attack command. The cat leapt two strides forward and bore that rider and horse to the ground with a growl and ripped apart the horse's throat with claws. Talon threw a dagger at the rider, who it struck in the eye, felling him.

Jenar slashed the back legs of the horse before her and it crumpled to the ground, one leg burned and the other frosted. Another swing and the rider's head rolled across the ground.

Talon grew alarmed on seeing the leader of the riders lifting the Shadow Horn to its lips. More riders converging on them would surely mean death. Without breaking stride, he desperately hurled Noren's black sword, which twirled end over end like all those daggers he had spent a decade practicing with. Only training and instinct gave him any hope that the longer weapon would fly as intended. It didn't, piercing the rider's leg instead of his heart, but that was enough. Green flames erupted from the sword and soon engulfed both screaming rider and frenzied horse. Both burst into a cloud of ash and fell to the ground, the magical horn and sword landing in the pile.

Only three riders were left, but two bolted for freedom. To Talon's surprise, Jenar shouted words he didn't recognize and both steeds stopped so violently that their riders flew over their heads to crash on the ground. He quickly grabbed up Noren's sword again and raced beside her to the fallen riders, who rose to meet their attack. They'd been Coiryn Riders before Everland and the Ever Fiend had corrupted them, and such horseman specialized in fighting on horseback. Afoot, neither was a match for the pair who now dispatched them in a dozen blows. Behind them, Nightwish had taken down the remaining horse and then clawed apart the last rider, several more dents on his battle armor.

Only two horses remained alive, if they could be called that. Neither had moved since Jenar's command and Talon got his first good look at them. Both were jet black, their coats shimmering with unnatural luster, almost beautiful despite their air of wild, evil vibrancy. On a hunch, he cut a strand from the mane of a dead horse and tucked it into his belt. Perhaps the mane of a Shadow Rider's horse had some value.

"Good for you." Jenar approved, grinning. "Maybe you're returning to your old, thieving self. Not everything here is so bad, is it?"

"Yes, it is. How did you stop the horses like that?"

She shrugged. "The words to command them came into my mind. How did you know to control Nightwish?" she challenged playfully, seeming amused by her new skills.

"My father was a knight and the cats are part of the military in Nybor. I learned their commands as a matter of course."

She patted a sable steed. "Let's ride these to the gate. They'll obey me. It'll be much faster."

Little surprised the Nyborian anymore and he retrieved the Shadow Horn before approaching a horse, which looked back at him with silvery eyes that left little doubt that it had drunk from the Poison Pond. He gave it the once-over as Jenar casually mounted hers, and then he did the same, half expecting the horse to bolt. It didn't. He barely had time to grab the reins and stow Noren's sword before Jenar shouted commands and they sped off, Nightwish loping along beside them.

As they charged over fields and through forests, nothing challenged the pair. Figures in the distance scattered on seeing them. Any vegetation that might've been alive and intent on molesting them did nothing. They leapt over black creeks, charged over hills, and cantered beneath that stormy sky that never unleashed anything but dread on the pair who trod under it. After a short time, they slowed on Jenar's command and soon saw an Ever Gate on the ground before them, its rectangular outline filled with light. While Talon had lost all track of time, it didn't surprise him that day had arrived on Llurien.

The pair dismounted before Jenar sent their hideous steeds galloping away. He decided not to ask the creatures' destination, for all that mattered now was a return to the normalcy of Llurien. One last glance around showed they were alone, and then the pair stepped into the opening, with Nightwish trailing along.

No sooner had they stepped from Everland into the shadows of Viland's courtyard than Talon felt relief wash over him. A blue sky had never seemed so welcome, the fresh ocean air off the coast of Talendor so invigorating. He took Jenar's hand and found her turning toward him, an excited light in her eyes. He crushed her lips in a deep kiss, pent-up longing for life and its more pleasurable pursuits overcoming him. But the coldness of that kiss startled him. He disengaged and was about to ask how she felt when a voice stopped him.

"Only the two of you?" asked Viland, sounding surprised, arms folded. "What of Noren?"

"Dead," answered Talon sadly, "or worse. The Ever Fiend has him."

The wizard's eyebrows shot up. "You met the Ever Fiend?" With a word of magic and swing of his fist, he made the Ever Gate behind them close, as if he were afraid something—or someone—might come through. Then he gestured for them to follow into the courtyard and back up into his tower and the living quarters therein. Along the way, Talon and Jenar related what had occurred, leaving out certain parts, like that Jenar had consumed the silver elixir. When Viland extended one greedy hand for the elixir vials, Talon hesitated.

"What do you do with this? I've seen it destroy men."

The wizard nodded. "Then you know that I was right in telling you not to touch it. Fear not, Nyborian. I merely use it in my spells. I certainly don't consume it or force others to do the same. As you say, it is death, or worse. A drop here or there in spells makes them stronger. Whether the spell is for good or evil makes no difference, so the elixir itself is not your cause for concern, but the character of the wizard."

Talon stared him in the eyes. "Now you know why I ask."

A chuckle escaped Viland. "I do enjoy a good repartee. I'd not expect such from you were it not for your upbringing. Years as a squire in the courts of Nybor has given you more sophistication than most would expect. It's a shame about your parents. You seem to have the makings of a fine knight. I inquired about you in your absence, you see. It is not too late for you, Stormbringer, given your honor." Seeing Talon frown, he added, "Hide it all you will. It lives inside you still."

"A poet," remarked Jenar with a snicker, one arm wrapped around Talon's waist. She jingled the sash holding the vials on his torso and looked at Viland suggestively. "Are you sure you don't want a sip? It's not all bad."

Neither man shared her amusement, the wizard extending a black hand once more. He didn't seem to realize her admission to having consumed some. "Those are mine by right, Nyborian."

Talon sighed and handed them over. He hadn't expected the wizard's comments about honor, especially those seeming to praise him for it. Maybe the rumors about the man were unfounded. Nothing he had witnessed personally seemed nefarious, other than the basic mission, and by contrast to the beings inside Everland, Viland was downright cordial, though Talon was no stranger to two-faced people. Still, there was nothing to be done for it and he had to just hope nothing evil came of his delivery.

When the wizard suggested that he return to the Poison Pond later for more elixir, Talon glared so forcefully that the wizard took a step back and dropped the subject before smiling as if to apologize.

The Nyborian made no mention of the other items he had collected along the way, though Viland noticed the Shadow Horn only to have Talon sternly shake his head that it was not for the taking. He also saw the sorelian sword at Talon's hip, making an inquiry about acquiring it only to be rebuffed. Talon intended to find a way to honor Noren, who had sacrificed himself for their lives, in defiance of everything Talon had ever heard about the sorelia. He would never look at another quite the same. Perhaps some good remained in those corrupted members of the noble karelian species.

Night began to fall outside and Viland offered them a pair of rooms, but Jenar made it clear she intended to celebrate life with Talon. They retired to his spacious suite overlooking the courtyard and that silent corner below where a portal to a dread world lurked unseen. Nightwish, who now showed all signs of having allegiance to a grateful Talon, lay silently at the foot of the bed while Jenar stoked a large fire, admitting she felt cold and wanting Talon to warm her with his body.

She insisted on pulling curtains around the four-post bed as if to shield herself from the light, acting coy about her shyness when teased about it. Only then did she undress, and in the black shadows, her skin seemed only as dark as his. The first touch of her cold skin no longer surprised him and he vowed to warm her up the old fashioned way. She otherwise seemed more alive than any woman he had been with in his short years, almost as if possessed. The drink flowed easily before and after their passionate tryst. He fell into a deep sleep with her nude body, still chill to the touch, pressed against his flesh.

He awoke sometime later, a growl from Nightwish disturbing him even as he realized the cat had climbed onto the bed, the ponderous weight shifting the mattress, the bed frame creaking. His eyes opened to find the black and green mynx about to lick his face. He pushed the beast aside and sat up, a glance revealing that they were alone. Where had the woman gone? To stoke the fire, which had died down? A moment later, the cat's ears pointed toward the window overlooking the courtyard. Talon caught the faint sound of words, the inflection telling him that magic was afoot. He rose, naked, and grabbed Noren's sword instead of his from the bedside, and gazed down to the ground.

In the courtyard's corner, the Ever Gate blazed with shimmering light. Before it, Viland stood with arms falling to his sides, his spell complete. Beside him, a figure with black skin and wild long hair stood with a dagger at the wizard's back.

"Viland!" Talon called, wondering what else to do from here. He had no bow to take out the creature beside the man.

The wizard turned his dark face up, an expression of horror on it. Then the figure beside him looked up, too, and Talon gasped. Something had transformed Jenar into a being not unlike those they'd seen in Everland, but she bore more resemblance to one in particular than any other.

She smiled obscenely at him, silver light shining from her eyes while she pressed one hand to her belly.

"You're to be a father, Talon!" Jenar called, her voice deep and hollow. "I feel him growing already. No telling what powers this one will have!"

He cried out in shock, desperate to save Jenar but powerless to stop her from carrying out her actions. Had the silver elixir been turning her into this all along? Had she known? Was everything she had done since drinking it just a ruse to deliver them one by one to the Ever Fiend? He didn't want to believe it, that this vivacious woman he had just shared a bed with had been a predator, possibly since drinking from the Poison Pond. Compassion made his heart wrench. If only he had a long bow, he could've destroyed her now rather than let her become some minion of the Fiend in Everland, possibly forever.

And a baby. He was to be a father of some unholy creature? It couldn't be true. And yet somehow he sensed it was. How was he to walk this Llurien knowing some abomination he had wrought would wander those Ever Pathways, possibly coming to Llurien from time to time to do who knows what to the living? Something must be done.

Jenar turned toward the Ever Gate and jabbed the blade in Viland's back, urging him forward. Talon turned and dashed from the room in all his glory, leaping down the steps with Nightwish close behind. On reaching the courtyard, he felt no surprise that both Jenar and Viland were gone, but the Ever Gate remained open and he strode up to it and peered through. Not twenty yards beyond, Jenar delivered the wizard to the waiting Ever Fiend, who grasped a vial of shining liquid and forced it to Viland's lips as he arched the man backward, the silver elixir emptying down his throat. Viland fell to the ground, clutching at his neck and convulsing.

Jenar paid him no mind as the Fiend draped a hooded robe around her, and she bowed her head. Then she raised her chin and turned toward the Nyborian. A brief flash of silver eyes came from within the dark recesses of the hood. She beckoned and the Shadow Riders came at her call, black steeds moving in tight formation once more. Only then did Talon remember the Shadow Horn, his eyes darting to the bedroom above. Jenar made no indication that she had taken it as she mounted one horse.

Silently, Viland stopped writhing and rose to his feet before the Ever Fiend draped a cowled robe around him. He climbed atop another nightmare horse and Talon wondered if he was the only person to see three Ever Fiends at the same time. That he could've been one chilled him, for it seemed clear that anyone with magic talent became a Fiend if they had consumed the silver elixir. What had become of Noren?

The horses wheeled as one and rode away. The master Fiend turned toward the gate and Talon beyond. It began to glide forward. Talon raised the black sword in his hand, fearing it would not be enough for the Ever Fiend. The Ever Gate might be another matter.

He slashed at its edge and saw the blade ignite with green flames as it contacted the seemingly insubstantial portal. The Ever Fiend stopped as black flame sprang from the portal frame and the Nyborian took his cue, swinging with all his might at every edge that shimmered before him. Time after time the blade cut into the gate. Soon a wall of black flame engulfed it from all sides as man and mynx backed away from the searing heat. As the gate hissed, popped, and crackled into oblivion, the Ever Fiend's final words came through it and sent a chill down his spine.

"I will find you, Stormbringer."

GLOSSARY

For more information on the world of Llurien, including maps and pronunciation audio files, please visit the official site, http://www.llurien.com.

Antaria: a continent in the northern hemisphere of Llurien, usually depicted on the left/west of world maps.

Asyander: a deciduous tree growing 30-150 feet tall, used for syrup and bows.

Chaos weapons: any magical weapon left inside Everland can become corrupted so that it's powers are unpredictable.

Coiryn: the god of courage, honor, integrity, pride, dignity, protection, victory, and heroism. He's the autumn/earth god of the green sphere and one of the creators of karelia. He's the patron of warriors and rules the first month of autumn in the Court of Gods.

Coiryn Riders: named for the god of courage, these expert horsemen are a major unit of defense for almost all cities and major towns.

Daekais: one of the original seven species of Llurien but now a race of the kais species. Created by the gods of the orange sphere: deception, greed, jealousy, and fear. Their teeth and claws are poisonous. See "kais" and "Deal of the Gods" entries.

Deal of the Gods: an agreement between the gods to allow ghosts to happen, to create morkais from a male and female daekais, to give magic to the species, to grant healing powers if species create religions, and give the karelia supernatural talents to resolve matters of undead and roaming spirits.

E'Kainum: the afterlife created by the gods of the orange sphere, reserved for the evilest, whose souls are shredded into oblivion without hope of recovery.

Ever Earth: soil found in Everland and which causes anything planted in it to produce an unusual and unpredictable yield, either in volume or properties.

Ever Fiend: the Ever Fiend is rumored to rule Everland and use Ever Gates to appear on Llurien to terrorize people.

Ever Gates: portals from Llurien to Everland. They are naturally occurring but hard to detect without the Reveal Ever Gate spell. Karelia can sense them. From within Everland, they are always open, but from Llurien, a spell must be used to open one.

Everland: a supernatural land ruled by the Ever Fiend and accessed directly via Ever Gates, or indirectly via Moon Gates. Everland, and everything in it, like the Ever Fiend, is not believed to be real by most people.

Ever Pathways: another name for Everland.

Humans: the eighth species of Llurien, humans were created by all twenty-eight gods and are the most variable species in temperament and disposition. Also called Antarians after the first man and woman, Antar and Taria respectively.

Jhaikan: one of the original seven species of Llurien. Created by the gods of the blue sphere: wrath, cruelty, cunning, and domination. They stand seven to nine feet tall, have a sinuous tail and reptilian skin that can change colors at will. They are man-eaters and are synonymous with evil.

Jhaikan Staff: a quarterstaff developed and used by kryll against jhaikan, it can be disassembled into three pieces for easier transport. Blades can be made to protrude from either end like a scythe, spear, or both.

Kais: this humanoid species has two races: daekais and morkais. Aside from disposition, they are largely the same, about four feet tall with feathery wings.

Karelia: one of the original seven species of Llurien. Created by the gods of the green sphere: truth, exuberance, courage, and intuition. They need only four hours of sleep a night and have a well-developed sixth sense that varies from one to another in just what they can sense and do. Appointed by the gods to resolve supernatural disturbances.

Karelian Sword: a double-edged weapon with a sharp tip, two and a half feet long, being a half foot longer than a short sword. The hilt is long enough for the karelia to use this sword as two-handed, but larger species may use only one hand.

Kerr: an ill-manned mountain bovine with two curved horns that are used to ram anyone or anything entering its territory. Prized for milk (used for cheeses), skins, and their wool. Their waste is known to be especially smelly, resulting in the popular expression, "kerr shit."

Kona leech: a predatory vined plant in the darkshade family. It slowly feeds on the blood of creatures it captures, which it renders docile with a secretion to calm them. Victims die of starvation or dehydration, as the plant wants them to live as long as possible. The plant is mobile, moving from tree to tree and hanging over trails.

Kryll: one of the original seven species of Llurien. Created by the gods of the red sphere: curiosity, aspiration, fairness, and peace. They prefer to live in large Evenorr trees and are extremely acrobatic, athletic, and masters of weapons. Every kryll has a subject to which they devote themselves, becoming an expert.

Kryllan Hand: a magical pair of bracers over the forearms. With a word, a metal gauntlet covers the hands, allowing for hand-to-sword combat. Also a fighting style of martial arts.

Kryllan Sword: equivalent to a bastard sword.

Leisiran: the afterlife conceived by the gods of the indigo sphere, reserved for the moderately good, who enjoy a paradise for eternity.

Llorus: a large continent lying mostly on the southern hemisphere of Llurien, south of the continent Antaria.

Llurien: the planet, which has two moons.

Linganore Trees: believed to only grow in Everland in a grove surrounding the Ever Fiend's Black Tower. Black trunks and blood red leaves. The trees are sentient and can move, barring passage, trapping people, or killing them.

Lochiare: the afterlife conceived by the gods of the blue sphere, for the moderately evil, who suffer eternal torture.

Maeryndor: an afterlife conceived by the gods of the violet sphere, for the least evil, who suffer boredom everlasting.

Magician: anyone with magic talent, whether they've become a full-fledged wizard or sorcerer or not. The term can be an insult to anyone of skill and power, since they should be referred to by their proper skillset: wizard or sorcerer.

Mandeans: one of the original seven species of Llurien. Created by the gods of the indigo sphere: innocence, passion, expression, and unity. They are water dwelling and rarely seen on land except by the shore.

Moon Gates: powered by the moon, Moon Gates are portals that allow nearly instantaneous travel between two Moon Gates, which are typically controlled by Priests of Scrylyn. The gates actually use the Ever Pathways at high speeds, meaning travelers are going through Everland, but most people don't realize this.

Morkais: a race of the kais species, they resulted from the Deal of the Gods and were created by all twelve "good" gods from a male and female daekais. See "kais" entry.

Mynx: a large, maneless, carnivorous cat (some as large as a horse) that can be trained in battle tactics and bonded to its owner. Mynx can wear armor, follow commands, and communicate threats to their owner with different vocalizations.

Orb of Vessyn: a sphere located in the Vanishing Tower and which causes the tower to randomly change locations.

Poison Pond: located in Everland, the Poison Pond is believed to have killed a group of riven who entered it for unknown reasons. The waters have since turned silver and are known as the silver elixir, a potent supernatural item.

Priest: members of a religious order. Within a priesthood, clerics and healers are more specific roles than the generic term priest, which not only refers to all of them, but to those who conduct ceremonies, listen to people's problems and console them, and interpret the will of the gods for the common people, though clerics and healers can also do this. Priests are the figureheads of a religion, while clerics administrate the religion and healers heal the wounded.

Querra: one of the original seven species of Llurien. Created by the gods of the yellow sphere: inspiration, empathy, rejuvenation, and patience. Three to four feet tall, they are playful, wise, and beloved by many.

Riven: one of the original seven species of Llurien. Created by the gods of the violet sphere: haste, hate, cynicism, and sloth. Three to four feet tall and often carrying diseases.

Silver Elixir: the toxic waters of the Poison Pond in Everland. Highly prized by magicians for its supernatural properties, which augment spells. Can be used to turn ordinary weapons into Chaos Blades.

Sorcerers: the class of magician which is capable of performing magic through force of will, rather than needing a spell.

Sorelia: a corrupted race of the karelian species, they were created when the goddess of corruption, Ronkainen, read the passage about creating karelia from the Book of Creation. Sorelia look just like karelia but have more variable eye colors. They are considered malevolent.

Species: while this can refer to animals, it usually refers to the humanoid species: karelia, mandeans, querra, kryll, kais, riven, jhaikan, and humans, some of which have multiple races.

Valenders: simple spells that any magician can usually do whether they've trained to become a wizard or not (or developed their talent for sorcery).

Valendry: the art of creating magical items.

Valend wizard: magicians who failed the tests to become wizards and are not allowed to perform magic except by creating magic items, known as valendry.

Wizards: the class of magician who needs spells to work magic.

About The Author

Randy Ellefson has written fantasy fiction since his teens and is an avid world builder, having spent three decades creating Llurien, which has its own website. He has a Bachelor of Music in classical guitar but has always been more of a rocker, having released several albums and earned endorsements from music companies. He's a professional software developer and runs a consulting firm in the Washington D.C. suburbs. He loves spending time with his son and daughter when not writing, making music, or playing golf.

Connect with me online

http://www.RandyEllefson.com
http://twitter.com/RandyEllefson
http://facebook.com/RandyEllefsonAuthor

If you like this book, please help others enjoy it.

Lend it. Please share this book with others.
Recommend it. Please recommend it to friends, family, reader groups, and discussion boards
Review it. Please review the book at Goodreads and the vendor where you bought it.

JOIN THE RANDY ELLEFSON NEWSLETTER!

Subscribers receive discounts, exclusive bonus scenes, and the latest promotions and updates! A FREE eBook of *The Ever Fiend (Talon Stormbringer)* is immediately sent to new subscribers!

www.ficiton.randyellefson.com/newsletter

Randy Ellefson Books

Talon Stormbringer

Talon is a sword-wielding adventurer who has been a thief, pirate, knight, king, and more in his far-ranging life.

The Ever Fiend
The Screaming Moragul

www.fiction.randyellefson.com/talonstormbringer

The Dragon Gate Series

Four unqualified Earth friends are magically summoned to complete quests on other worlds, unless they break the cycle – or die trying.

Volume 1: *The Dragon Gate*
Volume 2: *The Light Bringer*
Volume 3: *The Silver-Tongued Rogue*
Volume 4: *The Dragon Slayer*
Volume 5: *The Majestic Magus*

www.fiction.randyellefson.com/dragon-gate-series/

THE ART OF WORLD BUILDING

This is a multi-volume guide for authors, screenwriters, gamers, and hobbyists to build more immersive, believable worlds fans will love.

Volume 1: *Creating Life*
Volume 2: *Creating Places*
Volume 3: *Cultures and Beyond*
Volume 4: *Creating Life: The Podcast Transcripts*
Volume 5: *Creating Places: The Podcast Transcripts*
Volume 6: *Cultures and Beyond: The Podcast Transcripts*
185 Tips on World Building
The Complete Art of World Building
The Art of the World Building Workbook: Fantasy Edition
The Art of the World Building Workbook: Sci-Fi Edition

Visit www.artofworldbuilding.com for details.

Randy Ellefson Music

Instrumental Guitar

Randy has released three albums of hard rock/metal instrumentals, one classical guitar album, and an all-acoustic album. Visit http://www.music.randyellefson.com for more information, streaming media, videos, and free mp3s.

2004: The Firebard
2007: Some Things Are Better Left Unsaid
2010: Serenade of Strings
2010: The Lost Art
2013: Now Weaponized!
2014: The Firebard (re-release)